A BLAZE OF SPIRIT AND DREAMS

D. L. HOWARD

Autograph Page

Contents

Welcome to Eldritch

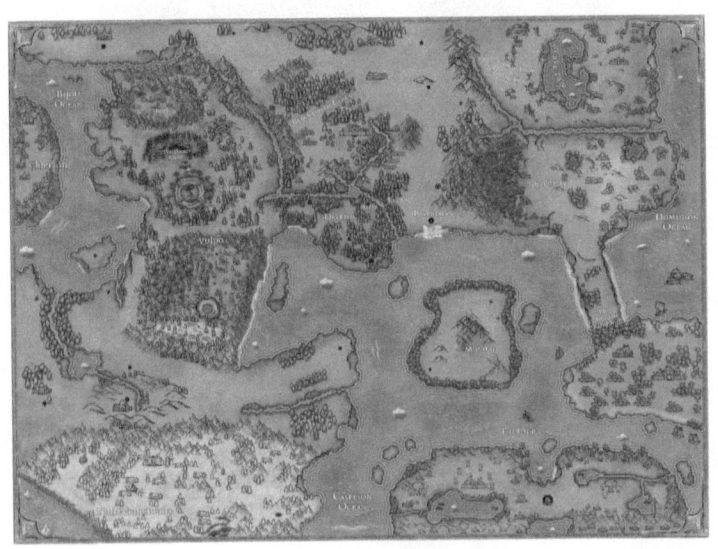

This is Vulpo

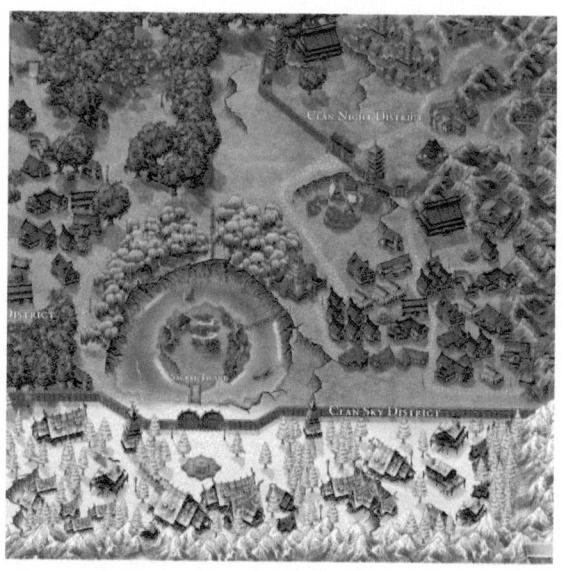

Vulpo is the land of the Vulpii, a magical fox like species composed of three separate clans. A deadly conflict between the clans is at its peak, and all secrets, old and new, will come to a head in this story.

Glossary of Terms and Gods

Vulpo: Country/Land where the Vulpii (Vulpiians) live.

Eldritch: The name of their world Elderton: Island where the trials takes place.

Eldish: Common spoken tongue in the Eldritch.

Zera, Mother Goddess: Creator of All Beings and Eldritch

Kho/Kha: Noble title... aka Lord or Lady

Vulpii/Vulpiian Clans

Clan Sky: Arctic type foxes. Prefer the cold regions (mountains, snowy, up high) Has a symbol (circle) for the sun on their foreheads to represent their clan. (white hair, blue eyes, typical of their features)

Clan Terra: Red type foxes. Prefer the forests & the small hills. Has a symbol (triangle) for the land on their forehead to represent their clan (reddish hair, red or yellow eyes, typical of their features)

Clan Night: Black/Silver type foxes. Prefer the mountainous region and caves. Has a symbol (crescent) for the moon on their forehead to represent their clan. (black hair, golden, gray, or dark brown eyes, typical of their features)

The Deities

Duara- Spirit Goddess of Dreams & Nightmares (Neutral)

Ibris- Spirit God of Shadows & Darkness (Dark) Dhasas- Spirit Goddess of Souls (Dark)

Vemnas- Spirit God of Storms (Dark)

Drekra- Spirit Goddess of Death & Decay (Dark)

Kheton- Spirit God of Fire & Lightning (Light)

Urdes- Spirit God of Forest & creatures (Light)

Esoi- Spirit Goddess of Sky & Wind (Light)

Iena- Spirit Goddess of Love & Fertility (Light)

Umjir- Spirit God of Mountains & Deep Places (Neutral)

Aku- Spirit Goddess of Moon & Night (Neutral)

Asis- Spirit God of Sun & Light (Neutral)

Common Eldish Curse Words

fuck = Jiiq shit = shezia damn = drakgo bitch = fatu you hoe= ma hezi dumbass= deplu

PROLOGUE

The long night was unusually dark and silent until it wasn't. Even on an evening like it was, there would always be someone scurrying around. Yet, the streets were strangely empty. His gaze slowly looked up at the darkened sky and his face twisted into a grimace at what he saw. Flashes of lightning illuminated in the distance. Revealing a smattering of dark gray clouds that were drifting across the mostly clear sky. The sight of them didn't sit well with him. There was something about it that made him uncomfortable with it all, even if he was protected.

Following in its wake, a deep rumbling sound reverberated through the air like a powerful drumbeat. It was reminiscent of the hard pounding cadence one heard during their sacred rituals. The volatile mix was nature's way of brewing a dangerous storm. It threatened the peace throughout the land that was accustomed to pretty things, including the weather. The storm meant more than just rain. He knew because what he saw threatened the harmony of the land and its vulpii. It was the nature of being in a cursed place.

Everything screamed Vemnas was present and the spirit of storms was working his storm magic late into the night.

Although Vulpo was ripe for what his spirit gods and goddesses demanded, it still wasn't time. Nothing could disrupt the delicate nature of what his work entailed, and an unnatural force of nature would do that. Shifting on his feet, he leaned against the brick wall of the building he hid beside. His dark cloak covered his head and ears, leaving only his face exposed to the elements.

The low light where he stood was courtesy of the two moons filling the endless dark expanse above. Countless pinpricks of diamond like stars peeked through the group of gray clouds. The large silver moon was still in the sky while its twin, the blue moon, had risen, matching its intensity. It was the holy hour on the holiest of days, Muda. It was the time where most were at home and tending to their altars. Praying to whatever spirit gods and goddesses who would listen to their greedy prayers in the forsaken land of his birth. He had nothing to worry about. His matron spirit goddess had already deemed him worthy.

The soft sound of footsteps approached him from the distance. There was no need to hurry and turn towards the sound because he already knew who it was. Even if they were late. He lifted his nose to the air and took a whiff. Their stench of low blood was mixed with cheap ale. A horrid and terrible scented concoction that made him wish he had chosen another.

A low growl of disapproval escaped from his chest. He stood in the deep shadows, watching with his glowing, golden eyes as the shadowy figures came closer to where he was. One stopped, but another continued on. Golden stepped out of the shadows to meet the one he was waiting for.

"Did anyone follow you?" he asked, as the other drew nearer to him.

"No, I traveled alone," the other said, before looking back over his shoulders. "Except for him."

Golden eyes simply nodded. "Do you have it?"

"I do," he said, and pulled out a wooden box from within the leather pack he wore across his shoulders. "Acquiring them was difficult, but I retrieved them. The previous owners won't even realize they're missing. Not for a long while. Especially with today being Muda."

Golden took the nondescript box that was being held from the outstretched hands and opened the lid. There, resting on soft, plush fabric, were two large raw gemstones. The stones were black as the darkest night. A living red flame glowed from within, making the stones look like a pair of eyes. Excitement filled him within. He'd searched long and hard for the gemstones, and once he discovered they were nearby, he set out to do whatever he needed to get them. He didn't care how many silons he needed to spend. Money was no object.

He reached out with his free hand to touch them, then stopped and decided against it. He could feel the heated stare of the one who brought the stones. Curious red eyes observed him too closely. Tampering down his enthusiasm, he snapped the lid closed and secured the box into the folds of his cloak. Still in disbelief that he now had possession of the rare gemstones.

"My payment," the courier said nervously, breaking Golden from his thoughts.

"Ah, yes." He reached into the folds of his cloak and pulled out a leather pouch. He handed it to the wide eyed Vulpiian. "All of your silons are in there. Including a little bonus for securing these quickly."

Red's grin stretched from ear to ear as he opened the pouch to count his coins. With the deft speed of his spindly fingers, he untied the leather throng and opened it. Red reached inside and pulled out a handful of coins and let them sift through his fingers. The motion reminded Golden of moving water.

"Is our business concluded?" Golden asked, more than ready to depart. A sneer formed on his face as he watched the greedy Vulpiian take a silon out and bite it.

The red-eyed courier's head bobbed up and down. A tiny kit like giggle escaped from his lips. More excited than Golden liked, he gave a curt reply. "Yes, it's concluded."

Golden watched with disgust. He never enjoyed working with the commoners, but sometimes, one had to do what needed to be done. Especially when he needed the utmost discretion. The courier looked back over his shoulders at the one who came with him and held the leather purse up. For some unexplained reason, the exchange made Golden uneasy. Unexpectedly, he felt a deep mistrust of the creature, and a quiet growl slipped past his furled lips.

Red turned back towards Golden and when he noticed his expression, the smile on Red's face slowly disappeared. He looked down into the pouch once more before tying the leather throng. "I-I'll be on my way then. If you need my help again, you know how to find me."

Golden doubted he would and said nothing.

Don't trust them.

The whisper of words rang clear in his mind.

Kill them.

If he was to get rid of them, then there would be no witnesses to know what have been done. He knew to never leave a job unfinished. Golden stood there and watched as Red Eyes darted back to his companion. Under the safety of his cloak, his ears perked up as he discreetly listened to the whispering chatter and banter between the two. He didn't like where their conversation was going. Something had to be done.

Kill them before it is too late.

Standing there, still as the wind, Golden reached within himself, seeking his powers. The low rumble of thunder above became a deafening booming sound. Touching his well, he used the spell stone he wore on his ring and pulled from it to amplify his strength. He drew on his magic and raw energy as it intertwined with each other. Golden whispered into the inky darkness that lurked in the crevices of everything, coaxing it to do his bidding.

The two others were so engrossed in their own conversation that they failed to notice what was happening around them. Too excited for the large purse of coins they had just gained to notice the night become darker, as if it was feeding on itself. Too caught up to see the tendrils of blackness as it curled around their ankles, then crept up their legs and eventually wrapping around their waist.

Golden sauntered towards the courier of his precious gemstones and stopped when Red and his friend ceased talking. They turned around and looked up, realizing much too late what was happening.

"Hey, what are you doing?" Red asked. His gaze nervously shifted to his friend, who shared the same troubled expression. "I-I promised I won't say anything about the stones or where they came from. I-I never go back on my word. My honor is of utmost importance to me."

"Let's get out of here," Red's friend said with a quivering tremble in his voice. Golden watched with amusement as the friend tried to leave but couldn't. When the friend's hands lit up the green color of his magic, Golden laughed out loud and the sinister sound made both Vulpiians caught in his clutches flinch.

"Honor is a thing of old when you're involved with me. I don't trust you will keep silent. After all, you brought someone with you when I said for you to come alone."

Golden lifted his hand, palm up. One by one, his fingers slowly closed into a fist. The Vulpiian standing behind Red Eyes suddenly let out a painful scream that sliced through the silent night. Red eyes turned to his friend and let out a choked gasp as the creature violently convulsed while standing there. His eyes rolled back into his head before he collapsed to the ground in a lifeless heap.

"Fari... get up," Red said nervously. "Fari, quit playing around. Get up!"

"I don't think your friend *Fari*... is going to get up or go anywhere," Golden said, with false concern etched in his voice.

Red attempted to free himself from the ever-nearing shadows, but all of his efforts were in vain. The darkness only answered to the one who called it, and that was the one who stood before him. The foul stink of fear permeated the air, which made Golden chuckle.

"Why are you laughing? This isn't funny. Wha-what's going on?"

Golden canted his head to the side and studied the Terran. Walls of snaking darkness built up around the two, blotting out the moon, and eventually sealing them together in total darkness. The sniffles of the commoner only made him angrier.

Soon enough, the red-eyed vulpii let out a bone chilling scream. No one would hear him, because Golden blocked off access the moment the shadowy walls went up around them. He moved closer to the courier, reached out and grabbed his neck, cutting off the screams.

Gurgling sounds came out choked, and Golden frowned even further. "Breathe through your nose if you must, but stop all the extra. Why can't you see your death is imminent and die like a proper Vulpiian? With honor!"

The terran eyes widened at the shadowy Vulpiian's words.

Golden continued. "This is my assurance that you won't speak about what you have found and delivered to me. I can't let you ruin this, *terran*."

Red tried to speak, but his words wouldn't come out. Golden loosened his grip around the Vulpiian's neck so he could hear the lies drip off Red's lips. "I swear on the Mother Goddess and m-m-my patron spirit god, Urdes. I wo-won't say a word," the terran promised in a frantic stutter.

"It's not a risk I'm comfortable taking. You almost made it out alive, but the spirits have decided. Ibris blessed us with his darkness and shadows. Your death belongs to Drekra while your soul belongs to her twin, Dhasas."

Red gasped, then whispered. "We don't speak those names."

"Allow me to let you in on a little secret, terran." Golden conjured a blade made of obsidian and black steel in his right hand. He lifted it to the Terran's neck and removed the glamour he wore that concealed his identity. "I speak those names and do their bidding with everything I am."

He quickly took his dagger and slit the throat of the Vulpiian he held in his clutches and watched as the life slowly bled from him.

The red-eyed terran recognized who he worked for and, with one last breath, he cursed the name of his murderer. "Night-song..."

Chapter 1

"Hurry, Blaze!" Icelia whisper shouted as she kept glancing back through the door. "I hear something."

"You always hear something," Blaze mumbled, but picked up the speed with what she was doing. The protection spell around the sealed chest wasn't dispelling like it was supposed to have been dissipating. She recognized the first two spells, but didn't realize they were cloaking spells until it was too late. A mistake she hoped she wouldn't regret.

"I thought you said you could disable those spells," Ice snapped. There was more fear in her voice than anything else. Blaze refused to let her friend's tone upset her.

"I *did* say that. The first two are disabled, but there is a third spell. They hid it underneath the first two. You and the others didn't bother to let me know it was a thrice spelled lock. I remember specifically being told it was a double lock."

Ice rapidly cursed in the tongue of her clan. Blaze recognized little of what Ice said, but she knew it was nothing good. Especially with the one curse word she heard. That alone gave it away to Blaze how unnerved her friend was. She never spoke foul words like she was right then.

Blaze pushed her on edge friend away from her thoughts and kept at what she was doing, trying to speed up, but nothing she did was working. She had practically exhausted every method she knew to remove the last spell. Whoever set it was a genius. A true master of spells. Spelled locks were nothing new, especially to her, but this one was one she had never seen before. She didn't like the uncomfortable feeling that blanketed her because of the situation she found herself in.

"I didn't know. I was just going off what Jinx and Hot Paw told me," Ice said, with a hint of worry in her voice.

Blaze groaned with frustration. Upset with her own mistakes. She couldn't believe she didn't check the job out like she normally would have. Ice was her best friend and, in most circumstances, she was a better judge of character, but this time, Blaze realized Ice made a costly mistake. Which ultimately caused her to err.

"You can't trust a word Hot Paw says. You know that. Jinx knows that. Even Stormi knows that and she's all about Hot Paw. Let me guess. He came to you both with this job." Blaze turned an accusatory glance in her friend's direction. "Am I right?"

"Umm... it's not like that." Ice's expression shifted to one of realization. Followed swiftly by something Blaze assumed to be remorse and something else she couldn't decipher.

Shaking her head, Blaze refused to say anything else about it. Instead, she focused her complete attention back onto the metal chest and did what she could to unlock it. Behind her, in the cramped room they were in, Ice had paced back and forth. She never understood why her friend took chances like she did. Blaze didn't care if they ever nabbed her, but Ice had everything to lose if they ever captured her.

"Hey, Ice."

Her friend stopped pacing the floor and looked up. Her crystalline sapphire eyes found hers, and in them Blaze saw a hint of fear.

"Yes," Ice responded. Blaze still detected the hesitation in her tone.

Blaze's complete focus was on the spelled lock, but she had a sinking feeling it was a test in futility for her. Nothing was working. It was only getting later, and the longer they stayed, the more dangerous it would be for them all. No one had to tell her it would be better if she were alone.

"You should probably get out of here," Blaze said, finally responding to Ice.

"I can't do that. I can't-" Ice stopped mid-sentence. Her ears perked up and twitched around. The sound of a door being beaten against faintly filled their space. Her eyes widened. "That's not good. I told you I heard something."

"It's probably Jinx," Blaze lied to calm her nervous friend down. "You know he's clumsy and a horrible lookout."

Blaze hurried with the spell, knowing her efforts were completely useless at this point. She tried once more but whimpered in pain when the lock whirred with a loud clicking sound, then glowed a bright red before going back to normal. She tried to remove her hands but couldn't.

Blaze's heart raced faster than normal behind its cage in her chest. Her hands shook against the spelled box. She quickly willed them still and looked over her shoulder. "You have no business being here if you get caught. Leave now."

Ice's blue eyes searched Blaze's face, but saw nothing but fierce determination. All too soon, her expression morphed into suspicion. "What's wrong? What aren't you telling me?"

"Nothing," Blaze said too quickly, while schooling her face to look neutral. Icelia had an uncanny way of telling when something was off with any of them just by a look. Her gift of intuition among her other magic was strong when she wasn't afraid, and that had everything to do with her bloodline. "Everything is fine. I just don't want you to get caught."

"What about you? Of all of us, you can't get caught, either. Your clan..." Ice shook her head. "I can't imagine what they will do to you. Especially being caught here, of all places."

"That's for me to worry about. Now please, go. I won't ask again, Icelia."

Her friend hesitated, then gave a quick head nod as if she came to some final decision. Ice spun around, then stopped in her tracks. She peered back over her shoulders. "Don't get caught."

Blaze didn't respond as she watched her friend shift into her true form and darted out of the small room. Of their crew, Ice was the only one who knew who she truly was. Around the others, Blaze wore a glamour to keep her identity hidden. Icelia knowing was enough for her.

Still staring off in the direction her friend went, even though the space was empty, Blaze knew the others would be okay. The crew had to be okay. There was a way out that would allow them to escape easily. She was good at being an escape artist and taught her crew the basics of slipping away. It was a necessary tool for their trade they weren't taught at the Academy.

Instead of the usual route, her friends opted for a secret passageway that hadn't been used in ages. *If the cobwebs were anything to go by*, Blaze thought to herself. They had found the path earlier when they were doing their research with the house schematics. Blaze had secretly thanked the spirits she suggested they retrieved them and that her crew went along with the idea. Blaze had an icky feeling about the job ever since the beginning. She didn't want to tell the others and had them worried about nothing. Looking for secret tunnels was her way of some type of insurance for hers and their safety.

Blaze heard Jinx's voice, then there was silence from her two friends. They had slipped out, leaving her all alone. The banging on the door continued until she heard the wood splinter and crack. Angry voices rose together in a chaotic chorus. By the second, the closer and closer it got to her, the louder those shouts were.

Any other Vulpii would have been unnerved, but not her. No, there was nothing she could do. Blaze cycled through all of her tricks and nothing worked. Her hands were stuck. As long as her friends didn't get caught, she would be okay with the outcome. Ice was more worried about what Blaze's clan would do, but Blaze wasn't, really. Being reprimanded was just another day for her. This would just add on to the already growing pile of bovek dung.

The hurried footsteps of guards running towards the room she found herself stuck in only had her steeling her backbone. Blaze straightened her spine as much as she could and let the stony mask of not caring find its way to her face. They would never see her weak, cowering, or showing fear. She was *Aku,* after all. A kit of Clan Night. They bowed to no other.

Clinking metal and then a splattering of bright light filled the room. Illuminating the space so the guards could get a better look at her face. Luckily, her glamour was still in effect. It would take them a while to see her true face unless they had a *Flayer* on the house's guard core. Knowing whose house she was in, Blaze more than suspected they had a few on the payroll.

She counted about ten guards as they encircled her. All wore the uniform and bright red armor of House Irontail. The crest on the chest of their armor was of a red six-tail that was covered in red iron surrounded by trees.

"My, my, my. What do we have here?" A male's voice, full of assurance, spoke from behind her. It was clear from their intonation that they were more than just amused. "I spy a Vulpiian who shouldn't be here. Caught in my little fox trap."

The male's comments drew laughter from all the guards. She didn't find it nearly as funny as they did. She recognized the voice the moment he had spoken. Blaze tried to ignore it, but inside, her heart kicked up the pace and was practically thumping an erratic beat in her chest. He wasn't supposed to be there. Hot Paw and Jinx swore he would not be there. That was the only requirement for her to do the job for them. Either they lied or they were intentionally trying to get her in trouble.

No, they wouldn't do that? Would they?

Too many dark thoughts filled Blaze's mind as she tried to figure out how to get out of the house, taking her down a path she didn't want to venture down. She had to believe her crew was loyal to her. To each other. If Hot Paw betrayed her or even Jinx, she made a promise to herself that they would regret it.

Blaze had a sinking feeling the moment his voice filled the room. Refusing to turn around to face her captor, she kept her eyes and face forward. Unable to face the one she had hoped to never get caught by.

"Come on now, turn around and look at me."

Blaze took in a deep breath, preparing her mind to handle whatever was about to happen. "Why should I? I'm just a thief who got caught in a trap."

"Do you really want me to believe you're just *some* thief?"

"That's all I am." Blaze shifted on her feet. Refusing to give more information than that. "A lowly, nobody thief. One who wasn't smart enough to not get caught. Obviously."

"*Obviously*." The male had repeated with amusement in his voice. "But we all want to know who we have caught. Don't we fellas?"

A collective chorus of yesses answered in return. She still refused to turn around.

"Don't you worry, clever little thief. We'll figure it out. We always do." Blaze heard the soft rustling of expensive cloth as it snapped behind her, then the perfectly timed footsteps as they walked away from her. "Take her to the chambers."

The two guards who stood beside her reached out and each grabbed an arm. Their grip was tight as they placed red steel arm bands around her forearms. She hissed with pain as they clamped closed. A jolt of magic traveled up her arm from the bracers, and Blaze nearly buckled under the pain. The voltage was much higher than the bands normally should have been. Something was off about the entire situation. It had been off ever since Hot Paw went to Jinx with the news of an amazing job opportunity. Everything told her to not do the job, but hubris got the better of her.

Blaze attempted to touch her magic, but it was just as she suspected. They completely shut her access to it off. The braces were doing their job as they barred and cut her off from the very magic that she had access to since birth. Luckily for her, judging by the lack of response from the guards, her illusion was still intact. Blaze let out a sigh of relief. She at least had that still.

"You can let go of the box now," the guard on her right had said.

She glanced at him from the corner of her eyes and was surprised. Most Vulpii around those parts had reddish brown skin tones. One of the many tells of Clan Terra. But this one was pale with snow white hair like those of Clan Sky, but his yellow eyes were that of Clan Terra. She looked at the mark on his forehead and realized it was a triangle. The Vulpii was a hybrid. Something that would have been worse than her if he was born into Clan Night. She quickly took him in and, from the looks of it, the hybrid was doing very well for himself. As well as one could be for being born into Clan Terra. To Blaze, her opinion of the Terrans had her considering them as the most peaceful of the three clans. Clan Sky was as chilly and cold as their lands, but nothing could ever compare to the likes of Clan Night.

The guards patiently waited for her. She returned her attention to her hands and noticed the pressure had vanished. Blaze yanked her hands away from the box and ultimately came to the unfortunate conclusion that she had really messed up this time. Icelia's worries about being caught may have been well-founded.

She couldn't touch her gifts. She couldn't shift and dart away. It was very apparent that Blaze's luck had finally run out as she was surrounded.

CHAPTER 2

B laze kept her head down as the guards led her away. At
the last second, another guard picked up the box she was
trying to get into. She watched him as he secured the ornate box
under his arms, then moved around the table to walk behind
her and her two escorts. Not knowing what was in the box was
going to bother her to no end. She was a curious Vulpiian.

According to Hot Paw, there was supposed to have been a
serious cache of raw infused gems that would have gone great
with the right sellers in Hallowbane Den. The market of illegal goods down in the Burrows that their Vulpiian leadership
constantly turned a blind eye to. Unfortunately for her and the
rest of the crew, that boat had left the dock and she wouldn't see
those gems.

What she didn't pay attention to before was now glaring
directly in her face. The job was a trap, and the box was the
sweet treat that enticed the sticky fingered Blaze. She surveyed
the room now that it was completely illuminated. Able to get
a better look at the place, she was intrigued by what she saw.

It was void of others except for her and the guards. The family who called the place home was nowhere to be found. Neither was the male who had only spoken to her just moments ago.

Everything blended perfectly with the land. Roots of the tree helped support the surrounding walls. Opulent furniture and priceless pieces of artwork covered the earthen walls. Rugs covered the floors and Blaze's mood steadily slinked further into darker territory. She knew it was a mistake to break into one of the Irontail's home, but it was too good of an opportunity to pass up. At least that was what she kept telling herself when she convinced herself to do it. Maybe she was too cocksure of her skills. Perhaps not. Whatever it was, she knew she was in deep trouble.

The guards led them past all the fineries and into a long, winding, barely lit hall. A cool breeze brushed over her skin, causing it to pebble. As Blaze studied it, the more she looked at the hall, the more she realized it was an unfinished tunnel. The bare walls were made from the land's soil and minerals. The floor was composed of light colored natural wood planks. Perfectly fitted together like tight puzzle pieces. All signs that this home was one of those that belonged to the major nine families and further proof she knew she had messed up. There were many Irontails in Vulpo, and Blaze hoped this was one of the lower-ranking members. But the house had to belong to someone higher in the family's hierarchy.

Blaze resigned herself to the fact that she was in serious trouble. There was absolutely nothing she could do to get out of this. Nor would she be able to explain herself, either. Her clan was strict and unforgiving.

Eventually, the small group found their way to a desolate dead end at the end of the hall. Blaze and her guards faced a thick, heavy set of double doors, engraved with scenes that she recognized as Irontail history. On the other side, she assumed, was some type of interior chamber. Blaze was afraid she was about to get a firsthand look at what the doors kept hidden.

She shifted on her feet, itching to get out of the guards' grasp. Wishing to make a run for it. "What are we waiting for?"

The sudden and unexpected nudge on her back had her stumbling forward, landing on her knees. "Shut up," the guard behind her snarled.

"None of that," the guard to her right had said while helping her off of her knees. "We do not act like heathens. We are better than that."

"Hmph. This one is a thief. They don't deserve any pleasantries," the guard behind her said in a smug voice.

"Well, praise be to the spirits that your opinion doesn't matter. Now back at attention."

Blaze couldn't see the guard behind her, but the rustling of armor and movement told her everything she needed to know. The hybrid was higher ranked than all the other guards. She examined the fascinating Vulpiian guard who lent her a hand. Blaze immediately thought it was possible that he could help her escape from the chaos she found herself tangled in.

She glanced slightly in his direction.

"Don't get any ideas, thief," the hybrid warned her.

She flashed a dung eating grin. "Oh, I have any ideas."

He stared at her before looking away. A silent moment had passed by between them before he knocked on the door then spoke. "Good. I'd hate to use force on you."

"I'm a model citizen of Vulpo. There's no force needed."

She caught a hint of a smile on the hybrid's face before it disappeared. "It'll be wise for you to be silent now," he cautioned.

The double doors before them opened, effectively cutting off any words she was about to speak. A deep voice from within told them to enter. The two personal guards on each side of her grabbed her arms and led her into the darkened chamber.

With each step they took, more and more lights came on, bringing a brightness to the previously darkened space. She wanted to gasp after finally seeing what the room truly looked like, but kept it quiet, as they warned her before going inside.

The chamber was beautiful. It was completely unlike how she thought it would look. The ground was blanketed with lush, verdant green moss and all around her were large-leaved plants and trees she never knew could grow underground. The entire chamber would have you thinking that you were outside, deep in the forest.

Directly in front of Blaze were two large trees, native to the lands of Clan Terra with its marbled blood red and dark green glowing bark. The branches from both trees entwined with each other, meeting in the center, creating a throne-like chair.

On it sat the Vulpiian from earlier. Watching her every move. She had recognized the voice, but now she could put the face to its rich, deep timbre. Mezal Irontail sat there like he was the lord of everything when he was only the prince of the Irontail clan.

Blaze steeled her spine. Lifted her chin in defiance. Mezal was a flayer. His magic allowed him to see past any glamours or illusions. It could also strip a person bare. Leaving nothing to the imagination and where everything was laid out in the open. A flayer's magic peeled back the illusions and left the vulpiian empty and void within. Unlike his fellow terrans, Mezal's disposition leaned towards the darker side. Which was an anomaly for his sometimes good demeanor family. They knew Mezal well around her clan's way. She remembered hearing her father over dinner talking about the prince. Once, he even mentioned that Mezal Irontail should have been born Clan Night instead of Clan Terra.

Mezal spread his hands wide with a charming grin on his face. "Welcome, Little Thief."

"*No*, I should thank you for the wonderful invitation," Blaze said. Her words were dripping with sarcasm. Mezal's eyes narrowed with annoyance. His lips curled downwards into a frown, then in an instant, it was back to his captivating yet fake grin. There were a few muffled chuckles from the guards behind Blaze, and the sound grated on her nerves.

"Do you think the situation you're in is funny? You are in serious trouble, *little thief*."

"Yeah, I kind of figured as much with you all bringing me down here to the dungeon."

"This is no dungeon, but call it whatever you like." Mezal snapped his fingers and her armed escorts all dispersed to different areas of the chamber. Leaving her standing there in the center, all alone. "Don't even think about trying to run. You won't get far."

"Wasn't even thinking about it," she lied. How Mezal knew what she was thinking, Blaze had no clue. What she knew was that his powers were one of the strongest in his family. She recalled her parents mentioning he was one of the most powerful in his clan. One of the rare ones with six tails. A fox born before they were cursed for one hundred years.

Blaze was becoming increasingly worried. Her eyes quickly scanned the room. They really caught her in a proverbial fox trap.

"Sure you wasn't." Mezal unfolded himself from the chair made of living wood and stood to his full height. His tails fanned out behind him, displaying his strength. Mezal's eyes flashed a bright red and his auburn hair fell low to his back. He wore a crimson tunic with forest green trousers to match. He had removed the cloak from around his neck and let it lazily hang off the arms of the chair he had previously occupied.

"I think it's time to know why you are here. Find out who we are dealing with." He took a step forward in her direction. "What is your name, thief?"

She looked him straight in his eyes. "Blaze."

Mezal stopped in his tracks. A moment of recognition crossed his face. Out of nowhere, he burst into laughter. "Blaze. *The* Blaze. The one who has wreaked havoc among the many houses of both Terra and Sky."

"The one and only."

"*Oh*, this is wonderful. But who are you really? You wear a nearly perfect glamour, and I am almost going to hate to dispel it. You have gone undetected for a long time now. Your name crosses the tongues of many of Vulpo's peacekeepers because you are hard to catch. And your name crosses the tongues of many nobles of Terra and Sky. You know the ones, don't you? The ones you have helped lighten their purses." He moved closer to Blaze and stopped directly in front of her. Mezal reached out and touched her face, gently caressing it before squeezing her chin tight. "But I can see past your disguise. If I wanted to. But not yet."

"You don't scare me, Irontail," Blaze said between clenched teeth. "I've endured worse things you couldn't even dream of putting me through."

Mezal's deep laughter filled the chamber. "*Oh*, I don't know about that."

Blaze yanked herself away from his grasp. Pulled her shoulders back. Rage filled her. She was many things. Done many things, but anything that a terran could do was nothing compared to her people and the fact that he implied it had her seeing red. "Try me."

Mezal's smile was crueler than those of her clan, which only solidified why her father was so impressed with the Vulpii. "First, tell me why you were trying to get into the box."

The sudden change of subject threw Blaze for a rapid loop. She shrugged, not wanting him to know the real reason, even though he knew who she was. "No reason, really. Got a tip that this place had a few trinkets that could go well on the market. You know... down there in Hallowbane Den. After weighing my options, I made the sound decision to hit it up. Hoping I'd get lucky."

"That's it?"

"Yes. I'm just out here trying to make a living. Provide for my family. You know, that curse really did us in. We lost everything during those tumultuous years. Now, we're just out here making it. Hoping to recoup some of our treasury."

"Hmm. If you say so, little thief." Mezal spun on his heels and walked towards the guard, who was the hybrid. He spoke in hushed tones to him before turning back and facing her. The guard took off. Blaze watched him leave before looking back at Mezal. "So you won't tell me the real reason you wanted inside the box."

"I've already told you," she said, feigning exasperation. Then faked a yawn. Unsurprised that he didn't believe her. He was too smart for his own good. "Do you think I can possibly leave sometime soon? It is getting rather late."

"You'll be leaving soon enough." Mezal looked at the door behind her and motioned for whoever to come forward. "I want you to meet someone first. A friend of mine. I think you two might click."

Soft footsteps had her ears perking backwards, then back forward. Mezal held a hand up, stopping whoever was behind her. She twisted around at the waist to see who it was and caught Hot Paw staring at her. In his hands was something, and he was wringing it tightly. He looked extremely nervous. His eyes darted between the guard by his side, Mezal, and herself.

Blaze schooled her face because even if she was angrier than she ever had been before, she refused to show it. Hot Paw had betrayed her. To her, this meant that he had broken the trust of the others, too. She trusted him when everything said not to. Now he stood there like he was caught in a trap instead of being the betrayer. Once she was free, she was going to make sure he knew exactly why it was bad to cross her. He would find out why she was called Blaze.

She turned back around and faced the one who was about to discover who she truly was. There was no running. Mezal was right about that. No, she was going to face whatever came her way. Destroying others afterwards, she would plot later.

Soon as Blaze faced Mezal, he was on her quick as she could blink. He had darted towards her so fast that she barely registered him even moving. She tried to scoot away, but discovered she was frozen in her spot. With the flick of his wrist, rope like tendrils of magic the color of deep green poured from his hands. The ground pulsated, then thick vines grew out of it, sought her out and wrapped around her feet and ankles. The only thing that went through Blaze's mind was how much she wished she could touch her magic. If she could, she wouldn't have been in the predicament she was in.

Mezal's voice lowered even more. "Before we get to the joyous reunion, let us first find out who you really are."

At first, the energy of his power was warm as a Sprig day, then it turned into the fiery heat of a mid-Sol day. Beads of sweat trickled down her face as her insides burned up. Blaze did her best to embrace the fire of his magic, but nothing she did worked.

Soon as the heat came, the icy grips of the cold appeared and swept it all away. Blaze's chest rose and fell as she tried to catch her breath again. The fading echoes of her piercing screams died away. She didn't even realize she had opened her mouth to scream.

After catching her breath, she eyed the fox, who watched her too intensely. Blaze was unable to decipher his expression, but she didn't care anymore. "You didn't have to do it that way."

"No. I didn't. But that is what you deserved for trying to break into my home. Steal from my coffers. It was what the crime demanded." Mezal gave her a look of disgust. He dismissed everyone from the room except the hybrid. He crossed his arms over his chest. "Now that we're alone. It's time we have a more productive chat. Don't you think... *Nightsong*."

Blaze said nothing. He knew who she truly was, yet he didn't let the others know. Just the hybrid, whom she glanced at, but his face was blank as well. She resigned herself to not getting help but also grateful that he kept her secret a secret still. Once free, Hot Paw would pay, but at least he didn't know who she was underneath the glamour she kept on around him and the rest of the crew. She glanced up at Mezal. "What do you want from me?"

Chapter 3

"Do you want to know what was in the thrice spelled box?" Mezal asked her. He had remained in front of her, but now he wore a look of determination. "Because I can tell you."

"You already know I want to know what's in the box. Why are you suddenly being nice? Why aren't you saying anything about who I really am?"

He shrugged with a bit of indifference. "In due time, but right now, I have other concerns."

"Okay," she said. "There is something else that I really haven't figured out yet."

"And what is that?"

"What do you want from me? Everyone knows that you're a connoisseur of pilfering knowledge. Whenever there's a need for information, there is always some type of exchange you demand in return. Monetary or by favor. So what is it, Irontail?"

He chuckled. "You're right. See, I told you that you were a clever little thief."

"That you did."

"I know who you are. The youngest of Diev's and Luya's little brood. How many of you are there? Five? Six?"

"There's seven of us."

"And you are the youngest, yes?"

"I am."

"That's what I thought. Those of Clan Night reproduce like we're dying out. My father always said it was one of the many unbecoming traits of your clan."

Blaze gritted her teeth together before schooling her face again. She refused to play games with Mezal anymore. "Here I thought that perhaps Clan Terra was better than those of Night and Sky. You just proved me wrong. It would seem that Clan Terra is just as rotten as the rest of us. Or maybe it's just you and the rest of the Irontails. You know what they say about your house, don't you?"

Mezal's eyes flashed a bright red before returning to its normal color. "You do not speak of my family like that."

"Then you don't talk about my clan like that. Listen, I may be who I am, but I am still a child of Night. You *will* respect us."

"You earn respect and loyalty, Nightsong. It's not easily given or received. You'll do well to remember that."

"I tire of this," Blaze said as she waved her hand around to encompass the entire chamber. "Let's get this chat done and over with so I can go home."

"I'm not so easily dismissed, little thief, but we do have something in common, I suppose. I tire of this conversation as well."

Blaze watched as Mezal ordered his right hand and only guard left to call for someone from her house to come pick up their problem. The guard left quickly, leaving only the two of them alone.

"Why not call the peacekeepers to come pick me up?" She asked, genuinely curious because she wasn't ready to deal with her family just yet.

"No need when we could just call your family. Besides, the peacekeepers already know. Pako, he's the hybrid, is a peace-keeper. The moment we discovered who you truly were, that was the moment the peacekeepers knew."

Blaze cursed in the tongue of her clan. The news was going to spread like a blaze and turn into an uncontrollable wildfire. Vulpii were nosey. They loved to gossip when it was about others and not themselves.

Mezal looked at her curiously. "Why did you choose the name Blaze? Did you become tired of always getting in trouble with your real name?"

"Something like that," she said with a quick shrug of her shoulders. "Didn't want all the drama my escapades caused to fall back on my family."

"Yet, now they will once word gets out that the infamous Blaze is actually one of the most hated—Liekki Nightsong."

"Well, like you, everyone will get over it, eventually. I couldn't care less."

"If you say so, young Nightsong. I can tell when I'm being lied to." Mezal clapped his hands together and smiled that cruel smile of his. "Let me show you what's in the box before you have to leave. After all, it is a gift for your father."

Blaze tried to think about what the gift could be. If it was for her father, it had to be some type of important gemstone. Slowly, the ramifications of what she was about to do earlier came crashing down on her. A storm of legendary proportions was about to rain down on her. There was nothing she could do to shield or protect herself from it. She was going to have to take the lashings when it came her way.

She eyed Mezal with curiosity as he went to retrieve the spelled box. Gems in the hands of Mezal were like seeing magic. He was considered one of the top master jewelers in Vulpo. He was just that good, and he knew it. She had seen a few of his pieces fetch for a fortune in Hallowbane Den. His skills with technomancy infused gems were leading the pack and most sought after in all of Eldritch.

He learned his craft at an early age because the Irontails had a couple of mines that did pretty well, but nothing came out of theirs like it did with her family's mines. The Nightsong family owned a few dozen mines and their gems and crystals were high quality and some of the best around Vulpo. Actually, her family earned the reputation as the best in all of Eldritch.

Mezal came back and held the box in his left hand. Blaze watched as he lifted the lid with his free hand. Inside was a deep burgundy colored plush liner that held three raw, uncut black stones. Inside the stones was an inner fire of red orange that glowed at every angle you stared at them. The stones reminded her of a pair of cat eyes. Stunned, no words immediately came to Blaze. She knew the gems could have gone for a fortune thrice over in the market down in the burrows.

Taking her eyes off the stunning stones, she glanced in Mezal's direction. His stony gaze pierced hers. "I'll give them to your sister, since I don't trust you enough to give them to your father. I mean... you were trying to steal from me, after all."

"How did you get those?" she asked with a force she didn't recognize. "Did you infuse them?"

"Does it matter?"

"Yes. Those things are worth a lot cut, but these are raw gems. Not everyone can afford them, and only the magic wielders who are strong with their gift can use those. On top of that, they're already infused."

The corner of Mezal's lips curled slightly upward. "I know all of this, Nightsong. Yes, I infused them, but it doesn't change the fact that they're a gift to your father. He knows I have them. Now imagine how he's going to feel once he comes to learn that the infamous Blaze, also known as his youngest daughter, was trying to steal them from me. That is something I'd pay money to see from behind a hidden wall."

Blaze kept a straight face, but knew he was right. The room seemed to get smaller and colder. There was nowhere in all of Vulpo she could go and hide. The luck she had in abundance have seemed to run out and Blaze didn't like how that made her feel. There was no doubt in her mind that she wouldn't get off free. Her father wasn't an easygoing fox. She would have to take the punishment she knew was lying in wait for her. It wouldn't be the first time she had taken a beating by him. The thought of it just made her even madder. "What makes you so sure that my sister is trustworthy?"

Mezal closed the box and looked at her sideways with a knowing smirk as he handed it off to Pako. "Senia will do whatever I ask her to do."

Blaze didn't like the sound of that because, to her, it sounded as if Mezal knew her sister on a more personal level. They stared at each other until it completely dawned on her. In a maddening blur, all the times her sister talked about the new handsome fox she was seeing crashed about in her head. There were too many times to count, and whenever their parents brought up the new love of her life, she brushed it off or changed the subject. Her sister always left and visited Ravenfalls with friends, too. She always assumed it was to visit her new love.

"Do you visit Ravenfalls often?" Mezal's knowing smirk was enough of an answer for her. Senia was *with* Mezal. "No... that's against the clan's laws," she whispered.

"What they don't know won't hurt and if you know what's good for you, Liekki Nightsong, you'll do well to keep that knowledge to yourself. Lest you end up some place where you would never be found."

Blinding rage flashed before her. She didn't doubt that Mezal Irontail meant every single word he said. Blaze begrudgingly nodded in agreement. It still didn't mean she couldn't use the enticing piece of knowledge as possible bait for blackmail. She and her sister, Senia, had always clashed, but now Liekki finally had something over her. *At least that was one good thing that came out of the day*, Blaze thought to herself.

"Come along now. Your ride should be here at any moment now. We don't want to keep them waiting." Mezal retrieved his cloak from the chair made from the living tree and put it on. Pako went and stood beside Blaze. Together they followed Mezal Irontail out of the chambers and through the twisted halls to reach the main level of the Irontail home.

Once outside, the cool Sprig breeze ruffled Blaze's hair, causing the thin hairs on her arms to raise. The moon was high in the sky and the dark clouds that were few were now too many as they crowded together ominously. She could smell a storm coming. More than one if Mezal's unspoken words had anything to do with the troubling and fast brewing turmoil.

Blaze's eyes darted all around and to the darkened areas. There was nowhere to run. Nowhere to escape. There were guards stationed all over the place. Blaze was stuck, and the look on Mezal's face said it all to her. He had suspected she would try to leave. Seeing all the suited up guards gave her second thoughts about running off and eventually she gave up on the idea of escaping. Defeated, she let out a heavy sigh. Blaze realized the entire endeavor was doomed from the start. There was nothing else she could do but face the situation head on and pray to the spirit gods and goddesses she made it out alive.

As Blaze stood there, she took a proper look around. Their small group stood at the top of the stone stairs, looking below where a well-manicured garden with a multitude of plant species started. The garden was massive. The largest she had ever seen. Everywhere she looked were a myriad of bright and luminescent colors. It was beautiful, even if she hated to admit it. She looked further to the back and noticed the garden ended with a thick grove of ancient trees. From her place higher up, all the paths in the enormous garden led to those woods, and she wondered what was in them. Considering where she stood, there was telling what lived amongst those dark trees.

"Senia should be here any moment now." Mezal descended the stairs as his cloak snapped in the wind that had quickly picked up. The sky had gotten darker. Blaze didn't think that boded too well for any of them.

Pako grabbed Blaze's upper arm and pulled her along with him as they followed his leader down the stairs and into the garden. All around were native and exotic flowers from other lands that didn't inhabit Vulpo. They were well taken care of. She knew that having those imported must have cost a fortune. The group reached the narrow path in a short time. Loose gravel crunched underneath their feet, breaking the monotonous sound of silence as they moved as one towards the Irontail's private grove of trees.

There was a low buzzing hum she felt skim across her skin before a crackle snapped the air like a whip. Blaze caught a whiff of her sister's floral perfume long before she ever sauntered out of the grove of trees towards them.

Senia was the epitome of what a Clan Night noble vixen should be and seeing her sister there in the flesh, Blaze scowled even more. Not only did they not get along, Senia always thought she was better than her.

Her sister wore a sly smile on her face as she glanced at Mezal. Her wide-set golden eyes were filled with mischief.

"What has the troublemaker gotten herself into now?" She stopped in front of Mezal and lifted her face to him. He leaned in and kissed her on the lips.

"Oh, this one here," he chuckled. "I caught her in a little thief trap."

Senia's hated gaze snapped towards Blaze. "Thief? Why steal when father and mother provide us with everything we could ever want? Stealing is beneath us, dear sister."

Blaze shrugged. Senia scoffed before rolling her eyes.

"The Peacekeepers know," Mezal said to her as he gently caressed Senia's face.

Senia's face scrunched up, confused. "Knows what?"

"That the terror of Vulpo known as Blaze has been caught." Mezal's smirk had returned. Sudden realization slowly dawned on Senia's face as she twisted around to face her younger sister.

"You are in so much trouble." Senia faced the Nightsong guards, who were silently standing behind her. Blaze recognized them as those loyal to Senia and would keep her sister's secrets until death. The grimace she wore on her face only had gotten more dark. "Take her."

"I would suggest you keep those cuffs on her arms. It takes away her ability to use her magic. She's as vulnerable as a little lamb right now."

"I'll have my father remove them."

"Speaking of your father…" Mezal handed her the box that Blaze tried to steal. "A token for Lord Nightsong."

Senia took it and held it close to her chest while watching her sister. "I'll make sure he gets it."

Mezal kissed Senia's forehead before stepping back. "I'll be away for a day or so. I'll contact you upon my return."

"As always, I will patiently wait for you," Senia replied with a softened voice. As quickly as her sweetness was for Mezal, it turned sour when she addressed Blaze. "Come on sister, we can't keep father waiting for too long, now can we?"

The Nightsong guards took quick steps and reached Blaze, each grabbing an arm. They marched her towards the grove to the transporter that would get them home. A low and deep, churning rumbling of thunder boomed across the night sky. A searing flash of lightning came quickly afterwards, making the dark seem like day for its briefest moment before returning to normal. Liekki didn't like the ominous feeling she felt within. The hairs on the back of her neck rose and her flesh pebbled. She knew that something was coming, and it wasn't just for her. It was coming for them all.

CHAPTER 4

"LIEKKI NIGHTSONG!" Diev Nightsong shouted. "You are the bane of this family's existence! Your mother should have covered your face with her hand after she saw you at birth."

Liekki took a step back from her father as she tried to rein in the simmering anger. Any other time she would have been horrified by the filth spewing from his mouth, but she had heard it so much, she had become immune to his tirades when it came to her. This was just another moment. Another notch on her long list of things of why she hated the vulpii. Her family. *Her father*.

"Dhasas should have snatched your soul," Diev Nightsong continued, his lips curled downward and his fists tightened at his sides. He paced back and forth like a predator waiting for its prey. His tails angrily switched back and forth. The actions reminded Liekki of an irritated cat. He abruptly paused, spun on his heels, and stormed directly towards Liekki, then stopped in front of her. His eyes blazed with pure hatred and rage. This was the true side of Diev Nightsong that none in Vulpo knew about, yet Liekki knew it too well. "Instead, Zera, our Mother Goddess, cursed us and let you be born."

Liekki took a deep breath and slowly exhaled. Never losing her calm. She let the anger simmer under her skin, but she knew she would never unleash it. No matter what he said to her. No matter what he did to her, Diev Nightsong was still her father. Head of the Nightsong House. All she wanted was the cuffs off of her arms.

"And there's not a thing you can do about it," Liekki goaded, knowing she was stoking the fire. "I am here and it's because the Mother Goddess wanted it so. I didn't ask to be here. You and mother did."

"Watch your tone, young one."

"I'm not young. I'm an adult and one of these days you will treat me as one."

"I'll treat you as one the moment you act like a proper vixen of Clan Night standing," he shouted.

Liekki held her arms out in front of her. "Are you going to remove them or not?"

"I ought to keep them on, but your mother still has a soft spot when it comes to you." Diev touched the braces on Liekki's arms. His hands glowed a bright blue. The longer he held on, the brighter his hands got. She felt a surge of magic flow up her arm before she heard the click of the cuffs unlocking. "You are not allowed to leave the house. Or this mountain. Not until we let this trouble you have caused blow over."

Liekki rolled her eyes, but knew better to test her father any longer. "Yes, sir."

"Good. Leave me be. I tire of your cursed presence."

Liekki sat on top of her favorite rocky ledge. Her feet dangled in the air while far below her the sound of the sea could lull anyone into a false sense of security. Of the many hiding spots she had, the ledge was her favorite place to go. It has been ever since she was a tiny kit and able to get away from her family. Even though the sound of the soothing ebb and flow of the water below wasn't too quiet, it was still the perfect and quietest place for her to retreat and think. Lately, she mainly used it to plot. Most times, Liekki's plotting comprised of thoughts for revenge. Tonight, it was how to avoid standing in front of the clan's elders. Everything that she had thought of wouldn't fare too well for her.

She picked up a small stone from the pile she had compiled after sitting down. The sharp, black rock was cold in her hand, but fit perfectly. Liekki tossed it up, caught it, and threw it towards the sea. Even with her keen sense of hearing, she wasn't able to hear the stone when it hit the water. She picked up another and did it again. Then again. The repetitive motions were soothing to her, and eventually it helped find her center. It had been off lately.

A strong breeze swept across the ledge and brushed the side of her face. Stray strands of her dark hair brushed against her cheeks before she reached up and pushed them back into the long braid she wore. A sudden sense of being watched hit her. Liekki glanced around to see if anyone was nearby, but she was all alone. Which wasn't anything new to her. Nevertheless, the uneasy feeling of being watched permeated her senses. She could have sworn someone was close.

The light of the second moon of Eldritch had made its debut for the night. The large blue orb had only risen a few hours ago, reminding her that time was flying by too quickly. Unlike previous nights before, the sky was clear over Vulpo. Yet the faint glow of the pale sapphire moon high above gave the world an ethereal glow. What few flowers and plants that grew in the part of the mountains she called home seemed almost unreal.

Liekki jumped up and made a rash decision. It had been days since they had ordered her to not leave the compound. She constantly felt the urge to get away. To escape. There was no way she could go back to the city. Her cover was completely blown. The Peacekeepers released the news that the thief known as Blaze was caught and reprimanded by her clan. Word had spread fast and caught on like a wildfire. It had been nothing but craziness once everyone realized it was her. Liekki's parents had been having to fend off heated calls for severe punishment. Including the calls from their leaders, the Sacred Three.

As much as her father hated her, he still refused to listen to the masses. She was thankful for that.

Liekki grinned. She wasn't sorry about what she did. The place needed some excitement away from the random murders happening lately, and she gave them what they wanted. The only person she wanted to see at the moment was probably her only friend, Ice. She hadn't talked to her since they escaped, leaving her to be caught by Mezal. The more she thought about it, the more she realized it was a trap.

Someone undeniably set her up. Liekki was determined to find out if Hot Paw was the only one responsible for setting her up or if there was someone else behind him to betray the group the way he did. Betray her in the fashion he did. The one thing she was sure about was that Ice had no part in it. More than likely, she discovered it was a trap afterwards. Her friend would help her figure it out. No matter what it took to get the information.

A terrible decision made, Liekki shifted into her true fox form and took off down the mountain. Checking her surroundings, Liekki darted across the rocky path, careful to watch her step as dirt and rocks flew from under her paws. Although she grew up in those mountains, it surely didn't mean they weren't dangerous. She knew plenty who fell and broke a bone or two. Even a few who had died from the fall.

Far ahead, the flickering orange-red glow from the pathlamp at the fork ahead told her she was close to where she wanted to go. Careful to avoid any of the guards on duty, she diverted to a darker, less lit path when she saw a guard standing still, head swiveling around as if he heard her.

Motionless, she slowed her breathing and flattened herself against the mountainside. She waited until the guard moved on. Being discovered at that moment would ruin everything. Time slowly ticked by and when she felt safe enough to venture on, she left the safety of the shadows and traveled back to the path she was trekking along. Constantly looking and sniffing around, checking her surroundings.

One could never be too careful.

Liekki rounded the curve and sprinted towards the bottom, careful not to disturb any other critters that lived in the mountains. It was Vulpii land, but the mountains had other things to say about who called it home. Dark nature spirits who didn't take kindly to being disturbed had been known to make their presence felt. More often than not, the presence being felt was deadly.

The further down she went, the more relaxed she felt. The guards near the bottom cared little about what she did. She could pay them off with whatever items they requested from the goods she supplied. Once in a safe enough place, she shifted into her two-legged form, shook out her hair and tails, then continued on by foot.

Not wanting to be seen as herself, Liekki brushed a hand down over her face, creating a new illusion of a different Vulpii. To everyone else, she looked like a fox from Clan Terra. She had auburn hair, yellow eyes, and a single bushy red tail with a white tip. She looked nothing like she belonged to Clan Night. Or that she was three tailed.

She hurried, but at a leisurely pace on the path, making sure she kept out of sight. The gates to the Nightsong compound would give her the most problems, but an idea had already formed in her mind.

"Hey you!" a masculine voice called out, startling Liekki, stopping her dead in her tracks.

Her head shot around to the sound to find two house guards on the ledge above her. Hidden against the dark stone, Liekki had missed them completely. She cursed silently to herself.

"Are you talking to me?"

The two guards glanced at each other before one came down another trail she didn't see. Thick brush and a couple of trees hid it from her. The closer he got, she realized she recognized the guard. One of her father's favorites. He stopped directly in front of her. "Who else would we be talking to? You're the only one on the path. It's late. What are you doing out here?"

"I'm going back home. To the terran district."

"Come now," he said with a raised brow. "That's not going to fly by us, Liekki."

The admission surprised her, but she refused to show it. "Liekki?" she said, trying to feign confusion.

The guard tilted his head to the side while wearing a smirk on his face. "I can see beyond your glamour."

Liekki let out a low growl. The guard was one of her father's flayers. She ran a hand over her face, dispelling the illusion. "It was a worth a shot."

"It was," the guard said with a smile. "Unfortunately for you, my job is to watch all the trails. Including the hidden ones you favor all over these mountains... and underneath, to make sure you don't step a paw off it."

"I wasn't going far. Tell you what — whatever you want, I can get it for you. Infused gems. Aged honey-wine. Vixens. I mean the really pretty ones down there in the *Silk Petal* district. Whatever you desire, I have access to it and can get it for you. All you have to do is pretend you never saw me. Let me go. I won't be away for too long. I promise I'll be back before my father or mother knows I was ever gone."

"You know that won't work on me. I'm here to do a job. I am loyal to this family and I never want to get on Leader Nightsong's bad side. Not right now, at least. Helping you run off will land me in hot water. I like my hide and tails exactly the way it is." The guard looked upward at the other guard and whistled for him. His partner jumped off the ledge and landed on his feet. "The younger Nightsong tried to escape just like her father said."

Liekki scowled even more. The fact her father had set up traps with guards all over the place was going to make it very difficult to get away, if at all. She couldn't take the teleportation gate.

They were highly guarded, she suspected, just like the rest of the mountain.

"Fine... I'll go back," she said, defeated. Liekki knew she wouldn't be able to do anything at the rate she was going. Not until the situation blew over after the meeting with the Clan's leaders. Something she wasn't looking forward to at all. "What's your name?"

The first guard who stood perilously close to her looked down at her. "Efrim."

"Nice meeting you, Efrim."

"As well, young one. Come on, let's head back. I promise I won't tell your father if you promise not to attempt to escape again."

Liekki really wanted to get away from there, but things were becoming clearer to her. The more she thought about everything, the more she realized, even if she left the compound, she wouldn't get far. Even if she made it to Ice, her friend's mother would see right through the glamour. Kalama Brightsun was no one to play around with. Especially since she was on the *Council of Three*, which was commonly known among all the clans as the Sacred Three. Her being a nine tailed also didn't help matters. Nine tails were the strongest among their kind.

She didn't fight with Efrim. Everything screamed at her inside to fight back the oppressive system she grew up in and do what she wanted to do, but Liekki knew when to pick her battles. The war against her family and the nobility could last a long time. She was a patient fox.

"Alright. I'll go back. Only because you have been nothing but nice to me. Unlike the other guards my father employs around here."

"Glad you're seeing it our way and making this easy," Efrim said. He pointed towards the path that led back up the mountain. He nudged her side. "We're going that way."

Liekki fell silent as they took a shortened route back towards the large house that went deep inside of the Hollow Spine mountains.

The path was rocky until they neared her home. That was when it became clearer. The frigid night air took a turn for the worst, which was unusual to her. She looked up to the night skies and froze. Efrim and the other guard with him did the same.

"Those clouds don't look good," Efrim said with a rough voice, observing the darkening sky above them.

Liekki's thoughts weren't too far off from his spoken words. Dark clouds always brought ill portents in her mind. An icy chill ran up her spine, making her shiver involuntarily. She wanted to get away as fast as she could. Something was very wrong. Not right. She didn't like it.

"No, they don't." Liekki took a step towards the stone stairwell, but Efrim stopped Liekki from moving when he held out his arm in front of her.

Efrim eyed his partner. "Go alert the others."

"Why?" the other guard questioned.

Liekki was curious too. "Yes, why?"

She never got her answer. A streak of blueish black and red lightning lit up the night sky, striking in the center of Vulpii lands. Thunder rolled like drums across the sky. Liekki swore she could feel the ground shaking.

"That's the sacred island," Efrim said, while pointing towards the center of the lands.

Even from the distance where they all stood, Liekki could see that he was right. One more bolt of pure white and bigger than the others hit hard, turning their night skies to day before quickly going dark again. She knew what it meant. Every single Vulpii knew what it meant. Efrim caught her gaze and that of his partners. Their eyes widened with nervousness. Possible fear.

All Liekki could think about was what it all signified. "You realize what this means?"

It was Efrim who answered. His ears twitched around before facing forward again. "I do, young Nightsong. Mother Goddess calls on our people yet again. For us to prove we've learned from our mistakes. She's calling us out for a second chance. It's our time to go through the Eldritch Trials yet again."

CHAPTER 5

E verything had been a blur in the Nightsong household. Liekki kept to her rooms because after the spectacular lightning show the night before, the guards had been all over the place. They were on double duty, constantly roaming the mountains and their home. Not an inch unturned could be breached. Liekki's father was on a rampage because he found out that she was attempting to escape, although it didn't work. Her mother, Luya, tried to keep the peace, but no matter how much she pleaded with Diev, it didn't work at all. Her siblings pointed and laughed at her when their father wasn't watching. Liekki was ready to smash them all to pieces. Her emotions were many things she couldn't quite put together. Frustration wasn't even the right word for how she felt during those moments.

Liekki felt utterly lost.

Alone.

Later on, Liekki learned Efrim had indeed kept his word and said nothing to her father. It was his partner that was there with them whose lips were looser than a high paid Vixen in a *flower house. Traitor.* In her head, she still could hear her father's foul words as they spewed from his mouth from that morning at breakfast. From when he confronted her about her attempted escapades. His words had the effect he wanted. They didn't make her feel any better. Her father wasn't taking any chances on her getting gone.

Liekki had finished dressing and walked towards the entrance of her private chambers. Efrim stood guard at her door when she stepped out finally. For the first time in a while, she was genuinely surprised. She didn't expect to see Efrim standing there with a smug smile on his face and a knowing glint in his eyes. Liekki slightly canted her head to the side, then opened her mouth to speak but was cutoff the moment the first word had slid off of her tongue. Efrim had beaten her to it.

"Kha Nightsong, how are you today?" His voice was more upbeat than normal.

Liekki's brows rose, wary of the strange mood she found the odd guard in. None of the other guards had ever been so formal with her before. Kha Nightsong was her mother. Not her. "Just call me Liekki. Or Blaze."

He smiled at her, eyes filled with mischief. "Alright. Kha Blaze it is. How are you today?"

She sighed and shook her head in exasperation. "Are you always this insufferable?"

He shrugged. "I could be doing something else, instead I am to guard you. I have to make the best of whatever my situation

43

is. If that means annoying you at times, then I have free rein to do that."

Liekki's eyes narrowed with distrust. "On who's orders?"

"Your father's, of course."

Liekki let out an aggravated hiss between clenched teeth. *This was the worst thing possible*, she thought to herself. "Why?"

"I guess he didn't want to take any more chances on you trying to disappear before the summoning today. Besides, from his guards, I'm the only one skilled enough to see past your exquisitely done glamours."

"Is that what this is all about?" she asked with a rapidly rising voice. "The stupid summoning?"

Efrim stiffened, then frowned at her words. "This is a serious matter. There's nothing stupid about the call from Zera, our Mother Goddess. This is our chance to redeem ourselves in her eyes. For us to move past the last one hundred plus years of being cursed because we failed."

"Wrong! *We* didn't fail. Kalama Brightsun failed. With her stupidity and greed, she doomed us all."

"Don't speak those blasphemous words about one of our sacred three!" Efrim rushed out. His eyes darkened, clouded with rage and pure, controlled anger. If Liekki kept up the tirade she was dangerously having, she knew that something bad would happen between him and her. Her father would become infuriated if anything were to happen again.

"Fine, Efrim. You're right, okay? I won't speak ill of her. Just know that she's not what she seems."

He shifted on his feet and eyed her carefully. "And how would you know?"

Liekki knew because Brightsun was Ice's mother. She couldn't tell Efrim that because he was her father's watchdog. Whatever he said would probably go right back to the daemon fox himself.

Or not... the random stray thought popped into her head.

She looked at her guard a little more closely and remembered that he didn't snitch on her about her trying to escape down the mountain using a glamour.

Liekki sighed. "Why are you being so nice to me? Really?"

"I'm a nice Vulpiian."

"But you're being extra nice. Why?"

"I have no clue what you mean, Kha Blaze." He stared at her wide eyed, daring her to challenge him.

"Sure you don't."

A smirk lifted at the corner of Efrim's lips. Liekki wasn't surprised, and silently questioned what the guard's true intentions were. She quickly scanned the hall where they stood, glad to find it still empty, before stepping closer to him. She leaned into his space where only he could hear her. "Can I ask you something?"

He inched closer to her, closing the gap. If anyone was to walk past them, it would seem they were engaged in an intimate moment. Efrim looked her straight in the eyes. "*You* can ask me anything?"

"Yeah, but will you actually answer this question? I mean, you didn't really answer why you're being so nice to me."

"If you recall, Kha Blaze, I said I was being nice because I'm a nice Vulpiian. Can I not be nice just for the sake of it?"

"I don't know. It's weird. Plus, you are my father's guard, after all."

"Ahh, I see," he said as he eyed her warily. "Kha Blaze, I *work* for your father. I'm still able to hold my personal opinions. I don't blindly follow like some others. There's something about you I find interesting. I can't take into account for others, I can only take into account my own actions. I am not like them. If you haven't noticed yet."

Liekki had noticed, but for some reason, it unnerved her. She stared at him for a long time. His eyes turned a different shade of colors before going back to his normal steely hazel flecked with golds and black. *Strange.* The energy and aura surrounding the strange guard had always been different, and for whatever reason, she didn't understand why it unnerved her so. "I've noticed. How long have you been with my family, Efrim?"

"Long enough," he said, evading her question. "The foxes of our clan aren't really nice to you, are they?"

"What do you think?" Liekki pointed to herself. "They call me cursed. My father said I never should have been born. Have you not noticed the stares of my siblings? I have black fur with reddish orange blended in with it. I have three tails when at my age I should only have one. Me standing here talking to you in my biped form says it all. I've been able to do this since I was born. I shouldn't have been able to do this until I am at least thirty to fifty years."

"All of that just makes you special and wise beyond your years. Not cursed. Not at all."

Liekki rolled her eyes. "You are the only one, then. Your opinion is the sore one out. Even I don't believe it."

"Perhaps you should. You are more than what you believe you are, Liekki."

A heavy sigh escaped Liekki's lips. She was thankful for Efrim being nice. It was a welcomed moment, considering everything she had to deal with that morning. The guard was still a mystery to her and even though she still didn't trust him, her opinion of Efrim had changed somewhat. Well, it was much better than it was the previous night.

"I'll think about what you said." Liekki reached out and touched Efrim's arm. "Thanks for the encouraging words. They're appreciated."

"Any time, Kha Blaze," he responded. "So where were you off to?"

"Just a walk down in the caves. You know, to clear my head. It's not like I can sneak off. My father has this place on lockdown."

"That he does. I'll go with you."

"You don't have to. I'll be alright."

Efrim cleared his throat. "I don't think you understand. I'm your bodyguard. I go wherever you go."

"You're my father's personal guard," Liekki reiterated, not understanding what he was getting on about.

"After last night, he thought I did such a great job in detecting you while you were using a glamour. He relieved me of my duty to him and made me your sole bodyguard."

Liekki couldn't believe it. All of her older siblings had their own personal guards, but not her. She wasn't worthy of one. That was how she could get into so much trouble. How she was able to sneak out as much as she did. But if the Sacred Three and the Vulpiian council, along with the rest of the important noble Vulpiian families, were screaming bloody murder about her actions, her father had to show faith that he was curbing her nightly activities.

She should have been excited that she was getting privileges, but in the end, it was nothing like that. No, this was way worse. This was her father's way of punishing her. Liekki glanced at Efrim once more. There were so many thoughts zipping through her mind. She would need a moment alone to decipher it all.

Liekki plastered on a grin that didn't quite reach her eyes. "Well then, congratulations on your promotion. I won't be down there long. I want to see the luminescent pools. They're beautiful and always bring me calm when it feels like the world is too much."

Efrim's eyes narrowed, and brows furrowed, but said nothing. He looked pensively at her, then pointed towards the left of them. "After you. I've heard about your family's luminescent pools, but never had the opportunity to see them. My duties have alway led to me to other places. And your family keeps it very well hidden from the prying gazes of others that are not a Nightsong."

Liekki led them down the winding halls, and towards the door that led to the caves. "Well, you are in for a treat. Our caves are the only ones that have them in all of Vulpo. It's a family treasure, so to speak."

She couldn't figure out why they had to wait until night for all three clans to come together to determine what was going to happen about the trials. Liekki's family traveled together through the teleportation stations. It took them to the outside edge of the cliffs that looked down at the sacred island. The most protected place for all Vulpii in Vulpo. It was the home of their government. It was where the sacred three also ruled together over all the clans of Vulpii.

All around the cliffs, Liekki could see the different clans gather in their cordoned off viewing areas. Clan Night differed from the other two clans. While Clan Terra and Clan Sky allowed all of their people to come to things like this, Clan Night didn't. Only the Nobles and high-ranking merchant families were allowed to come. The rest of Clan Night stayed back and would watch from the Summoning Stone area underneath the mountain, deep in the common caves.

Liekki's family was given special seating because of Diev Nightsong's leadership of Clan Night. They were the only ones who could sit in the first row. All six of her siblings, her mother and father, and their personal guard retinue. Her family strode into the clearing, chins raised, eyes forward. Unlike her family, Liekki's gaze searched the crowd and watched the others watch them. The Nobles of Clan Night and their families watched with awe and while more families than the usual watched them walk in with pure envy. There was no doubt in her mind that her father's enemies were in attendance. And extremely angry.

As they moved among the crowd, Liekki heard the heated whispers. She saw them pointing at her. It was hard, but she did her best to not let it get to her. She couldn't understand why, but lately she was finding it difficult to ignore the things she usually would and, unfortunately, she was in the worst place possible to act out her feelings.

In these types of moments, Liekki wished she could have a conversation with her best friend, Ice. She was her only close friend. Too bad it took her too long to figure that out. She didn't dare call her guard a friend. Liekki still thought it was suspicious that suddenly she was able to get a personal bodyguard. For so long, her father refused to let her have one, no matter how much her mother begged him. He was a hard and cruel Vulpii. A true dogfox, that much she knew for sure.

When they reached the front, Liekki sat down on the wooden carved bench near the end of the row. Her father sat at the opposite end of her and her mother, Luya, beside him, looking regal as ever. Ever since they had arrived, she felt a strange stirring in her stomach. Liekki didn't know what it was, but something was telling her it wasn't good. She shifted her body slightly to observe the crowd behind them, and there was Efrim standing straight behind her. She was oddly glad he was there by her side.

Flitting thoughts from earlier at the luminescent pools filled her mind. Seeing Efrim's pure surprise at the glowing pools and crystals had her laughing out loud. The way he acted, one would've thought he wasn't really of Clan Night.

Could he be something else? An eerie feeling skittered down Liekki's spine. As she turned around to face the front again, his eyes found hers, and he grinned. It was the same smirk that always seemed like he knew something that no one else did and wasn't going to divulge the secret he was keeping tight-lipped. She wanted to ask him if he was truly a fox of Clan Night, but the sky thundered and she knew there was no asking him now. Everything was about to start.

From where she sat, Liekki watched as three figures in robes the color of pure white walk out of the treehouse. They wore those colors to show they were neutral when it came to fairness and not beholden to the colors of their clan. The trio walked towards the center of the island in a synchronized motion.

Strong magic users, one from each clan, based on the colors of their cloaks, followed close behind the three figures before breaking off. Each went their own way to an individual designated point that created a triangle. Higher up from where she and her family sat, Liekki could hear the beginning of the chants from the three white-robed figures. The magic users from below stood at their spot and amplified the sound. As the tendrils of magic grew, Liekki felt it as it rose and entwined with each other to become one.

Their power called out to her magic, and she tried her best to tamper the call of it. The pull was strong, and she did everything to stay put. As the chanted words were weaving its spell, she slowly rose but was gently pushed down by the hands of Efrim. He helped to keep her firm in her seat, with no one being the wiser of the trouble she was having. The swirls and tendrils only had gotten larger and larger until it created a large mirror in the sky above the sacred island. Everyone gathered could see the Sacred Three from every single angle.

The spell complete, Liekki expelled the breath she was holding. It was a sigh of relief and the pressure of the curious magic had dissipated. Liekki watched as Kalama Brightsun, in her pure white robes trimmed with silver, made her way to the center of the small island. She knew that there was no leader of the three, but it was an unspoken, well known fact that Kalama Brightsun ruled the other two with an icy fist. Whatever she said went. No questions asked.

All the noise settled down, and a deafening silence filled the air. The pregnant silence was thick with a weary unknown that made Liekki even more uncomfortable. The tang of the magic workers magic was tangy and citrus like. It was clean and not corrupt like she would find in Hallowbane Den.

Liekki could feel the tension between the three clans. It wasn't very often the clans gathered together. Clan Sky preferred their snow and ice district, while Clan Terra preferred to hide away in their treehouses. Both of them looked down on Clan Night. The first of their kind. The true kits of the moon. Born of Aku. The Spirit of the First Moon.

All three clans were present, restless, and suspicious of each other, yet they knew had to be there. The situation was entirely way too important. They were on the precipes of something and she didn't know what exactly. Vulpiians didn't argue either. Apart from the few gloomy ones who thought the world was ending and their gods of darkness would take control. Liekki then frowned. Those same dark gods were the very ones that Clan Night worshipped.

Kalama Brightsun cast her gaze over the crowd and warmly smiled as she did. Liekki did everything to keep from growling out loud at the vixen.

"We gather here because our time has come. The time to prove ourselves worthy. Together, we have learned from the mistakes of our haunted past. Over the last ten years, we have grown together as a species. It is time to prove ourselves to Zera, the Mother Goddess."

A loud roar of cheers and chants went up from both Clan Terra and Clan Sky, but her tribe, Clan Night, sat there quiet. Stoic as ever.

Kalama Brightsun continued on. "Every eligible Vulpiian from each clan, their names have been added to the box." A hexagonal shaped box made with clear, crystalline glass appeared in front of her. It floated in the air and inside, thin slices of paper with written names on them, flashed and tumbled about in constant motion. "The qualifications are based on their overall rankings from the Vulpii Champion School. If you have finished the school within the last year or two, you are still eligible to be chosen."

Excitement drifted through the clans. She couldn't believe anyone would be excited to go through the trials. She never wanted to go through it. What if they failed? They would bring shame to them all, including their family. Her father would kill her himself if that ever happened to her or any of her siblings.

Liekki surveyed the area all around her. Everyone in Clan Night wore grim and solemn expressions. Their somber moods were the total opposite of the others. Luckily for her, she didn't have to worry about the trials thanks to her extracurricular activities; they had banned her from everything. Her name wouldn't be put in the box and for this one thing, she was thankful.

Kalama Brightsun and the two other elders walked in a circle. Each one going the opposite direction of the other on the outside. The trail they walked on the ground lit up in spectacular fashion. Their voices lifted together in a song of ethereal beauty. It started out peaceful, but gradually morphed into a mournful song of sadness. It pierced at Liekki's heart. Surprising to even her, a wetness pooled at the corners of her eyes. The three elders stopped all at once. Each one remained motionless, like the wind ahead of a violent and devastating tempest. Kalama Brightsun faced Clan Night while Elder Nikesh faced Clan Sky and Elder Salibas faced Clan Terra.

The Sacred Three had opened their mouths and spoke simultaneously. "Kheton, Spirit of Fire and Lightning, shed your flames of light so our champion can open their eyes and see the truth. Esoi, Spirit of the Wind and Air, breathe life into our chosen and allow them to live in righteousness and live that path until the end. Umjir, Spirit of the Mountains, give strength to our chosen, so they may stand strong as stone in the face of danger and temptation. Urdes, Spirit of the Forest, protect our champion and embrace them in your comforting shade."

Everything went still. The Sacred Three stared at the clans without expression, but not a word was uttered. The wind came to a halt. The waters below went still. Not even the smallest insect made a noise. Liekki knew the Spirits were working and walked amongst them. The feeling of the magic was different. Older. Ancient. The Sacred Three were strong, but this was much different. More than their gifts.

Liekki's skin pebbled all over. She wanted to run away from there, but she couldn't move. She attempted to move again, but remained fixed in her spot. Liekki glanced at the others and realized they were looking all around too, unable to move as well.

An overwhelming sense of wrongness blanketed Liekki, and she didn't like its feeling. Everything moved as if time slowed down. The Sacred Three all turned at the same time and faced Clan Night. A roaring sound filled Liekki's ears. The Elders' eyes widened. Their mouths opened wide and together, as one voice, they spoke.

"Liekki Nightsong. The Spirits have chosen. You are our champion. You will represent all Vulpii in The Eldritch Trials."

CHAPTER 6

The roaring in her ears stopped. The intense hold that had everyone in its grip was let go. Liekki sat there, stunned. She was at a loss for words. She didn't know what to do. Her entire family all moved around and fixed their gaze with burning glares. The expression on her father's face was one she had never seen before. It wasn't quite anger, but more that of confusion. Maybe some sick, twisted version of pride. Whatever it was, Liekki knew it was something that confused even her.

A deafening sound went up all around her. The maddening uproar was slowly taking hold amongst Clan Night and keeping them in it its firm grip.

"She can't be the chosen!"

"She should be in jail," someone from behind her yelled.

"She's a thief!" those sitting close to her family shouted. It was a rising cacophony of heated agreements that startled even Liekki. So much animosity surrounded her.

"How did her name get entered?"

"Isn't she supposed to be banned?"

"We need a do over!" Another shouted.

"Take her! Grab her! She's unworthy!"

Tension rose amongst her clan. Liekki could feel it. She saw it in their eyes. The way their lips pulled back in snarls, allowing their teeth and fangs to be bared.

"She's cursed! She will surely fail us!"

"We are doomed!"

Everywhere she looked, someone was furious and screaming. Her father rose from the bench. Liekki's mother and siblings followed pursuit. From across the way, she could hear the same outrage coming from Clan Sky and Clan Terra. In a mad dash of assiduous fury, they all rushed towards Clan Night's area. Malice in their eyes. Canine teeth bared. Their battle magic was hovering on the edge. She knew they were hellbent on trying to reach her.

Liekki felt a hand on her shoulder and she turned slightly around and looked up to find Efrim watching her. His eyes darted to the others, then back to her. He winked before he helped her up. "Kha Blaze... I think it's time that we should make an exit."

"I think you may be right," Liekki said, her eyes darting all around the clearing. "If not, they're going to shred me to pieces. This is wrong. How did this happen? I shouldn't have been chosen. I am more than a few years removed from the Champion School."

"The Spirits says otherwise."

"ENOUGH OF THIS!" Diev Nightsong shouted to his clan. "We will look into this further. She can not represent us. Something is very wrong. We'll get this figured out and fixed. Another will be chosen. Now, let us all leave this place before the other clans reach us and it becomes a bloodbath."

The discordant words were still being shouted, but not with the same enthusiasm as before. The Nightsong family and their guards departed in a hurry. The other families of Clan Night settled down and created a path wide enough to let their first family through. After they cleared, House Irontail barged into the area and began to fight. The rest of Clan Night broke apart and escaped the brawls that Clan Terra had begun.

Liekki and her family rushed to the stone pedestals that would transport them back to their home. Soon as she reached them, her father shoved her forward.

"You first, since you're the cause of this mess," he snapped at her.

Liekki didn't hesitate. She looked back once more and saw the other clans rushing after them. She wasn't ready to see her end quite yet. Efrim followed close on her heels and soon as they were settled, they were taken away and ended up in the Gate Room. A cavernous place with natural arches and stalagmites hanging from above.

She stepped off the glowing pad that was marked with magical sigils and onto the stone path that led away from the small underground island. Nothing but a long drop into the abyss surrounded it. Luminescent plants and flowers lined the stone path. It gave off enough light for her to see her way back to the safer zone and up the stairs that were carved into the side of the mountain.

The whispers drifting in the air to her ears weren't hard to make out. Her siblings were talking about her, which wasn't anything new. She didn't ask to be chosen. She didn't even ask to be added to the names. Her name wasn't supposed to have been in there. Liekki shook her head in disbelief.

Once she reached the top of the stairs, Liekki turned back to her siblings. "Just so you know. I didn't want to be chosen. I shouldn't have been chosen and I don't know what happened. I've been here this entire time so I couldn't have done any trickery. I can barely stand Clan Night, let alone Clan Sky and Clan Terra, so what makes you think I'd do this to help them?"

Her siblings glanced at each other, surprised that she would even speak up.

Liekki then stared at her sister, Senia, who was the main one spreading lies and talking about her. The mere thought of her actions made her even angrier. "At least I'm not sleeping with the enemy. I may be hated and even cursed, but no matter when it comes down to it. I am loyal to Clan Night. The true kits of Aku. You won't find me dipping my tails in other waters."

Her sisters and brothers gasped as they all turned to stare at Senia. Liekki didn't bother to stick around. She stomped out of there and headed straight to her rooms.

"Don't let the whispers of others get to you, young Night-song," Efrim said, as he kept up with her.

Liekki had forgotten the presence of her personal bodyguard, who had been with her the entire time. She rounded around towards him. "Why are you still here? I thought you would have left by now. Like the other guards."

He shrugged. "I take my duties seriously. I'm to protect you. Even if that means I have to protect you from your family. More specifically, your sister."

"You noticed that too?"

"I'm paid to notice everything. Including when a sister looks like she was ready to rip your heart out of your chest. I'd be careful around that one. Especially with the type of accusations you made. Your other siblings are going to whisper and they're going to get back to your father as your words."

Liekki laughed. She didn't mean to, but she couldn't help it. She thought back to the box she had tried to steal that got her in the mess she was currently in to begin with. Her father knew very well about Senia and Mezal. There was no doubt in her mind that he knew. He could pretend, but it was hard to pretend when one gave another an expensive rare gift like Mezal Irontail gave her father.

"Honestly, if it got back to my father, he wouldn't care. Especially since he already knows Efrim. You see, my words weren't an accusation. I was just stating facts. Now... after all the drama of today, I am going to bed. I need time for myself for a change and to rest my mind. Figure out how to get out of this mess I am in. This mess that is constantly growing and expanding."

"What the Spirits choose, who are we to go against it? Things happen for reasons, young Nightsong. You'll figure it out. Have a good night. I'll see you in the morning."

Liekki said nothing else, but turned and left Efrim standing there. She went into her room, closing the door behind her. She knew her father would probably come by her room eventually before he called it a night. Probably wanting to know how she did it, but she had news for him. She didn't do it and from the looks of it, the Sacred Three didn't do it, either. They were just as shocked as all the others. Including her.

Liekki jumped up from her bed and instantly shifted into her true fox form. Her fur stood on end all over her body. If she looked at herself in the mirror, she knew she would be extremely fluffy, and that irritated her. She hated when she had an uncontrolled shift. She let out a snarl, then a yip in frustration. The loud pounding against her bedroom had startled her awake, but they would know she was awake now.

She concentrated and shifted back into her biped form and shuffled towards the door and opened it. On the other side was her mother. Her fingers twisted and rubbed together as if she was nervous, but for what, she had no idea. Her mother's eyes scanned Liekki before she stepped inside of the room and shut the door behind her.

"What did you do? Your father has been on a rampage since last night. Fending off the other nobles from all the clans. They're blaming him for what happened. How did you do it?"

"I have no clue what you are talking about, mother."

"How did you get your name inside of the box? Did you use your magic?"

Liekki lifted her wrist so her mother could see clearly. The beaded black and orange gemstone bracelet she wore on her wrist shone under the light. "You know just as much as I do that I am unable to do major magic as long as I wear this. I can't even take this off. I can do basic magic like glamours, shifting, and hearth. My most basic self is cutoff from me. I'm just a shell mother. So how my name got entered, I have no clue. I am just as lost as you. Besides, we were all there. One moment, the glass box was empty. The next moment, it wasn't. If anyone needs to question anyone, they should question the Sacred Three."

Liekki's mother, Luya, made a face and scowled. "I don't know why you stand there and say you have basic magic. Even with the bracelet tampering with your magic, your gifts are still stronger than most Vulpii wish they could have. More than your siblings. More than me and I would never admit that to anyone else. That includes your father. He doesn't know how strong you truly are. We would all be in trouble if he ever do." She shook her head. "I don't know. Be careful today. I'm afraid of what Diev might do. Avoid your father at all costs, okay?"

Liekki's mother touched her face gently and caressed it in a motherly way before letting her hands fall back to her sides. "Okay, mother. I will." Liekki felt defeated. She decided she wouldn't argue. Not today. First off, she wasn't in the mood. Second, if her mother was in her room giving a warning, she knew it was extremely bad.

Luya smiled. "I'll stop by the kitchen and have food brought up here."

"Thanks."

Her mother started to say something, then hesitated. Liekki watched with curiosity. She had never seen her mother act like the way she was before. This was all new to her. It was weird, and she wondered what was going on.

"No need to thank me. I'm just making sure you are okay. How's Efrim?"

"Father's dogfox through and through."

Liekki's mother shook her head. "No. It was me who suggested that he come to you. No matter what you think, he's good. He's strong with his gifts and he is very intelligent. A good protector for someone like you."

There was something her mother wasn't saying, but Liekki couldn't figure out what it was.

"So, he's not father's dogfox?"

"No."

Now that was news, Liekki thought. "But I always seen him as one of father's guards. He reports to father. He even told me so."

Liekki's mother stepped closer to her. She tilted her head and snapped her finger. A spark of yellow came out of her fingertips. "I sealed the room from listening ears. So listen clearly, my darling kit. I've known Efrim for many years. Before I even met your father. He's always come and gone. He's loyal to me. Your father may think that Efrim is his lackey, but everything he reports to your father, he reports to me first. I let him know what he can tell your father."

"*Oh*. Well, that's some juicy news. Here I thought you just did whatever father said to do."

"I'm not some Vixen who wants to be constantly pampered and nothing else. I care about my children. All of you. Sometimes it's hard for me, but I have a role to play too. I know I'm harsh, but it's for your good. Truly. This world is so cruel. You are different and your path will be harder than anyone else. I knew that the moment I first saw you after you were born. Efrim, he is safe. He's a good guard, too. You'll see. I trust him because his magic is strong. He has five tails, Liekki, not the three you see. His glamours are the best. Top-notch. How do you think he saw you trying to sneak out?" Luya pointed to the bracelet Liekki was wearing. "That bracelet is courtesy of him."

Liekki had not expected to hear that, and her expression showed her surprise. It was obvious her mother was keeping secrets and now she wanted to know more about what her mother wasn't telling her.

"Who is Efrim to you? Really?"

"He's just a friend. His family is an old name. Pure Clan Night. It doesn't matter right about now. What does matter is that you stay strong. The Spirits are never wrong and neither is the Mother Goddess. You will do well. Somehow, I think you were born for this."

CHAPTER 7

A raucous banging noise wrapped against the door. Luya dispelled the privacy spell and frantically looked back at the door. "That's your father. I'm sure of it."

"What does he want?" Liekki practically growled.

"There's no telling but be on your best behaviour. For me, please?"

Liekki let out an audible huff. She didn't know what to think of this new turnover with her mother. For her entire life, she thought her mother was a pushover. Only to find out she wasn't. Things were becoming more bizarre to Liekki with each passing second. Things weren't as they should have been, and that was why she stayed to herself most days. Vulpo was becoming a cesspool of rot and moral decay. Even if she was a thief, some of her morals were better than the lot of Vulpiians she had come across lately. "Fine. For you and you only. I'm still unsure about everything, but if it keeps father off of yours and my backs, then I'll go along."

Luya smiled. "You know how to be a good kit when you need to be."

Liekki watched as her mother's face morphed from somewhat happy to that of being stern and stoic. What she normally saw whenever it came to her mother. Her back straightened and her shoulders pushed back. Luya's chin lifted and before Liekki stood vixen of noble heritage, who didn't brook any naysayers.

She was impressed.

Liekki took a step towards the door, then stopped when it burst opened. Her father, in his black and grey robes, stormed inside of her room and stopped just before her and her mother.

"Why weren't you opening the door when I first knocked?"

"More like banging on it, but I digress. You barged right on in as I was about to open it for you. I had to rush out of the way to avoid being knocked down."

He sneered. His face was a mask of disappointment and hatred. "Maybe it would do you some good."

Liekki swallowed her words, remembering what her mother had asked her just moments before. She stepped aside, allowing her father further entrance into her private space. With him in there, it felt like a violation and she knew that soon as he left, she would have to do a cleansing spell to rid the space of his erosion. She had enough negativity surrounding her. She didn't want his darkness around mingling in with hers.

Diev glared down at his daughter. His gaze was intense, as the gold of his pupils only darkened. She stared at him, never breaking contact, and watched as a shadow moved behind his eyes. It was so abrupt, she almost thought she was seeing things.

"You need to get properly dressed," he said with a snarl. "You have a visitor."

"I'm not expecting anyone," Liekki said. Shaken by what she had just seen. It sent a chill down her spine. Whatever was going on with her father wasn't right. She did her best to keep the words that always triggered her father to herself. Liekki had no clue who might have called on her so early in the morning, but she knew it wouldn't do her any good to show up looking the way she was.

"It doesn't matter. They're here for you. I suggest you hurry and get proper. You are representing the Nightsongs, after all."

Liekki opened her mouth to say something but glimpsed her mother barely shaking her head. No one had to tell her what that meant. She let out a frustrated huff. "Fine."

"Good. Don't take too long." Diev turned his attention to his wife and frowned. "I've been wondering where you have been hiding this morning, wife. Come along. We need to have a discussion before we greet our *uninvited* visitor."

Liekki noticed the way he said 'uninvited' and knew it was a Vulpiian he didn't like. She watched as her father spun around on his heels and stormed out the door, not even waiting for her mother. Luya gave Liekki one last glance, squeezed her shoulder in solidarity, and walked out. Alone again, Liekki flitted across her room, taking everything in. She didn't have time to cleanse it like she originally wanted. It would have to wait. There were times she could test her father, and there were times she couldn't. This moment was one of those times that she didn't dare cross him. Liekki ran a hand across her face, then went to freshen up. He made it clear her time was limited.

She was quick about what she had to do. Not too long after her parents left, Liekki stood fully dressed in front of the giant mirror mounted on one of her bedroom's wall. Flickering *lumo* lights were bright enough for her to see how she looked. To her, she looked like a presentable noble. She didn't want to wear a dress like her sisters would. She preferred the practicality of other attire. Helped her move around faster. Searching through her things, it didn't take long to find something presentable that her father would agree on. Liekki dressed in her typical attire. Loose fitting spindlesilk black breeches, matching midnight blue and black tunic, and a pair of comfortable leather boots.

Liekki gave herself one last look over, then departed her room to find her guard waiting for her. He wore a mischievous grin on his face and winked when he caught her staring.

"Kha Blaze," he said. "I'm to escort you to the receiving room."

"I know the way," Liekki said too forcefully, then instantly regretted how she sounded. She didn't mean to take her anger out on him, but she couldn't help it. Sometimes her father brought out the worst of her moods.

The guard chuckled. "I know you do. Your father assumed you probably had other ideas. I'm the surety that you'll get there in a timely fashion. A few moments longer, I would've been knocking on your door to let you know that time was up."

Liekki let out a sound of frustration. "Efrim. I'm not a small kit any more. In fact, I haven't been a small kit for years now. Long enough to start my own household, yet that won't happen because I have a controlling father. Seriously, nothing against you, but you're like an armored kit sitter."

He laughed out loud this time. "I've been called worse, young Kha Blaze. Let's go. You really have an important visitor."

"Who is it?"

"You'll see soon enough." Efrim left her standing there and went to the right and down the hall. He didn't bother to look back to see if she was following. Liekki had a feeling her guard knew she would eventually follow. She sprinted in his direction and caught up to him.

Liekki was over the cloak and dagger of suspense, but if she wanted to know what was going on in her house, she needed to make herself more present. "Hey, can I ask you something?"

Efrim slowed his gait. "You can ask me anything. Doesn't mean I'll answer."

She stopped. Efrim took a few more steps before halting and turned back towards her. "We don't have a lot of time. We must keep going."

"I know, but I don't want other ears to hear what I want to ask."

Slow recognition flickered over Efrim's face. "I understand."

He lifted a hand and a spark of white shot out from his palm and enclosed them in a cloudless dome. "What do you need to speak about?"

"My mother says I can trust you."

Recognition flared in his gaze. "Aye."

"Good. Have you noticed anything different going on in Vulpo?"

"Like what? There's always something strange going on in Vulpo."

"Vulpiians are even more quick to anger than anything. The clans are more closed off than usual. I've even heard the whispers. There's a rise in worship of Drekra and Ibris."

Efrim frowned at hearing those names. "We don't speak those names out loud. Dare we invite them in and cause trouble?"

"That's what I'm saying, Efrim. Trouble has already taken residence in Vulpo. It's not getting any better. In fact, I think it's worse. I've never known my father to be as cruel as he has been lately. You saw the mob at the summoning. The clans were rabid. Damn near foaming at the mouth. Something is terribly wrong."

"Then perhaps it's a good thing that Mother Goddess tests our people now. It's only right."

"I can't do this. I'll fail. Worthy... Hah! I'm far from that. They were right. I'm a thief. I'm not that invested in the well-being of Vulpiians. The only thing I care about is what it can do for me and how I can get out of this crazy trap of a life I'm stuck in here."

"You are more than a thief. The spirits chose you from all the Vulpiians, and for good reason. You are worthy. If trouble is brewing, then maybe it's a good thing you are the one to help us. You're not perfect, but we don't need a perfect champion. Just one who can see through the smoke and mirrors and prevail. Are you not that?"

Liekki opened her mouth to speak, then hesitated. "I-I don't know."

"You are more than what you believe. You've already said something is wrong with the Vulpiians. I doubt others have noticed it like you have." He smiled. "Let's go before your father sends another after you."

Liekki slowly nodded. Efrim knew how to say the right words, yet remained elusive with his tongue. He was a strange fox, but there was nothing she could do about it at the moment. He was correct about her father, which was why she agreed with him. "Alright."

Efrim gave her one last look before his lips curved into a smile. "Thank you for trusting me with your thoughts. I promise to not tell a soul."

"Even my mother?" She remembered her mother saying he told her everything.

"Not even your mother."

Liekki's head bobbed up and down, acknowledging what he said. "Good. Thank you for listening to me and not laughing."

"I wouldn't dare laugh." He tilted his head in the direction they were going before he stopped. "Come on."

She didn't need much convincing. They lingered long enough. He was right. If they didn't show up, her father would send another of his personal guards and they wouldn't be as nice as Efrim was. The duo walked down the hall, their steps echoed against the stone walls. Wavering flames from the lights on the walls gave the hall a dark, otherworldly feeling.

Liekki didn't feel the need to speak anymore. She let everything they said bounce around in her mind. He didn't out right agree with her, but hidden underneath Efrim's words, he agreed. There was something terribly wrong with the clans of Vulpo. She just didn't know how it was going to work out. How was being chosen as their champion going to help them all by going to the Eldritch Trials?

What if she didn't go? What if she ran away?

If they couldn't find her, then they couldn't force her to go through the trials and try to help them. For *Dhasas* sake. They wanted nothing to do with her. She wasn't even supposed to be on the list of suitable options. Yes, something was wrong, and she was going to find out what and how she got on that goddess forsaken list. There was no way she would help those who would rather see her in jail or dead.

Lost in her head completely, she didn't realize they had reached the receiving room until Efrim said something to her, jarring her back to the now.

"Don't worry, young Kha Blaze. Everything will work out just like it is supposed to."

"If you say so. Also, it's Blaze. No Kha. None of that extra fodder."

"As you wish, *Blaze*." He eyed the closed door before them. "I can't go any further. I'll wait out here until you're done."

"You still won't tell me who is in there?"

"No, you'll find out soon enough."

Liekki took a deep breath. "Alright then. I'll be back sooner rather than later."

Efrim's deep chuckle reached her ears as he moved to stand against the wall. "If you say so."

She didn't like the sound of that, but there was nothing she could do or say at the moment. Liekki closed her eyes, inhaled, then slowly exhaled. She reached out, opened the door, and stepped inside.

The room was bright, unlike the halls she had just come from. Double large arched paned windows let in the bright morning light. Rays from the sun cut through the room like a knife, but that wasn't what caught her attention. She had noticed her father and mother soon as she walked in, but it was the other Vulpiian there she wasn't expecting.

Kalama Brightsun rose from the chair she was sitting in and stood there, facing Liekki. Her hands were clasped in front of her while her cold, ice-blue eyes watched Liekki as she moved further into the room. She wore her elder's robes, but there was no doubt that she was there for personal reasons too. Her long white hair hung low to her waist, parted at the center. Fanned behind her were snow white furred tails, nine in total. Liekki could feel the old magic emanating off the old Vulpii even if she didn't look a day over fifty. Which was extremely young with Vulpiians.

"Kalama Brightsun, what do we owe the pleasure?"

"If it was a pleasure visit, trust me, I wouldn't be here consorting with the likes of you," she snapped.

Liekki flinched at the sharp and unexpected tongue lashing. She knew Kalama Brightsun was a piece of work, but she didn't realize how rude she was.

"Well, I'm glad Icielia didn't get that part of her personality from you." Liekki couldn't help herself, and the words were out before she could stop them.

Kalama's brows furrowed, eyes hardened and her lips pursed. Her chest rose, then down, and Liekki knew she had pissed the vixen off. She didn't care. She didn't like the elder enough as it was. There were too many reasons to count why she didn't.

"Liekki! You will behave or else there will be consequences," her father shouted.

She rolled her eyes, but answered. "Yes, sir."

"Leave us," Kalama ordered. "I need to speak to her alone."

Liekki caught the angered expression on her father's face. If the elder didn't think carefully about her words came out, she wouldn't be the one to help her. She stood there ready for the show.

"How dare you come into my home uninvited and order me around! If I had half the mind to throw you out of my home, I would, but out of respect for who you are, I won't." He grabbed Luya's arm. "We'll leave, but this isn't over, Kalama."

Kalama said nothing as they left the room. Liekki's mother reached out and squeezed her hand before departing the room with her father. Soon as the door slammed closed, Kalama spelled the room so no others could hear them.

"We have a lot to discuss, young Nightsong. I suggest you sit down."

She knew better to argue with the ninetail after she practically bullied her father while in his own home. She hurried and crossed the room and sat down on the chaise that was directly in front of Kalama. "I'm here. Sitting down. What is this about?"

Kalama faced her. "The trials. We have things to discuss before you are to enter Elderton."

Liekki swallowed any retort that was on the tip of her tongue.

CHAPTER 8

Liekki bristled at the tone Kalama had taken. The sky fox elder sat there with an air of authority and her nose stuck up so high she couldn't smell the hypothetical bovek dung clinging to the bottom of her shoes. As if she couldn't stand to be in the presence of those born under the moon. The sky foxes worshipped the sun and the spirits of light. Anything after twilight was like a horror show for them. Liekki always thought they were too pompous for their own good.

She wanted to tell the elder how she really felt. If it wasn't for Clan Night, the rest of the citizens of Vulpo would be a bunch of backwards backwater foxes still skulking about without a lick of common sense. But Kalama was a guest in her home, after all. If she disrespected one of the sacred three, then it would surely get out and spread like wildfire. If others found out she or her family wronged the Elder, then they would be the scorn of all Vulpii. It was bad enough she had already earned the ire of everyone. No matter how much she hated her family, she still somewhat liked them. Blood of blood and bone of bone was the strongest bond to her.

The air in the room took a sharp turn and dropped in temperature. It was much colder than when she first entered the space. A thin film of frost slowly spread and covered all the surfaces in the room. Liekki glanced at the elder before her and saw nothing but pure rage in Kalama's eyes. If she, a strong magic user, couldn't control her temper long enough to not allow her magic to do its own thing. Liekki knew she had no chance to go up against Brightsun.

"How did you do it?"

Taken aback, Liekki wasn't expecting those words to come out of the elder's mouth. She thought Kalama was there for something else. Not about what happened at the summoning.

"Did what? I don't know what you're talking about."

"Let's not play games today, young Nightsong. The situation is serious enough as it is. Do you not know that all of Vulpo is in an uproar right now? The clans are revolting and raging at the Sacred Three. There will be clans fighting against each other when we all should be united right now. Blood against blood. Friends against friends, all because of you."

Liekki hissed in warning. She refused to be blamed for the actions of others. "No, not because of me." Uncomfortable with Kalama's words. It hit way too close to what she was just discussing with Efrim. "I had nothing to do with this. I sat there like the rest of my clan. Happy because I knew my name wouldn't be entered. Because I wouldn't have to go through the trials and be the scorn of our people. I'm that enough already. Especially of late. Do you think I want to help our people when the majority of you think I'm cursed and should have died at birth? I'm not that crazy, Elder Brightsun."

Liekki leaned forward with her elbows on her knees and scoffed. "I would rather die than help the Vulpiians. May we all have another one hundred years cursed under the Mother Goddess' eyes."

Kalama had heard enough and rapidly got to her feet. Liekki felt the magic before she saw it. Her hands flew up and crossed her arms directly in front of her, trying to protect herself from the blast of icy wind that Kalama threw at her, but it was no good. The force of it pushed her and the chair she was sitting in all the way back to the wall. It hit with a thunderous clap. The door to the receiving room slammed open. Liekki grimaced at the sharp pain of Kalama's unexpected attack. She watched as Efrim walked in with both of his swords at his side. Black fire magic licked across its blades.

"KALAMA BRIGHTSUN!!" he shouted. "You will not harm my charge!"

With the flick of her left wrist, Kalama sent a flurry of sharpened daggers made from ice in his direction, but they failed in its attempt to reach him. Quick as his appearance in the room, he had brought up the blades from his side in a protective formation before him. The daggers melted to water, then evaporated before him. Efrim backwards kicked the door shut behind him and stormed towards Elder Brightsun.

The swords in his hands transformed into long, fluid whip like chains which he flung out towards her. One wrapped around Kalama's wrist while the other wrapped around her legs. She screamed out when the liquid metal touched her skin. Her teeth bared, her head snapped towards Liekki's guard. The elder wore a feral look on her face. Long gone was the cool as ice Vulpiian. No, her once crystalline eyes were now clouded and muddied.

"Who are you?" She uttered the words through her clenched teeth. "Why can't I touch my magic? What have you done?"

"I am who I am and you will not fight against me or my charge," Efrim said with a deadly calm.

He reached Kalama's side and touched her forehead. She yelped, then fell to the ground. She convulsed where she went down. Her eyes rolled to the back of her head. Kalama's breath was labored while her chest moved rapidly up and down. Efrim bent down and touched a bare piece of her skin. The convulsions stopped.

Liekki was slow to get up. Once on two feet, she brushed herself with her hands, then slowly approached the elder and her guard. She looked at him oddly. He was unquestionably more than he seemed.

"How?" She pointedly glanced at Kalama Brightsun. "How'd you do that? She's a nine tailed elder. She's a legend amongst our people. Her prowess with her magic is bar none amongst those in Vulpo."

"Doesn't mean a thing to me. She's a visitor, and disrespecting you isn't appropriate. She came here for a reason and attacking you isn't it."

She shook her head. "You don't know what I said. I provoked her anger. I deserved that, Efrim."

"I heard everything, Blaze."

"But how? She spelled the room?" Liekki really studied him. "Who are you, Efrim? Really?"

"In due time. Not right now."

Liekki glanced back at the elder and frowned. "She's going to tell everyone about this. She will say we were cruel to her and violated the rules of Vulpiian etiquette. My family will be ridiculed and possibly banned from everything."

Efrim shifted on his feet after he stood back up. Liekki was curious about the guard, but she didn't even know where to start. He finally looked at her with a curious expression on his face. "Do you really care about what happens to your family? I thought you didn't like them."

"It's weird. Normally I wouldn't give a crap, but under these uncertain circumstances, no matter how much we hate each other, I still oddly care. I don't want anything to happen to us. Not over her." Liekki kicked Kalama in the shin while she was sprawled out on the ground, completely out of it.

"Then Mother Goddess chose right. Perhaps your feelings and thoughts will change about the others of Vulpo, too."

Liekki rolled her eyes. "I seriously doubt that."

Efrim shrugged before turning his hardened gaze back to Kalama. "We'll see. Are you ready for the conversation she really came here for? Maybe she had enough time to think about her actions while down there."

Recognition dawned over Liekki. "You put her under a glamour, didn't you?"

Her guard didn't answer, and it didn't surprise her he kept tight-lipped yet again. She watched as he snapped his fingers. The sharp sound of his fingertips brushing against each other echoed slightly. Instantly, Kalama let out a small whimper. Her arms and legs twitched before her eyes shot open. They were back to the crystalline blue, and they stared directly at Liekki. She didn't shirk away from the glare.

Kalama slowly sat up into a sitting position on the floor and looked around as if to get her bearings straight. Once she recognized where she was, Kalama grimaced. Efrim held out a hand to help her up, and she almost slapped it away, but thought better of it and took the offered help.

"My duty and charge always comes first, Elder. I take my commitments seriously, as should you with yours. If this gets out, I'll make sure that everyone knows that House Nightsong of Clan Night was innocent. That you came to their home and provoked their youngest, who is no match for your prowess. How you attacked her and nearly killed her. You, a revered Elder of Clan Sky and one of the Sacred Three. The voice of our spirit gods and goddesses."

Kalama's mouth opened as if she was going to speak, but it seemed like she thought about her words and said nothing. Liekki noticed the slight tug of Efrim's lips at the corners. His smirk was just as devious as he was mysterious. Kalama took a deep breath, exhaled, and nodded.

"Good," he said. Efrim bowed his head in deference and pointed to the door. "I'll go stand by the door on this side while you discuss what you came here for."

Liekki wanted to laugh at the entire situation. Efrim had Kalama *the* Brightsun on edge. A feat that she had seen no one do. That was including her father. Kalama was angry at him, but she didn't dare go against him, and that made her wonder even more about who her guard was.

Kalama took the seat she had previously occupied. Liekki waited a few moments before retrieving a chair that was closer to her than the one she had originally sat in. Once she sat down and got comfortable, Efrim went and stood by the door and back to being the silent sentinel. A deadly sentinel. She wasn't that oblivious to his dangerous nature.

The elder leaned back in her chair and crossed her legs. Her clasped hands rested on her knees while her tails fanned out behind her. "Let us start over," Kalama said.

"I think I'm owed an apology first. I did nothing to you but tell you the truth and you still attacked me. In my home. It's the least you can do."

Kalama swallowed. Her slender throat bobbed. "You're right. Liekki Nightsong of Clan Night, I apologize for my unbecoming actions of a Vulpii of my station. Will you forgive me?"

Liekki glanced at Efrim, and he winked. She looked back at the elder. She didn't want to, but something told her she should. "I accept your apology. Don't let it happen again, Brightsun."

The elder's eyes narrowed, but she smiled. It didn't quite reach the corner of her eyes, but for Liekki, it was an opening to their rocky start. "I will make sure it won't. Now, for the reason I came here. We need to discuss the trials and your part in it."

"I've already told you I didn't add my name to the box. Everyone was there. You all are the strong ones who conjured up that crystal box."

"I understand."

"So choose somebody else," Liekki said. "I shouldn't have been entered into the pool of eligible Vulpiians, anyway."

"I understand that and agree, young Nightsong, but we just can't choose another champion. Although your criminal extracurricular activities were enough to ban you from the choosing, it seems the gods and goddesses saw different. There was no way you could have magicked your name into the box. I knew it yet, I still accused you. I would say my emotions got the better of me."

"I've noticed," Liekki said deadpanned. "So, how did my name get added?"

Kalama shook her head. "It doesn't matter any longer. Once a name has been chosen, we can not change the champion unless something happens to them. Only death will get you out of it. Now and during the trials."

The blood in Liekki's veins went cold. Death? She couldn't believe it. There was no way out of it. She couldn't do this. She would run. Liekki was unwilling to risk her life for the Vulpiians. For those who didn't give two tails about her. "I think you better start explaining yourself, Elder, because I am not liking what I'm hearing so far. This is starting to become unfair."

Kalama's gaze softened as it raked over Liekki. "I'm afraid life is unfair. If anyone should know this, it will be you. A Vulpiian born to Clan Night with the colors of red-orange and black. Able to shift to your biped form since you were just a wee kit. You don't think those outside of Clan Night hear the whispers. They say you're cursed. You are an abomination and an outcast among your own people. A menace to the other clans.

Your own father despises you. He has friends. They talk. So if any of us knows about the unfairness that is life, it is you and unfortunately, your stroke of unfair and bad luck continues. Our champion is you. You will go to the town of Elderton and enter the House of Vulpii. There are many houses, but you will know ours by the symbol of our kind. You will do whatever is necessary to survive and come out alive with the Hasking Stone."

Liekki exploded from her chair and paced the room. Her mind was a furious storm. A whirlwind of thoughts and emotions fought for prominence in her mind. She didn't want to be their champion. She couldn't do this. It was unfair. If she failed and died, then they wouldn't care. They would have gotten rid of their problem. Their headache. Liekki already knew they would call her a curse for real and they would banish her name from existence.

"I'm not prepared for this," Liekki whispered out loud. "I am not smart enough or strong enough to go through this. What if I died?"

"Then we're cursed for another one hundred years," Kalama answered with a hint of remorse. To Liekki, she had almost sounded dejected along with something else that Liekki couldn't quite place. "If it's any consolation, young Nightsong, in your class you had the highest marks while in Vulpii Champion School. You know this to be true. If anyone can do it, I know you can."

Liekki turned back towards the elder. It didn't slip past her that Kalama almost gave her a compliment. "How does this even work?"

"Come back. Sit down and let me explain the basics."

Liekki almost ran out of the room, but thought better of it. She went back to her seat and sat down. "Alright. Now talk."

Kalama seemed resigned to the situation and leaned back. "I'll be your mentor and I will help you as much as I can, but it's limited. You will only be able to reach out to me three times. I can only reach out to you once. So once you're in there, be careful with what you reach out to me for. Do you understand so far?"

Liekki nodded. She didn't like it, but she understood and said as much. Kalama continued. "You will be tested. Everybody's tests are different, so I can't tell you exactly what the tests are like and how they will go. You will need to figure that out. After entering the house, the challenge will begin. Challenges at every step you will have to endure. It won't be easy or pretty. You will learn and discover things about yourself you didn't even want to know. The most important goal is for you to find the Hasking Stone before time runs out. You'll know the stone when you see it. Trust me."

"What are these challenges I must pass?"

Kalama's shoulders rose, then sunk. "I don't know. Each eumen is different when they enter. One thing I know is that there are gateways that will appear once you pass a challenge. What they look like... ah, who is to say? You'll know when you passed that test and it appears."

"How much time will I have?"

"From the moment you were chosen, the clock had started. You have thirty days to reach Elderton. After passing the gates on the island, you will have forty-eight hours to go inside the House of Vulpii. Once you enter the house in Elderton, you will have four days to find the stone or fail."

"This is crazy. I shouldn't be doing this," Liekki complained, the sound of dejection clear in her voice. She had a tough personal decision to make. One that didn't involve the words and opinions of others. All she could do at the moment was nod her head and listen to Kalama Brightsun. Take in everything she could and weigh her options when no one else was around.

"I will help you as much as I can. You are already going down a dark and dangerous path that isn't good for you or our people. It's a collision that's wrong. I promise I'll do my best to guide you the right way during this trial, so you won't end up like I did. A failure. We must pass the trials together as a team or it will be bad for you and me both."

CHAPTER 9

Kalama Brightsun had left. Liekki sat there in her chair long after she had gone. Stewing thoughts and emotions ran rampant in her head. Overwhelmed by the turn of events after Kalama had come to her senses. Her guard stayed eerily silent, saying nothing to her, and for that, she was thankful. Liekki didn't think she could properly talk about anything she was going through. Most times, she wasn't afraid of anything, but dread and fear held a tight noose around her neck and heart. It was wrong, and she didn't know why.

The door to the chamber burst opened. Her momentary peace didn't last long. There was no reason to immediately look up. She already knew who was in the room. The oppressive pressure that exuded from the vulpiian filled the space and crawled across her skin. Liekki steeled herself for the tongue lashing she was sure her father was going to give her. He strode into the room, chest out, shoulders tense, and pushed back. His back was rigid as ever. He came in there with a purpose and she was afraid all the ire that lingered behind his dead eyes was going to be fired at her.

Liekki saw the warring emotions behind her guard's eyes when she cut a quick glance in his direction. He was wound tight and ready to uncoil unleashed anger if her father did something. A sudden realization bowled her mentally over. She somehow knew it like the air she breathed. Efrim would fight her father if it came down to it, and that was another thing she was confused about. Why was he taking his duties so seriously as her guard?

"What did that awful, high nosed vixen want with you? Did she get this problem of you daring to be our champion figured out? There will be another, right? It would be nice for them to pick an actual worthy soul from Clan Night. It could be one of your siblings. Just as long as it is not you. We need that so these clans can stop crying foul play."

"Elder Brightsun did figure it out," Liekki said with a calm she couldn't even believe she had within herself. The crying of their clans wasn't her concern. She had more concerning things to worry about and to Liekki, that took precedence. "Kalama Brightsun will be my mentor. That was the reason for her visit."

"WHAT!" Diev shouted. Enraged, snake-like veins protruded from his temple and the side of his neck. His eyes widened to where it reminded her of the buggy insects with enormous eyes. Liekki knew if her father wasn't more careful, he would blow apart something vital in his head. Anger like that was never too good.

"I knew she wasn't worth being a sacred three," he spat out. Words were so harsh, it was like a verbal dagger. But they were his true feelings, and it was obvious he didn't care who heard him. "I don't care if she does has nine tails. The vixen is an idiot."

"She's well liked and loved by everybody but Clan Night," Liekki said, surprised by her coming in defense of the one who just attacked her not too long ago. "Besides, there's nothing that can be done. Once a champion has been chosen, there's no turning back. The only way is if I am dead."

"I can make that happen," Diev said quickly, with a snarl, as he pulled out a blade hidden from the folds of his black robe. Light hit the dark steel and glinted under it. The blade wasn't the true problem. Liekki took a step backwards. She knew the blade was coated with poison. A rare poison that only her father had the antidote for and she knew he wouldn't dare use it on her if she was to ever need it.

"And if you do, you will doom us all," Efrim said too calmly from where he stood. He may have been still as a statue, but the anger behind his gaze told a different story. Liekki's father didn't know what he was walking into with Efrim getting involved with their conversation. Flashes of the altercation between him and Kalama flashed in her mind.

Diev's head snapped in his direction. "Who are you to speak to me? House guards are to be silent and know their place."

Efrim lifted his hands in a placating manner. "I mean no ill words, Elder Nightsong. I only meant it by saying that killing her will doom us all." Efrim glanced at Liekki, then back to her father. He gave her a look she didn't understand, but then again, there was something about the dark fox she couldn't quite figure out, no matter how much she was trying to. He continued talking to her father, his voice much stronger. "She's an abomination. A curse and should have died at birth, but here she stands. Unfortunately for us, the spirits have chosen her to champion our kind. If she dies before she enters or dies during the trial, she will be considered a failure. Vulpiians will be cursed for another one hundred years. Do you want to be the one to usher in another dark period in our time?"

A low rumbling growl came from Diev's chest. His tails flicked back and forth behind him. He was beyond agitated, but Liekki knew Efrim had him. Her father was a vain creature. He prided himself on being the best Vulpiian around and he wouldn't do anything to ruin his reputation in the eyes of others. She watched as he contemplated the guard's words. Liekki knew she was safe when he returned the blade back into its sheath, then stormed out of the room without saying another word. She let out an audible sigh of relief.

"Thank you," she said to the guard. "For everything so far today. I think I am going back to my room. There have been enough interactions for the day. I need to think and focus."

The guard opened the door. "You lead, I follow."

Time had flown by. The first moon of Eldritch was high in the night sky and she was free from the life sucking creatures that were her father and siblings. Free from the stresses and unrest brought on by her being discovered as Blaze and as her being picked for the Eldritch Trials. Liekki sat at her favorite spot on the cliff overlooking the sea. Her moment on the mountain cliff, the same as her home, had become almost a ritual to her because she had done it so much lately.

Next to her was her leather bag. Packed with clothes, food-stuffs, money and other things she thought she may have a need for on her journey. After Kalama departed, her decision became definite. She wasn't staying any longer. No matter what her parents or her guard said. Who even cared what Kalama Brightsun said? Vulpo was a cesspool of darkness. Liekki had enough of it in her life. She didn't want to dwell as a bottom feeder any longer.

Ravenfalls was as good a place as any, she thought to herself as she picked up a small rock and threw it. Nothing but good things have been said about the city that seemed as if it was floating. It was a modern place that wasn't defined by one species. The city welcomed everyone. Including lowly outcasts such like herself.

Her father thought he had everything under wraps. That she had nowhere to go. True, Liekki was a prisoner to his whims, but she was a smart vulpii and she could outfox the cruel, sinister dogfox no matter what he thought. From over the last few years, it always paid to be prepared for any situation.

Standing up, Liekki brushed the dirt and natural debris of small rocks off of her. It was time. Nobody was expecting her to leave anymore. She had to get away. Earlier, she was able to contact her friend, Ice, through the pools deep under the mountain, and explained that she was leaving. Liekki didn't explain where she was going, but she wanted her friend to know it had nothing to do with her. She wasn't worried about her sole best friend, who was closer to her than her own sisters, snitching on her to her mother. Brightsun would eventually figure out what happened and Liekki would be long gone. Liekki hoped they would be able to pick a better choice for the trials by then, because she knew she wasn't the one. No one had to tell her that.

"They could pick someone else. They had to," Liekki mumbled to herself. "I don't believe they can't choose another. That must be a lie to trick me."

Liekki picked up her satchel and put her arms through the loops before strapping it to her back. She took a deep breath to calm her nerves. Everything was about to go straight to the void, with all three clans fighting against each other. She didn't want to be around for the aftermath. Normally, Liekki had good instincts, and they were telling her to get far, far away from Vulpo. The darkness taking its hold over her home was like a vice grip on her throat. It was squeezing the life out of everything.

The surrounding air swirled and shimmered like the heat waves one saw over a blazing fire. A barely there snapping sound sluiced into the night, but she thought nothing of it. Once standing on two legs and feet, now Liekki stood on four paws. Her three tails swished back and forth behind her. Her eyes glowed a bright orange red as her ears rotated to the faint sound she heard behind her. She lifted her nose to the air and got a whiff of a familiar scent. She yipped into the night, warning whoever was out there off, then took off down a hidden crooked path as her tails merged into a single tail.

A hard resolve settled over Liekki as she traveled in her true fox form. Still in disbelief over the turn of events lately, she refused to let it sway her thoughts and heart. To her, leaving was the right thing to do, no matter what.

Right... she thought.

The path was a little tricky, but she took her time and moved as stealthily as she could. Avoiding larger creatures that made the mountains and crags its home. She did her best to avoid the traps that were out on the outskirts of the path and through the mountain crevices. She moved steadily down and through the winding path.

It didn't take her long as she crossed over a small bridge that spanned over a crevice. This was the way to the gemstone mines owned by her family. No one came this way anymore unless you were a mine worker. Even then, most of her father's workers were part of the deep ocean mining expeditions out in the treacherous waters of Dominion. There were a few deep ocean operations in the Caspeson ocean, but most of their rare jewels came from Dominion. The few that were found in the mountains were for special occasions. Even Liekki knew they could fetch a fortune.

Continuing on her trek, careful to stay away from the house guards, everything went smoothly for a change. Once she reached a fork in the road, she had to make a decision. Go left and run right into the miners and whoever else would snitch on her to her father. Or go right. Going to her right would take her straight down the path that would lead to peacekeepers at the end, but it was the way to get out. It was her best chance to slip away and make a beeline to Merchant's Row. There, hidden away in a dark corner in the back alley, she could give enough coins and hop a port to Ravenfalls without anyone checking her like they would at the official gates of transfer.

Plan and decision made, she padded towards the right and once she neared the gates; she stopped underneath a low level hanging rock formation. With the moon out, it created deep enough shadows to hide anyone. She shuffled towards it and stepped into the shadows. The gatekeepers wouldn't be able to see her. She quickly shifted into her biped form and placed a perfect glamour over herself. Sneaking past those guards was going to take everything she had.

Once Liekki felt like she was fine enough to leave Nightsong lands, she strode down the slight decline and towards the guards. They looked up at the same time. The one on the left with the gray eyes and dark brown hair she had recognized. He used to work the mines for her father as a guard, but it looked like he had moved up the ladder. The other one, she didn't recognize so much. He had the typical features of Clan Night. Black hair, cut short. Dark yellow eyes. A permanent scowl appeared on his face. He could have come from any of the families in the mountains.

"Halt," the brown-haired male shouted. "Who are you, and where do you go? There's a curfew."

"I'm headed back home. I was planning on catching a port back to Terra's side," she said. Her glamour had her looking like a Vulpii with dark red hair and pale yellow eyes from Clan Terra. If the triangular shaped mark she made sure to have on her forehead wasn't enough to get her to go past them, she also made it look like she had two tails, which was more than their one. That alone assured her they wouldn't contest her too much because she was stronger than them.

"Name?" the one with the scowl and black hair asked.

"Niazal," she quickly responded.

"Family name?" he continued. He took a step closer to her.

"Swiftfoot," she said. Using one of the nine major Vulpii family names, therefore, they wouldn't challenge her. Not as much as they would if she was to use a Clan Night name. "Ni-azal Swiftfoot. If you keep me any longer, I'll make sure to let my father know how you pathetic guards of House Nightsong kept me from getting home in time."

The brown-haired guard stepped in front of the other. "Excuse me, Kha Swiftfoot. No such thing is needed. Forgive my companion. He's just tired."

Liekki watched the guard give the dark one a look and then pushed him out of the way to allow her to go through. She held her breath as she moved past them and through the gates. After a few feet away from them, she exhaled. She didn't feel too bad for lying about who she was. Once her father learned she was gone, these guards were going to feel the brunt of his horrible wrath. But that was for them and him. If he really didn't want her to leave, he should have put better security on the gates. Liekki was even surprised that she had gotten away from Efrim's watchful gaze. She didn't think she could ever lose him. He was too smart.

It was as if an enormous burden was released off of her with each step away from House Nightsong.

CHAPTER 10

After getting away from the mountains and down into the valley, where all the action took place, Liekki knew what she was doing was the right move. The city topside was a place where everything went down. Up in the mountains was where the Clan Night nobles kept away from the common Vulpii. She didn't know how the other clans did it, but if their nobles were anything like hers, it was probably the same way.

The Burrows, which is what she and her friends call the underground network. It was a place where most of the Vulpii interacted with each other if they didn't do business topside. Majority of the nobles did their transactions down in the Burrows. The topside was for the commoners. At least, that was the way they taught her growing up. Trade from other places outside of Vulpo also took place topside. The Hallowbane Den was also down in the burrows. Located towards the darker and seedier side of the tunnels. Closer to Merchant's Row topside.

It didn't take Liekki long to reach the valley proper. More buildings came into view. Roads and their lumo road lights flickered so those traversing the streets could see. Many of the businesses were closed, but she knew that was to be for where she was headed. Her destination would be open. It was always open for the right price. Plenty of nightlife was still alive in Vulpo, even with a curfew. If you had enough money, a Vulpian could get away with a lot.

With her head down, Liekki kept her focus on the trek she was on. She passed by a few peacekeepers who said nothing to her, but eyed her suspiciously. Merchant's Row wasn't too far off, and she hoped to make it there without any problems. First, she had to get past the Silk Petal district. A lavish area with high walls and flowers crawling up trellises and upwards over the walls of buildings. Exotic and native flowers both grew alongside the roads. Scented night gardens were popular for the area, which was how it became known as the Silk Petal district. Along with other reasons she didn't want to think about.

The area was always busy and sometimes busier than Merchant's Row. Plenty of public peacekeepers and private guards for the many elite Flower houses kept patrol there. Liekki glanced at the fancy buildings closest to her. It was one of the many places where you could get anything you desired for the right price. Ironically, to Liekki, it didn't get past her that the silk petal district was right next to Temple row. Home to the sanctuaries and shrines of the mother goddess and the other spirits that were worshipped in Vulpo. Both Light and Dark spirit gods and goddesses like Kheton, Duara, Umjir, and Esoi.

Wonder how much they appreciated that, she thought to herself.

She scurried across the road, her speed increasing as she attempted to put as much distance between her and the city guards. Her breath came a little harsher, but she did her best to keep any noise down. She couldn't let anything impede her leaving Vulpo. Or her father knowing too soon that she had left.

Another peacekeeper with a lean face and beady, distrustful eyes watched her from the corner across the way. There was something about him she didn't like and did her best to not look at him, but couldn't resist. Liekki caught him as he eyed her for too long. The entire exchange made her very uncomfortable. His mouth moved as he said something to his fellow guard. The prickles on her neck told her it wasn't good. Not wanting to look back anymore, Liekki quickly passed the sweet-smelling flower district and took a shortcut down Temple row. An area she didn't frequent very often because it always felt oppressive. As if there was somebody watching her.

Soon enough, she heard the quick steps. There was a type of martial cadence to it. The rhythmic tapping of boots on the cobblestones felt like a warning to Liekki. With a glance over her shoulder, Liekki recognized the uniform. It was the peacekeeper who had eyed her for too long. He had chosen to follow her.

"Sheiza!" she whispered to herself. Liekki hurried at a faster pace and knew she could find sanctuary in any of the temples. There was nothing the peacekeeper could do once she entered one. Her people took the holy spaces seriously. Too serious, in her opinion.

Liekki thought about it and changed her mind. She didn't know about recently. With the dark undercurrent going on among the Vulpiians... it was obvious they were making deals with something not too ideal for a proper Vulpii. She was curious enough to see things and smart enough to not speak about it. Talking would have you becoming a dead Vulpii. Even with the strange dealings and too many stranger deaths happening in the Valley, she knew better. Liekki didn't want to be the next one found sprawled out in the gutter streets somewhere left there like trash. There were many ways that she could become dead now that all of Vulpo knew she was the thief who'd rained terror amongst the richer nobles and merchants. Unfortunately for her, the trials would probably take care of her on that front and they wouldn't have to lift a finger.

The footsteps of the guard behind her grew closer to her. The hollow sounds from their boots against the stone slightly echoed into the night. They didn't try to hide that they were following her, and she didn't let on that she knew they were behind her.

When she felt them getting closer, she quickly stepped to her right, reaching the entrance of the last temple in the area. She didn't look at who it belonged to. All she cared about was getting away from the guard. She scurried inside the dark, massive stone building. Once inside, she finally looked up at the ancient stone archway. Liekki recognized the old Vulpiic symbols carved into it and realized she was in Duara's temple. The spirit goddess of Dreams and Nightmares. Torch lights flickered against the temple's walls, casting a host of eerie shadows against the floor. Above her, the temple's ceiling was open aired. Allowing the night sky of dark blues, purples, and black with the moon and glistening stars to lend its beauty as its roof. Gentle sounds of trickling water from the nearby fountain reached her ears. She turned towards it to find the fountain perfectly placed in the center, which gave the place a deceptive semblance of peace.

Duara's temple was one that was not frequented by many. Not like the others. Many Vulpiians steered away from the place she supposedly dwelled in while in her physical form. Liekki's fellow Vulpiians also veered away from the two temples who belonged to the two Spirits no one liked speaking out loud about, or if they did, they spoke in hushed tones. They were twin sisters, Drekra and Dhasas. Spirit goddess of Death and Decay, while Dhasas was the spirit goddess of souls. The twins were dark as could be.

She heard the soft footsteps before she noticed the Vulpii. Liekki glanced up in time and was surprised when a priestess of dreams walked out of the breathing shadows and towards her. The servant of Duara wore an all black spindlesilk form fitting robe. Under the low light, the robe's design was speckled with what seemed to be stars and glistened with what she thought was possibly something surreal. Liekki didn't have to be told that magic was at play. She could feel it all around her. The priestess had golden orbs for eyes and long, black hair as dark as the midnight sky. Markings of Duara covered the side of her face. She smiled. It was gentle. Surprising for one of the temple they were standing in.

"How can I help one that seems lost?" The priestess's voice was welcoming. Warm and reassuring.

"I seek sanctuary," Liekki said, looking back warily towards the way she had just come from. "Only for a little while. If you don't mind." She already felt better about her decision to not hurrying out of the temple once she recognized where she was.

The priestess looked at her strange then nodded. "Stay for as long as you need, young Nightsong. Whether your time is short or if you need to stay for a few days. If you feel the need to talk, we are here. Duara welcomes you."

Liekki tilted her head and eyed the vixen a little closer. A sliver of a gasp slipped from her mouth. She was taken by surprise, which for her came in rare form. No one should have been able to see past her illusions. Her glamours were some of the best in Vulpo. Except for when a flayer was nearby, and she didn't think the priestess was one of those. "How'd you know who I was?"

"We see all in this realm or in Duara's. You're safe." The priestess' smile was genuine. "The one you're hiding from is still lingering at the entrance. He's trying to determine if he will come in or not. In the end, he won't step a foot in here. He will change his mind and go back the way he came from. He is too afraid of what he thinks is inside of here." The priestess leaned in closer to Liekki. "Let me tell you something important, Nightsong. Never be afraid of the sacred spaces. The dark spaces. Some may even find comfort while they dwell in those places. Leave when you're ready and feel safe enough to depart. You'll know when that time is."

"Thank you," Liekki said, her voice filled with raw emotion. She truly meant it. With everything that was going on, she was starting to believe that she was all alone out there, with no help at all. Besides, there was no way she was returning to the Nightsong household. If she had to go through the trials, the least she could do was see what she wanted to see before she ended up dead.

"You're welcome. Go in peace and may Duara bring you pleasant dreams instead of traversing the dark realms where her creatures of nightmares lives."

Liekki watched as the curious priestess departed, leaving her standing alone next to a thick basalt stone pillar. She had placed a hand on the cold stone for support. Although she was still tense and stiff, Liekki visibly relaxed a little, knowing she had sanctuary. Safety. Even if it was at the mercurial Duara's temple.

She didn't know the time, but Liekki knew she couldn't linger too long at the place of worship. She had to get to Merchant's Row and then down into the burrows to take the port out of Vulpo. Be gone before her father found out she had gotten away from the Nightsong mountain fortress.

Wandering through the temple, Liekki admired everything. From the smallest wax candle to the altar where the candles and incense burned. There were so many priceless sculptures and depictions of the spirit goddess for whom the temple was for. It all surprised her. She studied the multitude of expertly done murals that were painted onto the walls, that left no empty space. They were dark and haunting as they told Duara's story, yet they all had an ethereal beauty to them. This was a side she never knew about the spirit goddess.

Liekki hadn't visited the temples in a long time and wondered if she should have visited more before now. She loved the arts, even though no one knew that about her. Then again, it wasn't like they were running to discover more about who she was, either. She was cursed the moment she was born, according to her father and clan.

Staring at the magnificent building, she smiled. A rare thing for Liekki. To her, what are the temples, if not nothing but architectural art? But her momentary happiness didn't last long. Something else was there with her. She could feel it. Her eyes darted all around the chamber. The growing pregnant energy was becoming oppressive. It was the same as the other day. The fine hairs on her arms and back of her neck raised straight up. Somewhere deep within, no one had to tell her about how she got chosen. She felt the spirits as they surrounded her at the Sacred Island. She could feel them now. They did this to her and more often than not since that fateful day; she wondered which ones it was who chose her to fight for her people and why.

"The peacekeeper is gone," the priestess from earlier said. The voice had come from the shadows. Startled, Liekki's head snapped to her right where the sound came from, but didn't see the vixen. There was no one else there with her. The sanctuary was emptier than ever. "You must leave now, Nightsong."

"Where are you?" she asked. She took a step towards the voice, then stopped when she discovered she couldn't move any further. "Why won't you come out?"

The priestess voice faded as she spoke, but Liekki heard her loud and clear. "I am here and there. I am everywhere, young kit. Leave now. Be safe. You have my blessing tonight as you travel on your arduous journey."

"I am no kit," Liekki said with too much force. Tired of people saying she was a youngling when she was an adult. Her siblings weren't treated as such. "Who are you?" Liekki asked, the words trembling off her lips.

"I meant no harm, Liekki. I only meant to help. But compared to me, you are nothing but a young kit at this age of time. Now, leave this place lest you risk not making it to your destination."

Confused and conflicted. Her heart raced behind her ribs. A prickle of something she should know was at the edge of her mind. She glanced at the mural beside her and saw the image of Duara flicker and waver under the light of the flame. The face of the priestess flashed in her mind, then disappeared. They were the one and the same. Liekki searched harder and still saw nothing. Yet, there was an otherworldly emptiness to the place. Free to move again, she knew there was no more wasting time. She had to leave. Taking the spirit goddess of dreams' advice, she rushed out of the temple.

Faint sounds became louder as they reached her ears. She stopped and hid near the closest food cart, ducking low behind it. The faint noise was much clearer, and many Vulpiians were shouting and fighting with each other. The peacekeeper's whistles were buried beneath the clamor of the encroaching mob. Liekki peeked from behind the cart to find a wild and crazy scene unfold before her. The discordant sounds of chaos were close by, but what she saw truly alarmed her. Vulpiians from Clan Terra and Clan Sky brutally fought with each other. Even a few low born from Clan Night were out there sowing discord. Dark rage was in their eyes while their lips were pulled back with sharp teeth bared in snarls. The peacekeepers tried to intervene, but it was of no help. Everyone had an unmistakable look of hatred in their eyes. There was no way she could stay there. She had the strangest feeling they were after her. Careful of her steps and aware of her surroundings, Liekki looked all around before darting away.

Not wanting to waste time, she took to the shadows as she rechecked her glamour. She tightened the straps to her pack while moving at a steady pace to get away from what she had just seen. Liekki knew Hallowbane Den very well. She had taken many trips down there to market and sell her stolen goods. There would be a few Vulpiians who could help her, but doubt was a powerful thing and dug its claws into her thoughts. She wasn't quite sure anymore after being exposed to all of Vulpo, thanks to Mezal Irontail.

She reached the end corner of Temple Row. Where she needed was one block over on Merchant's Row. In almost a run, Liekki darted down the sidewalk. Once on the correct street, she searched for the alley that would lead to the entrance of the seedier side of the Burrows. It wasn't far from the Merchant's Guild. A garish looking building that was more in tune with what one saw outside of Vulpo and not keeping with Vulpiian architecture.

The path lamps were blazing in front of the building, casting off its orange glow and long shadows. Enough to keep her hidden still. Not a peacekeeper was in sight, and she was thankful for that gift.

"Perfect," she mumbled under her breath.

Looking both ways before dashing across the road, Liekki made it with no problems. Rushing to the side of the guild's building, she entered the darkened alley. To any other Vulpiian, if one didn't know what to look for, they would think it was just another dead end, but she knew better. At the back end, there was a wall and a door. The illusion made it seem like there was no wall at all. She kept her pace and walked right to it and whispered the word to reveal the door. As the door shifted, letting out a soft hiss of air, Liekki took a step towards.

"Not so fast... Kha Blaze," a voice said, halting her in her steps.

Liekki quickly twisted around. Her eyes widened and her mouth dropped open. "Efrim?"

She was shocked to see him there. Her personal body guard grinned his charming smile as he gave her a mock bow. He was wearing a nondescript black leather tunic and pants as to not give away his position of what house he belonged to. His dark wavy hair wasn't up in its usual bun, but flowed to his shoulders. There was amusement and mischief in his eyes. He smirked. "The one and only!"

CHAPTER 11

"**W**hat are you doing here?" the questioned stumbled out of her mouth. Surprise was evident in her raised voice and the expression she wore on her face. "I mean, how did you find me? Why are you here?"

"You normally don't ask so many questions. I thought you would be glad to see me." Efrim moved closer to her as he took in their surroundings. Eyes constantly darting to the dark spaces. Much like a guard, always being conscious of their environs.

"Not if you plan on taking me back home. You shouldn't be here."

"I can be wherever I want to be and right now, that's here as we go into the burrows." He touched her arms and tried to push her through the door, but she didn't budge.

Liekki's eyes narrowed. It didn't get past her notice that he conveniently ignored how he found her. Then she realized what he had said a moment afterwards. Liekki's brows furrowed with more confusion at him being there. "What do you mean... *we*? There is no *we*, Efrim!"

"You don't have a choice in the matter," he said as he grabbed her arm and guided her through the door. "There are eyes and ears everywhere. We must be careful with our tongues and words. It would be bad for me and even worse for you if you were to be caught out here. Tonight of all nights."

"What's so special about tonight?" she asked as she surveyed their surroundings. They were safe. For now. Tonight was like any other night when she had freedom, except for the crazed mob she had just saw, she thought. After the long morning dealing with Kalama Brightsun, she made sure she kept busy in her personal quarters for the rest of the day. Not wanting to draw the attention and ire of her father. When everyone had practically forgotten about her, she grabbed her pack and snuck out through the secret passage in her bedroom. No one knew about that hidden hallway. Not even Efrim.

Exasperated, he shook his head as he pulled her with him through the winding tunnels. The smell of fresh damp earth was more prominent the further down they went. The tunnel was dark, with the occasional lumo lamps lighting the path. After getting a better look at where they were headed, she thought it looked a little different. The tunnel they were in was unfamiliar to her.

"You really don't know, do you?" he said, voice low so it wouldn't carry. His face was still facing forward, but her hearing was fine enough to hear him clearly.

"Know what?" she said between clenched teeth as she tried to pull away from him. Tired of him tugging her along like some petulant kit, Liekki stopped in her tracks, putting all of her weight on her heels so she couldn't move any further. "What in the world are you going on about?"

Efrim let out an agitated huff and stopped. He rounded on her and stared directly into Liekki's eyes. "The leaders of the nine major houses had a meeting. Yes, that includes your father. They don't care what the Sacred Three elders said about you being chosen for the trials. They chose their own champion and want you dead, since it is the only way for their champion to compete in the trials."

"Jiiq!" she whispered with more force than necessary. "Kalama and the elders won't allow that to happen." Efrim gave her a look that said otherwise. This time, she scowled at the implications of everything. "What in Drekra's name are they doing?"

Efrim frowned and shook his head. "We don't speak that name out loud, Kha Blaze."

Liekki waved his superstitious words away. She didn't care about what names could or couldn't be said or whispered in fear of being hunted by said god or goddess. What she did care about was what the heads of Vulpiian society were up to. This wasn't like them. She wanted to know why they were so bent out of shape about who took part in the trials. She was just as competent as any other fox in Vulpo. If not better. Although she didn't want to do it because of many reasons, Liekki just wanted to know why they hated her so much. Or why should she even care enough to worry about what they thought of her?

"Let me guess, my father was the mastermind of me being murdered so they can have their chosen in place instead of me. That's why there's a crazed mob out there calling for my head." Her guard grimaced, but denied nothing. She let out a defeated sigh. "I'm leaving this place, Efrim. The choice is yours - stay here or come with me. Either way, I will not remain here in a place that wants me dead. In a place where the citizens or my very own flesh and blood don't believe in me and say I'm nothing but a curse. A burden to them. I refuse to stay here as they mock and ridicule who I am. That is not how I choose to live my life. I can find better out there. I'm done with Vulpo."

"You are not a curse. Nor are you a burden. I wouldn't be here if you were."

"No, you're here because of my parents."

"You're wrong again, Kha Blaze."

"Just Blaze or Liekki. No need to add my title. Especially not down here." They had stopped near the end of the tunnel before it spread out into the open cavern. There was one thing he was right about. The Burrows was a shady place and anything goes down there. It could be a lawless place. Especially if there was knowledge and information for sale. If she wanted to stay clear of the rampaging mob above ground, then she had to stay in character. Keep her facade and glamour until she was safely out of Vulpo.

"I can't call you either with that glamour on," he said. "What name did you use to get through the gates of your home?"

"Niazal Swiftfoot," she quickly replied.

"Until we're in a safe area, I'll call you Kha Niazal Swiftfoot," Efrim said with a grin. "Also, I'm here because I wanted to be here. I found your letter, then told your mother when your father wasn't around. She was distraught and worried because of what your father was spearheading. She will keep the letter from him and show him once he returns. I respected your privacy on that front. I didn't open it, therefore I don't know what the letter says, but I'm sure it's nothing that will make Kho Nightsong feel any better about this entire situation. To make sure you were safe, I told Luya I was coming to find you. She didn't ask. All she said was to make sure you got away safely and that you reach Elderton before your time is up."

Liekki looked at him strange. Besides, Ice, she didn't think anyone cared enough about her to help like he was. Or her mother. Lately, even her mother was acting strange. She discovered a new side of the vixen and Liekki didn't know how to feel about that development. No, this predicament she was in when it came to her mother was new to her. Then there was her strange guard. Her mother's family friend. Someone Luya trusted inexplicably. Liekki looked down at her wrist. She stared at the black and orange gemstone bracelet she wore. She had it because her mother trusted Efrim. He was the one who created the priceless jewelry for her. As a way to keep her safe from her hate filled father. If her mother had that much trust many years ago, why couldn't she do the same? Something kept telling her to take him.

"Fine. You can come along," she said. "Don't get in my way, Efrim."

"Like you had any choice, Swiftfoot." Her guard looked around before speaking back to her. There was a twinkle in his eyes. "Where are we going?"

Liekki chuckled softly in response to him. At least he was being careful. More than she was. She knew better, and she knew she needed to be more careful of her surroundings and her magic work to keep her glamour on. One mistake and everything could come crashing down. "Come on. I'm trying to hitch a ride to Ravenfalls."

He lifted a brow, but said nothing to her about her destination. He held out a hand in front of him. "After you."

Together, they left the tunnel and walked right into the crowded Burrows. The place was always busy, and it didn't matter what time of day or night it was. It was the complete opposite of what went on above ground on Merchant Row or any other area in the valley. The area where they entered was where a lot of illegal goods and wares exchanged hands. That included hard to find gems, creatures that weren't allowed in Vulpo, and even Vulpiians who were somehow caught up and owed the wrong Vulpii money. Now they were on the market block themselves until their debt was cleared. Which was always never.

The Assassin's Guild was also located down in the burrows and Liekki had to walk past the almost hidden cloak and dagger building to get to the Vulpiic Gates. It wasn't part of the

Aeroways above their land, but it was another way to get out of Vulpo undetected. And it was always available for the right price. Especially if you wanted them, the gatekeepers, to overlook the fact that you were a wanted citizen. Across Eldritch, in almost every major port city or harbor, wherever there was a Vulpiian presence, there was some form of the ancient Vulpiic gate system. A timeworn way of traveling before the Council and the Phoenixes created the Aeroways. The Vulpiian leadership no longer monitored the way through the gates. Liekki suspected they had forgotten all about it. No, the ones who watched and maintained the gates like a hawklen were the shady merchants who were on the payroll for the Assassin's Guild. The vulpiic transportation system and the shady territories were theirs through and through.

Liekki kept her face hidden as they wove through the massive crowd. Even with her glamour, a flayer could be anywhere and could detect her from a fair distance away. That couldn't happen on the night she was trying to escape. They continued down the way, and the crowd slowly thinned out around them. The lighting around Liekki became dimmer, letting her know they were getting closer to their destination. The rancid scent of stale, old ale filled the air, mixed along with urine and whatever else she didn't want to think about. It almost made her want to vomit.

She and Efrim had ventured into an area that was a breeding ground and a cesspool for the unsavory types. She hated being down there. Before everything went to complete shezias, back when Liekki was known only as Blaze, she had only ventured this far into the burrows to get rid of wares and then disappeared just as fast. Glancing at Efrim from the corner of her eyes, she was thankful he was there by her side, even if she didn't tell him out loud. There was no telling what would happen if she was by herself and they saw through her illusions.

As the duo neared the cave that held the gate, Efrim took the lead, with her following close on his heels. The sounds of water slowly dripping from the cave's ceiling and the low lumo lights inside the cavern added to the deceptive ambiance. At the entrance stood two male Vulpiians, wearing dark leather tunics and hooded cloaks, along with expensive boots. They both had the crest of the Assassin's Guild on the chest of their cloaks. One glance at their forehead with the crescent and triangular markings told them everything they needed to know. Both Liekki and Efrim knew the two were from Clan Night and Clan Terra. If anything, the dark auburn hair and black hair also gave them away.

The Terran stopped them, not allowing them to go any further. His slimy gaze lingered too long on Liekki before resting on Efrim. "What do you want? We're done for the night." His voice was a harsh, wet, raspy sound.

"We need a way out of Vulpo," Efrim said sharply, with no emotion in his voice. "We're trying to go to Ravenfalls."

The Terran shook his head. "Not going to happen. I said we're done for the night."

"I got the gemstones. I can pay," Liekki said in a rush, speaking up from Efrim's side. The guard gave her a weird glance, but she ignored him. She didn't care. Liekki had to get out of Vulpo no matter how she did it. There was no staying there. Not with a mob searching for her and wanting blood. "Look, we need to leave. Payment is not an issue," she said with a raised voice.

"I won't tell you again, you Fa-"

"Aom!" the other Vulpiian shouted, cutting off the words of the auburn-haired male. "Let them through."

The one called Aom's face turned a ruddy shade of red. "We were told not to let anyone through."

"And I said let them through or else it'll be my blade kissing the skin of your thin neck."

Aom growled, but took a step back. "If anything happens, it's all on you."

"I'm willing to accept any punishment," he said, staring at Liekki and Efrim. "Hurry and get over here."

The duo darted towards the waiting fox. Not saying a word. After they reached him, he observed them, then looked at his partner, before returning his gaze back to them.

"It's going to cost you," he said.

"Like I said, payment isn't an issue."

His grin was a sly one, but she knew his decision was made. "Alright then," he said. "I'll be back, Aom. Don't leave your station."

"Whatever," he growled with hatred in his eyes and clenched teeth. He turned around, his back facing them.

The dark-haired male laughed. "Come on. This way."

Efrim said nothing as Liekki moved to step in front of him.

"I'm called Shoam," their guide said to Liekki as he led them down a dark tunnel deeper underground.

It took them a couple of minutes to get to where they were going, but it was worth it for the view alone. The tunnel opened into a much larger cavern. Luminescent crystals were growing on the stone walls, giving off a soft light. To their left was an underground thermal pool with a soft glow on its floor, lending a sheen to its mirror surface. She could feel the low heat radiating from the waters from where she stood. To her right and straight ahead, Liekki counted quite a few blossoming trees with pink, yellow, and white flowers growing near the gigantic stone arch that took up the most space near the back.

"Thanks for this, Shoam."

"Nothing to thank me for," he said. "Aom can be thickheaded at times. Besides, I'm not helping you because of my good nature."

"What do you mean?" Liekki said, even though she suspected there was something else to him helping them.

Shoam chuckled. "Of course I'm helping because I want something from you."

Liekki pulled the pack off her shoulders and rummaged around inside of it. She pulled out three fist sized emerald green stones with what looked like a red flame in its center. "Is this enough to get us to Ravenfalls? Like I said earlier, payment is not a problem."

Both Efrim and Shoal let out an impressed whistle.

"That will get you very far. Just one stone by itself. You have three. How?"

"How I have my wealth is none of your concern. Do you want them or not?"

She held them in her hand for him to take. Shoam reached out and grabbed two of the stones.

"You'll need that third one," he said, with a cryptic tone in his words. He spun on his heels and quickly stepped towards the stone gateway. He placed one of the stones into a depression that she didn't see at the console next to it. After being inserted, a blueish glow lit up the Vulpiic runes etched into its surface around the arch. "Ravenfalls, I can't get you to right now. It's closed off because today is Muda, but I can get you halfway there."

"No," Efrim said. "We need Ravenfalls."

Shoam's hard gaze pinned Efrim to his spot, but her guard didn't care. He stepped closer to the dark fox.

"Listen here, you deplu. I said Ravenfalls is closed off tonight. Either you wait until tomorrow, or you go wherever I can get you. Unless you want to wait here until my bosses show up. Aom really isn't a loyal fox. I can guarantee you he already left his station to go snitch on me and what I'm doing." He held up the remaining stone in his hand. "From this stone alone and the way you two are trying to leave this late when there's a lot of crazy going on above ground. No one has to tell me you're running."

"Fine," Liekki said, while giving Efrim a stern look. "Where can we go this late?"

Shoam grinned. "Aster."

"No!" Efrim shouted. "We can't go there."

"Aster? Isn't that in Dryemia? I thought their lands were closed off to others, like our lands here in Vulpo."

"They are closed off. The only place they will allow non Dryem is Aster. It's a harbor city. You can catch a ferry from Aster to Elyium and take the aeroway or the next gate over to Ravenfalls from there. If you don't want them to catch you and soon, you better make your decision fast."

"Okay. We'll go to Aster."

"Good choice. You'll need a place to crash once you get there. Ask for Amiho. She has a small inn and tavern there. It's close to the ferry you need to take to Elyium. Tell her that Shoam sent you. She'll do the rest."

"Thank you for your help," Liekki said to him.

"It's absolutely my pleasure," Shoam replied.

Agitated, Efrim pulled Liekki away from Shoam and took her aside. Tiny wrinkles creased at the corners of his eyes and a scowl marred his face. "I don't think this is a good idea. You don't know about the Dryem like I do. They don't take well to outsiders."

"Neither do Vulpii, Efrim, yet we still have them come to our lands for trade."

"Do you think he's trustworthy?" He asked her.

"Absolutely not. But I've dealt with his kind before. Silons talk. Those gemstones are worth a lot of silons and he knows it. He will get us to where we need to go."

Efrim growled his displeasure. "You're doing this, aren't you?"

"Yeah, I am. Either you are in or you are out. But make up your mind now or go running back to my mother or father," she hissed.

He ran a hand through his silky tresses. "Fine. But you follow my lead once we get to Dryemia."

Liekki smirked. "As you wish."

They both went back to Shoam. "Are you ready to depart this place?"

"Yes. Aster is fine. Thanks for your help."

"Anytime," he said as he turned towards the Vulpiic Gates and turned the dial to a certain angle on the console.

The center of the portal lit up and let out a shimmery glow. From where they stood, they could see through to the other side. It was late and very dark, with a few lights. Just beyond, she could see a grove of trees.

"All you have to do is walk through. The gatekeeper on the other side will help you."

Liekki and Efrim walked towards the shimmering portal. "Let me go through first. Then you come right behind me."

She nodded as she watched him go through. Once she couldn't see him anymore, then it became her turn. She took a step before Shoam called out to her again.

"Hey Blaze," he said. She froze in her spot. His chuckle was dark. "I thought it was you."

She turned around to face him. "You are a flayer?"

"I wouldn't be part of the Assassin's Guild if I wasn't. Don't worry. Aom isn't. I recognized you the moment you came inside. Don't worry. Your secret is safe with me."

"Thank you," she said.

"Good luck out there. I hope you survive the trials."

She said nothing else as she went through the gates. All she knew was that she hoped she survived the trials herself.

CHAPTER 12

Going through the gates was like swimming through thick, viscous water. It was cold and unyielding, yet Liekki kept pushing through until she reached the other side. She emitted a tiny shout when she made it through the portal, bursting through, gasping for air.

Warm hands grabbed her and soft words comforted as she tried to get her bearings straight.

"I've got you," Efrim said in his soothing tone. "You're safe."

Liekki had bent over, hands on her knees, as she tried to keep herself from puking out her insides. Once her stomach settled, she straightened and got a better look around. They were in an opening, surrounded by a thick copse of trees. The ground was a sea of green grass and a rainbow of wildflowers. Not far away from them stood a Vulpiian of Clan Night origins and a creature she had never seen before, but only heard of.

The Dryem stood there staring at her with his arms crossed against his chest. His skin was the color of dark brown that one could find on the tree bark surrounding them. His eyes were the bluest of blues. They reminded her of the Caspeson Ocean. His hair was coiled and adorned with leaves and green vines wrapped around his blue tinged hair, giving it a unique look. He was all sharp angles, slim, muscular, and fierce looking. Liekki had gotten the strongest feeling that the male was someone she didn't want to make angry.

"I'm familiar with these lands and people," Efrim whispered to her, reminding her he was the expert. "Let me do the talking and only speak when they speak to you."

Liekki nodded, not risking herself from saying anything. This was a new place for her, and everything differed greatly from Vulpo. Efrim led her towards where the Vulpii and the Dryem were standing. They stopped only a few feet away from the ones who watched them with curiosity and disdain. The Dryem stared at her before landing his gaze on Efrim. The look he gave her guard was one that spoke of disgust and dislike. It was apparent to her they knew each other and Liekki wanted to know from where and how.

"Why are you here, Efrim? Last I remember is that Cirrha and I both banned you from Dryemia."

"I had no other choice, Xyrin. We were trying to reach Ravenfalls. The gatekeeper said the access to there was closed off. We had to come here or risk being caught."

The one called Xyrin made a weird noise, similar to one scoffing. "I don't care about the predicament you or your... companion is in. Our rules are not to be broken. Especially by one of *your* kind. I can't let you go any further."

"Excuse me," Liekki interrupted, knowing that Efrim told her not to speak unless spoken too, but she couldn't stand there and let him get in trouble. Not by the Dryem with a foul disposition. Especially since she was the reason he was there to begin with. "He really didn't want to come here. It was my fault. I made the decision, and he had to follow whatever I did."

"And who are you?" the Dryem asked with a sneer. "I don't remember speaking to you."

Liekki kept her retort to herself and instead plastered a smile onto her face that didn't quite reach her eyes. She ignored the looks that her guard was giving her. Liekki knew she was breaking the rules, but that was nothing new to her. She was a rule breaker all the way down to her soul and bones. "I am Kha Niazal Swiftfoot. Efrim is my personal guard."

Xyrin laughed out loud, which shocked Liekki. Despite being mocked and laughed at, Efrim remained still, saying nothing. But his rigid body posture communicated a different message. "You! You are a guard now? Look at how low have we fallen, old friend."

"We are not friends," Efrim said.

"But are we not? We were once. A long time ago. I'm sure you remember Efrim. Now, you come into my lands in the middle of the night seeking refuge until morning, when the sun's rays kiss the tops of our trees and our homes." Xyrin stepped closer to Efrim and got in his face. He was so close, they stood nose to nose. "Tonight, you are at my mercy and will do as I say. I think that makes you my friend. Considering that I'm taking you in front of Cirrha. You'll be begging for my friendship then, if I let her have her way."

Xyrin took a step back, then glanced at Liekki. He tilted his head slightly while his brows furred at the center while staring at her. "Why are you going to Ravenfalls?"

"To see what the city looks like. I've never been before."

"Hmm," was all Xyrin said. He lifted his right arm and made some strange gesture with his hand. Soft as a whisper of wind, more Dryem came out from the living darkness and surrounded her and Efrim.

Dryem, both male and female, from the looks of it, Liekki thought.

They were similar to Xyrin, yet different. They wore varied shades of blue and gold in their clothing, jewelry, and hair. "Grab them," he said.

Stunned by the sudden order, Liekki tried to get out of the way, but could not move. They were upon her and Efrim soon as the words slipped off Xyrin's tongue.

"What's going on?" Liekki asked while being jostled by two females. Both were wearing the color gold. They were beautiful to her, with their golden orbs for eyes and sharp, angular features that made them seem otherworldly.

Xyrin's grin teemed with a sort of ill will, and she suddenly understood why Efrim didn't want to visit Dryemia. If Xyrin was a representative of them as a whole, then they weren't amiable creatures. But neither were Vulpiians. The only thing about her people was that they seemed nice up front. Everything was an illusion.

Xyrin's chuckle was low and dark. "You are in luck, Kha Swiftfoot," he said. "You'll meet with Cirrha and then, with her approval, she may let you stay in Aster tonight. Or, she may not."

Liekki nodded. "I understand."

The wind picked up in the clearing. It started out as a low whistling sound before it gained speed and loudness. The Dryem that encircled them advanced on her and Efrim. Quick as they came, the gust of wind came faster and wrapped around Liekki and Efrim. Her captors' hands gripped her arms tightly, and they were lifted off the ground and higher into the whirling funnel of air. The air swirled around them, carrying them far away so some unknown destination.

They didn't last long while flying courtesy of the wind currents, keeping them afloat until they reached their destination. Landing softly on her feet, Liekki searched all around her to see where they were. Her group stood in the center of what looked like a town square. All around her were buildings and homes that were built into the trees. Very elaborate and beautiful tree style homes that blended well into the natural setting that wasn't intrusive, but instead, it was inclusive. They were similar to Clan Terra's dwellings, but had a twist of Elven architecture blended into what she assumed was Dryem architecture. She stood there and was in awe.

Xyrin landed in front of Liekki without issue and walked towards her, not missing a stride. His expression revealed nothing of what he was thinking. His smirk wasn't comforting when she saw his hardened, blue gaze lingering on her. The Dryem was an interesting group of creatures and the male before her was worse than Mezal. No one had to tell her otherwise. She always had a way of reading others and just knew it. Liekki returned the look, but kept quiet.

"This way," Xyrin said, and tilted his head towards the massive treehouse before them. The base had perfectly placed stairs wrapped around the immense trunk that led up to a wide, arched, open doorway. Lumo lights flickered everywhere, giving the place an ethereal atmosphere. Out of the shadows, more armed guards came and stood at attention. As Xyrin led them towards the enormous building, every guard lowered their head in reverence when he passed them by. Liekki glanced at Efrim from the corner of her eyes, but he said nothing. He didn't even look her way.

She had a strange feeling that Xyrin was more than what he seemed. It also had her confused and baffled as to why he was lingering and waiting by the vulpiic gates when they arrived. Did he know they were coming? The group and guards reached the top in no time and passed under the opened arch. They entered a hall that lead them all the way to the back, where it opened into an open aired court. Everywhere Liekki looked, there were living plants, vines, and sweet smelling blooming flowers. Well tended to and taken care of. In the center before them was a natural fountain and water flowed courtesy of the elemental's power in a never-ending cycle. The soft tinkling of its splash was the only sound in the large room.

On the raised dais in the large chamber were two thrones blended into one. They were crafted from the living vines, tree roots, and flowers that the entire dwelling was made of. It was a unique way to use what talents and resources the Mother Goddess gave them. It was also vaguely similar to something Liekki had seen before when she was taken down to Mezal Irontail's underground chamber. To Liekki's left, the seat of the shared chair was empty, but to her right sat a female Dryem that was beautiful beyond measure. Yet there was no doubt in her mind that this Dryem was more dangerous than Xyrin. Even from where she stood, the female Dryem sat there watching her every move. Her power was old. Ancient. It radiated off of her in droves and it made Liekki's flesh crawl with unease.

Her face was blank of any emotion. A crown of rich brown tree roots and vines with glowing blue stones embedded into the head piece rested perfectly on her head and forehead. Floral markings of gold and light blue marked both of her cheeks. Her face was angular and sharp like Xyrin's, while a metal ring adorned her nose. Leaves the color of burnished gold and auburn like the ones she saw during the beginning of the season of Win were entwined into her thick, silverish blue hair and hung down past her neck. Around her slender neck was a thick torc that matched her crown, using the same material with different shades of gold and blue stones worked into the design.

But it was her eyes that pierced Liekki's. They were the clearest amber, ringed with black. Without a doubt, Liekki knew she was the true power in Dryemia. She was the one even Xyrin bent his knee to.

Xyrin spoke in a soft tone that reminded Liekki of a whispering breeze. He spoke in the tongue of the Dryems and the female's gaze slipped past him to look back at Efrim, then Liekki, before she said anything. She motioned for the guards to release the captives and Liekki had never been more grateful. If she was to be at someone's mercy, she would like to have full access to all of her limbs, including her magic.

"Xyrin, my love. Come and sit next to me at your rightful place," the female Dryem said in perfect Eldish so that she and Efrim could understand. "This will need both of our attention."

Xyrin sauntered towards the throne and sat down beside her. They stared at each other as if they were communicating with each other mentally before facing forward at the same time. It was eerie in how sync they were, but beautiful all the same, Liekki thought.

"I am called Cirrha, Queen of the Dryem," she said. Her voice was strong, yet light as tinkling bells as it carried across the room so all could hear. "Welcome to my lands, even though you were not invited. If it hasn't been noticed, just like your lands, outsiders are only allowed in certain areas. Yet, you have the privilege to stand here in the center of Dryemia's heart. And it's without an invitation. Others have died attempting to see what you are seeing. Make sure you cherish this moment with what time you have left."

Liekki wanted to say something snide, but she deferred to Efrim. In Vulpo they had no queens or kings, but there were many other lands that did and she was taught and raised to respect them just as she did their own Elders and clan leaders. She swallowed any ill words that came to her lips and remembered Efrim's words when she slightly glanced at him. His smirk returned, even though he didn't acknowledge her staring at him. He kept his gaze forward at the two most powerful Dryem before them.

"Thank you for allowing us to enter your lands," Efrim said with a slight head bow.

"I wasn't speaking with you, Efrim," Queen Cirrha's words came out quick as a whip. Liekki felt the punishing sharpness from where she stood. "You are not welcome here and you know this. We will deal with your transgressions soon enough. I was speaking to your... companion."

Cirrha's golden amber gaze pinned Liekki in her spot. She cleared her throat. Her guard gave her a barely perceptible head nod, encouraging her to speak. She looked at Xyrin but her gazed ended on the Queen. "Thank you for allowing me into your lands. I will remember and honor this gift you have given me."

The queen's lilting laugh startled Liekki. "Ah, you are a smart one. What is your name, Vulpiian?"

"I'm Kha Niazal Swiftfoot," she responded, while trying her best not to shift on her feet. There was something other about Queen Cirrha's penetrative stare and for whatever reason, it made Liekki very uncomfortable. It was nothing compared to her father's or even Mezal's. No, this was more. The sooner they were able to leave Dryemia, the better she would feel.

Queen Cirrha shook her head slowly with disappointment. "You can't hide from me, Vulpiian. I see past your glamour. You are skilled, yes, but my gifts as Queen of these lands allow me to see through all nuances that could hinder my sisters and brothers. A way to better protect my people. You are no, what are they called... a terran. I see your true self."

Liekki said nothing while the Queen unfolded herself from her throne and stood to her full height. Tall and lithe. Queen Cirrha wore a sheer black dress with flecks of gold that hugged her body. It flowed freely as the slits showcased her legs as it went up both sides of her thighs. She sauntered towards Liekki and Efrim on bare feet and stopped directly in front of the pair.

"You are interesting, Vulpii," Queen Cirrha said low enough to where only Liekki and Efrim could hear her words. "You are from the Night clan, yet your colors are a mix of both Clan Night and Terra."

"But how?" Liekki asked, realizing her mistake soon after her words came out. "I apologize Queen Cirrha."

"No need to apologize. Those of your kind are a curious bunch. I am very well aware of the mischief you Vulpiians are prone to get into. Are you the one who put together this illusion?"

"Yes, I am."

"You are very skilled and talented." She looked at Efrim. "Did this one help you with your skills?"

Liekki shook her head. "No. I've only met him recently when he became my personal guard."

"Ah, Xyrin mentioned that you've become a lowly guard." Cirrha tsked between her teeth and said something in the Dryem tongue. Liekki remembered words being spoken aloud, but she didn't recall Xyrin telling the queen about Efrim being her guard. The longer she thought about it, the more she realized the connection between Xyrin and his queen, Cirrha. They were soul bonded and were able to speak with each other through a private mental connection.

Efrim turned a shade darker, letting Liekki know he knew exactly what she said. "There is nothing wrong with serving others, Cirrha."

"While you are in my home, you will address me as my title affords me, *Efrim*."

Efrim's jaws clenched tightly. "As you wish, Queen... Cirrha."

"Now, that wasn't so hard, was it?"

Safely so, Efrim didn't answer. Liekki couldn't believe she stood under the roof of the Queen of the Dryems. Never did she think she would step on their lands. The same could be said for her being chosen for the trials. Life had a way of taking what one knew and twisting it all around and making something new out of it. Yet, she didn't know if it was good or bad for her. Most times she didn't care, but lately, even if she hated to admit it, she cared a bit more than she wanted to.

"You have come at a most auspicious time. I would like to know why?" Cirrha said. "Come and share moshai with me. We will discuss it in my private chambers."

Liekki didn't have time to say anything. Queen Cirrha spun on her heels and walked away. Xyrin stood up from the living throne and rushed to her side. The Dryem guards that were closest to them followed right behind Cirrha and Xyrin while Liekki's and Efrim's keepers nudged their backs and told them to follow the others. Liekki stared at Efrim and he was still scowling, but he kept quiet as he silently encouraged her to move. She didn't know why, but something more was going on. There was something he was keeping to himself, and Queen Cirrha and Xyrin were keeping quiet about it. Liekki was determined to get to the bottom of it all.

"Duara, since you've helped me this far, continue to watch over me and lead me out of here... hopefully filled with breath still," Liekki silently prayed. Ever since being chosen, she found herself praying more to the spirits than she had in her entire life. *What was going on?*

She moved her right foot forward and then her left. Following the lead of the others. The Dryem were a fascinating group, and she hoped she could learn more about them if possible. Whatever this moshai was, she would do it to find out more.

Then, after that, she would make sure to get far away from Dryem.

Chapter 13

The group traveled up a set of curving stairs until they reached the top floor. Liekki shouldn't have been surprised, but she was. The scenery was breathtaking in its natural setting. A lush canvas of colors was atop the garden on the roof. Verdant green moss blanketed the floor, allowing a slight spring in her step as she walked on it. Vines of thick ivy cascaded down from the branches. The air was alive with the sweet fragrance of flowers and the gentle rustle of leaves in the breeze. Nocturnal birds sang their melodies, providing a backdrop of ambient music that perfectly complemented the rhythm of what she beginning to learn was the way of the Dryem.

The rooftop was open-aired with the top of the trees and their multicolored leaves being used as natural low walls. Bushes of rosenthyiums and jasliomus flowers were everywhere with their velvety looking petals. They were beautiful, yet extremely poisonous to the touch. Even if one was to ingest them, if not given the antidote in time, the poison could claim their life. A dangerous plant, even in all of its beauty. Finishing the ambience was the low flickers of light courtesy of the Lumoflies, as they, too, were in abundance.

Both the Silver and Blue moons of Eldritch were high above them, combining their silver and blueish light to the etherealness of the lumo lighting. Liekki remembered that for the three hours the two moons shared the night sky, it was a special and magical time. Many species across Eldritch did their strongest power workings during the holy hours. From what she could tell, that included the Dryems as well.

At the center of the rooftop, there was a low table made from carved wood. A dark wood with intricate markings engraved into its sides. There were no chairs, but a multitude of soft pillows around it. On the table was a carafe of what Liekki assumed was wine. Platters of fresh fruit, cheeses, and soft bread were there waiting, along with different types of savory spreads to go with it. It looked appetizing, and she recalled she hadn't eaten anything in a while and was famished.

Xyrin moved away from his guards and went and stood beside the table. After speaking to the ones who escorted them to the rooftop in their language, they all dispersed, leaving the small group alone. Queen Cirrha took her time and crossed the rooftop. She moved as if she were lighter than air. Her movements were filled with an ethereal grace that many couldn't duplicate. A grace that Liekki had never seen before. Not amongst her kind. The Queen reached Xyrin's side and lifted her face to his, with a deep type of love in her eyes. He bent down and kissed her lips gently before she turned around to face Liekki and Efrim.

"Moshai is a sacred time for us. It is the time we call when both moons share the night sky with each other. It's a time where the magic is at its strongest. For us Dryem, it's a time for us to bare our truths. No matter how dark or painful they can be. Being invited to share Moshai with us is rare and an honor," Queen Cirrha said, then pointed to the table and empty pillows. "Sit and honor me, Kha Nightsong. Share Moshai with me and my soulbind, Xyrin."

The shock on Liekki's face was one that she thought she was able to hide, but she was quickly learning, there wasn't much she could hide from the intuitive Dryem.

Queen Cirrha smiled and for once, Liekki didn't see any anger or malice in them. Only curiosity. "Yes, I know who you are. Your name carries on the winds and Duara herself showed your true self to me."

The night was getting weirder for Liekki, but if she wanted to know how Queen Cirrha knew everything, she had to share Moshai. Not waiting for Efrim to say anything, she went towards the Dryem and sat down where the queen told her to sit.

"Come, old friend," Xyrin said to Efrim. He wore a smirk on his face, with a mischievous twinkle in his bright, glowing blue eyes. "Come and share Moshai with me. Allow your truths to be told this night. It is the least you can do after how long?"

"It's been one hundred years," Efrim responded. To Liekki, it almost sounded like defeat. "But who's counting?"

Efrim reached Liekki's side in no time and sat beside her. Xyrin picked up an enormous green leaf from the bundle in the center of the table. He piled pieces of fruit, cheese and a large piece of the flat bread onto it, then served it to Cirrha. Then the Queen did the same and served Liekki while Xyrin served Efrim.

"Eat first," Xyrin said to them after pouring wine into the wooden cups. "Then we will speak of the darkness that is sweeping your lands and ours."

Liekki thanked them for the meal and then dove into her food, following the others. She thought the food in Vulpo was good, but even though it was only fruits, cheese, and bread, it still tasted wonderful and just as good as her food from home. It did not surprise her to see there wasn't any meat. Vulpiians were voracious meat eaters, but creatures like the Dryem were nature bound. She couldn't see them eating meat. Liekki didn't want to ask about it, thinking that it would be rude. Keeping her head down, she continued to eat.

Silence had blanketed them and it wasn't the uncomfortable kind that she often found herself in around her father or other Vulpiians back home. Liekki enjoyed the moment and let her thoughts run wild as she tried to figure out what was different about her culture and the one of the Dryems. It was obvious they knew of the Vulpiian spirit gods and goddesses. She didn't think they worshipped their pantheon, but she was wrong about many things. Although she was all over the place back home. Liekki was beginning to understand how young she really was, even though she was an adult compared to those sitting around the table. They have seen things she knew she wouldn't even begin to comprehend. Vulpiians were long lived and her short twenty-five years were still nothing but a blink of an eye for her kind.

"Efrim," Xyrin said, breaking the long silence while they ate. "Tell us your story. Why has it been so long?"

Liekki's guard sighed heavily after swallowing the piece of food he had just shoved into his mouth. He took a drink from his cup, then set it back down on the table. He stared at his hands for the longest time and, at some point, Liekki didn't think he was going to speak. She stayed silent because this was something he had to work through. Something he had to speak from his own heart.

"The lands were cursed when our last champion failed the trials."

"The one they call Kalama Brightsun?" Xyrin inquired.

Liekki took a bite of her bread as she watched Efrim nod in agreement. "Yes. One of the Sacred Three elders in Vulpo."

"Ah, I see. Go on."

"I couldn't leave the lands. If they were cursed, then so was I. Trapping myself in Vulpo, I considered myself cursed too. I could no longer wander the lands like I was used to. Then... *she* went silent. No words of wisdom. No expeditions. Nothing! No matter how much I reached out to her, I failed. It was as if my words and prayers had fallen on deaf ears. I had to find something to do to keep myself occupied. Or else I would go mad like the rest of the Vulpiians around me were doing."

Xyrin pointed at Liekki. "You became her guard."

"Not until recently. I knew her mother. I was around when my charge was born. You of all know I take my duties seriously."

Both Xyrin and Queen Cirrha chuckled. The sound was a surprise to Liekki. "That you do, Efrim," Cirrha said. "Perhaps too much."

"This was why you couldn't come? You couldn't reach out?" Xyrin asked. He almost sounded sad. No longer the angry one from when they first landed in Aster.

Liekki wanted to know the answer and set her cup down on the table and looked at him. His gaze found hers. She knew her mysterious guard was hiding something and even then; he didn't want to speak about it. Not while she was there. One of these days, she was going to find out the truth about Efrim.

"Xyrin. Queen Cirrha. I apologize for not keeping in contact with you like I should have. I promise, things will be better soon enough. For eleven years now, the curse had been over, yet my obligations wouldn't let me leave. Vulpo is in a state of despair, even if the crazy Vulpiians don't know it yet. Things must be set right before I continue my wanderings."

Xyrin picked up a piece of cheese and ate it before taking a drink from his cup. "And how will that be done if you couldn't fix it in the one hundred years plus you've been trapped there? Have she spoken to you again?"

Liekki was curious too. Her home was in a state of madness. Filled with the shadows and darkness of the spirit god Ibris. It blanketed their kind, and they were too lost to even know what was going on. The uncontrollable rage and anger. The random murders of citizens left in the streets with no one to know who was the culprit. Even the mobs they had to run from to get away only a couple of hours ago. Vulpo was in a state of chaos she had never thought to see in her life. She wasn't perfect by a long shot, but she refused to be as bad as a lot of the nobles she knew. The extent of her madness went to thieving, which she became a master at.

"No, she hasn't."

"I'm sorry, Efrim. Give it time," Xyrin said. Her guard shrugged.

"Never mind. When it's time, everything will all fall into place. Until then, how it will be fixed is not my story," Efrim said before staring at Liekki. "It's hers."

The Dryems' piercing gazes bore down on her like daggers, fixing Liekki to her seat with an unyielding force. All eyes were trained on her, watching and waiting for her next words. It was impossible for Liekki to tell what they were thinking or feeling. Their expressions remained neutral, betraying nothing of their thoughts and intentions. The silence was heavy, pregnant with unspoken thoughts and agendas. Liekki knew that much for sure. She could tell from the brief conversation she had just heard between the three others.

She swallowed slowly before sitting the piece of flat bread back onto the leaf plate. For a moment, Liekki felt completely trapped, as if she was at the mercy of these powerful beings. Glancing at Efrim, that included him, too. For he was more than what he seemed. Xyrin and Queen Cirrha knew what it was too. She was the odd Vulpiian out.

Liekki summoned her courage and words and met everyone's eyes with a fierce determination. Regardless of how much she disliked discussing herself or her experiences, she could do this. But reality was coming at her fast and no matter how fast she was trying to run. Life was going to catch up with her. The obligations that were chosen for her. The one thing she couldn't refuse, no matter how much she thought about it.

"Share Moshai with me, Kha Nightsong. Allow your truths to be told this night. How will you, a young kit compared to the others of your kind, be the one to help your fellow Vulpiians? Help to dispel the darkness that seeps from your lands and penetrates mine," Queen Cirrha said with a bite at the end. "The sickness of your gods and goddesses is a blight on my land and my sisters and brothers. The Dryem are not as we used to be and I blame you, Vulpiians. To better protect my subjects, I must know how you will fix the sickness that makes my Dryem ill. Or tell me what I must do to fix the situation we find ourselves in."

"I don't understand. Why do you blame my kind?"

Queen Cirrha leaned forward towards Liekki. "We Dryem don't pray to gods and goddesses, but the one who created us. Mother Goddess. We worship nature and honor the gifts and bounty it allows us, and in return, we are its caretakers. Somewhere down the years, your culture and blasphemous ways have crossed into our borders and now, altars of your spirits can be found all over Dryem. My sisters and brothers, my subjects are tempted by the whispers your spirits offer in return for their devotion. Tempted by the partaking of flesh, which is an abomination and goes against everything we are. My kind are no longer how they used to be. It's a perversion of who we are. A complete travesty, if I might add. If we are not careful, our lands will become a desolate and barren place. Nothing fit for a Dryem. So, Kha Nightsong. Why does your Duara speaks to me in my dreams? Why does your name fall off her lips and carry on the wind to my ears? Who are you and why are you here?"

Liekki swallowed, her throat suddenly parched. She didn't know what to say. The Queen said so much in that short span of time. It was enough to have her thoughts all over the place. Although she herself was a menace to her own kind, she realized that the rest of the world didn't see the Vulpiians in the same light. Just as she was a menace to the three clans, the Vulpiians were a menace to the rest of Eldritch. *No wonder they were being tested so soon again,* she thought to herself. Careful to keep those thoughts inside of her mind. More careful about what words came out of her mouth. This was deeper than she expected. Liekki took a deep breath and slowly exhaled.

"My intentions were to reach Ravenfalls. As I've said before. I had no intentions of staying or coming to Dryemia. I couldn't stay in Vulpo for another night. Unless..." Liekki's voice faded off as she left the sentence unfinished.

"Unless what?" Queen Cirrha asked, urging Liekki on. "What was going to happen to you?"

Liekki looked up and stared into the queen's face. The queen's gaze was damning yet, she didn't flinch when she spoke. No matter how much it hurts. "I would be dead. My soul resting in Dhasas' embrace."

Efrim clicked his tongue in a disapproving manner, followed by a scowl on his face. "We don't speak those names out loud, Nightsong. I've warned you about this before. Especially during these hours. To speak their names during the time of the spirits is to invoke their presence."

Liekki rolled her eyes. "I'm not superstitious, Efrim. How many times do I have to tell you that?"

"It's not superstition when it's the truth," Queen Cirrha interrupted. "Listen to your guard. He knows what he is talking about. Do you really think that your spirit gods and goddesses can't touch you? You've already been touched. Duara watches over you. One other does too, but they haven't unveiled themselves to me yet. Can you not feel them? I can feel their ancient power. If you can not, I am sure in time, all things will come to the light. Especially if those dark ones are afoot. Your dark spirits are a malevolent mess and whatever is going on, it needs to be stopped before it gets worse. All of Vulpo and Dryemia demands it."

"I don't know how to stop anything," Liekki admitted with defeat. The fiery hatred she had for her own bubbled to the surface. "I couldn't care less about Vulpo. Let the place rot in the deepest abyss."

"Then why are you running?"

"Because I was chosen," she finally said aloud. Queen Cirrha's and Xyrin's subtle glance at each other didn't get past her notice. "I was chosen for the Eldritch Trials."

Cirrha's brows furred with a knowing look, and then she nodded. "I see."

"The Mother Goddess sees what is going on in your lands and doesn't approve. Why aren't you happy? To be chosen is an honor," Xyrin said. "To be chosen to help rid the lands of what she doesn't approve."

"For you perhaps. Not me. I'm running from home because the clans want to make sure I never see another sunrise. So they can have their chosen champion go through the trials instead of me. I'm a dead vixen walking."

"You come from a noble house if I'm not mistaken," the Queen said. Liekki nodded, not surprised that Cirrha knew more about her and where she come from than she originally let on. "Why do they want you dead?"

"I'm a menace. A thief. I can lie with the best of them. I know I'm selfish and don't care. I don't even know if I want to go to Elderton when it's my time."

Queen Cirrha reached out her hand and touched Liekki's, that rested on the table. "You were running away from it all."

"I was." Liekki pointed a thumb in Efrim's direction. "Until somehow, he found me."

"Efrim has a unique talent for finding things. You'll learn soon enough," Queen Cirrha said, before looking up at the sky. The silver moon had almost disappeared from the sky. Liekki didn't know the time had moved so fast. "Moshai is almost up. I have one last thing to discuss."

Xyrin said something to Queen Cirrha in their native tongue before taking a drink from his cup. Whatever was said caused Efrim to react. He tried to keep still, but Liekki saw how his back stiffened at whatever was said between the Dryems. From the way he reacted, she could tell it was nothing good.

"Kha Nightsong, have you ever heard of the Carnaval du Malheur?" Xyrin asked.

The name sounded familiar, but she couldn't remember why or where she had heard it from. Or from who. Even hearing the name made her skin crawl. "No, I haven't. If I have, I can't place how I know the name."

"Don't worry," Queen Cirrha said. "It is something you'll never forget if you had."

"It's a traveling... carnaval of sorts," Efrim added. His voice lowered. "One you never want to visit."

They had her attention. "Why not?"

"It's a place where nothing is what it seems. Being so great at illusions, you should know something about that," Queen Cirrha said. "While you are out there traveling before making your way to Elderton, if you decide to go through the trials, only be careful. The carnaval only shows up after so many years or when the world is sliding into the dark crevices of Ibris. Never in the same place. My scouts alerted me that such a thing is back. No one knows where they come from or where they go to. If you come across it, don't enter its gates."

Even more curious, Liekki asked, "Why not?"

"Because you'll never come back. Sometimes you won't even make it out alive."

"Oh, sounds like the trials." Liekki had quickly put it together. Yet, somehow, she knew it was something more sinister and dark. Nothing blessed by the Mother Goddess. "A product of Drekra and her sister Dhasas."

All three hissed at her. Their scowls were so harsh that they could cut like the sharpest blade. Liekki flinched and realized her mistake when she looked up in the sky. Yes, one moon was setting, but it didn't mean they weren't still in the hours of the spirits. Realizing her mistake, she quickly apologized.

"I'm sorry." She glanced at Efrim before looking at the Queen and Xyrin. "I'm used to saying their names. It's kind of hard to stop."

"You should learn to stop before it causes any more harm. From what I know of your spirit gods and goddesses, those are the ones you don't want walking this realm." Cirrha finished her cup of wine. "Your spirits have done enough harm to Dryemia and my sisters and brothers. If any more harm comes our way, I'd be forced to do things that are unbecoming of my station and who I am."

Those words were a warning. Subtle, yet glaringly loud. Liekki knew that getting on the wrong side of Queen Cirrha's mood would be disastrous for her. Especially if she wanted to make it out of Dryemia in one piece.

"I understand loud and clear."

"Good," Queen Cirrha said. She looked at the sky once more before speaking in her native tongue. Xyrin answered with a short reply. She nodded, then looked at Efrim, then last at Liek-ki. "Thank you for sharing moshai with me. With my soulbind, Xyrin. The time for moshai has ended. You and Efrim are allowed to stay in Aster for the night. Leave for Ravenfalls soon as the light touches the morning sky. Do not linger in Dryemia. Get permission before you travel here again or you'll regret it."

Liekki bowed her head and let her know she understood. Xyrin stood and helped his Queen up before she left them all alone with Xyrin.

"She went easy on you, Kha Nightsong. I hope you accomplish everything you need to secure victory for your fellow Vulpiians. You passing your trials will help the darkness in your lands. In turn, it'll help the darkness in ours. If not, you will have gained a formidable enemy of the Dryem."

"But it's not here because of me."

"You are Vulpiian, yes?"

"Y-yes..." she said slowly, thinking about where Xyrin was going with his questions.

"Then you are at fault. Just as much as your other Vulpiians. Doesn't matter if you knew or not. Actions have consequences. From what I gathered so far during our moshai is that you are selfish Kha Nightsong. You have no sense of loyalty. Even to your own kind. As a thief, you are unquestionably not worthy to be trusted. Yet, your guard does. That is your one positive. You, as a Vulpiian, see the world in one way. But for the rest of

Eldritch, we all view the Vulpiians the same. As an affliction. A sore spot created by the Mother Goddess. Let me leave you with this. Change begins with just one. I wish you well in the trials." He looked at Efrim and for a moment, she saw a hint of sadness before his scowl found purchase on his face again. "I'll take you back to Aster myself. If you need to come back here, let Efrim know. He knows how to reach us. Nothing has changed."

With quick speed, Xyrin stepped closer to Liekki and Efrim, calling the wind to him, and swept them up. They reached Aster in no time, landing directly in front of the inn that Shoam from the Burrows had told her about. Xyrin didn't linger around, swiftly leaving soon as he dropped the two off.

Liekki could hear the gentle rush of the nearby river. The mirror like surface of the river glistened from where they stood, capturing the moon and stars from above. Reflecting what was above now low to where they were. There wasn't a river in Vulpo. Just the falls and the water around the elder's island in the center of their lands. The flowing waters reminded her of the crashing waves against the rocks down in the Caspeson Ocean, next to the mountains of her home. Still, the waters weren't enough to get her mind off what had just happened.

"That was interesting," Liekki said, more to herself than to her guard.

"With the Dryem. Things are always interesting. They have a peculiar way about them."

"Are they trustworthy?"

"No more than the Vulpiians. They're similar in their ways to the elves, too. Sometimes what they say isn't exactly what they mean. Almost like the illusions most of us Vulpiians are able to conjure up. Keep your wits about you in these lands, Liekki." Efrim glanced at her from the corner of his eyes. "I mean it. These lands are as treacherous as the ones we just left back home. They spoke true. There is a darkness about and it's seeping through Eldritch. Carnaval du Malheur is real and they always come about when those dark spirits of ours are on the loose. If the Queen's scouts saw evidence of their arrival. Be extremely careful. It's run by a nightdweller and a vulpii and they have a deadly way of messing with your mind."

Soft steps behind them had Liekki and Efrim turning around at the same time, ending their conversation. Efrim's knowledge of the carnaval intrigued Liekki and made a mental reminder to ask him how he knew so much later. At the top of the stairs to the inn, a beautiful vixen stopped just under the moonlight. The crescent on her forehead glowed a silvery color.

"You two have kept me waiting. I have rooms," she said. Her voice was strong and firm. She nodded her head towards the door behind her. "I'm Amiho. Shoam sent a message saying you would be coming. Don't take too long unless you want to be swept up by more Air Dryems."

Liekki slightly glanced at her guard, and his shoulders relaxed.

"Come on, Nightsong. We will be safe for the rest of the night," Efrim assured her before leading her up the stairs.

Chapter 14

Deep within the snow caves below, Kalama Brightsun paced restlessly back and forth in the cramped private sanctuary nestled close to her family's altar. She was more than agitated. Ever since the troublesome Nightsong vixen was chosen, there had been nothing but pure chaos in Vulpo. More than the normal amount of trouble going on.

She had pledged to help her mentee as much as possible, but how could she do that when Liekki was dodging her house guards and leaving Vulpo? The peacekeepers had searched far and wide for her soon after Kho Diev Nightsong realized she was missing, but it did no good. It was hard to use the resources for her and keep the peace in Vulpo all at the same time. Ultimately, the search had failed. Liekki was no longer in Vulpo, she was sure of it.

And then there were the deaths. The horrible murders. It seemed as if Drekra and her sister Dhasas walked the streets of Vulpo every single night. They were on a rampage, taking their fill of blood, death, and souls every night. It pained Kalama to see so many dead Vulpiians discarded like refuse on temple row every single morning. All of them had died the same way. All had their throats slit and left in front of the temple for Drekra.

She shuddered at the memory of the few she saw with her own eyes. There was no pattern to it. It didn't matter if they were male or female. Clan affiliation didn't matter either. Some were commoners. Some were part of the merchant class and even a couple were part of the noble houses. It was mass hysteria. Everyone was in an uproar, shouting for the Sacred Three to do something. Kalama didn't know what to do. She was too in shock to do anything, yet it all had a strange familiarity with it.

Kalama recognized the signs. It had been so long since anything like this had happened. A time period she had hoped to never see again in her long years, but life could be cruel in its vicious cycle. She remembered the many years before they were cursed. Before,whether they picked her as the perfect one to pass the tests because the other candidates weren't in any condition to do what needed to be done.

When the Vulpii were first chosen to go through the trials and prove themselves to Zera, the Mother Goddess, the darkness had started the same way then, too. She was blind to the situation like many were now, but no more. A failure on her part, Kalama couldn't admit to the others she saw the hints of turmoil and trouble long before it manifested as it did. They would have declared her as the source. Those of Clan Night wouldn't of hesitated to say she was the cause, the root of it all. No, Kalama knew she had to stay quiet. It wasn't like the other Elders would see reason. It was why she hated working with those from Clan Night and sometimes Clan Terra.

"What are you doing down here?" Her daughter's voice pulled Kalama out of her thoughts. She glanced up and saw her youngest daughter staring at her. "I've been looking for you. We have a guest."

"Who dares come to our house at this hour?" Kalama questioned, knowing that it was extremely late when she decided to pay a visit to the family's altar. Icelia's gaze swept the area as she tried to avoid looking at her, which made her even more suspicious. Kalama watched as Ice's entire body language changed. Instantly, she knew who it was. A feral, low growl slipped from the elder before she realized what she was doing. The sound was threatening enough that Icelia stepped back in a hurry, getting farther away from her. Kalama sighed and apologized. "I am just frustrated. I have to mentor his daughter who isn't easy to work with. Then he dares come here this late uninvited. None of this is right."

Icelia made a sound of disapproval, then slightly tilted her head to the side as if she could see directly through Kalama. The elder shifted on her feet but said nothing and watched as her daughter steeled her spine before saying what was truly on her mind.

"Liekki is not that bad," Ice said. "If you knew the type of things she had to endure dealing with that family of hers, you'd understand her more. She's a good vulpii, whether or not anyone believes it. I just don't become friends with anyone, mother, and you of all vulpii should know that."

"Bah," Kalama said, knowing the cursed vulpii was misunderstood. *But did she have to do all the things she did to get under her skin? Why couldn't she do better and stay on the right path? Like those of Clan Sky. There's something foul with Clan Night,* Kalama thought to herself before speaking again. "If she was so good, she wouldn't have run away."

Icelia spoke with certainty as she said, "You'll understand one day. When you do find her, because I know you will. Wish her good luck for me. That's all I ask."

Kalama hated her daughter was best friends with a Nightsong, but there wasn't much she could do about it. No matter how much she tried. She suspected Liekki was a foul influence on her. Ever since Ice began hanging out with Blaze, she kept staying out past what was acceptable for one of her status in their clan. Corrupted by Blaze's ideas, her precious Icelia began to steal and give her trouble at home. Kalama did her best to keep it within their walls, but others saw and had made comments about her upbringing. Kalama upset herself by thinking about it again. She raised her daughter with proper morals. She only hoped that all of her teachings would lead her down the proper path in life. Especially with her friend going to the trials. But she understood her daughter's words and promised she would try.

"Inform our guest that I'll be there shortly."

Icelia gave a quick nod and departed the small sanctuary, leaving Kalama all alone yet again. The coldness that was ever present in the snow caves finally penetrated her skin, sending a torrent of goosebumps down her arms. Any other time, the cold didn't bother her. This cold was different. Unlike most days, this cold brought with it a darkness that was wrong. She could feel its thick heaviness from where she stood. Heavily sighing, Kalama said her final prayer to the spirt of the sun, Asis, and the spirit of fire and lightning, Kheton. She knew who lingered upstairs in the waiting room. She would need all the strength she could muster to deal with the vulpiian, who was worse than his very own daughter.

With a snap of her fingers, the flames from the small braziers at the altar roared to life. Leaving the fire going, Kalama swiftly left her private sanctuary to deal with the daemon himself. Taking her time after reaching the stairs that led into her home, she stopped in front of the engraved double doors. Mentally chastising herself, she pushed it opened and stepped through the threshold. She climbed another set of winding steps that led her to the receiving chambers. Dressed in fine leather armour and furs, the house guards waited outside the receiving room, silent sentinels, every single one of them. They stood at attention and when they recognized Kalama. She quietly acknowledged them after they gave a quick head bow.

She ran her hands down the front of her dress, smoothing the creases out before she went inside. If anything, she had to look presentable. There was no way she would go in there looking like a commoner.

"I'm ready," she said to her guards. "Open the door."

The tiny sound of their leather creaking as they moved was the only noise in the hall before she went inside. Eyes forward, chin up, spine straight, Kalama glided into the room as if she was some Queen and the receiving room was her court.

"Have you found her?" Diev Nightsong shouted. "I thought the council would have done something by now!"

Keeping her temper in check, Kalama glanced at the head of the Nightsong house and leader of Clan Night. He stood there, tendrils of black slithering behind his pupils. She said nothing, but she knew the mark of Ibris when she saw it. Kalama hated to do it, but duties demanded it. She would have to inform the others about the latest developments. Not knowing how they would take it, Kalama understood the delicate situation would have dire consequences if approached wrong. She would have to tread lightly. Everyone in Vulpo knew that she and Diev didn't get along, and it went far beyond him and his youngest daughter.

"Hello to you too, Diev," Kalama said. She pointed to the empty chair next to her guest. "Have a seat. You don't come into my house and shout at me like I'm some low born commoner. You come into my home and show me the proper respect I deserve."

Diev scowled. "You deserve! I don't think so, Brightsun. If it wasn't for you, we wouldn't be in this mess. How hard could it have been? All you had to do was pass the trials from when you went! Now, my youngest daughter has to make up for your incompetence."

Kalama snarled. "Don't stand there and pretend to be righteous. Like you actually care about your youngest kit. I may not like Liekki, but if she was my daughter, I would try to show her a better way than the one she is going down. You haven't cared one bit about her ever since she was born! Don't you dare think that those outside of your clan don't know how the vixen is treated. We hear those words, Diev. The ones that said she was cursed from the moment she entered this world. How you and the rest of clan night feel is a direct correlation to how she is treated outside of those forsaken mountains of yours."

Diev froze in his spot as Kalama went on a tirade. She didn't care. If her words stung, then so be it. They were more than deserved. She wasn't perfect, but neither was he by a long shot.

"How dare you?" he spat out with more venom than a spindle spider that lurked in the dark spaces of the caves.

"I will take the dare any jiiqing time. Try me Diev. I. Dare. You!" Her visitor paced in his spot. Unintelligible words were mumbled under his breath. Ready for him to leave, she continued. "Tell me, why are you here?"

She stood there, magic waiting just under her skin in case she needed to call it up. She didn't trust the dark fox in front of her one bit. He was sly and cunning. Some would even say he was too smart for his own good. There was always an ulterior motive when it came to him, and she was sure there was a reason he was standing in her home. Why else would he come down his precious mountain and make his way to the ice and snow of her district?

A look of utter disgust crossed his face before replacing the stoic mask they knew him for. He cleared his throat, then adjusted the collar of his fine tunic. "We can't find her. All of my connections throughout Eldritch have not been able to find Liekki."

"It doesn't matter if you find her or not. She will make her way to Elderton. She knows how long she has before she must reach the gates of the island."

"How much time does she have? We can still switch out champions," he said with the sound of hope that Kalama had never heard before with him.

"It doesn't matter how much time she has. She is our champion. You and the others will eventually have to accept what is."

Diev and many others of his clan, and even in her clan along with Terra, still wished to change their champion, but it was a futile idea. It wasn't going to happen. They all wanted a new champion, even with the sacrificing of Liekki, to do it. She also couldn't understand why he was so brazen in his hate for his own daughter. Kalama had her limits. She wouldn't kill the young vixen for the needs of the others. No matter how much she hated the fox, she knew the Spirits chose her for a reason. Even if it was a reason that none of them wanted to hear or pay heed to.

"As I've told you and the others already. We are not sacrificing your kit for a new champion. How can you even call yourself a father? Standing here before me speaking ill of your own flesh and blood. Willing to kill her off. You are despicable!"

"It's for the greater good, Brightsun. This is bigger than all of us. This is for all the Vulpiians." He stepped closer to her. Their faces were close enough that she could smell the spicy scent of his natural aroma. The familiar scent of the ones born from the night clan. Their eyes met and the thin tendrils of shadows slithered behind the pupils and in the whites of his eyes. She withheld the shudder, opting to pretend she didn't see the disturbing sign of his true allegiances. "But you wouldn't understand that since you failed the trials the last time," he said, finishing his thoughts.

Anger bubbled up inside of Kalama. Tired of every single vulpiian against her, bringing up her past failures. Ever since her shame, and the dark times it brought upon them, she had done nothing but make sure her kind would succeed in the future where she had failed them in the past. They couldn't go back to the way they were. They were better than that. Which was why they were tested to begin with. Mother Goddess knew her children better than anyone. It was up to them to prove their worth. Or learn from their mistakes yet again.

But it was Diev's words that seeped into her mind and took root on her own secret fears. Kalama saw red after hearing Diev's accusations. In the few seconds that passed after him speaking, in her mind, she had already murdered the vulpiian standing before her in a million different ways. All gruesome and grisly, which shocked her to her core. She prided herself on being mostly nonviolent, but there was something about the Nightsongs' that brought out her most basic and primal nature, and she didn't like it at all.

Gathering all of her strength, she used it to speak what's been on heart for the longest time. "Let's get one thing straight, Nightsong. I failed because we failed together as a species. I was only a representative of who we were and was found unworthy. This is our chance now to redeem ourselves. Myself and others have taught the younger vulpiians over the years to be better than what we were. The Champion School gave them a chance. I have faith even when you and others don't."

"Hmph," he said in defiance.

"Don't you stand there and think you would have done better, because I can guarantee that you would have failed too. Your daughter, Liekki, has her flaws, but she was the smartest one in her class and the smartest one in the class before and after her. She is more than capable than any champion you would offer up instead. If we, as vulpiians, have a chance to pass, it's because of her and I'd be drakgo'd if I let her fail as her mentor."

Diev was seething, but she didn't care. She got the words off of her chest. Surprised that she took up for the wayward vixen, but everything she had spoken about Liekki was the truth. And she was determined to find her before her father found her. From the look in his eyes, he was determined to send her soul to Dhasas and didn't care about anything she had just said.

"It appears that we are unable to come to a mutual understanding. I'm sorry to hear that, *Elder* Brightsun," he said with as much fake sincerity as the smile he wore on his face. "I have other meetings, so I must leave *this* place. I am sure we will meet again soon."

With quick speed, Diev spun away from her. His cloak snapped behind him and he stormed out of the room. Kalama watched him and once he was gone, she let out a long breath. There was something wrong with Vulpo, yes, she knew, but there was something seriously wrong with Diev Nightsong. Perhaps her daughter was right.

"What is really going on with Clan Night?" she whispered to herself.

Chapter 15

Liekki and Efrim stayed in Aster a little longer than they wanted. After Xyrin transported them to Amiho's tavern, the skies quickly darkened, and a storm blew in soon after they went inside. It stuck around longer than they expected. The grey clouds brought with it an unusual chill, thick rolling mists, and a torrent of rain that wouldn't let up. Many patrons of the tavern kept saying it was unnatural, and Liekki did nothing but agree. They haven't had thunderstorms in a long while in Vulpo, then suddenly they did. In a land where creatures had dominion over the elements of nature, and they were saying it was unnatural, Liekki knew something was wrong and out of balance. By the end of the week, she was ready to leave. Extremely tired of the fickle weather.

Staying in Dryemia longer than they hoped didn't make Efrim's mood any better, either. Words had come along from Queen Cirrha by the swift currents of the wind. Due to the unfortunate weather, Liekki and her guard had permission to stay in her lands, but only as long as they kept to Aster. If the bad weather wasn't gone by the week's end, they still needed to leave and Xyrin would escort them out.

During the days and some nights when the rain would ease up, she would go out and visit the harbour city. It was nothing like Vulpo. From the buildings, the roads, and the open market shops. Everything was above ground or in the trees and its canopies. Nothing was underground like the vulpiians preferred to have, and it only made her wonder even more about the city they were to go to visit. Ravenfalls was known as a mecca of technomancy and a giant melting pot of different species. One could find anything or anyone they desired in a place that.

In her room, finally alone, Liekki ambled towards the window. The sun was slowly setting, painting what she could see of the sky, a watercolor of fiery reds and oranges. Cool, soothing blues and purples. The rain had slowed down to a near stop, and she knew it meant they could leave. The water elementals had managed to control the overflowing river allowing the ferry to resume its services. She was ready to leave. Liekki knew if they stayed too long in one place, her father's uncanny ability to find those and things that were hidden would find its way to where they were.

"Xyrin is waiting downstairs," Efrim said as he came inside of the room they shared. He closed the door behind him. "He'll ride the ferry with us to cross the river over to Elyium."

"We have a noble escort." Liekki slightly turned to catch the gaze of her guard. He seemed more relaxed than he had over the last few days. "They really want us gone, don't they?"

Efrim chuckled. "The Queen's orders. She wants to make sure we leave her lands."

"I thought we were doing well and being on our best behavior."

"We are, but there's so much going on here in Dryemia. Our presence here alone is causing a problem, according to Xyrin."

"But I've seen other vulpii here. I mean, Amiho has her very own tavern and inn. It's apparent she's well loved around here. She's a gracious host." Liekki said, trying to prove a point but knowing her reasonings were failing. Her guard agreed, but it didn't help the point she was trying to make.

"There are whispers. The spirits talk to those who listen. The Dryem are more in tune with nature than the vulpii are. We used to be in tune, but somewhere along the line, we are slowly losing that connection. When they tell you they hear the words of our spirits. They really do." Efrim moved closer to her and placed a hand on her shoulder. "I'm ready to move on. Ravenfalls is a wonder. Others won't look at you twice. We stick out like a sore thumb here. Even when you have a glamour on, they still stare at you too hard. Aren't you tired of that?"

Liekki knew he was right. She just hated to admit it to him. "Fine. I'll pack my things."

"Good. I'll be downstairs with Xyrin. Oh, and don't worry about paying for the gates. Xyrin is taking care of the trip."

She gave a nod, but said nothing else. Efrim had quickly picked up the small leather pack she didn't realize he carried with him and left her alone again. The music from below had drifted upwards and was cutoff soon as the door closed. Even with the unnatural rain, Amiho's tavern was a popular spot amongst the locals, merchants, and traders. Even the Whispers, what the Dryem called their storytellers of their histories, came by nightly and wove their tales of old and new. Captivating anyone who would stay and listen.

Liekki hastily gathered the few possessions she had. She checked the secret pocket inside her bag and made sure the remaining gemstones she had were still there. Along with the few silons she had to use once they reached Ravenfalls. Not taking too long, she quickly closed her bag and swung it over her shoulders. With one last look of her room, she left it and headed downstairs where it was loud and her guard and the Queen's soulbind waited.

The lively beats, kept in tune by the drummers' hands and the haunting vocals of the singers, had the crowd in a mesmerizing grip. She would have been lost by the melodic words of the Dryem's native tongue if it wasn't for Efrim waving her down when he saw her reach the bottom of the stairs. Xyrin stood next to him watching the entertainers, but his gaze met hers soon as her feet touched the floor. He was oddly aware of her and in tune with their surroundings.

"Hey, Kha Swiftfoot," Amiho's voice caught Liekki's attention. She turned around to see the Tavern's owner make her way towards her. She wore a traditional Vulpiian dress, in all black. Her eyes were lined with kohl. "I'm glad I could catch you before you left."

"Is there something wrong?" Liekki asked, concern etched in her voice.

"No, just wanted to give a few words to you before you left."

Liekki looked towards her waiting party, then back to Amiho. "Alright."

"Don't look so worried. It's not bad."

Liekki let out a breath. "Good, because I can't take any more crap from this place."

The tavern's owner laughed. "Dryemia is an interesting place. Be careful of these lands and those that dwell in it. In fact, be careful whereever you go." Amiho lowered her voice even lower, then spoke in the tongue of Clan Night. "The Dryems only care about their own interests and don't care who it harms to get what they want in the end. So be wary. Especially of the royal type. Take care of yourself and may Aku watch over you during your tests. There are those out there that wants to see you succeed. No matter what the others of our clan believe. I may not be home in Vulpo, but I know what goes on. Then there's Shoam. He always keeps me updated with the things that go on back home."

"I am deeply thankful for all that you have done. If I make it out of this, I'll return to see you." She didn't want to ask how Amiho knew she was the one chosen for the trials, but if she was friends with Shoam, the assassin back home, then of course she knew.

"I would like that." Amiho embraced Liekki in a hug, then disappeared into the crowd.

Liekki didn't know how to feel about being embraced by others. She never really was a touchy feely fox, and it was weird for her. She wasn't sure if she was okay with it. Like most everything else, she locked it up inside to think about later. Finding Efrim and Xyrin again, she sprinted towards them, making her way through the thick crowd of towering Dryems. They were a unique looking group. Some were thin and had elvish features with pointed ears. Others had features that resembled the plants and groves they lived around and in. Vines intertwined with their hair. Bright eyes and bark in the shape of horns on their chins or foreheads. Some even had plant like spores on their faces and arms. It was strangely beautiful to her.

"What took you soo long?" Efrim asked with a smirk on his face. They both knew she didn't take long after he left. She gave him a look, and he actually laughed, which took her by surprise.

"You're in a good mood," she said. "What's going on with you? You seem different somehow."

"Nothing is different, Kha Swiftfoot. I'm just glad we're leaving." Efrim had sounded almost relieved. It would be the first time this week he actually sounded somewhat happy or back to his normal self and Liekki was glad for it.

Xyrin turned around as if on cue. The stoic look he had, Liekki began to understand it wasn't him not liking her, it was just his resting *fatu* face. He really wasn't as bad as she had originally thought he was. When they first met, she secretly realized that Xyrin was hurt because Efrim hadn't kept in contact over the years, but then he showed up in Dryemia out of nowhere.

It was unexpected, and his emotions bubbled up to the surface fairly quickly. They were once close as brothers, but not anymore. Which made her wonder even more about the elusive guard of hers. Who was he... really? Where did he really come from? All questions that would need to be answered, eventually.

"Are you ready, Kha?" Xyrin asked her, using the prefix the Vulpiians preferred to use for their titles.

She looked around once more before answering him. "Yes, I'm ready. If we linger any longer, I'm afraid we'll have unwanted visitors."

"Hmph. We already do. It's why you must leave now," he said, lowering his voice, ushering them out of the door. "The Queen sends her regards and wishes you well during your tests."

When Xyrin announced the news of unwanted visitors, Efrim and Liekki exchanged glances before they trailed Xyrin out of the tavern.

"We keep watch at the edges of our forests. We have seen some of your kind creeping along near our outer borders. A small unit, nothing too large. My Queen is curious, so she allowed them entry to our lands and our scout patrols promptly picked them up. This was how we discovered they were searching for a fugitive. Lucky for you that you wear an almost perfect glamour. But since Cirrha saw your true face, she recognized who they wanted immediately and sent me here." Xyrin stepped closer to Efrim and Liekki and swept them up into his arms. "Hold tight."

She was getting used to the sensation of flying on the currents, but Liekki could say it wasn't her favorite thing to do. When they touched down on firm ground again, she almost bent over and kissed it.

Liekki looked around where they stood and realized they weren't in Aster any longer. The small harbor city seemed to be about the same size as Aster, but that's where the differences ended. The citizens of the city were a blend of Dryem and other creatures Liekki had never seen before. Still, there was no explanation on why Xyrin brought them to Elyium himself. Tired of waiting for an answer, she looked at the Dryem and asked him. "I thought we were taking the ferry?"

"The less who knows about your whereabouts, the better. We have an invested interest in you passing your trials. It fixes your problems there in Vulpo and alleviates some problems we have in my lands," Xyrin said. "So I brought you to Elyium myself."

"Thank you," Efrim said. "We appreciate it."

Xyrin grunted, then spoke in his native tongue. Efrim replied, leaving Liekki uncertain about what the two were discussing.

"The gates you're looking for are down this road, past those fruit pie carts. Take a left and continue down the street. You'll pass by a few taverns and a small park to your right. Near the end of that road is a dead end. You'll see an almost hidden door. It'll reveal itself to you as you get near it. Knock three times and tell them you're looking for Niro by way of Xyrin. They'll let you in. Niro is vulpii like you. You'll see that he has red hair and red ears. Like the clan your glamour says you're part of, so he'll be partial to your cause." Xyrin tilted his head to the side as if he was listening to the soft breeze that danced around them. From everything she noticed of the Dryem so far, Liekki wouldn't be surprised if he was listening to it. After a moment had passed, he straightened back up. "I must go. My soulbind calls out to me. Good luck on your journey."

Xyrin gave them both a quick head nod, then called the wind to himself and took off.

Liekki rubbed a hand down her face. She knew the signs. Red hair. Red ears. Niro was Clan Terra. Those were the trademarks markings of those born of them. She wondered what house he belonged to or if he was a commoner that was now part of the assassin's guild. She just hoped that Niro wasn't a flayer and that he didn't recognize her. Or was familiar with any of the Swiftfoots that she was claiming to be part of.

"Ease your mind. We will be fine," Efrim said, as if he read her mind. "Let's go before it becomes too late. I would really like to make it to Ravenfalls today."

"You and me both," Liekki said. "I want to see what the fuss is all about. Figure out what makes that place so great."

Efrim took the lead and followed the directions that Xyrin gave them. The scent of sweet dishes and savory meats from the street carts had Liekki's mouth watering. Her stomach grumbled in protest as they walked by each one without stopping.

"I could really use some food that is not just plants, vegetables and bread," she said, hoping her guard would catch the hint.

"Soon enough, Kha." Efrim looked around before they turned the corner. He whispered so only Liekki could hear. "Elyium may not be on the Dryem's land, but it is their territory, and the air listens to everything that is said. We'll rest and find food in Ravenfalls. Let's hurry and get out of here instead."

The duo continued down the road, eventually passing the park where it was filled with younglings playing. Curious about their greenish and brown skin with tiny tusks protruding from their lips. "What are they?"

"They're young orcs. The proper word for them is orclings. The orcs do a lot of trading here. They are not fond of tech-nomancy or tech period. Stuck in their ways, they prefer their hidden communities spread all throughout Eldritch. You may come across more in Ravenfalls, but I doubt it. You'll find them in the rural areas and hidden in the hills or deep in the flatlands."

"Oh," was all Liekki could say. She was curious about the new creatures and was even more curious about what other species she would find in the much larger city.

Liekki and Efrim traveled the block fast and finally ended up where Xyrin said they would end up. The dead end came upon them quick. On the brick wall before her, Liekki saw faint lines in the shape of an arc that glowed a strange blueish color before fading away.

"We're here," she whispered, looking around making sure no one was close enough to hear her.

Efrim knocked three times on the door just as he was told to do. He took a step back and waited. And waited some more.

Just as he was about to step up to the door again and knock, it cracked open. Liekki saw the red hair and yellow eyes before the male poked his head out of the door. He frowned when he saw them.

"We're looking for Niro by way of Xyrin," Efrim said in his gruff voice.

The male gave a curt nod, opened the door wide, and ushered them inside. He looked both ways outside of the door before closing it. Inside, he bolted it down. "This way," he said. Nothing more.

Liekki and Efrim followed him down the narrow hall they had entered in a single file line. The walls were void of any paintings or anything to indicate where they were. It was reminiscent of a long tunnel that kept going and going. Eventually, they reached another door and their guide opened it, pointing his chin at the opening. A blast of cold air hit Liekki in the face. Efrim glanced at her and she knew to go in after him.

It wasn't another tunnel, Liekki noticed. It was more of a stairwell that spiraled downwards. Stone steps carved from the natural rock that surrounded them. The further they went down, the cooler the temperature became. She didn't think the stairs would ever end and was thankful when they reached the bottom. Soon as the quiet guide met them at the bottom, the room lit up all around them.

"This way," their guide said once more, before leading them further into the darkness that faded away with each step as they got closer to their destination. The small group reached a tiny room, Liekki had thought until the lumo lights flared to life. There, standing by itself, surrounded by nothing but stone, was another vulpiic gate. Turned off and unused for a long time if the cobwebs had anything to say about it. The vulpiic gate looked like an ancient relic from another time.

"You sure this thing will work?" Liekki asked, her gaze roaming over the ancient artifact from another time.

Niro shrugged. He pulled a gemstone out of his pocket and took it to the console and inserted it. "It should."

Liekki watched as the gate flared to life and was always amazed at the magic at work.

"Where are you headed?" Niro asked, as he messed with the controls.

"Ravenfalls," Efrim replied.

Niro nodded. "I assume you know how this work? You know how to go through the gates?"

"Yes," Liekki said, then took a step closer to her guard. "We know how it works."

"Excellent." Niro pulled a lever down that was attached to the side of the console. A humming sound emitted from the gates while it shimmered in the void space. What looked like rushing water came down in a torrent. "This will take you to an area hidden behind the falls. The attendant will show you the way out."

"Do we owe you anything?" Efrim asked, mirroring what Liekki was silently thinking.

"No," Niro said. "Xyrin and Queen Cirrha have already taken care of the fee. Safe journey to you two."

He was a vulpiian of few words and Liekki was glad he didn't delve more into who she was.

Efrim exhaled a breath, then told Liekki he will go first like last time and for her to go through right after. She stood there and waited as her guard left her alone with the one called Niro. From the corner of her eyes, she took in the red-headed vulpiian. He didn't look at her or say anything else to her. After Efrim made it through safely, Liekki took a step closer to the gate before Niro said anything.

"I'm not sure who you are or who you are running from, but you must be someone important. To have the Queen and her soulbind at your side is both a good thing and a treacherous thing. Be careful of them. Careful of the Dryem period. They're not what you think they are. Whatever they do is for their own good. Their own purpose and devices. No matter how nice they seem."

Liekki wasn't surprised to hear the same again. First it was Amiho, and now it was Niro. "They're no worse than our own kind. I know how to be careful."

"Aye, you're right. Our kind have a reputation all around Eldritch. Especially in Ravenfalls. Watch your back. The city is the playground of Mezal Irontail. I am sure you know who he is. Well, he has eyes and ears everywhere. Just a little heads up for you if you don't want to be on his radar."

Liekki wasn't surprised, but she was thankful for the subtle warning and told him so. The vulpiian smiled, which didn't quite reach his ears. She pushed everything to the back of her mind and moved forward to the gates, and hoped her time in Ravenfalls was uneventful.

CHAPTER 16

The thundering sound of the cascading water was so loud that it was deafening to Liekki's ears. After she trudged through the unpleasantness of traveling through the vulpiic gate and its magical viscous fluid, she was relieved to be clear of it. A rush of excitement tingled throughout her body as she looked to her left at the falls. It surprised Liekki the spray of water didn't fill the chamber. Yet she could sense a vague hint of magic was keeping the water from entering and keeping everyone dry. A weak beam of sunlight broke through the falling water, illuminating the cave chamber she was in. Liekki couldn't believe she was finally far away from Vulpo. The furthest she had ever been. Away from her family and the others who wanted nothing to do with her. *Or to murder her.* For a first time in her life, she felt a semblance of freedom. She didn't know how long it would last, but she was determined to make the most of it while she could.

"Are you alright?" Efrim's voice came from her right, distracting her from her thoughts. A worried expression was etched on his face. "It should have been easier this go around. Each time you travel through a gate, your body becomes more acclimated to it, even though it's dangerous to us every single time."

Liekki didn't realize it at first, but he was right. She didn't feel as sick as she did the first time she went through it. Her stomach barely roiled around, but the wave of nausea wasn't there. Her hands shot up and touched her ears, then she brought them in front of her and checked her fingers. Everything was there. Liekki let out an inaudible sigh of relief. She knew the dangers of traveling through the ancient relics, but it was a necessary evil she had to endure. "Yes, I'm fine."

"Perfect," her guard said, then turned his attention to the vulpiian who was standing at his side. With a pointed stare, Liekki observed the one who watched her and Efrim. The gate attendant was a slender vixen who wore a black leather tunic with matching trousers that was a contrast against her smooth skin. Expensive looking daggers hung low at her waist. Her snow white hair was naturally wavy and fell down her back in rivulets with highlights of a few black and blue braids that had trinkets wrapped around them. Her eyes were a pale cornflower blue that twinkled with amusement. She was beautiful. The vixen wore a wide grin on her face, yet Liekki knew not to mistake the friendly smile for anything more than what it was. The gate guard was very alert, and Liekki knew by the deadly stance she was in that the guard was a weapon all by herself.

"Welcome to Ravenfalls. I'm glad you made it through just fine. I've seen some weird things when a traveler is ejected from those gates. You both came through whole, which doesn't happen very often. Be grateful you still have all of your limbs attached." Her stance eased a little, yet she was still alert. Staring at Liekki, she canted her head to the side, as if she was trying to get a more accurate feeling for her. "I'm Amiko. You've been here before?"

"No," Liekki answered quickly. It wasn't a lie. If she didn't have to go into details about why she was there, then she wouldn't give unnecessary information. "First time."

Amiko was quiet, as if she was trying to figure out what they were about, before she pointed a thumb in Efrim's direction. "I know it's not his first time. It's been a long time since the Wanderer has been around here."

"Wanderer?" Liekki asked, confused. Her gaze silently questioned her guard. Back in Dryemia, she discovered he used to wander the lands before he came to Vulpo, but she never knew that was the name they actually had called him.

"It's nothing," Efrim said, as he tried to steer the conversation away. His stance was rigid and not as lax as usual. No one had to tell Liekki he was uncomfortable. It was there for everyone to see.

"It's not nothing, Wanderer," Amiko said, with a slight hurtful edge to her words. Efrim winced but tried not to let it show it bothered him. Amiko reached out and intimately touched Efrim's arm. "It's been what... almost one hundred years or more. I last saw you right before you disappeared. A shame too. You should have kept in contact. I missed you. We had so much fun before you fell off the face of the land. You better find me before you leave this time. We have unfinished business. You know where I'll be. The same place as always."

Efrim cleared his throat. "We'll catch up soon enough, Amiko. My charge and I... we must go for now."

Liekki observed her guard as he tried to avoid making eye contact with her, which made her more intrigued. Was the vixen a former lover of Efrim? Amiko didn't seem to be too surprised to see him. She even touched his arm with such a gentle familiarity and couldn't keep her eyes off him. Liekki didn't know what to think about it. An unsettled feeling found a home in the pit of her stomach. She didn't like the vixen that was the product of Clan Sky touching him that way. It made her feel something weird inside, and Liekki didn't know how to deal with the emotions it caused. Was he not loyal to Clan Night? Why would he like her, a snow fox?

"Come on," Efrim commanded from where he stood. He didn't look back at Amiko or Liekki, instead, he headed towards the stone and wood steps that led upwards. He moved quickly and with purpose. Not wanting to be left behind, she said goodbye to the gate watcher and followed her guard up the stairs.

The higher they went up, the louder the sounds of the city became. When they reached the top of the stairwell, Efrim pushed against the latched roof. It didn't budge. He grunted, then searched around the tiny door and recognized what he did wrong. He unlatched the deadbolt, then pushed at it again with his shoulders. This time the door opened with a hollow thunk. Dirt and dust rained down on Liekki's face. She wiped it off but felt better with the blast of fresh air whisking over her face. Bright sunlight poured into the darkened space, blinding Liekki for a few moments before her vision went back to normal and she could see much more clearly.

Efrim climbed out of the space they were in first, before he reached back down and pulled her out. Liekki dusted herself off and suddenly wished for a hot spring bath. She searched the area and noticed they were in some alley, surrounded by extremely tall buildings. The alley was empty except for the two and, for some odd reason, she was glad for it.

"Where are we?" she asked.

"The guild district. You won't find much traffic around these parts. At least not during the day."

"Oh," was all Liekki said. Efrim closed the door to the way they had come from. She watched it disappear as the magic took over and it melded to look like the ground they stood on. "Is all of Ravenfalls like this?"

A soft laughter came from her guard. He was smiling, and that was a first for him in a long time. "Wait and see."

He led them out of the alley and into the streets. Liekki's mouth dropped wide open. "Wow!"

"It still looks the same," Efrim said, as he guided them further into the city. "Yet, I can see the differences. The growth."

Liekki didn't know where her guard was taking her, but the city was nothing like she had imagined. She thought it would be similar to the valley back home, but no. It was nothing like it at all. All around her were so many creatures from all around Eldritch. There were griffins strutting about. The elusive elves were dotted throughout the crowd. Tall and lithe, they moved about as if everyone around was beneath them. Above them, birds of all kinds flew around in the sky, and the Aeroways, which looked like tube shaped clouds, gave the sky a modernized look. Opposite of the skies in Vulpo. She could've taken the aeroways to get to the city, but she didn't want her father finding her that way. One of these days, she vowed that she would test it out as she wandered the rest of the world. But first, she had to pass the trials.

She attempted to take in all the various sounds and smells that pervaded her as they moved through the multitude of eumens, both citizens and visitors. The mingling scents of savory foods and spices from the food carts and stands they passed by to wherever they were going had her stomach growling and her mouth watering. Reminding her she hadn't eaten anything yet. As they continued their stroll through Ravenfalls, the sweet smelling floral aromas of the flowers from the city gardens and the pastries from the bakeries and pastry shop had her thinking about the perfumed air from the Silk Petal district from her hometown.

Liekki was in sensory overload.

The multihued cobblestone streets were a marker of the district of the city one was in, according to Efrim, as he occasionally pointed them out. Liekki looked down and loved the cerulean sea blue they currently traveled on. It reminded her of the Capseson Ocean that was on the other side of her mountains. The streets were filled with various sized carriages as they pulled their wares or passengers to their next destination. As she took it all in, she couldn't stop the grin that widened on her face.

"How could you ever leave such a place?" Liekki asked, as she hastened to his side to avoid being knocked over by a group of younglings running the streets.

She could only imagine her crew's faces if they were there with her to see the city. Icelia would keep cool, but she knew better about the others. Especially Jinx and Stormi's face. Not Hot Paw. She hadn't forgotten his betrayal. It was still fresh in her mind.

"This place is amazing," Liekki said.

"It only gets better," Efrim said, in a much better mood than he had been in recently.

He pointed out different points of the city while he gave her a guided history lesson to Ravenfalls. She didn't know where they were headed, but she really didn't care. She enjoyed the time, not worrying about the trials or her family. Even more so, Liekki wasn't worried about her cruel father. The fox who doggedly hunted her down so he could sacrifice her to the dark ones.

Trying her best to not think about it, Liekki focused her attention on the buzzing city around her. They leisurely walked, as she took everything in like a brand new kit when they're born into the world. Liekki felt so free and she loved every bit of her newfound freedom until the air took a drastic change around her. The once clean air had suddenly become oppressive and suffocating. Her lungs constricted as she gasped for the precious air, stopping her dead in her tracks.

"Efrim," she struggled to call out. Her voice was ragged and hoarse. She didn't know what was wrong. "E-Efrim. Help."

He didn't realize she had stopped and turned to find her struggling. Her guard was light on his feet and swiftly raced back to her, wearing a frown. Efrim's sharp eyes darted all around them, searching for the flayer they both knew was nearby. Their magic had a distinct feel to it. Liekki also knew the hidden flayer was a powerful magic user, too.

"Your glamour is gone," he said loud enough so only she could hear him.

"I figured as much," Liekki replied, before grimacing with pain. "Wherever that flayer is, it's not too far. Their magic is warring with mine. "

"Shezia!" Efrim grabbed her arm and pulled her along as they sped through the crowd. Weaving in and out of massive throngs of eumens as he took Liekki deeper into the city. "I should have been able to feel them, at least. How did they even know we were here already?"

"I don't know," Liekki huffed between painful breaths. A stabbing pain shot through Liekki's chest. "Efrim, they're still nearby."

"I know. Hold on. We're almost to where we're going. We need to lose them, and the only place I can think to do that is there."

Liekki looked up in time to see Efrim pointing at an out of commission airship. It was painted black, with a colorful multitude of flying beasts painted on its exterior. It was permanently docked and had a roped off area with a long line of well-dressed patrons waiting to go inside. "What is that place?"

"The Winking Raven. It's a place that's crowded day and night. Easy for us to become someone else and get lost."

"Are you sure?" Liekki said before her vision went blurry. She reached up grabbed the sides of her head with both hands. A quiet moan escaped her. Sharp, piercing pain filled her head. "I don't think I can make it, Efrim. I need to sit down."

Efrim spun towards her and placed a hand over her chest and the other on the side of her temple. Heat flowed from his hands, warming up the longer they stayed on her. Everywhere his magic touched, the darkness faded away, and she became more like herself.

"Thank you," Liekki said, sighing with relief. "I was only seconds away from passing out."

"Not on my watch. Come on."

The guard grabbed her wrists and led her to The Winking Raven. Instead of waiting in line, he cut through the waiting patrons, much to the disregard of those waiting. A trail of curses and angry threats followed them, but Efrim didn't care. Liekki was worried at first, but then she remembered how he put down

Kalama Brightsun with barely a touch and she was an old nine tail. Glancing over her shoulders, looking at the scowls of others, she was sure he could do the same there.

The two quickly reached the front of the line. At the front entrance, a male vulpiian with black hair and odd green eyes with gold flecks stood there letting others in. He was dressed in black leather pants and a fancy royal blue tunic. He looked up and was about to yell at Liekki and Efrim before he stopped mid-sentence.

"Nooo," he said with a look of surprise on his face. He smirked. "Look at what Duara dragged in. Is this a dream?"

"It'll be one of Duara's worse nightmares if you don't let us in, Rion." Efrim pulled Liekki closer to him. "We're in a jam and need to catch our breaths. If you know what I mean."

Rion looked at Efrim, then at Liekki. His eyes narrowed, and Liekki didn't understand why until she realized her glamour was gone

Liekki panicked. She didn't have the energy to do any magic after that last assault.

"Are my eyes deceiving me?" Rion leaned in so only they could hear. "The one and only Blaze is here. You know there's a hefty reward for your capture. Your father really wants you back, you know. He has the assassin's guild searching for you."

Liekki's worried gaze met Efrim's, but her guard was the epitome of calm and collected.

"I will owe you big if you let us in, Rion," Efrim said, trying his best to bribe the door guard. "Even throw on extra for forgetting you ever saw us."

A moment passed between the foxes. Liekki's skin crawled. She rubbed them, trying to ease the sensation and not scratch. All it told her was that the flayer was close by enough for their magic to affect her the way it was. Shifting on her feet, she leaned in so both Rion and Efrim could both hear her. "Can you two hurry this negotiation up? I don't have much time."

Efrim glanced at Liekki's hands as she feverishly rubbed her arms.

"Now or never, Rion," Efrim said to the door attendant. "Our time is about to be up and this lovely establishment is going to be a war zone in a few moments if you don't let us in now."

Rion muttered a vulpiian curse under his breath. "You owe me big, Wanderer. I'll come collecting soon enough."

"You know how to find me." Efrim's words were solemn and Liekki wondered what the payment or favor was that was being discussed. The look on his face had her keeping her lips closed.

Rion stepped aside and let them in. Liekki had never been more relieved than she was at that moment. They rushed inside and she didn't have time to look at everything because he pulled her to a dark corner beyond the dancing floor.

The inside of the dance hall was crowded and loud. She had never heard of or seen a place like it before. Any other time, if she was feeling any better, she would have ditched her guard and went exploring.

"Sit down here," Efrim commanded in a voice that told her not to argue with him, as they reached an empty table. "You want something to drink?"

"Not yet. I want to stop feeling like the cruds."

"I understand and plan on helping with that," he said as he directed her to sit on a soft chair. A Dryem with soft green eyes and brightly colored leaf like hair came up to them. Efrim turned to her and held up two fingers. "Two dwarven whiskeys."

The Dryem smiled, acknowledged his order, then walked off towards the bar on the other side of the dance hall.

"How long will we stay here?" Liekki was curious. She didn't want to leave so soon after they just gotten there. The airship was massive and had so many levels for her to investigate. "Maybe after I catch my breath, I can go explore this place."

Efrim chuckled. "I'm not surprised. This place is probably creating a sensory overflow for you."

"It is..."

"Are your paws itching to go scrounging these well-to-do patrons..." He looked at her with a raised brow. His expression was serious, but his eyes glistened with mirth.

Liekki crossed her arms over her chest. She didn't want to admit the truth, but he was right. It had been a long time since she had the itch to pickpocket, and being around all the wealthy citizens of Ravenfalls triggered the once banked longing. It would be so easy to take a trinket from one, maybe two, patrons, she thought. Instead, she lied to her guard. "It's not like that."

This time Efrim let out a deep laugh, but the music drowned it out. "If you say so, Kha Swiftfoot. I know you're probably in pain still, but I can't give you poppyweed to ease it. You're going to have to deal with it. For now, I want you to conserve your energy. I am going to use my magic and place the glamour back over you. A flayer will have the hardest time trying to dispel it since it's my magic."

Liekki wanted to keep her Swiftfoot persona. She was growing accustomed to it, but then she really thought about what he said about his magic and him replacing her illusion. "Wait... you remember what I looked like?"

Efrim stared at her. Liekki couldn't make heads or tails of the emotion that passed through his eyes. He cleared his throat. "I'll never forget what you look like, Blaze. No matter what form or illusion you have covered over you. I will always know who you are."

Liekki was unsure of how to interpret his words. She took them and locked them in the small mental room she labeled for him. Her guard was a fluctuating storm of things, and she didn't know which one she was getting at any moment.

"O-okay." It was the only word she was able to get out. He chuckled as he placed a hand over her chest again.

"Don't move. Let me help you the best way I can."

And he did. Amazed. The transference of magical healing energy had her feeling better than ever. After the top off, she felt like she could run for miles and not be winded. "Whoa," she said. "That's some powerful mojo you got going there."

"It's not that powerful," Efrim insisted.

"Do you feel like this constantly? How did you do that? I never knew healing magic could feel like that. What did you do to me?"

The barrage of questions rapidly being fired out of Liekki's mouth was uncharacteristically her, but she couldn't help it. She had to know. If she ever needed healing back home in Vulpo, she didn't feel the way she felt right then.

"You ask so many questions, Swiftfoot." He chuckled and turned to the Dryem server, who took their drink order earlier. She had returned silently to their table. He grabbed the two tumblers of whiskey and gave her a golden silon.

"Thanks," she said before wandering off.

"Take a drink. You need it," Efrim said.

"What about you?"

Her guard picked up his cup and downed half of it. "I'm already on it."

Liekki picked up her cup and took a drink. The liquid felt like fire going down her throat. She coughed as the alcohol burned through her chest. "Holy Mother Goddess and God of Fires. That shezia burns."

"Language, Kha Swiftfoot."

"Really?" She rolled her eyes and took another drink. This time, her mouth and throat were numb to the whiskey. "After everything we have gone through, you're getting onto me about language? I'm not a kit, Efrim."

"I'm well aware of this, Kha Swiftfoot." He glanced away from her and scanned the room. "I need to go take care of something. Let's get this glamour replaced."

Efrim downed the rest of his drink and moved closer to Liekki. "This won't hurt at all."

Liekki laughed. "It better not hurt."

She sat there as he made quick work of the illusion, replacing it so no one could be the wiser about her true identity.

"There we go. Much better. You look like a proper Swiftfoot now."

"Thank you."

"No need. You can stay here or wander around, but don't go too far. I'll try not to be gone too long." Efrim took two steps, then stopped and looked back over his shoulders. His long black hair framing his face, giving him a mysterious aura about him. "Oh, and... don't get caught."

Liekki smirked. "I have no idea what you're talking about."

"Sure you don't," Efrim said with a grin before he walked off.

Liekki waited for a few moments, then tapped into the mentality she used as Blaze. Feeling much better, she finished her drink and set the cup on the table. She meandered through the crowd and found her way to the dance floor. The strange music was loud. No one paid any attention to the red-headed vulpiian as she danced her way across the floor, occasionally swiping a few things from their pockets. When she reached the other side, she headed straight to the bar, securing her newfound goods and trinkets into the bag she was carrying.

She would assess what she collected later, but for now, she would celebrate by ordering another drink. Liekki found an empty space at the end of the bar and waited patiently. Eumen watching was becoming her new favorite pastime. There were so many creatures, she didn't know what to think. What fascinated Liekki the most was the dragons in their two-legged partial forms. They weren't quite full dragon, but not quite fully other, but unique all the same.

The same dragon she was staring at just moments ago came over and took her drink order. Liekki kept it simple and ordered another dwarven whiskey. At first, she didn't like the taste, but it grew on her after a few sips. She liked the burn of it against her tongue and throat. She sat there and drank her drink and continued her eumen watching while the music continued to blast.

Twenty minutes must have passed and still no sign of her guard. Efrim was still gone and taking care of the business that he kept to himself. Nursing on her drink still, the empty seat next to Liekki was suddenly filled. A young looking female fairy came and sat down beside her. Liekki knew of the fae from the Aolani Kingdom, thanks to the gossip courtesy of her sister, Senia, who always spilled about the world to their siblings. She was a living, breathing gossip paper all by herself. Senia lived for the news of the nobility around the world. And the Fae beside her looked very familiar.

The fae kept staring at her without trying to hide it. Liekki recognized the curiosity twinkling in the newcomer's eyes, but she still didn't like the way it made her feel. To Liekki, the fae's staring felt intrusive and rude. What if she was able to see past Efrim's glamour? Could that be why she was staring? Shifting in her seat, Liekki took a deep drink from her cup, emptying it, hoping her neighbor would ignore her, but it didn't stop.

Tired of being gawked at, Liekki looked back up from her drink and snidely asked the fae, "Want my autograph or something? You keep staring."

Startled, the fae quickly turned her head and looked away. "I-I'm sorry."

Liekki smirked at how easily the fae was apologetic. She seemed too bright eyed to be a regular in Ravenfalls. She wondered if she looked the same when she was staring at others, too. "Hey, it's okay."

"I'm new to town," the Fae said. "Where I'm from, it's just a bunch of Fae folk. Even with so many eumens around, I feel as if I could disappear. I like it."

Liekki canted her head to the side. Curious about the fae beside her now. "You want to disappear?"

The fae heavily sighed. "Sometimes. Doesn't everyone?"

Thinking about the question, Liekki used to want to escape. Wasn't that the reason she ran away? The reason she ended up in Ravenfalls. But now, she wasn't so certain. Liekki shrugged. "I'm not sure. It's a complicated idea. I like being forgotten about, but being found or seen is appealing. Maybe, there's something I need to find."

Liekki took a drink from the second glass beside her. A bright green thing that the bartender surprised her with. From the corner of her eyes, she watched the Fae again and suddenly knew why she seemed familiar looking. She turned to her. "Hey, don't I know you?"

"No," the Fae lied.

Liekki chuckled. "Yeah, I do. I've heard about you. Even seen your face before. Aren't you the Fae princess?"

The fae fidgeted in her spot before speaking. "Unfortunately, you're correct."

"Nothing to be unfortunate about. You are *Princess* Kaia, after all. A true royal. Aren't you about to marry the Elven Prince?" Liekki remembered the entire story from Senia not even a month ago at the dinner table. Apparently the news was all the rave, and she remembered not caring one bit.

The Fae stirred her drink. "That is what the rumor mills are saying, I suppose."

"What brings you to a city like Ravenfalls?"

"My... significant other is from here?" Princess Kaia said with a little hesitation. Liekki noticed and was even more intrigued.

"Prince Cyrus?"

Kaia bit her lip, then grumbled. "It's a long story. I just wanted to get away for a while."

"I understand. I come from a family that's part of the Vulpii nobility. Things tend to get messy around my home."

Kaia nodded, but her eyes drifted away and lit up. Liekki followed them to find a handsome male come walking their way. "Messy indeed," Kaia had finally replied.

The princess introduced the male as Tayo, her handsome vampire significant other. Liekki kept her amused thoughts to herself. He was definitely not Prince Cyrus. They chatted a bit. Liekki made sure she kept her answers vague. She couldn't give too much away unless her father's eyes and ears found out. They could be anyone or anywhere. Especially in a place like Ravenfalls.

Soon enough, the odd group wanted to dance and Liekki turned down the invitation when it was offered. She was glad for the company and the opportunity to actually feel normal. Not being judged by her clan and others thinking she was cursed. All she really wanted was her moment of solitude. When they asked if she was alone, she lied, not wanting anyone to know that Efrim was there with her.

"Are you ready to leave this place?"

Liekki spun around on the chair was sitting in. Efrim stood there, hands at his side, but there was a nervous energy about him. There was something wrong, and she didn't know what.

"Not really?" she said.

He frowned. "I'm sorry Kha Swiftfoot, but we don't have much time. I've secured us a place to stay while here. Let's go before your father's and Mezal's people find us. I've spotted them both inside of this place."

"Well, that's all you had to say. I can always come back and visit this place later."

Efrim smiled. "That you can."

"I'm also not trying to get caught by my father's people." Liekki hopped off the chair and followed her guard out of the Winking Raven. She saw what he meant as they neared the entrance. She could spot the roughnecks her father called his associates a mile away. They rushed out of the mega tavern and kept to the shadows. Slipping away into the crowd.

CHAPTER 17

Liekki pushed the few stray strands of her hair out of her face. She stood near the falls on the edge of the cliff as the water thundered down into the ocean far below. The sun was setting and painted the sky in oranges and reds, softly lighting the land beneath in a warm glow. A gentle breeze blew across the way and brought with it the fresh scent of the salted air of the Caspeson ocean. It was their last day in Ravenfalls and Liekki had enjoyed herself entirely too much. She was fortunate to take it all in and experience everything there was to offer.

Exploring the food markets was one of her favorite things to do. She sampled new foods from all the different cultures she had become familiar with during her stay. In one of the many parks around Ravenfalls, Liekki was able to shift into her true four legged form and played with a few young vulpiian kits she saw. The things she had the opportunity to do were fun for her and was a much needed respite, considering everything she had been going through. Surprisingly, Efrim was the perfect city guide, and there was no way she could thank him enough.

"Where to now?" Liekki asked.

The time had gone by in the blink of an eye, and Liekki had nearly forgotten about the trials. Instead, her mind was seared with the memory of her father's rage and the clans uniting as they marched through the valley. Their voices raised and hands clutching blazing torches. That was the one thing she didn't think she could ever forget. That they were hunting her. Although there were a few times that she and Efrim had come extremely close to being found out and caught by bounty hunters. Luckily for them, Efrim's magic held up. The glamour did its job, and sure enough, it kept her hidden. The ickiness and wrongness she would feel whenever a flayer was nearby, she didn't feel anymore.

The screeching of the white feathered and yellow beaked sea birds pierced the silence. Liekki peered over her shoulder to see if Efrim heard her. All she saw was his profile. His inky black wind swept hair fell down to his shoulders. Efrim's gaze was pinned forward and his expression was lost, deep in contemplation.

"Is everything okay?" she asked. He had been unusually quiet, and she didn't know why. Which was odd for him.

He looked at her and rubbed a hand over his chin. "Everything is fine."

"Are you sure?"

"Very." He cleared his throat. "We should consider departing this place. Aren't you due to report to Elderton soon?"

He made an excellent point and was very right. She had to find her way to Elderton even if she didn't want to do it. Ever since she left home, the days passed by in a blur. Now the fun was ending, and the craziness was about to begin. Was she ready? She wouldn't know until she stepped foot into Elderton. "Yes. Have about three days left," she said solemnly.

His eyebrows shot up in surprise. "Three?"

Laughing nervously, Liekki then gave a shrug. "Just about. I'd rather not wait until the last minute to arrive. I want to show up early so I can investigate the area and figure out what I must do."

"Didn't Brightsun tell you?"

Liekki gestured with her hand, shaking it with indifference while making a face to match. "She did. Somewhat. Not much."

"Typical of the elder. I never understood why they couldn't just be more forthcoming. We all have an investment in you surviving and passing the trials." He ran his fingers through his hair. "I'm sure you'll figure it out. You're a smart fox."

Her guard went unusually quiet again. Liekki didn't know what it was, but something was weighing heavily on Efrim's mind. "I can tell when something is wrong, Efrim, and you're not acting yourself. What is going on? Can you at least give me that?"

"Blaze," he said, exasperated. Rarely did he use that particular name, and with that tone, it alone made her ears perk up. He continued, "We really should get back to the inn and gather our things."

Liekki refused to move and shook her head from side to side. Needing to know what was wrong, she stormed closer to him.

Standing directly in front of the solemn guard, she poked him in the chest with two fingers. "No, you're not getting off that easy. Now what in Drekra's horrible hellscape is going on?"

Efrim frowned at her for speaking the dark spirit's name. His voice lowered an octave. "I've told you about that."

"Yeah, yeah, I know. Sorry."

He let out a heavy breath. "If you must know, I saw Mezal Irontail late last night and earlier today. There was no doubt he recognized who I was. If anyone can pierce through my magic, it's him. He doesn't have to touch you to find out who you are."

"But.." Liekki started, remembering how he discovered who she was, but was interrupted by the guard.

"I'm not finished. The way he dispelled your glamour was a painful and cruel way. He did that on purpose to teach you a lesson. He's not to be trifled with. So, I suggest we leave sooner rather than later."

It was like a ball of ice was sitting in the pit of Liekki's stomach. She didn't like Mezal, not one bit. There was something about the prince of the Irontails that rubbed her the wrong way. Ultimately, she knew she was at fault for breaking into his home, but Efrim was right about how he did her. She still remembered how much it hurt when he ripped through her magic and battered at her mind, trying to break into her thoughts. The fox was a menace, and no one seemed to care. They were too worried about her thieving when there were worse vulpiians roaming the land. More sinister things taking root in the dark alleys of Vulpo's streets. In the private quarters of the vulpiians homes.

"Point made. Let's head back." She didn't want Efrim to know how much his words unnerved her. Honestly, everything about Mezal Irontail unnerved her. She wished she could use her magic that was battle tested and ready instead of doing minor glamours and hearth tricks. "Hey, when we get back to the inn, remind me to ask you something."

"What do you want?" he asked. Efrim looked at her, his eyes seeing and knowing all. He was too intelligent to not know there was something she wanted. It was like he knew her too well. Possibly better than herself, and that was another subject she wasn't ready to discuss yet.

Putting on a brave face despite her worries, she tried to pretend she was alright. "Aku's tits... how did you know I wanted something?"

His brows rose, but the smirk on his face broke the tension that hung between them. "Aku's tits? That's a new one I don't think I've heard before."

"Stick around and you'll learn all the new expressions I come up with." She smiled and was glad when he smiled back. Things were starting to feel normal again. "Hey, everything is going to be okay. Let's not worry about Mezal. We'll go back to the inn, grab our things, then do whatever we need to do to get out of here. Preferably unseen and unharmed. If Mezal is here, I already know my father has something to do with it."

"Alright. Then you can tell me what you wanted once we're back at the inn. For now, let's keep our wits about us."

The two retraced their steps and left the calming atmosphere of the waterfalls. Keeping close to her guard, after making sure her glamour was still intact, they caught a carriage to ride back to the northern part of the city. Although she wanted to travel back by walking the streets, her guard had other things to say about it. He had made very valid points, but she still grumbled and fussed about it. When they reached a newly emptied carriage, Liekki gave in and hopped inside right after her guard.

Everything was going well on their way back until they neared the northern part of the city. The roads were congested and filled with the shouting citizens and visitors. From inside of the coach, she could hear the screams and yells. The acrid stench of burning fire reached her nose, causing it to twitch before she sneezed. She rapped her knuckles against the side of the carriage, hoping the driver heard it amongst the brewing chaos.

"Hey, stop, will you!" She shouted loud enough for the driver to hear her. The carriage came to a slow crawl, then an eventual stop. She quickly shot up and opened the door to peek outside to see what was happening. She cursed under her breath. "Hey Efrim, I really think you should take a look at this. We're not going any further in this ride of ours. At least, not this way."

He surged from where he sat and reached her side in no time. She moved aside just enough in order for him to view out the door. "This isn't good," he murmured.

Liekki sucked in a breath and couldn't keep the sarcasm out of her voice. "No, you don't think?"

"You need to stay inside the carriage," their driver warned them. "The crowd is getting wild."

"What's going on?" she asked, glancing up at the one driving their carriage.

The driver, who looked like a low born elf, didn't bite his tongue. "Those damn vulpiians are causing a ruckus in the northern locality where all the lodging and taverns are located. It started about two hours ago. It looks like it has gotten worse."

Liekki tilted her head slightly to the side. "What do you mean, '*those damn vulpiians*'?"

The driver had the nerve to look sheepish when his eyes focused on his passengers. First, he found her ears, then the mark on her forehead. And finally, his gaze landed on her eyes. The driver's eyes widened into an almost comical proportion.

"My apologies..." his voice trailed off, but Liekki could tell he really didn't mean it.

"Kha Swiftfoot." Liekki put authority and anger behind her words. Even a little magic to add to the heat of her words.

"My apologies Kha Swiftfoot."

"Much better," she said, before looking around as more and more people were starting to crowd around in the road. "Can you get us any closer? Even if you have to find an alternate route. I'll pay you handsomely."

"I don't know..." he said slowly. "I can try, but it gets worse the further in we go."

"What was the catalyst for this?" Efrim chimed in. "I smell burning smoke."

"One of the inns went up in flames. The innkeeper had words with a patron. That particular patron's anger got the best of him and he set the place on fire without a second thought."

"Didn't the peacekeepers arrest him?" Efrim asked.

The driver scoffed. "Even I know better to mess with an Irontail. He walked out of there like his tails doesn't stink. Nothing will happen to him. Nothing ever does to those uppity vulpiians."

Her widened gaze met her guard's anger filled ones. He looked at their driver. "Which inn went down in flames?"

"The Lyon's Crown Inn and Tavern," the driver said, ignoring the looks he was getting from both Liekki and Efrim.

Liekki's gaze slid towards Efrim while their driver continued to give his opinion about Vulpiians were a bane to everyone's existence. He really didn't pay attention to who got inside of his carriage and that would eventually land him in a bunch of hot water if he wasn't careful. She knew her guard was getting angrier, and when Efrim's lips thinned into a firm line, she knew he was near the edge of exploding. She had to do something. The Lyon's Crown was the inn next to theirs. Was it coincidence that Mezal was in an establishment next to theirs? It couldn't be a coincidence at all. There were too many lodgings located in the city for him to end up in the one beside theirs. She didn't like that new development at all.

She looked at the driver. Liekki had enough of his unwanted opinions and harsh words. "You know, you keep saying '*those vulpiians*' like it's a bad thing and you have two in your carriage." Liekki's voice turned bitter. "I'm starting to wonder if you have a bias against those of vulpiian origin. You wouldn't disrespect your passengers like that, would you? I surely hope not, because although you are an elf, you are still lowborn and I am not a lowborn Vulpii. My power will outrank yours any day for getting on my bad side.

The driver cleared his throat and quickly changed the subject. "I think I know a way. Return inside and I'll take you there."

"That's more like it," Liekki said with a wide grin. The driver quickly sat back down in his seat and grabbed the reins to the carriage.

Efrim yanked Liekki back inside the coach just as it jerked and moved again. She fell into her seat and laughed. He scowled at her. "You didn't have to do that."

"I know. Don't care," she said. "He deserved it. I'm tired of everyone looking down on us because of our heritage and origins. The elves are no better than the Vulpii and the eumens of Eldritch will need to learn that one of these days. Mother Goddess doesn't have favorites. If she did, then the trials wouldn't have begun. We all would have been created and evolved equally."

"You really don't care, do you?" The guard whispered under his breath. "You really can't see, can you? It's more than us being looked down on or not. I had hoped you would have come to your senses by now. Sometimes you're good, but then, we have moments like these."

"I don't know how many times I've told you, Efrim. I don't care much about anything lately." She turned away from him, no longer wanting to talk, and instead she looked out of the window as the city passed them by in a blur. Twilight was quickly turning into night. The driver took them down a less crowded road, but the closer they got to reaching their destination, the worse the situation had gotten.

"You may not care, but there's an entire skulk of foxes that are depending on you. I really hope you get your sheiza together, Swiftfoot."

His words stung. She was sure that was the effect he wanted, but she wouldn't let him know that. The entirety of Vulpo was depending on her. Even if the majority of them wanted her dead.

The carriage came to a jerking stop. The silence was thick between the two and was disturbed by the door opening. Fading sunlight and encroaching darkness filled the inside of their car. Their driver stood to the side with a frantic look on his face. "I can't go any further," he said in a rush. "You have to get out of here. You're only a couple of streets away from your destination. It's an easy walk."

The muted sounds of chaos reached their ears, but it was not like it was moments before when they were going in the main direction. Liekki knew there was something else going on, and she didn't like the fluttering in her stomach. Something was off. It was almost like a warning. "Why can't you get us closer?"

"There is a checkpoint. The peacekeepers are checking the carriages. I don't know who or what they are searching for, but I can't let them do that. They can't check mine. I must go now before they setup these checkpoints all over the city. Hurry, please." He stepped to the side while constantly searching all around them. More than once did he look back over his shoulders towards where the peacekeepers were located, checking the other coaches.

"Alright," she said and hurried out of the coach. Liekki had just pulled out enough coins to pay their driver when he hopped back onto his perch. He grabbed the silons and shoved them into his pockets.

"Have a good evening." The driver waved and then took off in the opposite direction, the carriage tilting on its side as it hit the nearest corner from going too fast.

"Why do elves have to be so weird? He was definitely hiding something."

"Wait until you actually meet a dragon. They're worse. They're always hiding their hoard," Efrim told her. He glanced around the area where they stood. There was a growing crowd, but nothing like the other side. "Let's stick to the crowds and slip through the checkpoint to get to the inn. There's a back way to get inside. We can slip in that way and grab our things. If I didn't know any better, this smells like a trap."

"I was already thinking this was a setup."

He pulled Liekki towards them and held her hands to make it look like they were just another couple needing to get through.

Liekki didn't want to think about the fluttering feeling when he held her hand. It was Efrim. Her guard. Nothing more.

The two noticed a family of fae who were making their way beyond the checkpoint and slipped in with them. Efrim asked the father a question and while they moved through the line. The peacekeepers didn't notice a pair of vulpiians who looked odd walking along with the family of fae. Once they were in a safe enough distance, Efrim and Liekki thanked the family and wished them well.

The sky had darkened even more and the first moon was slowly rising. The unsettling feeling that Liekki was becoming used to had only gotten worse. When they reached the road where the inn they were staying was located, she stopped in her tracks, causing Efrim to jerk back towards her.

The sky and everything around them were filled with black smoke. The bright angry colors of orange and blue consumed the inn that was on fire.

"How come they haven't stopped the fire yet?" Liekki asked. "I know in a city like this they should have some water elementals or water magic users around here."

"I don't know," her guard responded, then he inspected the blaze. "That's not normal fire. Look closer."

Liekki stared harder and realized he was right. It wasn't a normal fire and whispered what she knew it to be. "That's fox fire..."

"Knowing Mezal, he more than likely did a spell that would keep the fire roaring until he says otherwise. This is madness. A natural fire would've consumed all the surrounding buildings by now, but this fire only consumes that building. Even if they had a powerful water magic user or an extremely strong fire user to quell that disaster, it wouldn't work. Be on the lookout. If you notice anything unusual or if you notice any vulpiians, don't give them cause to look your way. Keep your head down until we get inside."

"Alright," she said. Efrim took the lead, and she followed close on his heels as they moved towards the side of the building. It was chaos out in the streets. There was fighting and shouting. Peacekeepers doing their best to keep the citizens calm. It was perfect for them to sneak in and sneak out.

They reached the side of the inn and went inside the entrance designated for the workers. It was an empty hall, void of the staff, just as she expected it would be. Maneuvering threw items on the wood floor that were left behind in a hurry. She did her best not to step on anything valuable. Everyone was outside watching the disaster roaring next door or blaming each other for the commotion..

The servants' stairs were empty too, and they rushed up them to the third floor where their room was located. Efrim looked out into the hall first to make sure they were in the clear. When he gave the okay, they darted down the darkened hall to the very end and quickly entered their shared room.

Soon as she went inside, something told her to duck. She tugged at Efrim's tunic from behind and yanked him to the floor. A loud twang echoed in the darkness, followed by a double thunk. A whoosh of air occupied the space they had just vacated. Her eyes adjusted to the darkness, and she looked up to find two daggers lodged in the door where her head would have been.

She cursed under her breath. Efrim pulled her into his arms and rolled them out of the way when a large meaty pair of legs and big hairy feet came crashing down, causing the floor to shake.

"All ye doing is making it harder for yerselves. Come out while you can. I promise it'll be quick and painless," the gruff voice said with a chuckle from up above them.

The arms around Liekki loosened and gently and placed her behind the one they belonged to. She could see well in the darkness, but it didn't look like their attacker could. Efrim placed a finger over his lips, making sure she didn't say a word. He pointed to the other side of the room where their leather bags were stored, then back at her. She knew what he was telling her. He pointed to himself and then back up at the invader. Liekki took a better look at the intruder. He almost looked like an orc, but he wasn't as tall. He talked like one of the highland dwarves. Then it dawned on her. He was a hybrid.

What on the Mother Goddess's green land did the hybrid's parents think would happen if they hooked up and did the mattress tango and spat out a pup, she thought with a frown.

Efrim held up three fingers, and she knew the countdown was on. They had to fight their way out, after all. A shezia eating grin spread across her face and when Efrim pulled down the third finger, it was on. He sprung up, taking the hybrid by surprise. While they were occupied, she hopped off the floor and darted to where their things where and quickly grabbed everything and shoved it inside of their bags.

The hybrid was bulky. He had that size as a plus for him against Efrim, but her guard was a well-oiled machine. He was lithe and deadly as he moved fluidly, going through his forms, taking the hybrid down. The Dworc, because she didn't know what else to call the assassin, grunted and cried out as his weapons fell to the floor. He didn't even know what hit him. She almost felt bad for the thing, but thought about the reason he was there, hiding in the dark in their room. The echoes of the cracking sound of multiple bones breaking from where she stood had her glad it wasn't her. She winced in solidarity because it sounded painful. The dworc cried out in a high-pitched voice she never expected from someone of the male species. Yet, she was impressed at the skill and the quickness it took Efrim to do what he just did without breaking a sweat.

The dworc groaned where he lay while Efrim stood over him. "You br-br-broke my bones," the dworc stuttered.

"Who sent you?" Efrim demanded with a deadly calm she had never seen before. The dworc mumbled and curled into a fetal position. Efrim kicked him in the chest. Blood spat out of the dworc's mouth. "If I have to ask again, you are not going to like what I do."

"Okay, okay. Wanderer, I'll tell you."

Efrim froze. "How do you know that name?"

The dworc laughed. "I know a lot of tings. Yer not the only one who knows tings, Wanderer."

"Then I suggest you tell me who sent you or I'll send you to whatever forsaken god you orcs worship."

The dworc growled in warning. "I'm not an orc."

"You're no highlander either. Your tongue says you're a highlander, but they hate orcs just as much as orcs hate the highland dwarven clans. To both of them, you're an abomination. You were probably kept hidden away from both of them because they would have killed you while you suckled from your mother's teats." Efrim knelt down with his knee on the dworc's chest. He brandished a dagger from his waist and held it against the dworc's throat, slightly piercing it. A thin sliver of blood oozed out. "Now, tell me what I asked or I'll remove your head from your body."

The dworc's eyes widened. A wracking cough rattled from his chest. "It was another of your kind. A red-headed one. With multiple tails. He dressed in fine clothes. Black slithered in his yellow eyes. It wasn't normal. His smile was cruel, and darkness filled his heart. He wasn't a good fox."

"Did he give his name?"

The dworc shook his head. "No. I asked, and he said I didn't need it, then he handed me a pouch full of coins."

"Are you going to meet him again?"

"Aye, to let him know the job was done. Then he will pay me the balance."

Efrim's solemn gaze met Liekki's when he looked up at her. It felt like ice filled her veins. The dworc couldn't go back to Mezal. There was no other who fitted the description he gave. They had to get out of there before more of Irontail's lackeys came looking for them. No one had to tell her it would be better if there were no witnesses to seeing them. She knew what had to be done and gave the silent approval of what her guard asked without words.

He looked down at the dworc. "What is your name?"

"I'm called Lum'do." He coughed again.

"Well, Lum'do. Let me invite you in on a little secret of mine. I know the healing arts and there is no help for you. Blood is slowly filling your lungs, and there is internal bleeding in the rest of your body. When I hit you in the legs and chest, I did so to incapacitate you. The symptoms are unpleasant. What you will experience is a slow and painful death. It will get harder to breathe. Even if you didn't have broken bones, you wouldn't be able to move. It could take hours before what I did, take you and you succumb to the deep sleep. But I can make it easier for you. Allow me to finish this and send you on your way. May you come back in a better situation. I know life must have been hard being of two, yet you're only one, and not loved by either. Orcs and dwarves are not known to be pleasant by the rest of us. I'm sorry, but you got a double crap hand."

The dworc stared at Efrim for a long time before coughing again. More blood bubbled at the corners of his lips. Liekki could see the sad resignation in his face. There in his eyes there was even a little bit of fear. "Aye. Yer aren't wrong. You promise it'll be quick and painless?"

"I promise. I'll make it painless for you."

"Alright then." Lum'do nodded and then tilted his head back as much as he could, exposing his neck to the guard.

Efrim heavily sighed. "May our Mother Goddess take you in her embrace, Lum'do."

A single tear slid down Lum'do's face. Liekki watched as Efrim slid the dagger across the dworc's neck in one quick slice. Lum'do lifeless eyes stared at nothing. Efrim reached up and closed them. He wiped his blade on the dworc's tunic, stood, then looked at her. His face was void of any emotion. "Let's get out of here."

Chapter 18

Death was one of those things that many of the races in Eldritch never thought about until it was their time. For the long-lived races, it shouldn't happen for hundred's if not thousand of years. That included the highland dwarves and the orcs. Lum'do didn't have a chance once he took the job from Mezal. He forfeited that right to a long life when he took the bag of silons he wouldn't be able to spend.

Seeing someone die had Liekki in her emotions. Had her in her feels. It was a first and there was always a first time for everything. All the time she and her crew went out on jobs in the dead of night to steal what didn't belong to them, she never once thought about being caught or murdered. The things she went out and did, it was like a dangerous game of chances to her. To her crew. This was a way for her to stick it to her father. Her siblings, especially Senia, the darling of the Nightsong brood. A way to stick it to the entire Vulpiian society.

"Don't feel sad for Lum'do. He chose his path. May he choose better in the next life," Efrim told her as they went back from the way they had come.

"But..." Liekki started. "It's not fair... almost."

"That is the way of life and the way of death. An unfair, vicious cycle. For some of us, it's a long continuing, never-ending revolution, but those that choose the path of chaos... well, they endure many of those periods. Lum'do was born into a chaotic cycle. He had no other choice but to live it and die by it." He stopped. His ears twitched around. "We have company. Probably those who were part of Lum'do's unit searching for him. Keep quiet. They're not coming through these stairs. We will be safe as long as they don't hear us."

Liekki flattened herself against the wall and slowed her breath, trying her best to be as invisible as possible. There could be no excuses. It seemed like forever, but only moments had passed by. The sound of two male voices, one low and rough, while the other was raspy, as if he hadn't spoken in a long while, reached their ears. They were arguing with each other over if their companion could get the job done. Raspy voice didn't believe Lum'do had what it took, the other had a little more faith. Liekki agreed with Raspy. Lum'do had no chance against them. She glanced at Efrim and realized the truth. Lum'do had no chance against her guard.

Once the voices faded away, Liekki and Efrim crept out of the stairwell and down the narrow hall until they reached outside. The first moon of Eldritch had fully risen, and the night had turned considerably cooler than it was when they went inside. The fire next door was still blazing out of control, but the heat from it didn't help the chill. There was an unusual fog that covered the ground. No one had to tell her it wasn't normal. When she pointed it out to Efrim, he agreed.

He signaled for her to keep quiet and led her around the side of the inn where it was void of anyone, as they kept to the dark shadows. Liekki didn't know where they were headed, but she also knew now wasn't the time to question their new direction. She just wanted to get out of the city perfectly healthy and preferably with all of her limbs attached to their proper places. She had grown quite connected to them.

"There is someone out there," Efrim whispered.

Liekki looked all around but didn't see anyone. "Where?"

"Use your senses. Close off the outside world and touch your magic. Widen your reach and search for what is attempting to stay concealed from us."

She did as he told her and cleared her mind. Liekki reached down and touched the tip of her magic and spread her awareness by pushing it outwards from her. She could feel Efrim and see his warm colors that hovered on the close edge of black. But it was the other that she felt that unnerved her so much more.

Continuing to move slowly, Efrim and Liekki used the building as their guide to lead them to the street. When they reached the end, he looked back at her. "Do you feel them? *See* them?"

She did. They lingered to her right. A dark and violent color of black and gray filled her mind, and the other was muted.

Almost neutral. There were two waiting for them. "I can sense them."

"Good. One of them is Irontail."

"Let me guess. The dark colored one."

"Exactly." Efrim looked in the direction where the two vulpians hid. "This won't be easy. They can see us. We both know they're going to come out fighting. You need to be ready. Think of this as a preparation for the difficulties you will face during the tests. Survival. Fighting for your life."

Her face contorted into a frown. "I don't want to think about the trials, Efrim."

"You better. You only have three days left. Two and a half now. Once inside, no one can help you but you. Learn to use your talents now."

Liekki didn't want him to know she could reach out to Kalama if she needed her mentor's help. That was limited, too. She would practically be on her own. She glanced towards the area where the two hidden silhouettes waited. Something in her wanted to say it surprised her to know that Mezal was there, but it would have been a lie. A wave of revulsion and anger instead filled her heart and mind. All she wanted to do was incite a lot of violence towards the dogfox who was hunting her at the behest of her father. There was no doubt Diev Nightsong was the reason Irontail was there.

Out of the shadows stepped the thing that frightened her the most lately. He was illuminated by the silvery moonlight and she could have sworn his eyes had glowed a red before returning to their normal coloring. The brilliant moon cast half of Mezal Irontail's face in harsh relief. If he wasn't so cruel, she would say the dogfox was beautiful. She could see why her sister chose him. Two dark spirits made perfect for each other.

Too bad he was of Terra.

Mezal's grin was full of malice. His eyes had gone dark red with black swirls in them where the whites should have been.

"That is not natural," she said under her breath and shook her head. "Nope, not natural at all."

"Where are you going, clever little thief? Don't leave so soon. We've only just gotten here. Let's play catch up."

At Irontail's side, his fingers were twisting and moving in odd, jerky motions. She could feel the air changing. Charging with his magic.

"Run!" Efrim shouted, not bothering to be discreet about it.

No one had to tell her twice. Liekki took off in the same direction as Efrim. She ran hard into the night. Her feet led her far away from the two Terrans that were hunting her. She and Efrim darted into the crowds, pushing and shoving so many out of their way so they could put as much distance between them and Mezal. They didn't care if they looked crazy running like they were being chased down. When she looked over her shoulder behind her, Mezal's hybrid, Pako was hot on their tails. Those that were still lingering seemed just as confused and lost to what was going on around them. She recognized the signs of an illusion and the eumens were lost in one. Except for the few peacekeeper patrols out on the streets. They were coherent enough to shout a warning, but she and her guard ignored them.

"I told you we only want to talk, clever thief!" Mezal shouted.

"I won't look back. I won't look back," Liekki chanted under her breath. She made the mistake and turned around. A flying ball of inky black came hurdling her way. She quickly sidestepped to her right to avoid it. The peacekeeper who was in front of her didn't have the luxury of dodging it in time, and the inky, swirling blob smacked him in the face. A loud scream erupted from his mouth as smoke rose from his body. The inky orb that Mezal threw was eating the peacekeeper alive. He had no chance of surviving. It smelled so bad to Liekki. The stench of burning and melting flesh was enough to make her gag.

"Running like a coward to fight another day is not a bad thing," she kept whispering to herself, hoping the words actually got stuck in her mind. Convincing herself was the hardest, because what she wanted to do was turn around and fight back. Even in her right mind she knew fighting Mezal and even fighting Pako in the state of mind she was in was a death sentence.

Another inky orb came whizzing by her head, barely missing, but hitting another peacekeeper. Liekki kept running and not realizing her guard had stopped in front of her. She ran right into his back, sending them both flying towards the ground. They landed hard. The ground scraping her leg. She could feel the blood oozing down the side of her knee. There was a throbbing ache in her arm. Liekki had a strong feeling she probably hurt her shoulder on the way down to the ground.

"This is for the birds," she said under her breath. "Why do we have to run from them?"

Efrim groaned as he shoved Liekki off him, sat up, and pointed. "Because of that."

Liekki looked up just in time as both Pako and Mezal were about to be on them. The dark rage that filled Mezal's face was that of absolute horror. She froze in her spot. No words could come out as she sat on the ground with her mouth gaping wide open. She couldn't believe that nothing came to mind for her to do anything. This wasn't like her and she didn't like that she froze up the way she did. It almost felt cowardly to her.

Arms encircled around her waist and warm breath by her face. She slightly moved to see who it was, but honestly, she recognized who it was the moment she got a whiff of him. Efrim always smelled like home to her in some odd way.

"Perhaps another time, Mezal. We have prior engagements to attend and can no longer play with you today!" Efrim then whispered in Liekki's ear. "You may want to close your eyes..."

Before she could even answer, everything around them spun. The angry shouts coming from Mezal were extremely loud, but then faded into a buzzing sound. Almost like the sound of a thousand bees in Liekki's ears. An invisible force seemed to draw the air away from them. Their movements were so fast she had to do her best to keep her stomach from revolting and throwing up everything that was in it.

Landing in a dark room with a loud thump, Liekki rolled over with Efrim wrapped around her before coming to a complete stop. She winced in pain as she removed herself from his tight embrace.

"What in the world was that?" she said with too much calm that bordered perilously close to hysterical. Her head was still spinning as she adjusted to being still again. "What just happened?"

"That was me saving our plu's," Efrim answered. He let out a heavy sigh, then stood up. "Come on. Let's get out of this place before Irontail and his lackeys find us here."

"But how?"

"You always ask a lot of questions Blaze," Efrim grumbled before realizing which name he used, then mumbled something she didn't understand. "Let us get out of here and I'll tell you. Once we get you safe. That's my main priority."

"Where exactly is here?" Liekki looked around, but all she noticed was they were in a room. Small and closet sized. It smelled of dust, mold, and something else she couldn't quite figure out. The door being closed wasn't helping it air out the pungent smell.

"The gates. Our time in Ravenfalls has finally come to an end. We need to get out of here. Now!" He reached out a hand to her. She stared at it for a beat, suddenly hesitant, but she pushed back whatever those feelings were, then took it.

"This doesn't look like the gates," she said, grunting as she rose off the ground. Wiping her hands on her pants, Liekki watched him open the door, curious about what was behind it. It didn't take long to discover what it was. The brightness from the vulpiic gates filled the once darkened space. "Ooh. Nevermind."

He chuckled before leaving the room first. She didn't mind small spaces, but she didn't prefer them. Not wanting to be left alone, she hurried after him, leaving the claustrophobic room. The gate attendant from their first time they had entered Ravenfalls was standing there with a too wide grin on her face.

"Wanderer, I was getting worried about you. Especially since you didn't come down the normal way most travelers through these gates do."

"You know how it is, Amiko. Sometimes the unconventional method works best for me."

"So you have always said. Luckily for you, the gate is already fired up."

"Thank you for this. For everything."

Amiko looked him over and smiled once more. "It was nothing. You know, anything for you." She walked over to the gate's controls. "We outcasts gotta stick together. Now, where are we headed today?"

"Far away from here. Make sure the signature is gone by the time Mezal and his hybrid show up. We can't be followed. We have got to get Swiftfoot as close to the west as we can."

Amiko looked at Liekki after she emerged from the closet room. One brow rose as if questioning what her guard said. "Come now, Wanderer. Is that what we are doing right now? You know I know that your charge is not a Swiftfoot. Why else would you be traveling west? Or better yet, why else would you be running from an Irontail? Those two houses are allies. He wouldn't dare harm one of theirs."

"You were always too smart for your own good," Efrim said with a smirk. "I don't want you taking the heat for us. That's why we are not confirming anything with you. All we need for you to do is get us somewhere safe that isn't in Dryemia."

Amiko's laughed filled the chamber even with the noise of the waterfall. "Still on Xyrin's and Queen's Cirrha's blacklist?"

"Maybe..." Efrim said, his shoulders shaking from the laugh he was trying to suppress.

The gate made a whirring noise, nothing like before. Liekki edged nearer to it and then halted. "Why is it making that sound? It doesn't sound safe."

"If you haven't noticed yet, the gates aren't safe. I'm honestly surprised you haven't lost a limb yet. Each time you make it through with everything intact, you better thank the Mother Goddess for bringing you through these things whole. The vulpiic gates are ancient and this was why they were shut down by our ancestors. They could never figure out the magic. Figure out how to make it work without someone dying."

Liekki swallowed. She had heard the tales, but she didn't think about how true they were. Too worried about leaving home. Too absorbed in thinking of only herself. She didn't really calculate the dangers she would encounter. Still, she knew it would be nothing compared to the dangerous trials she was about to endure. For her kind, who didn't care one ounce if she lived or died. All they cared about was not being cursed.

Quick and fast, like Kheton's lightning, she had a sudden thought. Liekki turned to the gate attendant. "Hey, Amiko. Have you been to Vulpo recently?"

Amiko stared at her strange then followed up with another question. "Why do you ask?"

"I wanted to know about the atmosphere." Which was true, but she really wanted to know more about what her father was doing. How he factored into all of this.

"Oh," Amiko said before schooling her face to the impassive. She didn't take long to speak what was on her mind. "It's a place where I don't want to be daily. Even worse, now that the clans are fighting with each other. If you're anything other than clan night, you better stay away from the valley or keep to your trees or snowy tundra and mountains. Diev Nightsong is going on a deadly rampage and his followers don't care about anything but what he says. Things there are worse than anything I've ever seen before. Lucky for me, the guild keeps me away more often than not. And I'm glad they're staying out of the game of politics. It's not who we are. If you can, stay far away from there."

Liekki made a scoffing sound. "Don't have to worry about me going back soon. I plan to stay far, far away."

Efrim interrupted the conversation. "We really should be going. Can you get us as close as you can to the shoreline of the Bijou?"

Amiko messed with the controls to the ancient gate. "Not the shoreline, but there's a town not far from the coast. It's between the Lyew lands and beyond the western borders of

Vulpo. There's a gate there if you can believe it. An odd place, but the town has a mix of every creature imaginable there. I must warn you though, the town there, it's a lawless and rough place. I would tell you to seek out my inside contact, but he went silent on the guild weeks ago. More than likely, he's dead or got caught up in the Carnaval du Malheur. They always show up when the world has gone mad. They're on the constant move. Last I've heard is that they've taken up residence right outside of this forgotten town of bandits and thieves. Either way, my contact is no longer around, but if you play nice enough, I'm sure you can find someone to help you. After all, you are the Wanderer."

"I don't know about all of that," Efrim said, yet again down-playing the name that everyone who knew him kept calling him.

"If you say so. But in all honesty. Be careful. The both of you. Things aren't right back home and there is something lurking in the darkness. Getting caught up in it can twist your mind to become what you are not. It's like a sickness that one can't get rid of. Safe travels and good luck out there," Amiko said.

The whirring of the gates stopped, and in the center of its opening appeared a town with stone and wood buildings. Lumo lights were sparse, but it gave off enough light so they could see. A thick fog seemed to cover the ground like a blanket. The ominous feeling Liekki got from just seeing it through the gates had her wanting to hightail it out of there and go in the opposite direction. But from what she could tell, the place wasn't entirely busy. It reminded her of one of those sleepy towns where the residents went to bed early, right after the sun had set. Then again, it was a town for bandits and thieves. More than likely, something was happening inside the buildings. She could see the town being the perfect place for hiding if it wasn't for the warning blaring inside of her head.

Efrim cast a glance in her direction. "One last time through the gates. Are you ready?"

She didn't want to say what she really thought about going through the doorways, but she had no choice. Time was no longer on her side. And that was made even clearer when a loud crashing sound startled the three. Their heads all sharply turned toward the noise. Shouting followed afterwards, and it was at that moment, Liekki realized what was happening with the commotion up the stairs.

"Well, our time is up." Efrim said. "Time to go, Swiftfoot."

"I'll hold them off long enough," Amiko said, working the controls as fast as she could. "Don't worry, they won't know where you're headed. I scrambled the signature to random, but you'll make it to where I send you. It's a little trick I've discovered how to do working these things."

Liekki moved quickly to his side. Rather than letting himself pass through first, Efrim kept her close, and they moved forward through the gates together. Like before, the same sensation of heavy, sticky water suddenly overcame her as it rushed over her. Liekki's stomach did flips and the abrupt wave of nausea rushed up her throat. She could taste it in her mouth and did her best to keep from gagging before pushing it back down. She knew it was gross, but she refused to look weak. Especially in front of the one who was supposed to be protecting her.

A frigid breeze brushed past her, providing some relief from the discomfort that seemed to follow her everywhere she went. The sound of nature, birds calling, and creatures in the woods howling almost had her feeling like she was back home in her beloved mountains. Only thing missing was the sound of the waves far below. The faint scent of salt water reached her nose, but it wasn't prominent like it would have been back in Vulpo.

Liekki looked around. There was something different about the gate they came from. The gate was nestled between two large trees. A dirt path led away from the gates, into the woods, before it led who knew where. She scanned the area, and that was where she spotted the dark lump on the ground. She pointed to where she was staring.

"Over there," she said low enough for Efrim to hear. "What is that?"

"Stay put. I'm going to check it out."

Efrim left her where she stood and went towards the dark lump on the ground. It took him a few steps to get there before he stopped next to it. He looked down, then frowned. Liekki already suspected what it was, but when he twisted around and whispered it was a body, her suspicions were confirmed. Instead of rushing back to her, he called Liekki to his side. She was able to get a better look at the unfortunate soul vacated corpse. This one had reddish brown hair and the markings of a fox from clan terra. Liekki watched as Efrim knelt down and felt the neck of the deceased vulpiian.

"He's still warm to the touch, but there is no life in him. This is a fresh kill." Efrim glanced up and looked all around their surroundings, knowing the killer could still be out there. "We need to leave this place. It's not safe. I think he was the gate attendant. He has on the guild's colors. His killer is probably out here hiding and watching."

"Why doesn't this surprise me? Who in the world knew we were coming to wherever this place is?" Liekki said. Her eyes darted back and forth, searching the trees to see if there was anyone watching. Many times before, she could tell if she was being watched or if someone was near to her. Perfect skills to have when she was on a job with her crew and it never failed her. But now... she was beginning to wonder because everything said they were alone, but her instincts were screaming the opposite.

"I don't know who would know. Whatever this is, I don't like it, Swiftfoot, but there is nothing we can do." He searched further down the path. "Lawless places like these are not to be trusted. Included those who call it home for however long. If we have to find shelter outside, then we will. We aren't going into that town."

"Whatever you say," Liekki said. "I'm following your lead on this one. Thieving I can do. Murder isn't exactly on my list of not so Kha like talents."

Efrim rounded her and looked at her curiously. "Huh, that's a surprise, considering who your father is."

Liekki regarded him oddly. "What is that supposed to mean?"

"Exactly what I said. Now keep quiet and follow me."

Liekki didn't want to let what he said go, but he was right. They had to be silent. She could ask him later. A list was already being compiled. She couldn't stop thinking about what he said about her father. Had he really murdered someone?

They darted with urgency on the desolate path, veering away from the ancient gate that loomed ominously behind them. The moon, veiled by a shroud of menacing clouds, cast an eerie glow, granting them just enough visibility to navigate their path. Yet, even in the dim light, their surroundings exuded a malevolence that clung to their very souls.

The dreaded feeling was so palpable that it settled deep within Liekki's gut. Whatever it was, it refused to relinquish its tight grip. She was never one to be afraid of anything. Whatever danger or trouble they were walking towards was only the tip of the ice usually found high on a mountain. Something was terribly wrong.

Every creak of a branch, every whisper of the wind carried a grim warning. The tiny hairs on the back of her neck and arms rose as the flesh on her arms pebbled. Thinking about everything, Liekki wondered if the very fabric of the world was unraveling. She knew it to be that way back home in Vulpo. What type of place would it be if she passed the trials and came back to a home filled with carnage and bloodshed? Was she a sacrifice for the Vulpii? A sacrifice by her father? There were so many unanswered questions. To her, they were in the midst of a living nightmarescape of Duara's. Life was filled with so many horrors and dangers they were to face, but the true horror was in the unknown that awaited her. The trials were a malefic trap of despair. Who cared if the Mother Goddess was the one who sent her along the Stygian path? She had to make sure that whatever she did was that she came out alive in the end.

CHAPTER 19

T he winding dirt path took them far away from the gate and right to the edge of the dark coastal town. Surprised the town wasn't the thriving and bustling thieves' den than what she expected it to be. No, the lively town in her head was nothing more than a place of emptiness. As Liekki emerged from the depths of the foreboding woods, she realized the lights weren't coming from the town, but from the carnaval. It had taken up residence on the outskirts of town. The small rural coastal town itself had gone completely dark. A sense of unease, perhaps even fear, settled upon her.

Liekki had heard the noise before she saw the dark wonder.

"What is that place?" Curiosity got the best of her as her mind whirled around what she was seeing. She knew it with everything inside of her it was the carnaval the others had mentioned, but she wanted to deny that it was an actual thing. How could something like that exist in Eldritch? *How could many things that are unexplainable exist in their world*? She thought. The two slowed down their pace but continued walking forward.

"The one thing both Queen Cirrha and Xyrin advised us to stay away from," Efrim told Liekki. "That is the Carnaval du Malheur. A product created by followers of Ibris and Duara. An insidious and twisted tribute to the spirit of shadows and spirit of dreams and nightmares."

"Have you ever been?"

Efrim stiffened at her question. Something passed over his face, but she wasn't sure what it was before he finally answered. "No. And pray you never find yourself inside of those tents. The vulpiic gates have nothing on that place."

She and Efrim stopped at the edge of the forest, hidden in the shadows and behind the branches with its larger than normal sapphire colored leaves. It was the perfect cover as they watched from a distance. Crimson, orange, and shades of violet flames flickered within clear lanterns. The laughter of the young ones that drifted to her on the wind sounded eerie and wrong. In a town where thieves and bandits called home, little ones shouldn't have been mixed in with their dangerous activities.

In the short distance, giant sized red and black big top tents were strategically placed in a circle. Iron gates surrounded the entirety of the carnaval. She was curious to know what was underneath those giant tents as they snapped in the wind. Her mind was battling it out because she didn't know why she had the strong desire to visit the carnaval. Everything was saying it would be perfectly fine, but there was that one voice that sounded so familiar that kept telling her no.

The inexorable pull was stronger, faceless shadows whispering in her ears about all the oddities she would find beyond their iron gated walls. How she could discover priceless items that would fetch a fortune for her and her crew down in the burrows back home? Promises of how many silons they could reap for their coin pouches. They would be rich beyond measure. Richer than her father. Her crew would be set for their long lives. Liekki smiled at the thought. Going there would be a good thing. She had time. She didn't need to reach the island for a few more days. The Queen and her soulbind were wrong. Efrim too.

Muted melodies, chords that were discordant and distorted, drifted to her ears. Tempting her. Luring her to come behind the iron gates. Promises of everything she could ever want or dream of were waiting for her. All she had to do was make the first step. One small step to a lifetime of happiness. Liekki nodded, as if she was agreeing to something. She would show them it's not as bad as they claimed.

"Liekki no!" the familiar voice shouted, but her decision was already made. Ignoring everything, it was time she did something she wanted to do and not what others told her to do.

"No... don't!" This time, the voice was feminine, yet it was still familiar, even if they sounded out of breath. Her lips furled into a snarl because this voice was similar to another she didn't like. She just couldn't remember the name of the person. Or why they were there.

Liekki's mind felt like it was being torn in two by another presence, but there was nothing she could do to oust it. Her gut feeling was doing the thing that said something was wrong. But the other part of her mind kept whispering and the words and things they were promising sounded so much better than going to her death in the trials. Blaring alarm bells went off in Liekki's head, but it was as if her body had a mind of its own. The small logical part of her mind kept telling her to wake up, but she knew she wasn't sleeping. It warned her not to move, but she couldn't help it. In a mental battle of wills, she fought hard but was losing. Small beads of sweat rolled down her temples. Liekki really didn't want to take the first step, but her feet moved anyway. Then another step. Before she even realized what was happening, Liekki had moved only feet away from the carnaval's entrance.

Familiar shouts came from behind her and she found a way and forced herself to stop to see who kept calling her name. Liekki contorted her upper body, twisting halfway around, and recognized the unmistakable features of the black-eared Vulpii. Efrim was always by her side. A warm smile graced her face as she reached out a hand to him. In a voice that didn't quite sound like hers, she said to him, "Come on, this place should be fun for a bit."

"I got this," the feminine voice had said, interrupting Liekki.

Liekki's eyes darted toward the annoying noise, and a low growl slipped from her mouth. She had finally recognized who the voice belonged to. "What are you doing here, Brightsun?"

Kalama said nothing but ran faster towards Liekki. As she neared her and wrapped her hands around Liekki's waist, she finally spoke. "I'm here trying to save you."

Liekki couldn't move to protect herself. Her body tried to continue to move forward, but it was a failure. Liekki grunted as Kalama pulled her backwards. They landed in a tangled heap in the dirt far away from the carnaval's entrance. Dark and sinister laughter filled the air as the fog that had taken over Liekki's mind cleared. Able to see clearly, she focused on the vixen who was still holding her.

The wind suddenly surged, swirling fiercely around them. "She will be ours..." this time, the voice became a collective many and melded together, hissing in a spine-chilling crescendo. "She's promised to us. She'll be ours. One way or another," the voices echoed before dissipating and leaving an unsettling presence in the air.

"What in Zera's name-" Liekki glanced around the small clearing they were in before catching Kalama and Efrim staring at each other strangely. Not liking how they obviously knew something, but weren't telling her. Over the secrets, Liekki was determined and tried to shrug her mentor off of her but failed. "How did you find me?"

"Are you clear-headed? Can I let you go and you won't go tromping off towards that place?" Kalama tilted her chin upward, towards the carnaval, ignoring the questions Liekki threw her way.

"I'm fine. No more fog brain." And she was. This was the most clear-headed she felt in a while. Glancing back over her shoulder, she still didn't like how whatever it was that hijacked her mind with the will to do anything tried to make her to go to the carnaval. Queen Cirrha and Xyrin warned her to stay away. Next time, if there ever was one, she promised herself she would listen.

"Excellent," Kalama said, before removing herself from her mentee. "I set up camp not far from here. Closer to the gates."

Efrim clenched his jaws and swallowed. "Was that you watching us in the forest?"

"It was. I was trying my best to become invisible. It was one of those creatures from the carnaval that murdered the gate attendant. It wasn't me. You both know how I feel about the murder of others. Which makes what is happening back home that much worse."

Liekki stood up and brushed the dirt off of herself. "Did you take the gates? How did you get here?"

Kalama pressed her lips together. "Shh... we are not safe here. Come with me. We have things to discuss. All three of us."

Liekki and the others followed the trail back the way they had come from, then veered off the main path to a more narrow, rarely used trail. The call of the Hootz birds was the only sound they could hear besides the occasional crunching of dead leaves and underbrush underneath their feet. Wherever Kalama was leading them, it wasn't far enough from the carnaval du malheur, Liekki thought.

"Right through here," Kalama said while pushing back a smattering of branches, revealing a dark hole. She climbed inside first while Liekki stood there and watched, not too sure about going in. She still didn't trust Kalama all that much, even if she was one of the sacred three. For all she knew, they could be walking into a trap.

"Look harder," Efrim said with a grin. "This area is wrapped in an illusion, although the little hideaway isn't. We'll be safe, Blaze."

"I must be tired or I need to figure out this magic of mine," Liekki mumbled under her breath. Trusting her guard once more, she stepped through the opening. She mumbled once again under her breath, sure as night and day that Efrim heard her. "I thought I was doing fine until I started to hang around you and her."

His low chuckles confirmed he did.

After entering the hideaway, Liekki's eyes widened. Everything shifted, revealing the once dark space for what it was really was. The interior defied the outward appearance from what she saw at first. The inside was much larger than she had initially thought. To her left, resting against the wall, was an unrolled bed pallet. She was sure it belonged to Kalama. Her gaze continued to scan the space and in the center, a small fire pit had crackled to life with the snap of her mentor's fingers. A bluish spark jumped from Kalama's fingertips, causing the fire to roar to life. Suspended over the dancing fire with magic was a black teapot. On Liekki's right were two more bedrolls that were placed against the wall, as if her mentor already expected extra visitors. Overall, the small hideaway was cozier than she had expected and the warmth from the fire was perfect and just what she needed from the growing cold outside.

Liekki hurried around so her guard could come all the way inside and all three settled down next to the fire. The silence was pregnant with an unknown she didn't like. She would rather there would be noise. The crackling of the flames was a good start, but she could also feel the unasked questions from both her mentor and her guard. Liekki's mind was filled with so many questions and so many thoughts. Things she thought she knew were turned and flipped upside down and around. Nothing was as it should have been, and that was what disturbing her the most.

"Tea?" Kalama asked while dropping a few tea leaves into the mugs that were sitting beside her. Both Efrim and Liekki nodded their agreement and watched her while she poured hot water into the mugs. Steam rose from the cups as Kalama handed each one their own.

Liekki held the mug and relished the warmth from its sides. "Thank you," she said.

"You're welcome," Kalama responded before taking a sip from her own cup. "There's nothing special about the tea. It's just something to keep us warm with the weather taking an unusual turn out there."

"Warm is good." Liekki took a sip from her cup and loved how the heated drink went down. The flavorful, spicy scent of the tea indicated it was one of the darker teas she enjoyed drinking when she was home. The kind that would give you a kick when one needed the energy.

"How did you find us?" This time it was Efrim asking the question that plagued his mind and surely Liekki's, too. "We made sure to keep off the grid by using an alias and glamours."

"Hardly did you any good, now did it? In case you have forgotten, Blacktail, I'm more than just being one of the sacred three. I've got a few tricks of my own if I want to know certain things. Things like when an Irontail and a retinue of Nightsong's most trusted leave together through the aeroways. I have eyes and ears all around Vulpo, too." Kalama's unreadable gaze met Liekki's. "Your father and Mezal teaming up were something I wasn't expecting. They really want you dead. I believe there is more to what they're saying. What is it you know?"

"Don't remind me of how much they want me dead. I've been living it the last couple of weeks since I've left home," Liekki told her. Mezal and her father working together was nothing new. Especially since he made it known that he was with her sister, Senia. "Although, I don't get why. The trials would see me dead if I'm not careful. If I fail, I won't have the chance to stay alive like you, Elder. In Clan Night... I am an abomination because of the way I look. My home is a prison. All my father has to do is wait, and he and the rest of my clan will get their wishes. If I fail and come home, I won't see the next morning. Trust me on that. You wanting to know what secrets I might know," Liekki shrugged. "Your guess is as good as mine, Elder."

Kalama took another sip of her drink. "I came to make sure you get to Elderton without hindrance. No matter what I think about you, I want to see you succeed, Liekki. I know firsthand how it feels to fail. You will be tested harder than you have ever been tested before. You will it feel it physically and mentally. The trials aren't easy. It will be no walk in a park."

"That's not giving me much hope, Elder. But I understand where you are coming from."

"Good. Then we have quite a bit of work to do before you leave tomorrow."

"Tomorrow?"

"Yes, tomorrow," Kalama said. A slow grin spread across her face, and her eyes twinkled with mirth. "After what I just saw with that horrible carnaval, I am resolved to make sure that you learn how to protect your mind. You can do the most magnificent glamours and some illusions. But that won't be enough. We need to teach you how to harness your foxfire better. How to control it."

Liekki absentmindedly played with the orange and black beaded bracelet she wore on her wrist. "Good luck. Besides my small illusions, I can barely call foxfire or lightning to me."

"Yet there's so much power in you." Kalama gestured to the bracelet around Liekki's wrist. "I know about that. I know you have three tails, which is unusual for one your age, and I know how your family and clan keep that piece of information hidden from the rest of us."

Liekki's head shot up, alarmed at Kalama's words. "How? Who told you?"

Kalama sighed and set her cup down. She shifted the way she sat on the floor, crossing her legs underneath herself. "Your mother. After you left, Vulpo became extremely bad rather quickly. There is no doubt in my mind that this insurrection has been in the making for a long time now. Your mother sent word for me to meet her in the temple of Duara. Apparently, she wanted to speak with me since I am your mentor for these trials. She told me things about you and your magic. It was why I left to find you. Well, one of the reasons. I didn't want your father finding you before I did. What I found curious while with her is discovering that the mistress of the dreamscape is your mother's matron spirit? Did you know?"

Liekki shook her head, surprised to hear that small tidbit. She never really spoke with her mother for fear of her father doing or saying something to hurt her. Diev Nightsong was a daemon of a fox and didn't care who he hurt. That included his wife and children. Thinking back to their private altars they had in their family's sanctuary, the only ones they were allowed to give prayers to were Aku and the Mother Goddess. Not Duara or any of the others. It would seem her mother was keeping secrets, even from her father. And she knew for a fact her father was keeping secrets. Deadly ones for sure. "I didn't know about that, but then again, there's so much I don't know about my mother."

Efrim looked over his cup at Liekki with an unreadable expression on his face. "We're safe now. What was it you wanted to know or ask back in Ravenfalls?"

Thankful for the sudden change of subject, she remembered what she wanted to ask him before everything went crazy. "I wanted you to teach me a few moves. Your footwork... the way you move when you fight is something I could use. Just some basics. Nothing too fancy, at least not yet. I'm a quick learner and I think it would come in handy for the trials. I don't know, I just have a strange suspicion. Any type of help I can get means it will be better for me there. I'm going in blind and anything is better than my lousy training."

"Of course. We have a day. You can get the gist of things before you leave," Efrim said with a smile. "And when you survive, we'll continue the training."

"I'm also hoping that we can also get some training in," Kalama said right after the guard. "I can work with your magic and the limitations you have. Or," Kalama glanced towards Efrim. "Find someway to undo the magic that was done on that bracelet."

"The bracelet's spelled and can only be removed by it wearing the magic wears out or there's a great need for all her magic to be at hand. There's no way to undo the spell. We will just have to do the best with what she has at her disposal."

"One could hope." Kalama released a heavy breath. "The bedrolls behind you are for you two. Get some rest. I'll keep watch. You could use some sleep before we start your quick training."

"Thank you," Liekki said, with relief she didn't know she was needing.

Kalama grimaced. "Don't thank me yet. We haven't even begun and trust me, it won't be easy."

Liekki had woken at the break of dawn to her mentor's foot on her chest. The pressure startled her. Brightsun leaned over her with a mischievous smile on her face and a wicked gleam in her eyes. It didn't make Liekki feel any better about the upcoming learning session.

"Rise and shine, Nightsong. We have a lot of work to do and not enough time before you have to leave today." Liekki groaned but got up after her mentor removed her foot. "Meet me outside."

Liekki cursed under her breath about getting up early with hardly any sleep, but she wouldn't dare say those words near the Elder. She hurried outside and found Kalama speaking in hushed tones with Efrim. It was odd seeing those two looking like they were the closest friends after the incident between back at home, Liekki thought. She knew that even in troubled times, sometimes one had to set aside any differences to reach their common goal.

"Glad you can join us. I figured this would be a suitable spot to work on your wards and shields. Efrim will takeover this afternoon," Kalama said.

"I'm going to scout the area. Make sure the small fisher's boat I saw near the coast is sturdy enough to get you to the island. It is about an hour from here. North, but the currents can be rough out there." He walked towards her and placed a hand on her shoulder, then he winked. "Have fun this morning."

She watched him walk off before turning and facing her mentor. "Is this going to be hard?"

Kalama's smile faltered, not quite reaching her eyes. "Nightsong," she began, her voice laced with a more serious tone. "Anything of true worth or significance is going to be demanding and hard work. If it comes easy or is handed to you without any effort on your part, then it is something you don't require or truly desire. Now, let's get started."

The morning went quickly. By midday, Liekki was mentally tired and drained. Kalama was serious about training her mind to be stronger and her being able to call and use her foxfire with ease. Thanks to her mentor, Liekki had a much better grasp of how to use her foxfire as a weapon. How to shield her mind from attacks which gave her hope, little as it was, for the trials she would soon be enduring.

After a small meal, Liekki's training with Efrim began, which was just as hard as working with Kalama. In a clearing that was next to their hideaway, Efrim showed her the basics. How the movements she was learning flowed naturally into each other until it almost felt like a dangerous dance. He taught her how to use low and high kicks. Quick strikes with her fists and hands. He showed her where on the body a strike could cause the most damage and stop a heart from beating. She was taught the proper technique for blocking an attack. With Kalama's help, they both taught her how to incorporate her magic into the movements she had learned.

In the beginning, Liekki kept stumbling, and frustration bubbled up inside of her. She thought about everything she had dealt with over the last month. She refused to give up. No one had to tell her that her life possibly depended on the skills she picked up from the two foxes.

Soon enough, the first moon of Eldritch was starting its ascent while the sun was still low in the sky, creating a hazy, mystical effect. Her time was up with them. It was time for her to depart. Liekki wasn't ready, but she had no choice. Efrim and Kalama escorted her to the Bijou coastline. Thankful that they were a distance away from the empty town once claimed by the bandits and thieves. Instead, they were claimed by the darkness that was the Carnaval du Malheur.

"Here we are," Efrim said, when they slowed to a stop. The rushing of the water gently lapped against the side of the small boat that had two oars inside of it. "It's sturdy enough to stand the currents and get you to Elderton."

"The trip shouldn't take you long," Kalama said, cutting in after Efrim. "An hour at most."

Liekki stared at the small boat. "How will I know where to go?"

"You'll know," the Elder assured her.

So many thoughts flitted through Liekki's mind. She didn't know what to say to either of them. The anger she still felt in her heart hadn't left. It festered like a wound that had gone rancid. Why did she have to sacrifice herself for the betterment of vulpiians? It wasn't fair. Then again, life wasn't fair. How many times had she heard her father tell her the exact same thing? She didn't care about them, except a few. Those few she would do the trial for. She didn't want them to suffer for everyone else's mistakes.

"Guess I should be going," Liekki said, then looked up at the two foxes beside her. "Don't want to be late to the games."

Efrim's expression was grim, but she knew he kept his thoughts to himself. He reached out an arm to her, and she embraced him. "May the spirits watch over you. You will do fine. I'll be here waiting for when you come back."

"If I come back," she said.

"Don't think like that," Kalama admonished her with a sharp click of her tongue. "Remember everything we went over. Use your training from the champion school. You are strong enough to win this. If you must, reach out but remember, even that is limited. I'll do my best. I'll keep watch by the Hasking stone back on the sacred island."

"Is that even safe to go back to? With the way my father and his followers are acting in Vulpo, it doesn't seem safe."

"Nowhere is safe. I'll be alright. Now go."

Liekki stood there, still as the wind. With a head nod, she said nothing and walked towards the tiny contraption that would transport her to the trials. Rocks and sand crunched under her feet as she moved closer and closer until she was next to the boat. She took a deep breath, then exhaled before climbing inside.

"Nightsong," Kalama called out. Liekki looked up. Her mentor took a step closer to where she was. "Icelia asked for me to give you a message. I didn't tell her I was searching for you, but she knew I would. She told me to tell you if I found you, 'may you have good luck and she will see you when you come back'."

A flicker of happiness ignited within Liekki and spread throughout her. Kalama couldn't know just how much what she did meant to her. She didn't get to tell her best friend goodbye, and she had felt so bad about leaving without seeing her. Icelia wasn't mad at her, and that was enough. Ice had faith in her even when she didn't have it for herself.

"Tell her I will do my best," Liekki said while settling down on the seat inside the boat. She knew what the elder thought about her hanging around her daughter. She didn't have to relay the message, but she did anyway. "Thank you for telling me."

Kalama held out a hand and flicked her wrists and fingers towards the boat. A rush of air swept by, circling the craft, then propelling the skiff forward into the waiting water. "You're welcome."

Liekki took out the oars and began rowing toward the direction of where she needed to go. On the banks, she could still see Efrim and her mentor as she moved further and further away from them. Slowly, they became nothing but shadows and silhouettes. Going north wouldn't be as hard now that the gust of air that Kalama sent at her helped the journey go easier.

She had to pretend that she was okay when she took her leave, but it was all an illusion. Liekki had felt nothing but dread as it wrapped itself around her heart and soul. Everywhere she looked, she saw shadows that had a sentient presence. They lived and breathed the darkness and it beckoned to her. She was tempted yes, but she resisted. Every step toward this moment weighed heavily on her. Blaze wasn't afraid to admit she was scared and fearful of going to the trials. The things they taught her in the school about it were enough to send a shuddering chill down her spine. No one had to tell her. She could feel it hovering around her and waiting. Biding its time. She was going to her death and there was nothing she or anyone else could do about it.

CHAPTER 20

The sun had completely set by the time Liekki neared the island of Elderton. It loomed in the shadows of the moon. The closer she got to it, the more her heart raced. The island was enveloped in a dense shroud of fog, making her unable to see what was there. As she neared the old dock, the mist dissipated, revealing to her what was once hidden from all eyes except those chosen to be there.

It was nothing like Liekki had imagined. Brass fencing surrounded the entire island of Elderton and gates soared twenty feet high. She could sense the old magic from where she was as she reached the dock. There was a pregnant silence that seemed to expand over everything. Liekki paused for a moment, absorbing everything around her before stepping out of the skiff. With deft fingers, she quickly tied the rope into a secure knot around the wooden post on the dock, ensuring that the small boat wouldn't drift away.

Wanting to get a better look at the gates, she turned and faced them. At first Liekki hesitated, but the ancient magic called out to her, like a breathy whisper on the wind. It wasn't malicious as it was back on the mainland with the carnaval, no there was something familiar about this presence that called to her.

With quick steps, Liekki approached the closed gates, which were adorned with the symbol of the Mother Goddess in its center. A beautiful circular knotwork with its seamless loops and twists, merging into the next to create an abstract looking tree. There was beauty in the curves and details that whispered to her very soul. She was in the right place; it seemed to say.

Beyond the gates, it was darker than night, unable to see anything, even with her excellent night vision. She stood there in front of the imposing barrier, at a loss for how to pry it open, when a gradual creak startled her. Shattering the silence, the gates swung open, groaning in protest as it invited her inside. Liekki stared into the darkness and didn't know what she should do. She could turn around, but that would make her a failure. Something everyone already believed her to be. Liekki straightened her back and, with steel resolve in her heart, she took the steps forward and walked into the waiting abyss.

The otherworldly darkness turned to a drab charcoal gray, allowing her some type of light as she continued forward through the gates of Elderton. The ancient magic she felt the moment she neared the island had only grown to where she could feel it deep in her bones. Although she couldn't see anything in the gray shadows, Liekki could still feel something watching her. She had felt it ever since she passed through the gates. Somehow, she knew it didn't want to cause her harm, no it almost felt like it wanted to talk to her.

Ahead of her, a small orb of silvery white light winked into existence, then grew larger until it almost blinded her. She raised her arms to shield her eyes, but it wasn't very effective. Liekki came to a slow halt, freezing in place, unwilling to risk toppling over because of the brilliant light blinding her.

A soft rustling of fabric caught her ears and from behind her arm, she noticed the once bright light dimming to a tolerable level. Liekki slowly lowered her arm to find a vulpiian standing before her. She couldn't stop staring at the vixen. She was beyond beautiful. Liekki's eyes raked over the vixen and took in everything. Her long, ebony hair flowed just past her shoulders, while a few small braids adorned in silver framed her face. Her fox ears and nine tails spread behind her were black as the darkness she traveled through. The vixen's beautiful dress curved around her slender form. The fabric was black as the void, but when she moved and the light hit it just right, the dress glimmered with specks. It resembled the celestial tapestry of stars one saw in the night sky.

Wrapped all around the vixen was an old, primordial magic that pulsated with secrets of the unknown. The overwhelming moment was enough to make Liekki tremble where she stood. Made her want to fall down to her knees and show reverence to the one before her. Succumbing to the desire, Liekki found herself going down on bended knee. The vixen reached out a hand to stay her motion.

"No, don't. Please stand," the vixen said. Her voice was strong yet gentle. Almost mother like.

Liekki rose and got a better look at her. She reminded her of their spirit goddess, Aku. Clan Night's Matron Goddess. "You look like Aku... but you're not. Who are you?"

The spirit goddess smiled and the warmth it exuded filled Liekki within. "You know who I am. Open yourself and see."

Doing as she was told, she opened herself to the old magic. Instead of the raw force of the ancient power she sensed, Liekki felt a warm caress. It swirled around her mind and continued to flow through her. It was like a balm to her heart and soul. A promise that one knew would never break. The gentle embrace one gets from their loving mother when all else seems lost. The moment was everything to her. She couldn't even put it to words or thoughts as it overwhelmed her totally. With the sharpest clarity, it dawned on her. A gasp slipped from her lips. Liekki's eyes widened. "Zera," she whispered. "You're the Mother Goddess."

"You are correct," Mother Goddess replied, her eyes piercing Liekki's as if she was searching deep into her soul. "I can feel the questions burning inside of you. I can see the darkness of your hate for your kind slowly corrupting your spirit, yet there is still hope for you. In time, the answers will come to you. Right now, you are not ready for them. You're not in the proper place on your journey to receive the answers you have been seeking."

There were so many things Liekki wanted to ask her, but when she opened her mouth to voice her questions, Liekki found herself silent. She shuffled around on her feet as everything swirled around in her mind. The good feelings she was riding on had quickly turned into something sharper. Colder. First it was like ice before it turned into white hot rage abruptly surging in her veins. "Then when?" Liekki spat. Words came to her, but they weren't the ones she wanted earlier, but the ones she needed right then. "Why must I endure the things I do and you sit back and do nothing? You watch when you could have helped me all of this time."

"There are things you must learn and you haven't yet. Soon enough, you will. Go forth and be a blazing instrument of truth for you and your fellow Vulpii." Mother Goddess stepped aside and the gray mist parted like a curtain, allowing a glimpse of what truly lay beyond the gates. "Believe it or not, I want to see all of my children succeed. Sometimes, it's better they learn through trials and tribulations before they come to an understanding. Now go, I'll be watching you."

Liekki stood there as the Mother Goddess departed. The ethereal figure walked away until she became nothing but a blip of silvery light and winked out of existence. The raw and ancient power she felt when Mother Goddess first appeared gradually faded to a constant hum that she attributed to the magic of the island. With a resolute and echoing thump, the gates closed behind her, sealing her fate. There was no going back. Only way now was forward.

Stretched out before her in the distance were the shadows of odd shapes. Stationary though they were, she still didn't know what it was. Following the long path of dirt and rocks, Liekki realized the buildings were a campground of sorts. Once she was closer, the odd shapes turned out to be shelters with a conical frame as it reached upwards. Made from a simple yet durable type of canvas and sturdy wooden poles to shield the eumen from the weather and sun.

Spread out before here were rows and rows of tents. She reached the campground and noticed a few other champions walking around. None looked up at her and she was glad for it. Liekki didn't feel like interacting with anyone. The shelters weren't assigned. She walked around until she found one she could use. When Liekki found an empty one, she stepped inside to find a spacious interior. Moonlight filtered in from the hole at the top, casting a glow, lighting the space. There was a central fire pit with provisions that appeared beside it. She went to the woven basket to find bread, fruit, cheeses, and dried meat. Next to the wall of the tent was a cot with bedding that looked soft and inviting

The night was early, and she knew she didn't have much longer before she needed to enter her house. She stood there and debated if she would go searching for her house, then come back and rest for a few hours or not wait and start the trial. Her aching muscles and weary mind chose for her. She moved next to the fire pit and bent down to arrange the wood in its center. With a snap of her fingers, the fire magic she learned to control sent a spark to the kindling, and a fire began. She blew on it until it grew and grew into a sizeable blaze.

Liekki searched through the basket of provisions and took out a piece of the dried meat and a piece of cheese for now. At first, she wanted to search for the House of Vulpii, but decided against. She wanted a nap. She would rather feel rested before going inside. Liekki had a strange feeling she was going to need all of her wits about her. Or else she was going to end up on the other side of the living.

Liekki had been at the camp for less than a day and she knew by waiting any longer, she was putting off the inevitable. Sitting alone in her tent on the edge of her cot, she got up and went and banked the fire that was keeping her warm. While other trial aspirants were sleeping, she decided there would be no more waiting. After pouring dirt over the fire to extinguish it, she wiped her hands on her pants and stood up. Grateful for the food, she was full and rested.

She stepped outside of the tent and looked at the night sky. A slight chilly breeze whipped around, lifting her hair all around her face. Although it was Sprig, the nights were still cold. It wouldn't get any warmer until it was the season of Sol. The first moon was still up, but the second one was also making its ascent. She guessed she had slept for at least four to five hours. There was no point in waiting any longer. It was the hours of the spirits. No better time than ever. She was more than ready to get these trials done and over with.

Liekki looked both ways before she carefully weaved her way through the circular camp of tents. The stench of fear was ever present, and she didn't want to be around it any longer. She could only take so much. After settling down earlier, she noticed that there on the island, her magic was more sensitive to others and the world around them. Even then, she didn't want the fear of others to find purchase in her mind. There was no room for that. She had to stay focused on the end goal. Get out alive.

Moving easily through the camp, she made it to the outer edge, where she heard someone talking in a strange tongue. She slowed down, curiosity getting the better of her to see who it was. Eldritch was a place filled with mystery and so many creatures she hadn't even known to exist, so when she caught a look at the female euman they intrigued her.

Moving closer to get a better look, she stayed behind to avoid being seen. The euman was talking to the Umital bird, a messenger who could carry letters to anyone anywhere in Eldritch. Liekki thought about the letter she wrote, but instead of using the Umital bird, she left her letter back home in a place where her father and mother would find it.

Everything all went to the void when the euman hurriedly spun around. Liekki tried to get out of the way, but didn't move fast enough and the euman crashed into her. Liekki couldn't stay upright, and stumbled to the ground and landed on her backside with a grunt.

"I am sorry," the euman said, quickly apologizing in the common Eldish tongue. "I did not see you passing."

A sharp pain radiated up from her backside, and Liekki cursed under her breath. Nothing seemed to go right. Even as she tried to be invisible. It was the same in Ravenfalls. She had a glamour on there and still was found out. Remembering the euman who ran into her, Liekki looked up at her and let out a frustrated sigh. "It's okay. Most eumen I've noticed walking around here are in a daze," she said and settled herself on the ground, not bothering to get up. "I was hoping to get by unnoticed."

Liekki sat there and rested her forearms on her knees while the euman looked all around them. There were a few more trial aspirants walking around. The way they were looking, Liekki knew they were probably as restless as she was. The strange euman turned back around peered down at Liekki. Something passed over the euman's face as she stared at Liekki. She lowered herself to almost eye level and extended an offered hand.

Not wanting to be that type of vulpii, Liekki accepted the kind offer and allowed herself to be pulled off the ground. "Thank you," she said.

"My pleasure. It was my fault you were down there to begin with," the Euman said.

Liekki kept her thoughts about it to herself because she was just as much at fault as her.

"I am Ayinda of the Vermilion Fibanyon," Ayinda said, introducing herself. "I hope I didn't hurt you."

Liekki shook her head. Getting a better look at the creature before her. "You didn't. I'm Liekki, by the way. A vulpii from Clan Night." She pointed to the crescent mark on her forehead. "What are you?"

"I am a Lyew from Tarac. My home borders the Bijou Ocean directly across from Elderton," she explained.

"Oh, I've heard of your lands. I passed the Lyew lands before getting here," Liekki told her, remembering when Efrim said the coastal town was between their homeland and the Lyew lands. Now she knew what he was referring to. "They're north of Vulpo. That's where we Vulpii are from. Although, on my journey, I didn't come across anyone that looks like you."

"You wouldn't," Ayinda clarified. "Tarac has charms that repel outsiders. If you are not Lyew, you wouldn't find it."

"I see," Liekki said, thinking back to how something like that could have come in handy. "Wish I could have had a charm like that this last month."

"You and me both," Ayinda agreed with a small giggle.

A silence descended between them both as the weight of what they were about to do settled down over them. Their gazes met with a soul deep knowing that everything in their life was not about to be the same. Liekki didn't know what Ayinda had to go through to be there, but she hoped she came out alright. She seemed nice in an innocent type of way. Nothing like the way Liekki had to endure ever since she was just a little kit. A rush of memories tried to flood her mind, and she did her best to push them back into the locked room she liked to keep them in. She didn't need them to make an appearance now. Definitely not there, right before she was to enter the trials. She needed to be focused on the task before her.

"Good luck," Ayinda said. Her words were truly sincere. She reached out her hand again, this time offering a friendly handshake.

"Same to you," Liekki said to Ayinda and accepted the gesture.

When their hands touched, Ayinda took a small step towards her and blew a stream of steady air onto her face and chest. Startled, Liekki's eyes widened with surprise as the sudden gust of wind brushed across her face and chest, causing her lashes to flutter. She didn't know what to think. *Could it be some weird Lyew custom*? she thought. Not wanting to be rude, Liekki returned the gesture and blew into Ayinda's face, then smiled. She hoped she did everything right. Ayinda's bright grin gave Liekki a small measure of relief. She released Ayinda's hand and gave an awkward nod.

"I'll be on my way then," Liekki said before taking off. The small encounter wasn't much, but it was enough to make her feel a little better. Why couldn't more Vulpii be kind like the

Lyew she had just met? *Someday*, she hoped. Leaving the campground behind her, she shifted into her true form, and Liekki made the heavy trek to find the House of Vulpii.

CHAPTER 21

D arting through the circular rows, Liekki's three tails bounced behind her as she searched for the house she was about to enter. Going all the way to the back, searching the last row closest to the mountainous wall, Liekki's heart raced faster. When she spotted the one from her earlier reconnaissance, she slowed to a stop in front of it. Thankful it was far enough away from the house that was burning. She didn't know what had happened, but she recognized the signs of someone who had failed. Whoever it was, they cursed their eumen for one hundred years. The idea frightened her. Made it seem so real when before it was just words told to her by Kalama.

House Vulpii was made similar to the homes of those who lived in the mountains. On the outside, it looked like a noble's home, but it went back far enough that it looked as if it was designed and carved from the side of the mountain.

She yipped before going closer to it, carefully stepping over the gravel and loose stone that was under her paws. When Liekki reached the door, she shifted into her two-legged form and reached for the door's knob. She held her hand over it as if she was rethinking going in. Rethinking everything. She was still filled with anger. Dark thoughts and whispers had slowly crept inside of her mind again.

"Why do I have to do this when they don't even care about me?" she said out loud to no one but herself. "This is ridiculous!"

Unsurprised at the silence for a response. She was lonelier than she had ever been before at that moment. The quietness lingered around until she couldn't stand it any longer. Even then, the stillness and absence of noise had a way of becoming loud in her ears. It was accusatory, and it was oppressive. A frustrated exhale escaped her lips. "Guess that's answer enough."

Liekki turned the knob on the door to the House of Vulpii and entered, stepping through the threshold. Inside, the home was empty of anything. She went further inside and the door behind her slammed closed. Liekki glanced back over her shoulder in time to watch the door disappear. There was no way out. She had to go through it now.

She squinted as she tried to get a better look around. The interior was windowless and shrouded in darkness. Despite having the ability to see in the dim light, she wanted to get a clearer look. Figure out what she would need to do next. There were no rules. The only instruction given to her by Kalama was to locate the Hasking stone, a mysterious stone she knew nothing about. Liekki lifted a hand, palm facing upwards, and called the foxfires to her. The reddish orange flames danced and flickered without burning as she held it up to see all around. Spotting a sconce on the wall to her right, she directed the flames from her palm towards it, igniting it, illuminating the room.

Bathed in a warm glow, Liekki could see the room clearly. She scanned the space, noting everything for later. There were no furnishings. It was entirely bare. Nothing but an empty room and the strange shadows formed from the warm glow of the lamp on the wall.

Ahead of her was a long hall. She walked towards it and stood at the beginning of it. She noticed each side of the wall had a row of doors.

"I wonder..." she started and stopped.

Did she have to go through one to start her trials? It should have been obvious as the two moons, but she didn't know.

Her eyes darted to each door, hopeful that one called out to her, but none did. Not even the barest of a whisper. There was only silence. "Which one to choose?"

Liekki didn't know what to do, so she did the obvious. She aimlessly strolled down the long hall and would occasionally touch a closed door, hoping for something to happen, yet it never did. She chose another random door to her right and pushed to open it, but it wouldn't budge. Faint light from the sconce on the walls in the front room reached the hall, but not quite, lending an eerie shadow to it all.

She continued her trek down the narrow hall, hands up, lightly brushing against the doors as she passed them. None of them calling out to her, souring her mood. By the time she reached the end of the hall, her anger was blazing hot. Not even the coolness of an unexpected breeze was enough to bring her to heel. Or the sudden door that appeared in the space of the blank wall that was in front of her. Mumbling curses of her clan that didn't translate to the common Eldish tongue, Liekki stood there and examined the new development.

"Why do all the weird things happen around me?" she said out loud to herself. Frustrated, she hadn't figured out what to do yet, even though she had just gone into the house.

The newly appeared door had a light purplish glow all around it. Ancient looking runes that were etched around the door lit up brightly, but she didn't understand what it said. None of the writing was familiar to her. Nothing she had seen before, but she was sure if Efrim was there, he would have some pretense of knowledge of it. Her wayward guard always knew more than what he would reveal.

She stopped directly in front of the arched door made from the innards of the house. Liekki didn't know where the thought came from, but she acted on it and reached out a hand and let it hover just over the new door. Warm against her palm, she felt the ancient magic from earlier. *This was the way.* Placing both hands on the door, she pushed hard, shoving her shoulders and all of her weight into it. The door groaned before it budged, releasing a puff of dust motes and stale air. The room beyond was dark. Still, something told Liekki she was going in the right direction. She listened to her instincts and crossed the threshold and tumbled off a cliff into the unknown.

A blood-curling scream tore from deep within her soul as she plummeted to her imminent demise. Her eyes were wide open, but she couldn't see. It was as if she was completely blinded. Total darkness had surrounded Liekki. Lacking her sense of sight, she was thrown off balance. She had no idea where she was headed. All she knew was that it was too fast. If this was her end, she prayed she would die a quick death, but even that wasn't a surety with her luck lately.

Giving in to the thoughts that she failed after barely just getting started, Liekki abruptly hit what she assumed was the ground. She cried out as the force of the fall had her tumbling and rolling, unable to stop herself. Still blinded by the darkness, she didn't see the stones and trees. She hit her head against them in a collision where the sweet darkness and promise of sleep took over.

A painful groan slipped out of Liekki's mouth as she emerged from the painful slumber. Slowly, she opened her eyes and blinked a few times as the startlingly bright light hurt. Lifting her arms over her face, she gave herself some semblance of shade as she tried to look around. Her head was pounding like drums and there was nothing she could do about it. The pain was an intense pulse that pounded to the beat of a melody that she couldn't even hear.

She had only felt it.

Gingerly, she touched the back of her head and felt the knot that had formed. As she made another attempt at shifting her position, the relentless pounding resonated inside of her skull, causing her to wince. Dark spots filled her vision. With painstakingly slower movements, Liekki managed to sit up, and once upright, a wave of nausea surged through her. Threatening to expel the contents of her stomach. Taking deliberate deep breaths, she focused on not getting sick. After a few moments had passed, so did the sickness she was feeling.

After Liekki deemed herself okay, she glanced around, trying to determine where she was, but nothing looked familiar. True, there were trees everywhere that said she was obviously in a forest, but which she didn't know. The leaves were deep red as the blood that spilled out of one's veins. Its bark was black as the midnight sky. The one she had collided with was the largest one by far that she had ever seen before. Its trunk was wide as five adult vulpiians standing side by side. And tall enough where the night sky was partially blotted out, allowing little moonlight to filter through its canopy.

The sound of the forest's creatures was silent, but she could sense an otherworldly presence there with her. Something was watching her, and she didn't know what or who it was. At least she was alive, she thought. Getting to her feet, Liekki swayed a bit before the spinning in her head stopped. She dusted her pants off from the debris and took a better look around. A small trail, almost hidden by brush and fallen trees, led away from where she was. Liekki didn't know where it was going to lead her to, but anything was better than standing there like a lost bovek.

She shifted into her true form, hoping it would help the healing and the excessive throbbing in her head. Like most of those who could shift their forms, she and her fellow Vulpiians could heal faster in their true form. After shifting and yipping at the moon in the sky, her way of honoring the spirit of the moon, Aku, Liekki, took off down the path. She jumped over the fallen hollow tree log that had verdant moss growing over it. Already feeling her body heal itself thanks to the shift, she ran the trail, careful to watch her steps. The further she went, the more the sensation of being watched grew, but the inhabitants of the forest were no longer silent. For that, she was grateful. The silence was beginning to unnerve her.

The path curved around, then dipped into a downturn. She followed it until she reached the end. On the side of the path, she noticed a dark spot, but heard the soft whimpers that sounded like someone was in pain. She leaped towards it and came to a stop when she realized the still form was a dryem. Moving closer to the unmoving form, she sniffed around the creature, but she couldn't smell any foul sign of infection. Quickly shifting into her two-legged form, she bent over the whimpering figure, looking at it with concern.

"Are you okay?" Liekki asked in the common Eldish tongue.

The curled up form whimpered, but rolled over to her side to face Liekki. Her eyes widened at seeing the strange vulpii. "Aren't you a sight for sore eyes," the dryem said, her voice cracking a little from no use. "I guess I'm in a bit of trouble. I was coming down that slight hill there and took an unfortunate tumble. My leg... it's hurting something fierce, but I don't think it's broken."

Liekki glanced at the dryem's leg. It was bent at a weird angle. She wanted to help, but there was nothing she could do. Her magic wasn't of the healing sort. Destruction... yes, she thought. "I don't have any healing magic. I can't help you there. It looks broken even though you say it's not. You would know best. Maybe I can help make a splint or some crutches for you."

"It's alright," the dryem said with a smile that was etched with pain. She shifted in her spot and grimaced. "There's a healing pool not far from here. If I can get to it, all I would need to do is submerge my injured leg. The waters can heal anything."

"Seriously?" Liekki asked, her jaw dropping with surprise. She had never heard of healing waters before, but perhaps it could help with her insistent headache that came back when she shifted to her two-legged form.

The dryem laughed, and the sound was light. Airy. It reminded Liekki of bells. "Yes, really. I can show you if you're able to help me get there. It's not far. I promise. We are practically next to it."

Liekki looked around and saw nothing, even though the feeling of being watched was ever present. With all of her strength, she helped the dryem off the ground. Completely upright, the dryem hopped on one leg before she attempted to put weight on the injured one. She hissed in pain, but told Liekki she was good. Together, the two traveled the rest of the path that veered off to a fork. Liekki didn't know which way to go.

"We go right," the dryem said. She pointed with the jutting of her chin. "It's just beyond those trees there."

"Then it is to the right we go," Liekki agreed and led her new unlikely companion in the direction the dryem had pointed.

They traveled a few minutes, deep off the path, until Liekki could smell the scent of fresh water. They were close.

"There." The dryem's gaze penetrated a group of trees. "Just beyond that small grove of trees lay the healing pools."

They hobbled together, making their way slowly but surely. Liekki helped the dryem as best as she could. She pushed through the dense foliage that created a tunnel from thick vines and interwoven tree limbs. Underneath their feet, the path gave way to a soft carpet of fallen black leaves. Contrasting against the rich brown dirt and purple and blueish moss-covered stone. The trees thinned out and beyond it there was a pool glistening under the silvery moon above. Liekki's watchful gaze searched the area and noticed the slate colored wall of a bluff behind the waters, hidden by the few trees.

The natural pool was fed by the spring that led into the mouth the cave that was carved out of the side of the bluff. It was there for shelter if ever one was needed. Somehow, Liekki felt at peace for a change and that put a ghost of a smile on her face. Everything was serene. Peaceful, and she wondered more than once if the waters could heal the anger that threatened to consume her at the most inopportune times. It was a sickness after all, and she knew if she didn't get her emotions in control, it would consume her like her father. She didn't want to be like Diev.

"This is a sacred space," the dryem said with a reverence. "A secret place known only to the Dryem. Blessed by our gods and goddesses."

A confused expression crossed Liekki's features. She couldn't believe it. The door she walked through had taken her back to Dryemia. She didn't know why she thought all the tests were going to be on Elderton. The doors reminded her of the Vulpiic gates, yet she couldn't choose her destination. If it sent her back to Dryemia, then the Hasking stone must be there. She had to make sure that Queen Cirrha and her soulbind, Xyrin, didn't find out that she had come back while she searched for it. What the dryem said had her mind reeling. "I thought your kind worshipped only the Mother Goddess and the very nature of Eldritch."

The dryem chuckled. "Yes, we do. But... we like the vulpiians have our own that we speak of only with our kind. To speak of the *Primordials* to any that is not us is to be anathema to the dryem. I am only a humble servant of our mother goddess and of our Queen Cirrha. I can't say more because I don't want to jeopardize being cut off from the lands of my birth. You understand, yes?"

Liekki understood more than what she said. She was beginning to understand with a strange clarity. She hated what her kind had become, but Vulpo was her home. Despite her brief absence, she had come to secretly miss the place. Miss her crew. Vulpo was an enchanting place. It was home.

"I understand more than what you know," Liekki said with a deep sincerity.

The dryem's blue gaze met Liekki's. "Come and let us pray these waters heal my injured leg."

Liekki helped the dryem to the edge of the pool. On her own, the dryem limped into the pool and waded into its water until she was standing in its center and the water had risen to her breast. Liekki had found a spot on the ground, not too far from the edge, and sat there. She kept watch as the dryem took to the waters. Too many thoughts flooded her mind after discovering the dryem had their own pantheon. Yet, she remembered clearly that Queen Cirrha said her subjects were starting to listen to the spirits of Vulpo. The dark spirits that even they didn't speak out loud. It was no wonder the Queen and her soulbind were upset. If their own gods and goddesses were jealous gods, then Liekki could see how that would create problems for the Dryem. It didn't bode well at all.

The darkness that was infecting Vulpo really was seeping its tendrils into Dryemia, Liekki thought.

Time had passed as they talked a little. Mostly, Liekki kept to her own thoughts and didn't know how long the dryem kept in the healing waters. After a brief silence, there was a muted scuffling sound that alerted her they weren't alone. Her ears twitched towards the tiny noise. The feeling of being watched had tripled in that brief span. She looked to the dark spaces beyond the trees and could have sworn she saw a pair of amber eyes staring at her. Liekki quickly hopped off the ground and moved closer to the waters. "I heard something. I'm not sure of what it is," she whispered so only the dryem could hear her.

The dryem's eyes widened. Her head looked to the left and right as she scanned the sacred space. "No," she whispered. "He can't have found me this fast."

Liekki's eyes narrowed. "What are you on about? Who are you talking about?"

"Quiet," the dryem hushed as she hurried out of the waters. Her leg had healed completely and allowed her to move about, unencumbered. "I'm afraid I haven't been that honest with you. I'll tell you once we're safe. I beg of your help once again."

Liekki didn't like the situation at all. She hadn't forgotten what she was supposed to be doing. She had to find the Hasking stone and hopefully get out of the trials alive. Once she figured out what she was supposed to do for her tests. She hated being clueless. She should have known that there was something more about the randomly injured elemental on the side of the path.

The dryem grabbed Liekki's wrist and pulled her to her side. Liekki wrested herself away from the dryem, stopping in her tracks, and frowned at her. "What are you doing?"

"I'm saving both of her backsides, now come on. He can't find us. Not like this." The dryem's troubled gaze shifted towards the bluff. "There. We must go inside that grotto and find cover. Trust me."

Liekki didn't have any choice and followed the dryem into the dark cave. She wanted to know who this '*He*' was because she wasn't so keen on running without reason. Lately that's all Liekki had been doing was running and hiding from trouble, and there was no doubt that whoever was watching them was trouble. She could taste it in the air.

Their breaths hung in the air. The gurgling whispers of the flowing stream, coupled with the eerie silence, had Liekki on edge. Her eyes constantly darted around in the dark. She could sense an unspoken warning in the air and didn't know what to do about it. Any other time, she would have left. Leaving the dryem to her own devices and troubles, but for some reason, the thought of it didn't sit right with her. Decision made, Liekki remained at the dryem's side. Sensing the ever presence of danger that had haunted her since she went through the mysterious door.

Liekki suppressed the urge to call for her flames, using caution, knowing the light from it would betray their hidden whereabouts. Following the Dryem, they went back far as they could go in the enchanting grotto. An enormous boulder wide enough to hide the both of them stood near the flowing stream. The dryem pulled Liekki behind the large stone, using it as their cover.

They crouched low, and the dryem placed a finger over her lips, signaling they should be silent. Liekki looked into her eyes and saw a cloud of uncertainty. Long gone was the calm and vibrance she had originally seen. Now fear and worry mirrored back at Liekki. Whoever the dryem was running from was a dangerous foe, for sure.

From the moment she found the elemental creature, she never once sought her name, nor did the dryem give Liekki hers. She stared at the elemental creature now and wondered who she really was. She had rich brown skin like Queen Cirrha, but her eyes were bright blue like gems. Her hair was silver and gray, like the storm clouds right before they darkened in the sky. Twisted branch like horns protruded from her scalp while lights of gold sat upon her head like a crown. There were markings under her eyes, gold and blue, while a gold torque made of stone and vines wrapped around her neck. Oh, Liekki could see the resemblance between the two, but how they were related, she wasn't so sure.

"Who are you? Really?" Liekki whispered low enough so only the dryem could hear her.

A heavy sighed escaped the dryem's lips. Her shoulders slumped, resigning herself to whatever troubled her. "I am Varaila. Daughter of Cirrha."

Chapter 22

Liekki had frozen in her spot, taken by surprise by what the dryem had just confessed to. She suspected the two were kin, but to have a grown daughter that was close to her own age was surprising news indeed. Although Liekki considered Queen Cirrha an interesting dryem, she didn't think of her being exactly the motherly type. *No wonder she was so concerned about the spreading darkness*, Liekki thought. She met Varaila's gaze. "Daughter of Queen Cirrha? Are you serious?"

Varaila nodded somberly, not saying another word. A flickering reddish-orange light lit up the grotto, giving it a warm glow. It chased away the semi-darkness. All the while, heavy footsteps once far away inched closer and closer as they echoed against the cavern's walls. Varaila peeked from behind the boulder and let out a slip of a gasp before her hands quickly rose and covered her mouth. She moved closer to Liekki's side and crouched even lower to the ground, as if she was trying to fold in on herself. The footsteps neared their hiding spot, then they paused in the center, not too far from where the waters flowed. There was a shuffling sound. A sudden breeze filled the cave. The flames had cast a dark shadow against the wall and stuttered before winking out.

"I know you're in here, Varaila. I can smell the fear seeping out of your pores from where I stand and it smells so delicious," a deep and menacing male voice said before he chuckled.

He called the flames back to his hand, filling the grotto once more with low warm light. He moved closer to where they hid. His footsteps were much slower, but they were louder all the same. Liekki carefully balanced herself on her feet and placed a hand against the cool rock, then leaned forward to the right. She couldn't resist the curiosity that burned inside of her any longer and peeked around the boulder. From her hidden spot, Liekki took a sidelong look at his face. He was tall for a dryem and well built. Dressed in black linen type pants and only a matching vest that was left open, baring his chest. She made out intricate markings on the side of his face and complex patterns of swirls scored his arms and chest. His long hair hung past his shoulders and was twisted into tight coils. They were the color of purple and silver ombre with occasional green flecks in them that reminded her of pollen from a flower.

"I can only imagine what it will taste like," he had continued from where he stood. "As I devour your soul. Your spirit. Your entire being until there is nothing left if you don't give me what I ask for. I'll even spare the friend you've collected before coming here. Just come out from behind the stone."

Varaila's shoulder shook from a silent cry. Liekki hurried back into her hiding spot and watched Varaila from the corner of her eyes. Tears fell down Varaila's face. She looked like all hope had fled from her. Utterly defeated.

"Don't you want to help me?" The dryem asked with sweet venom.

Liekki glanced at Varaila and mouthed, "What is it he wants? Who is he?"

Varaila kept her lips closed and shook her head, refusing to say anything. Liekki knew that hiding behind a rock and keeping quiet wouldn't get the job done. It was apparent the male had no intention of departing. They needed to get away from there or else they were both going to end up dead. There was one thing the newcomer had right. Varaila was too frightened to do anything. She was crouched with her arms wrapped around her legs. Liekki knew it was up to her. She couldn't leave Varaila there. It was a strange predicament they found themselves in, but there was no way Liekki could let her die. Not while she stood by and watched.

"I helped give you life, you crazy fool. I was the one who spent my precious seed inside of that fatu of a Queen you call mother. Then she decided to send me away after you were born. When she discovered I followed the ways of my heart and not the old and outdated ways of our kind. The Mother Goddess doesn't care for us or our kind. I follow those who answer our pleas and reward us for our obedience. If only she had let me teach you, then you wouldn't be weak and cowering behind a rock." He laughed, loud and harsh. "Don't worry, my lovely flower, she will get what is coming to her too. Cirrha will learn the ways of the shadows or she will learn what death eternal is."

Too much was said and not said in his words. Trouble was brewing and, more than once, Liekki didn't like what it implied for her. What it meant for her fellow vulpiians and possibly the Dryem. She couldn't understand how she played into all of it. She was only a thief. Nothing special.

The dryem released a heavy sigh. "Since you want to be difficult like that fatu Cirrha, it seems I have no choice. Too bad you have doomed your companion to an untimely death. I'll only ask once more, my little flower. Give me what I want and I may let you both live."

Liekki closed her eyes and called her magic to her. The feeling of controlling the foxfires was strange, but she enjoyed it immensely. The heat of the fire flowed through her body and hovered just under her skin, itching to burn its way out. She wanted to free it. Liekki felt a hand on her shoulder and she opened her eyes to find Varaila staring at her.

"No," Varaila mouthed. "Don't. He'll kill us both, no matter what."

"I don't know about you, but I'm not quite ready to die just yet," Liekki silently mouthed back. "I'm going to distract him and you run out of here to safety."

"No... don't," Varaila pleaded.

"Too late..." Liekki said.

With a wide grin and, to Varaila's dismay, Liekki hopped up from her crouch, revealing their hiding spot. She wasn't one to listen to the rules much, anyway. Keeping her hands down at her sides, Liekki didn't want to reveal her magic just yet. "You know... you really talk too much. If you were going to kill us, you would have done it by now."

The male's head snapped around and found Liekki standing there glaring at him. She stood there, unafraid and determined to do whatever needed to be done to get out of that cave. A malicious grin slowly crept across his face, stretching his lips into a wicked curve, revealing white sharp eye teeth. His darkened eyes sparkled with a sinister gleam as his gaze met hers. Shadowy tendrils snaked around his arms and legs, moving lazily as if they were waiting for his command.

"What do we have here?" he said, while he continued to stare at Liekki. "A vulpii... from the night clan. Yes, you would understand the shadows as they speak to us."

Liekki didn't know what he was talking about, but she had seen what those dark, silky tendrils could do when Mezal was wielding them back in Ravenfalls. She didn't want any part of it. "Yeah, I'm not sure I understand what you're talking about, but Clan Night doesn't cling to the shadows. That is the domain of Ibris, and I'd rather not cross his path. He can be a vengeful spirit."

"I can get you to change your mind," he spoke aloud, his words laced with malevolent promise. The dryem extinguished the flames in his palms, quickly descending the grotto into total darkness. Swiftly, he commanded the shadows to obey his will. He guided them with relentless speed and attacked Liekki.

Flames instantly burst from Liekki's hands as she flung two large blazing orbs toward the dryem's way. She dropped to the ground and pushed Varaila and herself out of the way and further back into the cave behind another boulder. Lighting a path in front of her so she could see. The dryem behind them dodged both as they hurdled towards him. A gust of air surrounded him, lifting a stream of water. The dryem directed it towards the flaming orbs, dousing them. The cave went dark again.

Liekki cursed in her native tongue. Her eyes adjusted to the darkness and Liekki watched as their attacker melded into the shadows and rushed towards them. Without time to think about what to do, Liekki gave in to the magic that was her own and did what came naturally to her. The air crackled around them with charged energy. It smelled of damp earth and decay, ripe with tension. The heat within Liekki burned hotter until she couldn't contain it any longer.

Bolts of sky blue and white lightning crackled and arced through the air inside of the cave. Flashes of light were enough to allow Liekki to see their attacker. He stood there transfixed and distracted by the storm that filled the cave. With deadly precision, the bolts zigzagged, striking all around as he danced to avoid being struck.

The damp atmosphere was filled with electric energy at Liekki's command. Leaving Varaila behind, Liekki inched closer to their attacker. Dodging the shadows, he flung her away, not wanting to be touched by its cold and slimy tendrils. She carved a path towards him, doing her best to strike him, but he proved it more difficult than she had expected.

"Who are you? Why do you come after her?" Liekki asked as she hurled a flaming orb of blue fire his way, then darted out of the way when he responded with a gust of air. It caught her and slammed her against the wall. She fell to the ground and groaned at the pain blossoming in her lower back.

"If you should know, Vulpiian. My name is Acoris, of the Twilight Grove," he said before rushing towards Liekki and pinning her in her spot. Shadowy tendrils slowly snaked around her ankles and arms as another gust of wind swirled around her, lifting her up. "And now you are going to die."

Undeterred, Liekki reached for her magic, then she reached out and touched Acoris on his arm. He was confused as he stared at her, yet it didn't stop the assault on Liekki. The shadows squeezed tighter around her limbs while she did her best to not cry out. The wind blew her hair all over her face, slashing against her skin like tiny blades, cutting it. Droplets of blood fell and swirled around her.

She couldn't fail. If she was to fail, Liekki knew they would die, as sure as the air she breathed. A slow, cunning smile spread across Liekki's face. Acoris didn't recognize the look on her face, but it was there in her eyes for all to see. Mischief glinted in those amber gems of Liekki's. She couldn't kill him, no matter how much she wanted to. No, but she could make him wish he was dead. Not letting go of his arms, she accepted the assault and did her best not to cry out.

Her strength wasn't with foxfire, not yet, but her illusions were top tier, and Liekki knew it was her key out of the grotto, alive with Varaila. With the depths of power, she wove an intricate tapestry, conjuring a dreamscape that even Duara would be proud of.

Acoris grunted. His eyes glazed over and Liekki knew she had him. The slithering tendrils of his shadows disappeared. The cutting wind halted. She didn't let go of his arms as she tumbled to the ground. Maintaining contact was the most important.

Liekki created visions of despair and torment inside Acoris' mind. His eyes darted back and forth as he was pulled further into the vision where the sound of anguished cries pierced his ears and his soul. She made sure he saw the groves he favored as they burned to nothing but cinders. A desolate, charred landscape where death lived. Grotesque figures that were once was his fellow dryem from the Twilight Grove of his birth and home ambled aimlessly as they cried out.

She twisted the very fabric of what he thought was home into a nightmare he truly believed was nothing but the truth. Liekki let go of him once she knew the illusion was part of the very fabric he believed to be his reality.

A deep bellow came from Acoris, filling the cavern with its resounding timbre. "Noo. No! What is this?"

She watched as he reached up and tore at his hair. *Let him enjoy this torment*, she thought. Liekki ran to where Varaila hid and grabbed her arm. "Let's go. He won't harm us anymore. He doesn't know the real from the fake."

Varaila hesitated, but eventually rose from her hiding spot and looked directly at where Acoris stood. His face was twisted into a painful grimace. His eyes rolled to the back of his head as he stumbled around. "What did you do?"

"Instead of fighting with my foxfire, I sent him a sending. One even the spirit of dreams would be proud of." Liekki grinned. "Come on and let's get out of here. I wasn't going to let him harm you or me."

Varaila stared at Acoris with her arms wrapped around her chest. "I don't know what to say."

"Thank you is a start."

"Thank you," Varaila said with a chuckle. "I appreciate what you've done for me more than anything. You didn't even know who I was yet and still you helped me. A stranger. I don't even have that type of loyalty back home in my grove."

"I don't know what's going on, but we will have time to discuss it later." Liekki gestured towards the door with a slight inclination of her head. Loyalty. Was she loyal to Varaila? She could've given her up, but even thinking it didn't sit right with her. Mayhap it was loyalty that drove her to help her? Images of Efrim, her family, and crew churned around in her head. Even thoughts of Kalama plagued her mind. Could it really be loyalty to her fellow friends and family that bound her? For her clan and the rest of Vulpo for why she decided to go through the trials? She didn't know. Liekki glanced back at Varaila, no longer wanting to think about it. "We really should leave this place."

"Okay," Varaila said without hesitation and followed Liekki out of the grotto.

The two retraced their steps that led them to the healing pools and once they reached the narrow dirt path, they stopped.

"Where to now?" Varaila asked. "I have to get far away from here. Acoris is my father, yet he isn't the only one who's searching for me. There's more. A lot more. Especially since the Twilight Grove had gone rogue and entered a contract with that dreadful Timos."

"Timos? Who is that?"

"He's the soulbind... what you would call life mate of the one who controls Le Carnaval du Malheur. Timos is a dangerous creature, born of the shadows and darkness. He feeds on the essence of those who lives. The very spirits and souls he consumes gives him life. He's similar to vampires, but he doesn't require blood to survive."

An icy chill skittered down Liekki's spine as she thought about the coastal town that was empty. The carnaval was there. She remembered the pull it had on her and she didn't want to go near it. She wanted to stay far away from there. "Where are we? I know you said we are in Dryemia, but the last I saw of that dreadful carnaval was near the Bijou. How did it get in Dryemia?"

"It moves. It's on the edge of our borders now, unable to pass through our wards. Not far from the Twilight Grove and where Vulpo begins."

The news didn't sit well with Liekki. She had an inkling that the carnaval was the key to what she was looking for. Kalama's words rung clear in her head and she knew that she would have to not heed them. Then it dawned on her. "You know how to take the wards down, don't you?"

"Yes," Varaila said. "I will take the knowledge to my death before I let it fall into the hands of Acoris and the Twilight Grove. That dreadful carnaval can not get what it wants. It's not a product of this world."

"No, it's a product of Drekra, I believe."

Varaila shook her head. "No... this is older. Much older"

"Whatever it is... I think I need to go there to find this stone. I don't believe in coincidences. I keep hearing about this carnaval and that is a blazing sign in my eyes."

Varaila stood there silently while she stared off into the distance. Liekki could see the thoughts running through her mind because those same thoughts were scouring through hers. This hasking stone, it had to be inside the tents of that carnaval.

"I never got your name, friend. What is it?"

"It's Liekki, but my friends call me Blaze."

Grinning, Varaila held out her arm. "Blaze suits you."

Liekki clasped Varaila's outstretched arm before she brought her in for an embrace, then released her. "So, Princess, where to now?"

Varaila let out an exasperated groan, tinged with a small laugh. "Don't call me Princess. I hate that title so much. Just call me Varaila or V, if you will."

"V it is," Liekki said, before squinting at the sudden emergence of a stone archway. Odd and out of place. The center of it was clear, allowing Liekki to see right through it. "What is that? It just appeared out of nowhere."

Varaila looked at where Liekki was staring. "It's no telling. These woods of ours are enchanted and always seem to know what one may need when they don't even know what they're looking for."

Liekki moved away from Varaila and walked towards the arch. She put her hand through its center and there was nothing there. Just an empty space. She looked over her shoulder and shrugged. "It's just a stone arch," she said, then stepped through it.

The arch was triggered, and its magic grabbed hold of Liekki. A loud scream escaped from her lips as something pulled and tugged at her from behind, pulling Liekki away. The world around her rushed by so fast that everything was a blur. The last thing she saw was Varaila staring at her with her wide cobalt blue eyes and her name falling off her lips.

CHAPTER 23

U nder the cloak of night, Kalama and Efrim had returned to Vulpo. They traveled fast as they could from the coast of the Bijou. Traveling through the wind currents, she and Efrim reached the sacred island in the dead of night. There was an eerie silence that permeated the atmosphere, and it had reached the heart of Vulpo. Even in silence, Kalama could hear the unspoken. The words that were and were no more. The melodic trills of the nightingales or the rhythmic chirps of the thrushes on the tiny island were absent and missed. Even the haunting and eerie screeches from the night hawks and nightjars that found solace at night were silent. It was a deadly silence that had Kalama's nerves on edge.

As they took their time crossing the bridge, she was met with the smell of death on the wind. It had a metallic tang to it, causing her lips to curl when it hit her tongue. Kalama stopped midways and held up a hand. Her ears twitched forward, and she took a better look at what they were walking into. The small island was dark and not just because it was nighttime. Usually there were lumo lights all around the cliffs, so one would know where they were without slipping over the side. Even those weren't lit, giving off any light. No one moved about and finding the first guard post empty didn't reassure her feelings. Thinking hard, she knew that time was precious, and she had to come up with a plan. A thought crossed her mind, but she quickly dismissed it. No one had to tell her because she had been around long enough to know that something was very wrong.

"Keep your eyes open. I don't like this," she told Efrim. Kalama glanced backwards at the Nightsong guard and look beyond where he stood. Back to the empty space that should have had two of her guards on duty.

"My eyes are always open, Elder." He pulled out the daggers from their sheaths he wore at his waist. The steel glinted under the moonlight. Efrim looked at the elder. With a calmness that didn't seem natural, he spoke a promise. "Let whoever comes for us taste the sharp metal of my blades. It's been a while since I've bathed them in blood. For they are thirsty and I want to let them get their fill while getting drunk off the scarlet life essence of my enemies."

Kalama stared at Efrim with a strange look in her eyes. "I pray we don't need them. Bloodshed isn't the answer to everything."

"Yet, it's the answer to what will happen if need be tonight." He jutted his chin forward. "I'll watch your back. Nothing will happen to you."

Kalama laughed. She clasped both her hands together and slowly spread them apart. Creating what looked like a long staff made from hard ice. Azure tendrils coiled around the staff, constantly in motion. "You know I can handle myself just as well. Trust me. Although my staff is made of ice, it's strong enough that it won't break."

Efrim acknowledged the unspoken words. "Even yet, I will still be back here, watching your back."

"Very well," Kalama said, leaving well enough alone. "Stay close."

She guided him the rest of the way on the swaying bridge, while the soft lapping waves in the waters below were deceiving at a glance. They were treacherous and its currents were deadly. If one were to fall into the waters, very few would have survived it.

Reaching the entrance to the small island proper, Kalama's gaze darted around before proceeding forward. She stuck to the path that would lead them beyond the sacred tree and to the small building where she and the other two elders kept watch.

"Where is everyone?" Efrim asked. "Where are the acolytes?"

He got his answer after a few more steps. The few acolytes who were under the Elders' watch were spread out on the ground, forming a circle. Each one had their throats slit. Their lifeless eyes stared upward at the night sky, forever unseeing. Kalama gasped at the sight. The vice grip of pain squeezed her heart. They were innocent vulpiians who did everything to honor the Mother Goddess and their spirit gods and goddesses. She didn't understand who would do such a thing. She had prayed that the island would be untouched by the foulness that had seeped into Vulpo. Looking around at the dead, she knew that the time for inaction had long past.

"Why would anyone do this?" Kalama whispered. Angry that she was too late to help her acolytes. "What is the meaning of this?"

"I'm not sure why, but we need to find the other Elders. It's too quiet. Shouldn't they be here too?"

Kalama's head shot up. When she left, the others were secure because of all the unrest and rioting that was going on. There was no reason for them to have left the sacred island unless they were betrayed. Alarmed, "The guards!"

She darted towards the small sanctuary. No one knew the inner workings of the sanctuary but the sacred three and their sworn acolytes. Together, they entered the small temple. Efrim stopped to look around, but Kalama ran straight to the back. Elders Nikesh or Salibas were nowhere around.

"I don't see the Elders," Efrim said.

"There's one more place they could be," Kalama said while shoving furniture out of the way. "Watch the door."

"Already done, Elder," Efrim assured her.

After searching his side of the small sanctuary, he turned back to the widely opened door and stood watch. At the back of the small temple behind an altar, Kalama shoved pieces of furniture out of the way. After making some space, she knelt down and pressed a button that was discreetly hidden at the lower bottom of the wall. A release of air sounded, then a grinding noise replaced the puff of air. A door hidden in the wall slid open, revealing a stairwell that led downwards.

Kalama had an inkling of what she would find in their quarters, but she didn't want to face it alone. Seeing her acolytes, all strewn about like pieces of trash, had her in a dark mood. She looked back over her shoulders. "Efrim," she called out. "Come with me."

The guard only gave a curt nod and went to her. Choosing to keep his daggers out, he reached Kalama's side. "Are we going down there?"

"Yes. Down there are our private quarters if we must stay on the island for more than a day. It is our living spaces whiles here. If Nikesh and Salibas aren't up here, they would be down there. If they're not down there, then I'm afraid we... no, they have betrayed me."

It was something she didn't want to think about, but she did, anyway. She and the other elders didn't quite get along, especially after the choosing ceremony. She didn't know how many times she told them she didn't want Liekki 'Blaze' Nightsong to be their chosen, but there was nothing they could do about it. The spirits had chosen, and it was their duty to follow.

Kalama followed the stone carved spiral stairs to the bottom with Efrim close at her back. It was dark where there should have been lumo lights giving off enough light to see. She bit her bottom lip, worried even more. Danger was on the wind and she didn't know in what form it was coming.

If there were still intruders, she didn't want to alert them to her presence. She motioned for the guard to follow her. Thankful that they could see fine in the dark. Together they moved in silence, careful to watch their steps as they maneuvered through, knocked over and destroyed pieces of furniture. Kalama had prayed that no one would have found this place, but it was evident, it was tainted too.

Who would do such a thing?

Moving down the hall, everything below was circular in design. For one new to the island, the mazelike halls would be confusing, but not to her. She knew exactly where they were going. Reaching the second ring, she found the room that belonged to Salibas. Carefully, Kalama opened the door, but had trouble opening it all the way. Something heavy was pushed against it. Lowering her shoulders, she put her weight behind it and pushed harder.

The door opened and Kalama slipped on something wet underneath her feet. She flailed as she tried to regain her balance. Efrim was right behind her and reached out and grabbed her, steadying her, so she wouldn't fall to the ground.

"Thank you," Kalama said, a little breathlessly. She looked down at what was blocking the door and let out a sigh of defeat. "Oh no. Not you, too."

"Elder Salibas," Efrim confirmed. He stared hard at the dead vulpiian whose eyes someone plucked out. His throat was slit like the others. "Look at his neck. His throat was slit, too."

"Yes. Just like the ones who were found dead at the temples entrances on Temple Row. This almost has a ritualistic feel to it. I don't understand why anyone would do this. Especially now."

"We will figure it out soon enough," Efrim assured her. "This can't continue on."

"You're right. This can't continue on. Seeing poor Salibas here like this, I've already come to the conclusion of how we might find Nikesh," Kalama said, dejected. "His room is just a few doors down."

Kalama left the room and went further down the hall. Her mind was filled with so many thoughts. Both ill and good, but mostly ill thoughts. Wondering on who would do such ill deeds on holy ground. Someone who didn't care about blaspheming everything they as Vulpiians were. A name popped into her head at the thought and she prayed to all who listened that she wasn't right.

She stopped in front of another door and took a deep breath, then opened it on the exhale. This time, it wasn't hampered by anything and opened smoothly. Kalama went further into the room to find Nikesh dead as well. He wasn't strewn about on the ground. They propped him up against the wall. His hands were cutoff and placed in his lap. His eyes were staring forward and his mouth was opened wide in a frozen scream. She looked closer and found that his tongue was missing. Kalama shuddered at the sight. It was wrong and horrible.

"There's a darkness here that I didn't truly feel until we came into this room. His throat isn't slit like the others." Kalama's eyes searched until she spotted what she suspected and pointed. "His heart is missing. You know what this means?"

Efrim shifted on his feet, careful with what he wanted to say. "Yes, unfortunately I do. Let's get this stone you came here for and get out of here. Whoever did this will come back looking for you because it's not done until all three of the Sacred Elders are dead."

Kalama nodded in agreement. "My quarters are in the next hall. It should be there."

They left Nikesh's room and hurried to the next hall. They didn't come across anyone else, and Kalama was thankful for it. She reached her room and was careful as she entered the space. Her personal wards hadn't been disturbed. Whoever attacked the island didn't make it that far. She rushed around her space while Efrim kept watch at the door.

Kalama found her leather bag and grabbed the few items she would need. She also picked up the Hasking Stone that was tied to the one that Liekki was searching for in her trials. Efrim looked back at her as she grabbed the stone off the shelf. It was glowing the color orange as she picked it up.

"She's entered the challenge," Kalama stated. "It has started. Liekki has four days to find this one's counterpart."

Efrim stared at the crystalline stone and watched as the glowing orange morphed into a shade of royal blue. "It's turning colors."

The Elder let out a cry of joy. Her eyes sparkled with a hope she didn't have just moments ago. "I think she passed her first test. Blue means she is in good standing and will stay this way if she continues to pass them. If there's trouble, it will change colors. Pray it never turns black." She carefully put the stone inside of the bag she was holding. "Once we get to safety, I'll tell you all about it."

"Where are we to go? No where is safe in Vulpo right now?"

"We're going to my home. I have safe places underneath. We won't be found. I just hope you don't mind the cold."

Efrim chuckled. "No Elder. I don't mind the cold at all."

CHAPTER 24

L iekki landed on the hard packed ground with a loud thud. This time she was aware and covered her head with her arms, protecting it from getting hit again. Too bad she couldn't say the same for the rest of her body. Everywhere hurt all over. Laying on her back, Liekki looked up at the strange portal she had gone through and watched it disappear.

Slowly, she sat up and stared all around. She was still in a forest, but these woods seemed more familiar to her. Just as familiar as the mountains that were in the distance. A surge of joy washed over her. She was either in Vulpo or close to its borders. Not that it mattered, because she was close to home and that was enough for her.

Standing up, Liekki checked for any injuries and found none. Once she was sure she wasn't being watched, she took off and searched to see exactly where she was at. Liekki wasn't a stranger to hiking because it allowed her to think, and thinking was good for her. It gave her time to put into perspective everything that had happened so far. Ever since she had entered the house and opened the door that led her back to where she was.

She remembered something about four days to but was unsure exactly what or why. Glancing up, the night was giving way to day. Flashes of her needing to find something started to fade from her mind. Thinking back to what happened with Varaila and Acoris, there was no doubt in her mind that when the strange door appeared, it meant she passed some test. She did something right. Was it because she was loyal to a stranger she had never met before? Varaila was nice. Liekki knew the dryem princess didn't deserve the unfortunate luck she had. With Queen Cirrha as her mother and Acoris as a father. Varaila almost had it just as bad as she did.

Liekki came to an abrupt stop.

The correlation between Varaila's situation and her very own was too close for comfort. Diev Nightsong was as wicked as could be, yet her mother was a victim, just like Liekki thought of herself. Despite her rebelliousness, her mother still tried to keep her safe in any way she could. Even her mentor, Kalama, had come to her senses and did her best to help her at the end so Liekki could protect herself. Liekki understood that being loyal to one didn't mean the end of all. She was loyal to her crew, even if one of them betrayed her to Mezal. She gained a deeper understanding of herself from the encounter.

A faint and subtle sound carried by the wind had caught Liekki's attention and pulled her out of her thoughts. She listened carefully. Her head swept back and forth as she quietly searched the area. Needing to know where the sound was coming from. Without thinking, prompted by the whispers, Liekki followed the soft voices.

On the outskirts of the forest, she trekked along a narrow stretch of an old trail, more than likely made by a group of wulverns. Creatures that were similar to an ancient breed of wolves and dark hound hybrids. She knew they kept to the edges of the forest and normally kept to their small packs unless something or someone bothered them.

The sun slowly made its ascent across the sky, giving her plenty of light to see. It was a long walk. Uneventful, but it was enough that her body had grown tired and hungry. It had been a long time since she had eaten anything or had anything to drink. By the time she reached the end of the trail, the sun was fully up, her mouth was parched, and her stomach twisted with hunger. She needed to find food.

She could shift.

Even in her true form, she didn't want to taste the raw meat of a hunt. She hated it and only did it when it was absolutely necessary.

She leaned against the trunk of a tree and rested for a minute. The whispering voices had stopped. After catching her breath, Liekki looked up while her back was against the tree and muttered a curse under her breath. She couldn't believe it.

"How do they move so much?" Liekki said out loud while staring at the very thing she had hoped not to come across again. From afar, she stood there and listened to the whispers that called to her on the wind again. This time, they were much louder. It was the siren's sound that was as dangerous as a dagger being held to her throat. Kalama and Efrim both said to not go anywhere near the carnaval, but she needed to know if they were hiding the stone. She always trusted her gut instincts, and they were telling her what she sought was beyond those finely made wrought-iron gates. There had to be a reason the blasted thing kept showing up wherever she was.

Her stomach made obscene rumbling sounds and was the answer to the unspoken question sitting on her tongue. She had no choice. She had to go inside. Besides, Kalama nor Efrim were nearby to stop her. It couldn't be that bad? Maybe they had food.

Driven by hunger, she glanced around to make sure she wasn't being followed. Liekki made the first step towards the black gates that stood tall and imposing. There was an eerie ambiance that hung thickly in the air. The hair on the back of her neck rose a little. A prickling sensation rippled across her skin, which made her feel slightly on edge. There was so much wrong with what she saw, yet Liekki pushed down the urge to run away.

She took another step forward and another. Behind the dark gates was a thick cloud of gray fog and mist, but she knew they only hid what couldn't be seen to an outsider. She could hear the voices. They whispered sweet words and harsh threatening ones, but no words ever put fear in her heart like her father's words could. There was no comparison. The laughter and the strange music that wove a tempting tale through its notes invited her in. So, Liekki took another step. And another.

The only thing Liekki could see beyond the mists was the giant tent towering above shrouded buildings beside it. Unable to see what they were from outside, she knew the only way was to go inside. The snapping of cloth in the wind drew her cautious gaze back to the gigantic structure. Its black and blood red striped dome was high enough that dark spires made with the same finely made wrought iron marked each side of the dome. As if it was a cradle holding it up. She looked closer and found the iron spires were oddly shaped into creatures that seemed to watch everything. Quickly looking away, her gaze continued downward until the building was lost in the fog hovering over the ground. It had obscured everything from the naked eyes.

Liekki moved closer until she reached the metal gate with its creaky hinges. It slowly opened for her. An invitation. A warning echoed in her mind, but she brushed it aside. The heavy rhythm of her heart pounded a fierce beat behind her ribcage. The sound thundered in her ears. She hoped it was only the excitement that had her anxious and her blood flowing with anticipation. But she knew better. It never failed. Her body always reacted this way before she had a job with her crew. This time was no different. Just a different type of job. Finding a gem was all the same, yes. But this was a giant gem that would get her out of the trials.

The odd trickling of something in the back of her mind told her she needed to go back, but it warred with the well known stubborn streak of hers. Without another thought, the unrelenting gut feeling propelled her to move forward. It was as if an external force controlled her legs and feet. Even if she tried to fight against it, it wouldn't do any good. Giving in, she let them lead her beyond the gates and inside of the Carnaval du Malheur.

Everything was dark and muted. Varied shades of gray smoke and mist surrounded her. There was nothing she could do to make it go away. She tried conjuring her foxfire, but it did no good. Frowning, she tried again. Every single time she called it to her, it sputtered out. Leaving nothing but endless fog in its wake. She turned in circles as she continued forward. Her mind wandered and her thoughts raced. Imagining what awaited her once, she pushed through the veil.

It didn't take long to find out what it was.

Her breath caught as everything came to life before her and the mists parted to reveal what lay beyond. Her amber-colored eyes darted from one thing to another. Twisting paths led the festival goers down many directions. Each one passing by the many tents and rugged buildings that ranged from large to small. Each had a life of its own and strange, runic type symbols on the outside of them. If she stared long enough, perhaps she could decipher them. There was something familiar about the runes, but she couldn't figure out why or where she had even seen them before.

Along the winding paths were carts with prizes of all sizes and games for every age. Every kind of race of creatures that made up

Eldritch was in attendance. It was full of eumens and silently she mouthed a word of thanks that she wasn't alone. She saw a few werewolves, elves, orcs, and even a dragon. Shifters of all kinds and even the striped skinned felines that walked on two legs.

The air carried a hint of excitement. The scent of savory foods and extremely sweet breads and treats. Yet there was something else underneath. A hint of decay that reminded her of death. She looked around and there were so many that mulled about, but they walked past her as if she wasn't there. Lost inside of their own dreamscape. Oblivious to anything around them but what they were seeing or feeling.

Dreamscape...

Liekki studied and focused on everything around her. Seeing but not seeing. At the corner of her eyes, something was there, but what? It seemed like a familiar shadow had passed her by, but couldn't tell for sure. She didn't know. Then whatever it was, had flitted away. Maybe it would come back. Would she remember what it was if it did?

No longer comfortable standing still like a statue, Liekki moved about. When she became stuck between going left or right, she chose the left side. There were larger buildings and less eumens in that direction, which made her decision a little easier.

"Would you like a pie? They're filled with the most delicious meat," an older dryem female called out.

Liekki had considered passing her by, but she stopped and stared at the dryem. The old one's eyes were milky white. A subtle hint of old magic surrounded the dryem that she almost missed it. Tilting her head to the side, she couldn't stop staring. She never seen an old dryem before. The euman must have been ancient. The dryems were a long-lived race, just like the Vulpii.

Liekki's gaze softened after chiding herself for seeming rude. How would she know anything about dryems when she hadn't seen many of them before in her life? Still, she was curious about the old one. "How long have you been here?"

The dryem chuckled, then coughed. It sounded harsh and filled with phlegm. "I reckon I've been here a long time now." A faraway look crossed her face. She went silent for a few minutes before she spoke again. "Long enough where I can't even remember."

"Are you well?"

The dryem shook her head. Years of pain and worry filled her eyes. She smiled, but it didn't quite reach her eyes. Her voice lowered as she spoke. "No one is well if you've found yourself in this place. No one leaves this place either. Do well and guard your spirit, lest the darkness snatch it away."

"Wh-What? What are you on about?"

"Excuse me?" the old one said. "I asked if you would like to try one of my meat pies? I made them myself. They're really good."

Liekki's head tilted to the side. An uncomfortable thought formed, then disappeared. "I didn't think Dryem ate meat."

The old one shrugged. "Does me no good if I did or didn't anymore. I'm no longer connected. The land and the primordials are no longer within my reach." She grabbed a flaky pastry puff and held it up. "Meat pie? They're really tasty. I made sure you can taste the spices. One bite won't hurt. Come on and try it."

Liekki took a step backwards. She didn't know what was wrong with the old one. All she knew was that there was something wrong with her and she didn't dare eat her pies. "I'm not hungry," she lied. "I best get going."

The old one chuckled before it became a full-blown laugh that made Liekki shudder. She rushed away from her, but the old one's laughter still rung in her head. She stumbled into someone and she looked down to find two kits staring at her. One had bright yellow eyes and the other sky-blue eyes. Both had white, fuzzy ears and fur. They were twins. Their tales were bushy and the mark of Clan Sky was on their foreheads. They yipped, then hopped around in their spots before turning around and ran away from her.

"HEY," Liekki shouted. "Wait up. Stop!"

They didn't listen. She muttered a curse under her breath. "I'm probably going to regret this," she said and ran after them.

The two vulpiian kits darted between the legs of others on the path without stopping. They kept going, intent on getting away. Everything passed by in a blur as Liekki chased them down. She didn't know where they were bound to but she wanted to know who they were and how did they get there. Maybe they could even help her. Eventually, the twins came to a stop and yipped again. Liekki skidded to a halt, dust flying underneath her feet. "Why did you run off?" she asked them in the common Vulpiian tongue.

The two kits yipped again but didn't shift to their two-legged form. She couldn't tell if they were old enough to shift yet. "How long have you been here?"

They didn't answer. Instead, they sat down on their haunches. Their wide, jeweled like eyes stared at her as if they could see right through her. The one with yellow eyes stood up and trotted towards the building that Liekki didn't even see was there until at that moment.

The building was isolated, and there was no one else around them. It stood tall and regal. Made of dark stone. Long, narrow windows that reflected everything in like mirrors. In front of it stood a crumbling water fountain that, surprisingly, still worked and had fresh running water.

The blue-eyed kit stood on all fours, shook out its fur, then went and rubbed the side of Liekki's leg with its body before it trotted towards the fountain. It glanced back at her and yipped, then took a drink from the fountain. Mouth still parched, the water looked incredibly refreshing to her. She desperately needed a drink.

"Are you sure it's nothing wrong with the water?" Liekki asked the young kit. It hopped up and down and yipped again. She was pretty sure that its latest yip was a yes. It couldn't be as bad as the pies were. Everything about those pies and the dryem was just wrong. She could find food later. Water was more of a pressing need. She hurried to the fountain where the kit waited and shifted to her true form and drunk from the water. It was cold as it went down. She drank until she couldn't drink anymore. She yipped back at the kit, giving her thanks. It wagged its tail before taking off toward the yellowed eyed one.

Liekki glanced up and realized the two sky foxes were standing in front of the door of the building with mirrored windows. She darted towards them and stopped next to the two. Above the door were those same runic symbols she saw everywhere else. This time, the runes shifted from the distorted fuzziness to that of words she could actually read.

Shocked, she shifted to her two-legged form and read the words out loud. "House of Mirrors."

The twin kits yipped before both going to the door and rubbed up against it. Liekki stared at the door. It was a glass door with the same mirrored reflections. She pointed at the door and looked down at the two sky foxes. "Am I to go in there?"

Both hopped up and down, then yipped again.

She released a long breath. "Fine. Will I see you two again? You really shouldn't be running around in a place like this. Where are your mother and father? Your family? How'd you get here?"

They both sat on their back haunches and stared. A weird sensation brushed against her mind before a few images flooded the inside of her head. Trees. A forest. Snow was everywhere. Stained with bright red blood. A female vulpii lay dead in the snow next to a large stone near a cave. The two kits huddled beside her.

Another image flashed in her mind and it was further inside of the darkened cave. A male vulpii with yellow eyes wide open lay dead with its throat sliced open. A familiar thought tugged at her mind and she couldn't figure out what it was. She hated the unclarity.

"Your family is gone," she said to the twin foxes. That much she could tell from the mental images sent to her. "I'm truly sorry. Is that how you ended up here?"

More images brushed across her mind. The two kits running off when a mob of Clan Night vulpiians came their way, flinging death spells in their direction. They ran hard. Traveling across Vulpo into the north, where somehow the strange gates appeared to them. The twins knew they had no other choice. Either end up dead like their parents or take their chance with the mysterious iron gates. They took their chance and went inside. The two had been there ever since.

Liekki knew she couldn't leave them there by themselves. The twisted carnaval was a perversion of what normal festivals should look like. Whatever was going on in Vulpo wasn't good, either. Somehow, it had something to do with the darkness that permeated this place like a sponge. Lifting her head, getting a better look at the House of Mirrors, she knew what she had to do. "I gotta go in there, but you two stay out here. Be on watch and I'll come back and find you. Then we'll figure out a way to get out of here."

Kalama would know what to do with them. They were from her clan. She may have known the twins' family. All she could do was try to get them to safety. Excited, the twins both yipped, wagged their tails, then got comfortable on the ground. Smart enough to not get too close to the door, but far enough where they could get up and run off if they needed to if there was any danger. Not wanting to waste any more time, Liekki reached out, opened the door, and went inside.

The entrance was elegant. Luxurious, if not a touch old and outdated. They covered the furniture under white sheets. Unused for a long time. Cobwebs were everywhere, and she knew the only occupants now were spiders. She shuddered. She hated spiders. The house reminded her of those she saw in Ravenfalls before her visit turned sour. Still, something told her not to linger in the foyer.

Liekki moved quickly beyond the front of the house and made her way towards the hall. The house was a likely place for the Hasking stone, even though she had no clue what it looked like. She wandered all the way down the hall until she reached the end. She could only go two ways. Left or right. She took the right and kept going. Reaching another area, she entered what looked to be a study or a receiving room. Carefully looking around, she noticed an enormous fireplace that took up one side of the wall. It was cold and unused. The rest of the room was exactly why the place was called the House of Mirrors.

Mirrors covered every single inch of wall space. Her eyes darted around before she looked up to find the ceiling was covered with mirrors, too. She took a step further into the room when the door behind her slammed shut. She jumped nearly out of her skin. Before she could do anything about the sealed door, a blazing fire roared to life in the fireplace, lending her light to see.

"This isn't good," she whispered. Alarmed, she spun around, her back to the fireplace. Liekki stared at the thousands of reflections of her mirrored self. Their amber gazes glared at her as the flames danced behind her. Suddenly, she didn't like the room or house and wanted to leave. Liekki hurried to where the door was, but in an instant, it was no longer there. Just another seamless mirror.

"What in Drekra's name..." she said, before rushing to the center of the room, examining all the mirrors. "There has to be a way out of here. There has to be."

She darted towards the mirrors. Ignoring how the shadowed reflections of herself made her extremely uncomfortable. Ignored how some reflections didn't move exactly how she did. Probing the mirrors with her magic, looking for any weaknesses. Searching for any gaps where air could come through. Liekki searched every corner and crevice until she couldn't anymore. There was no hope for her. She was stuck in that chamber room.

Frustrated, Liekki let out a soul weary deep scream. The sound bounced off the mirrors and strangely echoed back to her. There was no way she could fail. Determined to get out of there, she went back to studying the mirrors while doing her best to ignore the strange feeling of being watched. She knew there had to be a way out of that damned room, and she was determined to find it.

Sweat beaded down her face as the room became warmer. The heat from the fireplace quickly washed the coldness away. Now, she prayed she didn't burn up. At first, after coming into the room, Liekki didn't feel comfortable touching the mirrors, but now something was tugging at her mind. She had to get out of there. She had to find a way out of the room, and then out of the house. What she was looking for couldn't be there. The house was a trap, and the twins led her to it.

"I'm a damned fool," she said while touching the mirrors and pushing, hoping that some were false and were actually doors.

"A fool. Yes, you are…" a voice that sounded like hers but not quite hers said.

Liekki looked into the mirror she was standing in front of. Behind her, one of the thousand reflections smiled at her. Distorted and wrong. The blood in her ears roared. The shadowed reflection stepped out of the mirror and stood there watching her. Liekki stilled. She could feel the darkness curling around the shadowed imitation of herself. "Who and what are you?"

"I am you. You are me."

"NO!" Liekki shouted. It was wrong. There was no way she was that thing. "You are not me."

The thing smiled her smile, yet it wasn't. It was cruel. Evil. Malevolent. "No, perhaps not. I am a better version of you."

"I doubt that," Liekki said, taking another step back."

The thing cocked its head to the side as if listening to something only it could hear. Its eyes darkened. "Since you don't believe me, allow me to introduce myself. I am called Fear and now you will learn why I'm the better version of you."

Faster than Liekki's eyes could see, the shadowed reflection conjured up a perverted version of her foxfire. It was black and purple, reminiscent of the shadows surrounding it. Before she could even move, it lashed out like a whip and attacked Liekki. Unable to move out of the way in time, the shadowed fire struck across her chest. She let out a loud, pain filled cry as she stumbled and fell back to the mirrored wall. Her chest felt like it was on fire. She gasped for a breath and even that hurt. The pain was unbearable.

"The only way you're leaving this room is with your death," the darker version of herself said. "And your death is mine to claim."

CHAPTER 25

"This isn't real. Can't be real. Reflections can't talk."
Liekki tried to reason with herself as the pain throbbed from the reflection's attack. A paralyzing grip took hold of her. She couldn't breathe. Everything hurt all over. Liekki wanted it all to stop.

"Oh, it's very real."

"You," she gasped. "You can't be real. You are not me."

The shadowed reflection laughed as it attacked her again. There was nothing she could do but take the assault. Take the beating that shouldn't have felt real. The thing grabbed the front of her tunic, lifted her off the floor, and flung her across the room. Her back crashed into another mirror, but it didn't shatter. Radiating pain shot out from her spine. She hit the floor with a loud grunt. Liekki tried to reach out to her magic. Anything to help her, but it wouldn't answer. She couldn't even feel it. There must have been something she could do.

Focus... Harness your calm.

Liekki remembered the words from Efrim. Words he taught her right before she left him. She took a deep breath to steady her nerves. Everything around her was so chaotic while she was there on the floor in the middle of the storm. She couldn't fight if she was unfocused. Efrim kept telling her over and over that her mind had to be clear from all clutter. She didn't truly understand then. Now she understood. Liekki continued her deep breaths, then exhaled when she finally had found her center.

"You aren't good enough to be like me," the shadow taunted.

It paced back and forth next to her. Unaware of the change that had taken hold of Liekki. "What makes you think you can defeat me? Look at you. You can't even counter anything I throw at you."

The thing scoffed as it paced in circles in front of her. Liekki tried to sit up, but everything swirled around her as she collapsed back to the ground.

"You are worthless," the reflection said, continuing its tirade. "Try as you might, you couldn't even stand up to our father when he berated you. You have no courage. You are a weakling. Fodder for the spirits. For the gods. You can't even be honest with yourself about the truth. The truth is that our father was right. Our mother should have covered your face with her hand and smothered you when she saw your face at birth."

The shadowed reflection words had hit home. Her father didn't know how much those words hurt when he said them to her. Yet, they stayed with her and constantly replayed itself in her head ever since. Try as she might, there was no way to purge them. It was a wound. A scar that was on her soul.

Liekki knew the truth of the reflection's words. It hurt just as much as she physically hurt. Was that her problem? Unable to be honest with herself and her abilities. Was this why it was time for her kind to go through the trials again? Did her kinsmen even know what being honest was about? Or how to be trustworthy? So many questions that beget more questions. But none gave her the answers she wanted to know. How to get out of the horrible house.

Vulpii faced constant disdain throughout Eldritch. Yes, Liekki knew there were good ones out there, but it was always the foul ones that made the rest look bad. Looking within herself, she wasn't one of the good ones either, if she were to be truthful. She may not have been as bad as the others, but taking things that didn't belong to her was a crime. Sneaking into homes that didn't belong to her was wrong. Those actions were the reason she ended up in the mess she was in back home and had her on the run. Her family, for sure, even if they were nobility, didn't get out of this untouched. The head of her family lived his life as an upstanding citizen, but underneath all the smiles and laughs was a vulpii filled with darkness, hatred, and cruelty.

Yes, there was something terribly wrong with Vulpo and its citizens.

A drakgo shame.

The shadow was right about her, but that wasn't all who she was. Liekki refused to let fear of the truth plague her anymore.

It was important for her to confront the truth about herself. She glanced upwards at the distorted reflection that was an imitation of her and shook her head. Finally, taking the steps to be a better version of herself. Going on the way she had been wasn't the right way. She understood that now. It wasn't who she was or how Vulpiians should be.

"*My* mother, she was right about one thing. My mother had love in her heart and let me live." Liekki slowly got to her feet and stood upright in front of her reflection. No longer afraid of its words, she knew in her heart she could fight the thing and win. She didn't want to die there in that twisted house filled with distorted pieces of herself. It could drive a vulpii insane.

The perverted version of herself took a step back. Its eyes darted back and forth. Liekki tapped into her reserve of power. The inner strength to survive and protect herself from the new attack. Once the shadow realized what was happening, it renewed its attack. This time, Liekki went on the offensive instead of taking it and praying the assault would stop.

"I am not weak," Liekki said through clenched teeth. She raised her right arm out in front of her, palm facing forward. "I know I'm not perfect, but who is? I am a product of my environment, but no more. I no longer fear that part of me. I know I can be honest with myself and I accept that."

Flames burst from her palm in a roaring stream. The shadowed reflection tried to ward itself, but was too late. The thing's piercing screamed was so loud that Liekki's ears bled. She fell to her knees as she kept the raging outpouring of flames coming from her. She wanted to get rid of any evidence of the thing that was her, but not her.

Exhausted and still in pain, Liekki called back the fire once the screams stopped. She fell over, her hands hitting the ground to keep her steady from completely stumbling over. She gasped for air, doing her best to catch her breath. Once her racing heart was under control, she looked up at the dark smudge spot on the mirror. Fear was gone. She sighed with relief.

Still looking at the mirror, it began to wobble and shimmer. The distorted black smudge disappeared and the familiar arch appeared. It called to her. This was her way out. Liekki got to her feet and staggered towards the portal and stepped through.

It was night. Her head felt like it was stuffed with cotton. Her entire body hurt, but she didn't know why. Couldn't remember why. Slowly, she turned around, trying to recognize where she was, but nothing was familiar. Two Clan Night Vulpiians stood outside of an all black tent in front of her. They watched her every move, but they said nothing to her.

The sounds of eerie music were everywhere. Laughter and screams reached her ears. A strange mix. Wherever she was, the place was crowded. It wasn't the burrows. There were too many non vulpiians lingering about.

She considered asking the guards, who were still keeping an eye on her. Liekki went towards them and stopped. "Can I ask a question?"

The one on her left spoke. "You can ask all the questions you want, but they're waiting for you inside. You are late."

"Late for what?" She didn't know she was late for anything.

"The meeting. Don't you remember? Kho Nightsong sent for you."

"My father sent for me?" She repeated, struggling to remember. Nothing was coming to mind. It must have been true. "Where are we?"

The guard shifted on his feet before eyeing his partner. "We're just outside of Vulpo, Kha Nightsong. The Rogue and her mate invited the Sacred Three and your family to meet with them. They are the owners of this strange place."

Liekki took a better look at her surroundings. She took a step away from the dark tent and its guards. Wanting to get a better look, she moved with the other eumens. If she was already late, then a few more minutes wouldn't hurt. She passed by a booth that had what she guessed was a seer sitting behind it. The old fox beckoned to her, but Liekki quickly darted away from her. She never trusted them and in this place, it didn't seem right to hear what words or lies she would spill. There was something not quite right with her. With the entire festival grounds. It wasn't festival season, so why was it set up? Unable to understand why it kept bothering her, but she really wanted to know where they were.

Not paying attention to where she was going, Liekki ran into another euman's back. They weren't vulpii, but something else. When they turned to look at her, Liekki realized the euman had pointed ears and long, black braided hair with trinkets entwined in each braid. She had a heart-shaped face. Compared to the others around, she looked as if she was in the wrong place. Strange scars marked her face under her gray eyes. She looked Elven almost. Like she was one of the fae. The euman stared at her, then a pair of blue black feathered wings emerged from her back. Liekki looked even closer and realized there were hints of purple feathers underneath the larger ones. Almost in an ombre colored fashion. The winged euman had dressed in colorful clothes that matched the color of her wings.

"Excuse me," Liekki said in Eldish. "I wasn't paying attention to where I was going. I think I'm lost."

The euman stared before speaking. Her voice was strange and melodic. It was like listening to bells as she spoke. "It's okay. This place is big and easy to get turned around. Which way did you come from?"

Liekki pointed in the direction she came from. "What is this place?"

The euman's lip curved upwards into a smile that didn't quite reach her eyes. "This is the Carnaval du Malheur."

The name sounded familiar to Liekki, and she couldn't remember why. She hated when she forgot things. It drove her crazy. "What are you? I've never seen one of your kind before."

"It doesn't matter what I am any longer, kit of the moon." She cocked her head to the side and closed her eyes. A moment passed before she spoke again. "Your name is whispered on the winds. You are wanted. The others are waiting."

"What others?"

"The ones you tried to run from. Go. Then come see my show afterwards. I'll be in the big tent."

"Your show?"

"Yeah. It's fantastical. You won't want to miss it. It's the biggest show ever. I promise you've never seen the likes before. Trust me." The winged euman looked behind Liekki, then back at her. "I must go. Take care of yourself."

Liekki watched the winged euman take flight, leaving her standing there alone. If she didn't get back soon, those guards were going to come after her. Retracing her steps, she hurried back to where the guards still waited. They pulled the tent's flaps back and allowed her entrance.

Braziers were stationed in the four corners of the tent, giving off enough light to see it was filled with vulpii. Her mother and father, along with her sister, Senia, stood to her left. Efrim was standing near them. To her right, Mezal Irontail and Kalama Brightsun, along with the two other elders, watched her with accusatory glares. Her best friend, Icelia, stood close to her mother and even she wore a frown.

A black wooden table was directly in the center of the tent. Immediately in front of it stood two eumens. One was a Vulpii with black hair and black ears. The crescent mark of Clan Night glowed a strange red on her forehead. Her eyes were a dark red. She wore a black spidersilk dress, and a black chocker about her neck. Behind her, nine black tails fanned out, and each one swished slowly like they were under water.

Next to her was a tall, euman male. His skin was dark as night and his eyes were red as blood. There was a savage and cruel look about him that made her skin crawl. His lips spread into a thin smile that sent chills down Liekki's spine. He wore a matching spidersilk vest and pants that was the same print as the vulpii at his side. She knew then who they were. Rogue and her mate.

"So glad you could finally join us," the strange vulpii said. Her tone was condescending. "I don't have all evening and wasting my time with you is beneath me."

"Then why are you?" Liekki snapped back, not caring if it came out rude.

"Because I was summoned. I must abide all summons."

"What is your name?"

The rogue met Liekki's gaze, her eyes firm with a glint of knowledge that she would never divulge. "My name isn't important. But, if you must insist, you can call me Rogue. It's what I am, based on the rules of our kind."

Her father murmured something under his breath, but she wasn't surprised. He always had something to say. His focus shifted to Rogue, then crossed his arms over his chest. "Can we get this done with? I have business as well. I don't see why our presence is needed."

Her mother placed a soothing hand on her father's arm. His expression twisted into a scowl as he looked down at her. Luya whispered something to him, and his body stiffened. Her father's face scrunched up, before being replaced by an emotionless mask. He patted her hand with his free one. A kind gesture which was odd for him.

"My apologies. Continue. My business can wait."

Shock rippled through Liekki. Her father never apologized to anyone. Who was this vixen that could coax an apology from her cold-hearted father?

"Apology accepted Kho Nightsong." Rogue gestured to the empty seat at the table when she turned back to Liekki. "Take a seat. We don't have much time."

Liekki looked to her mother, then at her father. Their faces were blank. There was no help to come from them. She turned towards the elders and Mezal. Their faces bore the same blank expression.

She didn't like this and didn't want to do it, but something kept tugging at the back her of mind that insisted she had to do it. "Fine," she huffed. "I'll play along with whatever this is." Liekki gestured to the chair and table.

"Good," Rogue said too calmly. "Come and sit. Let this little game begin."

"Game?" Liekki asked. Her brows narrowed with confusion. "I don't like games."

"Life is a game. Whether we like it or not, we all must play it. When we take breath no longer, we have lost. Now sit," Rogue ordered.

No longer wanting to argue, Liekki dragged the chair out and sat. Long shadows cast off from the flames in the brazier gave the inside of the tent an otherworldly atmosphere. She scanned every eumen in the room, meeting their stern gazes and deceptive miens. Whatever this was or whatever they expected of Liekki, she knew she couldn't fail.

She ran a hand across the wood table. Runes were carved around the edges. They seemed familiar, yet she couldn't read what they said. In the center of the table. On its top, deep gouges marred an otherwise pristine surface. Whatever the creature was, Liekki didn't want any parts of being around it with claws like that.

"The name of the game is called *Shadows of Truth*," Rogue said, bringing Liekki out of the mental road she traveled down. "It's a long game, but with our time restraint, we'll leave it to three questions." Rogue looked at everyone standing in the room. "Are you all okay with this?"

A chorus of agreements filled the small space, except for one. Icelia.

"Three isn't enough," Ice said. "Why not five? That should be sufficient and can be done in the allotted time."

Rogue stared at Icelia before shifting her gaze to the others. "Very well."

Shadows passed behind Rogue's eyes, causing Liekki to flinch. She hoped the vixen didn't notice. It reminded her of a time she saw it before, but it wasn't there. No, it was at home, but who was it?

"The game, Shadows of Truth, is a way to discern truth from lies. Your answers will determine if the Elders will cast you off as a rogue. Forever a pariah to Vulpo and the Vulpii. You are what they call a menace to their society and don't value the laws. You do whatever you want to do. Your leaders say you believe you are above them. A thief has no place in Vulpo, Kha Nightsong. Answer truthfully, and you might get to stay in your precious Vulpo."

"If I lie, how would you know?" Liekki asked, not sure of the validity of the game.

"Because I can sense a lie from the truth. It was why I was summoned by the spirits and the Elders. These are your witnesses, so you can't say it wasn't fair when you ultimately fail at this, too."

"I won't fail," Liekki said, determined to make her words truth, even though she didn't feel comfortable with them as they fell off her lips. She took a deep breath and said it again, but with conviction. "I won't fail."

Rogue looked at her mate, whose smirk was wickedly evil. An unspoken understanding passed between the two. She looked at Liekki and snapped her fingers. "Let's get started then."

CHAPTER 26

The darkness that surrounded the festival was nothing compared to the pure enmity and hatred Liekki felt directed at her inside of that tent. It was so thick and palpable she could cut it with her dagger. It crawled over her skin like a thin film of sweat. Irritating physically and mentally.

A harsh wind blew outside of the tent, making the tent's walls shook. The flap of the door flew open. The door's guards quickly closed it. Liekki look behind her, then looked back at the others and Rogue.

"Have you ever stolen from those who could not afford to lose what you took?"

Feeling the weight of everyone's accusatory stares, Liekki wanted to tuck tails and run out of there. But there was no way she could leave. She had to answer the questions. She knew if she told the truth of why she stole, her answers would get her cast out. No longer welcome in the land of her birth. She may have hated the place, but she loved it too. Her relationship with Vulpo was a complicated mix of love and hate.

Her beloved mountains came to mind. Her special place when life became too much. It was her solace and now, if she told Rogue the truth, then being honest would be her downfall. Liekki thought about it even more and knew what she must do.

"I have always been mindful of the ones I targeted," she said. It wasn't a lie. Liekki's targets were always thoughtfully chosen because of who they were. "I made sure my actions didn't put them at risk unnecessarily. What I took, believe me, they wouldn't miss."

Rogue's gaze bore into Liekki. Penetrating the veil of her words. Liekki hoped that the perceptive fox took her answers for what they were. She spoke true. That was what the game was all about, wasn't it? Speaking and telling the truth.

"Your words are gray," Rogue said. "Truth yet not. It seems I may have misjudged you. Yet, I do not detect a lie, because there is more truth than anything. We'll continue."

"What do you mean 'gray'?" her father asked. "There are no gray answers. The answers should be clear as black and white. I already know what those foul words of hers are. They're lies! We will have what we came for Rogue. Don't you forget that."

Rogue's voice was otherworldly, hers and not hers. "You forget your place, Kho Nightsong. You are in my domain and you will respect me while here. Or else."

A loud boom clapped outside the tent. The lightning illuminated the sky so brightly that it was visible from inside the dark tent. Everyone stilled, looking around at each other. Wondering who had lost control. It wasn't normal lightning, no, this was magic made. Liekki could still taste the citrus like tang of it in the air.

She knew who the magic belonged to while everyone else was still trying to figure it out. The same vulpiian had turned around and glared too hard at her.

Under Rogue's uncomfortable gaze, Liekki squirmed under it. Not meeting her gaze, she looked away and found Kalama's ice blues instead. "Can we hurry this along? I have nothing to hide."

Rogue dipped her head in a bow. "Question two. Do you feel remorse for the pain and suffering you have caused your fellow vulpiians when you steal their things? Things that don't belong to you. Priceless heirlooms that belonged to their families and will never see again."

"No," Liekki answered truthfully. "No, I don't. Those vulpiians live in excess. The items may be priceless, but they don't miss them. Whenever I offload those gems and jewelry, the funds and proceeds from the sales go to those who are in need. To those who have no help or pedigree name to lift them up in hard times. Especially after the last one hundred years our people had to deal with."

Liekki turned slightly towards where Kalama Brightsun stood. She hoped her words had some effect on the vixen, but she stood there cold as the ice district she lived in. If it wasn't for her failing, then their people would be better off. She knew this. All of Vulpo knew this. It wasn't fair for those who lost everything during the dark times to be spat on.

She didn't know where the anger rose from, but it was there. Hot in her heart and blood. How could she really sit there and answer the questions thrown at her when it was Kalama who should have been sitting there in her place instead? Every single time anything had gone wrong in Vulpo, the whispers always mentioned her name, Blaze. They blamed her for doing things she didn't even do.

Blaze was a name Liekki was proud of. How come the vulpi-ian leaders and her family couldn't see that? She knew why. All it took was one look at her strange eyes. Her strange fur and hair. Her being different shaped what her life would be the moment she took a breath. Inside the wall of her family's home, life was worse. She knew if one listened to the stone of the mountains of House Nightsong, they would hear her anguish. Feel it. They would breathe in the rage that festered in Liekki's heart.

Every day and every night, the abuse never stopped. If she wasn't being scolded by her father, her siblings sneers and scowls made up for it. There was no rest for the wicked. Liekki knew it. So many days had gone by in her life where it was nothing but chaos. She would kill for a moment of peace. She would steal for that moment of peace.

And she did.

When she couldn't take it any longer, that was when she began to steal. Figuring out the many ways the nobles tried to hide their things from thieves. But Liekki was a clever thief. A smart one who knew how others did things because of the way her father hid things. She started with him, then worked her way to other Clan Night houses. Eventually, all of Vulpo got a taste of Blaze's handiworks. She really didn't feel any remorse. Those nobles got what they deserved.

"And yet, another true," Rogue said. "On to the third question. Have you ever betrayed someone you considered a friend or ally?"

Liekki answered immediately. The answer was a simple one. As far as she was concerned, she could be trusted. "No. I value loyalty. I've never betrayed a friend or ally knowingly."

"You speak of valuing loyalty, yet you aren't really that loyal, are you?" Rogue crooned. "How should others trust you or even consider you trustworthy if you can't even be honest with yourself?"

It was as a red hazed covered Liekki's eyes. "I'm loyal!" she shouted.

Rogue's sinister laugh did nothing to soothe Liekki's nerves. Her brief outburst did nothing for her case. It was she who was on trial, not them. She suddenly didn't want to be there anymore. She wanted to leave and go as far away as she could.

Liekki shot up from her chair and darted to the door. Nervous murmurs filled the tent. But she didn't care. If she left, they couldn't banish her. All of her answers had been truthful. The moment she reached the tent's door flaps, a sharp, needle piercing pain shot through her head. She clenched the sides with her fists as the excruciating ache continued, intensifying with each pulse. Liekki let out a pain filled cry and fell to her knees.

Nightsong. Liekki. Listen to me.

The voice was inside of her head. It sounded familiar, but she was in too much pain to recognize it.

Nightsong!

Liekki cowered as the voice shouted.

"If you walk or crawl out of those flaps, Kha Nightsong, you will fail and become rogue. The mark of your clan and your heritage will burn red as the blood that spills from your veins. Never able to walk the lands of Vulpo ever again," Rogue warned.

"I don't ca-" Liekki started, but was interrupted by Rogue.

"I'd be careful what you say next."

More intense and debilitating pain arced through Liekki's head. She didn't have to worry about finishing the sentence. The world was darkening. She opened her eyes and looked up to find Kalama standing over her. Her gaze piercing hers.

NIGHTSONG!

The room went dark and the only sound Liekki heard was her own harsh breaths. The pain had subsided, but there was no way she could move.

"You are in trouble. What is going on? I can try to help to the best of my abilities," Kalama said.

"Brightsun?" Liekki asked. "Where are you? I can't see you."

"This is the only way. It took too much of my energy to break through to you. Your mental walls are well fortified. Any other time, that would be good and I'd be proud. Right now, not so much. I came to help. You're in danger, kit."

"My entire life is filled with danger. This isn't anything new."

"I had a feeling you wouldn't remember. Sometimes it is a fickle thing."

"What are you on about?"

"I don't have long. Focus. What is going on?"

"I'm about to be banished for being truthful," Liekki shrugged, and even that small motion hurt. *"I feel they rigged the game."*

"What game are you playing?"

"Shadows of Truth."

Kalama cursed under her breath. "Be careful of your answers or you will never get out of there."

The pain had resided.

"But I'm telling the truth."

"Sometimes, the key to being trustworthy to those that matter, Liekki, is deceiving the enemy who would do you all harm," Kalama told her. *"I can't keep this connection any longer. Stay strong. You can do this. If anyone can, it's you."*

The connection broke. Everything slammed back into Liekki. Her back arched off the ground, and air came rushing back into her lungs as she gasped for deep breaths.

What in the world?

"She's back. Let's finish this thing already. I'm going to be late as well," Mezal Irontail grumbled from where he stood.

"Very well," Rogue asked. "You can stay where you are, Blaze. This is another simple question. Can they depend on you on to prioritize the well-being of others over personal gain?"

"Yes. What kind of question is that?" Liekki answered too harshly. But soon as the words slipped off her tongue, she knew them to be a lie.

Rogue nodded. Saying nothing else, the vixen in her spider-silk dress walked around the runed carved table. She made her way towards Liekki and stopped only inches from where she was. "Another lie veiled behind the truth. Do you even know how to be honest? How to be trustworthy to others?"

Rogue's laugh was harsh and condescending. The grating sound irked Liekki's mood. "You're never getting out of here. You will never see home again." Rogue turned to the others. "She is not worthy."

"I knew it," Liekki's father said from afar. A sick satisfaction gleamed in his eyes. "She is the worst of us."

"I should have listened to you, love," her mother said, tears in her eyes. "I had hoped you were wrong. She's not worthy to be a Nightsong. Our daughter."

"She has never been a daughter of mine. Senia is my daughter and true heir. The other children are just spares. This foul thing is an abomination," her father declared.

"Mother!" Liekki yelled. She couldn't believe the words that came out of her mother's mouth. What her father spewed was normal for him. Her mother words- they had stung deeply. Disbelief was etched upon Liekki's face as her head shook from side to side. Denying what her mother had admitted to. "No... this isn't right."

"You are no longer of the vulpiians," Rogue said, as she knelt down beside Liekki. "That is all that matters now. Forever anathema to home. To your family. To your friends and loves."

Rogue's fingers brushed across the mark on Liekki's forehead, leaving a searing burn that sent waves of pain coursing through her. The stone arch door had appeared as she scooted far away from the vixen. There was a gentle pull at her chest. It called to her, but she had to reach it first.

Angry still. Liekki didn't understand how she could have failed. She answered the way of the game. What was she missing? Liekki shifted to her true form and ran towards the mystical door. She hoped for an escape, but as she neared the shimmering gate, it seemed to move further out of reach. Casting a quick glance around, the tent appeared to have expanded. Stretching wider and wider the more she ran towards the mystical door.

Liekki wondered if it was all a trick.

Laughter erupted from behind her as she gave up on the portal that had once pulled at her with a sense of peace. Now the notes were discordant and sharp. Liekki switched directions and darted through the canvas flaps that made up the door of the tent. The fresh, sweet smell of night was a relief compared to the stifling, stale air inside of the tent. Outside, the weighted stares didn't bother her as much. Only thing on her mind was to get far away from them.

Under the forever night sky, Liekki scurried away, trying her best to avoid the guards who hunted her. They gave chase soon after she barged through the tent flaps. She always counted on her instincts and they were screaming at her to get far away from the festival as possible. Dashing between festival goers, Liekki didn't know which way to go. Everywhere she had turned, there were eumens. Tents. Another tent. Another cart. More festival goers. More of everything.

She spotted an unmoving large wagon cart and ran towards it. She jumped into the back and sniffed around. They filled the back with metal poles and sealed boxes. Curious about what was inside the boxes, she shifted back to her two-legged form, keeping one hand partially shifted into a paw and unsheathed her claws. Not worried about others, she couldn't help herself and clawed the box open to see what was inside.

Peering inside it, all she saw were expensive costumes and clothes. From the feel of the costumes, they were spidersilk and could probably fetch a few coins in the burrows.

"No wonder you lost at the game," Icelia said, startling Liekki.

Her head shot up to find her best friend standing there watching her with a disappointed look on her face. "What are you doing here?"

"I came to find you, but I'm not surprised you are going through things that don't belong to you."

"It's not what it looks like. I was just being nosey."

Icelia shook her head. "No, you weren't. I know you better than your own family. Those won't catch for a lot of coin. That's imitation spidersilk."

Liekki shrugged, pretending she didn't care. "I don't have to wear it."

"Walk with me," Icelia said, before stepping away from the cart.

"Alright," Liekki said. She jumped down from the cart and followed her friend.

They walked side by side on the path was empty of others. "You must do better, Blaze."

"Why should I?"

"Because this is not who you are. Stealing is never good and I know. I used to do it with you, but not anymore. This is more than about stealing."

"I don't see how it is more. I'm not the only thief in Vulpo. Why do I get picked on?"

"Because of who you are. Your heritage and your name. Because of your differences. They all go against you right now. You'll always be scrutinized closer than others because of it. I know you do this to rebel, but is it worth being cutoff from all that is you? Be honest with yourself. Can you be transparent with yourself? Can you acknowledge your mistakes? How can you turn these from being a negative and make them become your strengths?"

Liekki heard her friend. She spoke the truth, and the answers came swiftly. Her heart hurt. She was wrong. There was no doubt in that and the fact was, she cared. Even when she said she didn't. She did what she did because she was hurt and inflicted pain on others to make herself feel better. To make what she did seem righteous, when it was nothing but selfish.

"You're right," Liekki agreed. "I can do better than what I'm doing, Ice. This isn't truly me, but I let anger and pain drive my actions. And I've hurt others in the process. It was wrong. I can be better. I promise I will be better."

Icelia smiled and embraced Liekki in a hug. "Now you're starting to see what I have always seen in you."

The familiar pull of peace and joy tugged at Liekki's center. She looked up to find the mystical shimmering door had reappeared. Long gone were the discordant notes. This time, it urgently called out to her. Liekki eyed her friend.

"Go," Icelia said. "We'll hang out soon enough."

Liekki nodded, then walked to the portal and stepped over its threshold. Everything faded behind her until it was solid black.

CHAPTER 27

The air was heavy and thick. Liekki twisted around to face the direction she had come from. The strange stone archway she had just passed through had disappeared. Wherever she was, she was stuck. There was no way back. At least, not from the way she arrived.

"Hello," she called out, but her words and voice echoed back to her.

She was in a cave or underground somewhere. In the distance, she could hear the faint sound of water dripping. Liekki took a step forward, after calling foxfire to her palm. The fire emitted enough light for her to see only around her, but not any further. The darkness was deep and barely unpenetrable. Underground caves could be dangerous. She knew this, but there was no other way out. Liekki carefully took another step forward and hoped she would find a light or a way out soon.

Too much time had passed, and there was no ending. Tired and hungry, there was nothing she could do but keep going. The underground cave seemed to go on forever. Rubble and loose stone crunched under her feet when everything went deathly silent. She froze in her steps. Whispers carried on the faint breeze she was happy to have.

"Hello," she called out again. "Anyone there?"

Something brushed against her arm, and she jumped.

"Who are you?" she demanded.

Tiny tendrils skittered across her feet and she stomped the ground, trying to get rid of whatever it was.

"Show yourself," she shouted. "Quit playing games!"

From the corner of her eyes, she could have sworn she had seen someone move past her. The oppressive weight of the darkness was taking its toll. Negative thoughts found purchase in her mind. Doubt and fear slipped in the cracks of her resolve. Threatening to unravel her completely.

You are alone in this world.

It was a whisper, but she heard it clearly. Goosebumps rose on her arms.

You're worthless, and no one would ever understand or support you.

Another whisper that struck at another thought she never spoken out loud. What was going on? She moved her hand about as she tried to see who was talking to her. But there was nothing there.

From her left came another whisper.

You are weak. A failure.

"I AM NOT WEAK. I AM NOT A FAILURE!" Liekki shouted into the empty darkness. But how could it be empty if she kept hearing the voices? Was she going insane?

From her right came another whisper.

You are flawed, and that makes you worthless.

You should be dead.

Should be dead.

Dead.

The whispered voices came faster and faster. Surrounding her. Filling her head with regret. Doubt and a sense of hope-lessness. They fed on her insecurities and she didn't know how to stop them. It was too much. There was nothing she could do but take the verbal and mental beating.

Extinguishing her foxfire, she collapsed to the ground and curled up in a fetal position. Tears fell out of her eyes and the sobs deep from her chest. It hurt more than anything because the whispers were truth. She was a failure. Weak. Worthless. Painful words that cut like a dagger. She refused to move. Liekki gave up, letting despair cover her like a blanket.

Liekki didn't know how long she was on the ground, but it was long enough that her body was stiff when she finally took control. She was all cried out. She wiped the tears from her face and sat up. Her back rested against the cool wall of stone. The whispers had continued, but she tuned them out. They couldn't hurt her anymore than they already did. They weren't words she hadn't heard all of her life.

Although doubt had its claws stuck deep within her, but with a surge of defiance, she cast off the haunting whispers. Refusing to let the words do any more damage. True courage was not giving up, but persisting despite the horrible odds.

She knew she was far from being perfect. She was a flawed vulpii. Inside and out. She couldn't control the way her eyes were. The colors of her fur. It wasn't her fault that she had shifted to her two-legged form ever since birth, and not when she reached fifty years like the rest of the vulpiians. She couldn't help that she had three tails at her age when most didn't get their second until they were much older.

It was who she was.

If she couldn't accept herself, then how could she expect everyone else to?

All of those things made her vulnerable in so many ways, yet she was more than her flaws. She was stronger. They made her stronger because of the things she had to deal with. Beneath her flaws and imperfections, Liekki was strong and capable. How could others see it if she kept it hidden? With another surge of defiance, a sudden peace she had never felt before settled over her.

"I am more than just fur and magic. I am more than a thief because I am as good as any in Vulpo," she said to the darkness. With courage, she was ready to face whatever came her way. She wouldn't let her past or imperfections hinder her any longer.

The whispers faded to nothing, and in the darkness, the stone arch shimmered in front of her. Lighting a path to it. Unfolding herself from the ground, Liekki got up and walked towards. Not once looking back at the darkness that had almost consumed her.

Liekki landed on the ground with a hard thump. Groaning, she sat up, then stopped. She was on a solitary platform in the middle of nothing. Unable to really say it was nothing, but it looked like nothing to her. Liekki didn't think she was in Eldritch anymore. She could feel the magic. Distorted with powerful emotions. It was an ethereal realm that was fluid and ever changing. It reminded her of a passage she read in a book about the dreamscapes and nightmarescapes of Duara.

The plane was enveloped in swirling mists that shifted in colors and density. The colors ranged from fiery bright reds and oranges to thick smoky grays. From deep blues to multiple shades of purples. All undulating constantly, blurring and blending together.

There was something else in the mists, an energy like she had never felt before. She reached out to touch the vibrant tendrils.

The misty energy pulsated when her fingers touched it and a jolt shot down her arm. Fleeting images of vulpiians faces filled her mind. Raw emotion barreled into her and she couldn't stop it. Liekki quickly removed her hand from the tendril and the images and emotions she had felt disappeared.

"What in the world?"

Curious, she reached and touched another tendril. This time a red one and the emotions that raged against her were anger and fear. Liekki quickly removed her finger, not liking how that felt. All around her, the colored mists pulsated from light to dark, and she could guess that it had something to do with the strength of the emotions behind the energy.

Within the swirling mists, windows appeared and disappeared. She couldn't go to them, being stuck on the platform, but she wanted to see into them. One such window popped up next to her as if it had read her mind. Liekki moved closer to the window and touched the glass.

Everything churned around her, lifting her up as an image slammed into her head. She stood outside a house. There was something familiar about it, but she couldn't place what it was. She was in the receiving room of a noble's home. A minor family from Clan Night. It took a minute, but she remembered now. It was the home from one of her first jobs as a thief.

The vixen was sitting in the chair crying while an older male, who Liekki assumed was her husband, whispered words of comfort.

"Who would do such a thing?" the vixen said in between sobs. "Why would they take my grandmother's jewel? It was a family heirloom, Vikna. It's always the eldest daughter's duty to pass it to their eldest daughter upon marriage. My mother was the eldest, and she passed it down to me. I hoped to pass it down to our daughter, but I can't. Grandmother went through so much for that jewel and now it's just gone."

Shock hit Liekki dead center of her chest. The jewel was a beautiful sapphire. A rare and unique blue gem that fetched a ton of silons in the burrows. She thought she was doing well and was so proud of that job. Now, she recognized the errors of her ways and knew she was terribly wrong.

A wave a pain washed over her as she watched the couple who were in turmoil behind the actions of her thievery. To see their suffering was an eye opener. She never cared about the consequences of her behavior before now. As she stood there, the scene faded away, and she landed back on the platform. Another window appeared, and she touched it.

It took her to another scene. Another instance where she had to see the ramifications of her actions. It came almost instantly after she realized the enormity of her ways and situations. Liekki realized she helped others, but in the end, she destroyed so many, putting them in the situations she was trying to fix. A vicious cycle that she'd gotten caught up in.

"How can I make this right?" she asked. Horrified by everything she had just saw. "How would I feel if I were in their shoes? I would be miserable. I thought I was doing good, but

I wasn't. I didn't have enough compassion before to see and understand that I was the one who was wrong in all of this. Mother Goddess, oh, what have I done? I don't want to be like this anymore. Forgive me."

Liekki knew what she needed to do. The first step started with one vulpii. Her. If she could change for the better, why not all of them? She needed to rectify those that she did harm to. She would do what she needed to help get their items back if she could.

The ground shook beneath her and the small platform she was on spread into a narrow strip before her. At the end was the stone arch door she knew she had to reach. All it took was one foot in front of the other. Liekki walked across the narrow strip and into the shimmering portal, leaving the ethereal plane of empathy behind.

CHAPTER 28

"I've been looking everywhere for you, Kha Blaze," Efrim said. He frowned as the scent of decaying food hit his nose. "Your father searches for you."

Liekki glanced up from her hiding spot in the narrow alley off of temple row. The rioters and looters had trashed it from earlier, which made it the perfect spot to hide in. "Get over here, Efrim. They'll find me if you're standing there staring the way you are."

Efrim glanced around, a confused looked fell over his face. "What are you on about?"

She cursed under her breath while reaching out and grabbing the front of Efrim's tunic and yanked him to her. "I know my father's guards are hunting for me. Mezal Irontail and the peacekeepers of Vulpo are looking for me. There's not a safe space anywhere in these blasted lands."

"Ah, so you got my message."

"Of course I did. Why do you think I left in a hurry? I didn't even pack a bag because I needed to get out of here. I can't go back to Ravenfalls. Not after being banned the last time we were there." She side eyed him. "You're the Wanderer. Where can we go where I won't end up dead or as food for some creature larger than me?"

He shifted on his feet so he could get a better look at where they were. He looked both ways. To their right, and down the road, were peacekeepers who had their weapons drawn. There was no use in wearing an illusion. Every single one of them were Flayers.

"We can't go right. The Flayers will see right through our illusions and glamours," he said to her.

"What about the left?" Liekki asked. She placed a hand on his back for support and got up to see what he was looking at. He was right about going right. It was a death trap.

To her left was Duara's temple. She had been there before and found sanctuary. She could ask for it again. There was something about the spirit goddess of dreams and nightmares that called to her. "Do you think we can make it to the temple of dreams?"

Efrim looked to his left. There were one, maybe two, peacekeepers. "We could make it. If we kept to the shadows. Between you and me, we could take out the peacekeepers."

"Then it's to the left we go," she said, not wanting to voice her true feelings about it. A foreboding sense of unease had fallen over her. It was why she had hidden, hoping it would go away. She tried to shake it, but she couldn't. Decision made, she hoped that having Efrim, her guard and friend by her side, that it would be safer for her.

Efrim grabbed her hand and entwined his fingers with hers and left the place that kept her safe. She followed at his side as they traversed the shadows. Cloaked in its icy embrace. The smell of burning buildings and embers from the many fires choked the air. The two stayed as low to the ground as they could.

"Perhaps if we shifted to our true form, it would be better to breathe," Efrim said.

Liekki liked the feel of his hand entwined with hers and secretly she didn't want to let go. She felt safe with him. Surprised that she could finally admit it.

"If you think it would be better," she said reluctantly. "Then we can shift."

He looked her in the eyes, then touched the side of her face gently with his free hand. "I'll always protect you, Blaze."

Her heart stammered in her chest. She didn't know what was going on. All she could do was nod. He told her to shift first and then he would. Liekki did as she was told and shifted as he stood over her. Once on all fours, she shook out her fur. He looked at her, amused. Under his watchful gaze, she didn't feel uncomfortable. No, with Efrim, she felt free and proud of her colors. He accepted her for who she was. He was one of the few who did.

He looked both ways out on the road before he shifted to his true form. He stared at her like he was trying to tell her something, but she wasn't understanding. A slight tingle brushed against her mind. Images of the temple followed it.

"Follow me," he said, but the words were projected to her mind.

She froze in her spot. Her tails swiped back and forth behind her. No one has ever spoken to her that way before. Only through the language of vulpiian yips.

"How?" she asked.

"Doesn't matter right now. One day you'll understand."

Efrim always gave her vague answers when he actually knew and didn't want to say. At those times, she had always had to figure it out on her own and she really didn't want to do that. But for now, Liekki couldn't worry about it. The situation they were in was a matter of life and death. The wrong move or mistake could cost both of them their lives. He circled her, then brushed up against her, then barked low enough for her to move.

Swift as the wind, the two darted from beside the building they had taken shelter, and ran towards the Temple of Dreams. She ran slightly ahead of Efrim, feeling safe that he was there by her side. A dark protector in the face of immense danger. Perhaps it was the only good thing her father had done for her.

Maybe they would be safe after all.

Liekki didn't see the flaming ball of fire being lobbed in her direction. Everything happened in slow motion. By the time she realized what was going on, it was too late. The fiery orb hit her side with force. The impact knocked her off her feet. Stumbling, she hit the ground, writhing in agony. The smell of singed fur filled her nostrils. Explosive pain wracked her body in pulsating waves.

Unable to stop the shift, her body fluctuated between her two-legged form and her true form. She was could not keep one form or stop it from happening. She cried out in pain as it did a number on her body. Chaos erupted all around her. Darkness threatened to take over. In her mind, all she could hear was Efrim's voice.

"Keep your eyes open," he said to her.

Obeying, Liekki opened her eyes to find him standing over her, calling down his foxfire as it struck a peacekeeper. The ground trembled with the force of the lightning strike. Efrim ran towards the second peacekeeper. He pulled out his sheathed dagger right as he reached the city guard, and stabbed him in the chest, forever silencing him. The shocked peacekeeper looked down at where the blade was, then crumpled to the ground when Efrim snatched it out. He bent over the dead peacekeeper and wiped the blood of the blade on the guard's uniform before replacing it back in its sheathe.

Efrim rushed to her and placed a hand over her heart. He whispered words she had never heard before. His hands warmed and power flowed from him to her, easing the agonizing pain. Her involuntary shifts stopped, then she shuddered after the last one.

"Are you alright?" he asked.

"I am now, thanks to you."

"Can you get up?"

Liekki nodded. "I think so."

Efrim put his arms around her and helped her to her feet. The sound of a crowd shouting alerted them to more danger. "We are almost there," he said. "Just a few more feet. Once on the temple grounds, they can't do anything to us."

He held her up with his arm wrapped around her waist. Liekki only wanted to lie down and sleep, but she knew it wasn't coming anytime soon. They had to get to safety first. Together, they slowly made their way to the temple gates. To where they could claim sanctuary.

Cloaked in darkness, they didn't see her father standing before the gates that would allow them entrance onto sacred ground. But they heard him loud and clear. Liekki's head darted around, searching for him, but couldn't find him.

Diev Nightsong's voice cut through the air like a razor-sharp blade. "Where do you think you two are headed?" he sneered, his words dripping with malice. "I think I like you exactly where you are."

His voice echoed through the living night as he summoned the very shadows and darkness that danced around them. They answered swiftly and enclosed around Liekki and Efrim. She tried to call her magic to her, but it was so far out of reach, it was like she didn't have any.

Efrim shoved her backwards while he stepped in front of her. "You should leave this place. Let us be."

Diev barked out a laugh. He walked out of the shadows. "I don't think so. She belongs to me. She is the blood of my blood, no matter how much I despise the mere thought of it."

"No, she doesn't belong to you. Liekki belongs to no one but herself," Efrim countered.

"You either let her go, Blacktail, or you will die in her place." Diev flexed his fingers at his side. He cocked his head to the side, then his eyes widened. His lips spread into a bone-chilling grin. "After seeing her for what she truly is, you still want her? How sweet."

Liekki watched the exchange, confused. What was her father talking about? "What's going on?" she asked Efrim.

"Leave it be," he warned.

"I'm standing right here!" she shouted. "How are you two going to talk to me like I am not right here?"

"I said, leave it be," Efrim said between clenched teeth. He glanced at her. "Please."

"Oh, she doesn't know, does she?" Diev asked, knowing the answer.

Efrim turned back to Liekki's father. "What do you want from us, Kho Nightsong?"

Diev Nightsong lifted his hands. "I've already told you. I guess we are going to have to do this the hard. You were an excellent guard, Blacktail. Too bad you fell for the vixen. Vixens are always a dogfox's downfall."

Warning bells were blaring inside of Liekki's head. Her father's twisted smiled widened as thick tendrils of shadows had snaked itself around Efrim's legs. Efrim nor Liekki didn't know what was happening to him it until it was too late. Efrim tried to move, but couldn't.

"My magic..." he cried out in a panic. "I can't feel it!"

Still in pain, Liekki moved through the agony and tried to make her way back to Efrim to help him. The grip around his legs tightened, and Efrim howled out in a pain filled moan. With a flick of Diev's hand, another tendril wrapped around Efrim's neck. His eyes bulged as the tendrils restricted the air from his lungs.

Horrified, Liekki hobbled her way towards her friend. She couldn't do much, but the least she could do was try to protect him the way he would do for her. There was no way she could lose him. She refused to. Liekki stood in front of him with her arms spread out wide, protecting him as best as she could.

She faced her father and stared him down. "Take me if you must, but leave Efrim alone. He did nothing but what he was supposed to. That was to guard and protect me. Leave him out of this, father. This is between me and you! Please."

Diev let out a chuckle, amused at the scene playing out before him. "Alright... if you really want this."

Time crawled. Her father's magic tore from his hands and crossed the way towards her. Tears welled up in the corner of her eyes. She looked back at Efrim and realized she cared for him more than she had wanted to admit. Yes, she would do this if it meant he would live.

The tendrils around his neck loosened. His voice was raw. His words came out urgently. Frantic. "Liekki, don't do this. I can fight him."

Thoughts of what could have been filled her heart and mind. *It wasn't meant to be in this life*, she thought, but perhaps in the next. She surrendered to the peace in her heart and soul. She gave him a lazy smile. "Until the next time, Efrim."

The force of the magic hit her hard. Instantly setting her on fire. Her screams had mixed with the sobs and shouts of Efrim as he did his best to try to heal her.

Dark laughter surrounded Liekki. Powerless to stand upright any longer, she looked at the ground and kind of recognized the design on the road. It was a vague outline of a stone arch.

Odd, she thought, until it shimmered to life. A faint tug pulled at her. Like a siren's call, it called to her. She would be okay if she touched it. She didn't know how or why, but she knew. Liekki slipped from Efrim's hands to the ground and was transported through the portal. Everything passed by her in a blur and eventually faded to nothing. Tired of everything and hurting all over, she succumbed to the call of sleep and peace.

CHAPTER 29

The luminescent pools were more vibrant than normal. It emitted a glow that touched every inch of the cave. The strange lights danced along the rock formations, weaving patterns of color that couldn't be seen anywhere else in Eldritch. Her family's caves were a magical place and always had been. The perfect atmosphere when she wanted alone time, but it had been forever since she visited them. She loved exploring the underground caves. The pools were always one of her favorite places underneath the mountain. Liekki visited them more than anyone else because she never tired of them. Unlike the rest of her family.

Liekki made her way through the labyrinthine path, worn into the ground after so many years of use by her ancestors. As she rounded the corner, Liekki noticed the pools weren't empty. She drew closer to the northern edge and recognized the outline figure of her mother sitting on a stone next to the waters. Liekki couldn't remember the last time she had seen her, but with everything going on in Vulpo, it wasn't out of the normal.

Liekki didn't want to interrupt her, but a strange desire to talk with her had overcome her. Careful to watch her steps on the slippery stone, she made her way towards her mother.

All around her, Liekki admired the scenery. This part of the cave was bright with color. Crystals, large and small, was everywhere. It took them many years to form and grow to be the size they were. Big and small enough to cover the slate walls and ceiling of the cave. Hanging from the same ceiling were stalagmites. Covered with bioluminescent moss, which enhanced the ethereal feel. Its light reflected off the crystals, giving a rainbow effect near the pools, and Liekki dared anyone to say these pools weren't extraordinary.

The mirrored waters were still, but she could see the tiny fishes that found refuge in its water swimming around. Simple creatures to survive in such an environment.

Luya looked up and grinned when she saw it was Liekki. She patted the empty space on the stone slab beside her. "My precious kit, don't mind me. It's been a long time since I've been down here. I needed a moment of peace. Will you come and sit?"

"I can leave and come back later," Liekki said, suddenly too nervous to talk with her.

Luya shook her head and smiled. "No, come on. I don't bite."

Liekki's steps closed the distance between the two. Her mother stood up and when Liekki reached her, she embraced her in a hug. It felt like time had stopped. All that existed was the warmth of her mother's touch and the soothing words she whispered in Liekki's ear.

Tears coursed a salty trail down her face. Liekki didn't notice them until her mother brushed a thumb across her face and wiped them away. A flood of emotions threatened to overtake her completely. For so long, Liekki yearned for a connection with her parents. In time, she grew to understand it would never happen with her father, but her mother had showed promised. Now she was there, accepting her for who she was, the emotions she couldn't contain.

Despite their differences, Liekki saw that the love of her mother was always there. Hidden underneath flashes of cruelty done in her father's presence to protect her. A bond between a mother and kit could never have been broken, and Liekki should have realized it when her mother first defied her father after she was born.

The little things over the years flashed in her mind. Tiny, but caring gestures, when Liekki thought she was all alone in the world. Her mother's embrace was like a much needed lance to a wound that was soul deep.

"Don't cry, my sweet one. I will always be here for you," her mother said. "I know I haven't been the perfect mother. There are things I regret, but I was the best mother I could be, considering the situation. Now, I know it wasn't enough, and I am so sorry Liekki. I'm so sorry, my love. Can you forgive me?"

Liekki stared into Luya's eyes. There was remorse and pain there. Being married to her father was no easy feat. Liekki didn't know what exactly her mother had to go through, but she was here now. Trying to make it better. It was a step. A good first one.

Holding on to grudges wasn't her thing. She couldn't be mad at her mother anymore. Their relationship was broken, but it would take two to fix it. She wanted this for them. Her mother wasn't the perfect vixen, but the goddess wouldn't have given her to her mother if she didn't think she was the right one. Liekki knew she could have been born to anyone in Vulpo, but Luya was who the goddess chose. A perfect fit for her.

Could she forgive her mother? It was a simple answer. One she couldn't answer before now. She was too blind by rage and hate to see it. Now, the answer blared before her. Her heart pounded in her chest. The words she and her mother needed to hear rang loudly in her ears and sat on the tip of her tongue. Liekki couldn't help the smile that formed on her lips.

"Yes, I forgive you, mother."

Light filled her heart and soul. Joy and peace filled the dark scar that festered within her. An understanding and renewed sense of purpose had taken hold of her. Liekki felt the burden of everything lifted and the joy of her mother's love replaced the desolate feeling. The walls around the two that separated them had disappeared.

This was what she needed.

What they needed.

Liekki closed her eyes and did her best to memorize this moment. It was everything she wanted, but didn't realize she needed. Their embrace lasted longer than she expected. She was okay with that. When they finally pulled away, Luya led her to the stone slab she was sitting on earlier and pointed to it.

"This is for you," she said, her voice filled with love. "Take it."

"Take what-" Liekki had said, but stopped as she watched the large slab transform.

The magic of the caverns ebbed and flowed as she stood there transfixed, watching the scene before her. After the transformation, long gone was the slate slab, but in its place was a large crystalline stone. It was clear, but she could feel the pulse of the magic within it. She didn't know why, but she stepped towards it and reached out for it, then stopped. At the back of her mind, something told her it was hers. There was a familiarity to it, but she wanted to be sure.

Liekki glanced back at her mother. "Are you sure?"

"Yes, love, it's yours."

She nodded, then reached out and grabbed the beautiful large stone. Soon as her hands touched it, everything came rushing back to her as it pulled her away from the caverns. Outside of the House of Vulpii, Liekki found herself on her back, looking up at the bright blue sky with its puffy white clouds dotting it. She blinked more than once.

Liekki couldn't believe it. She was a winner. She passed most of her tests. The memories of the one she failed were there at the forefront of her mind. But she passed, and she lived. That's what mattered most. The curse wouldn't hinder her kind for another one hundred years. They wouldn't be able to blame her for their failures anymore.

Her body ached, but it was nothing a hot soak in the springs could fix. She sat up and groaned at the sharp pain. Her chest burned fiercely. Liekki reached up and pulled the top of her tunic aside to find markings on her chest.

"What is that?" she said to herself. Alone, she lifted her shirt all the way to get a better scope of what she was seeing. It was the symbol of the mother goddess. Tattooed on her skin, from her shoulder down to her chest, the ink matched the colors of her fur. Shades of orange and black swirled together. The mark was a knotwork of two trees, entwined with each other. To have the mark of Zera emblazoned on her skin was an honor and all the proof she needed that she truly passed the Eldritch Trials.

Liekki made her way through the campground in Elderton and towards the gates. They were simple this time. No gray mists. The spirit goddess Aku wasn't present. Just the land and creaky old gates. As she approached them, they opened and let her pass through them. She made her way to the docks and found the small fishing boat she used to get to the island still moored.

She hurried to it, ready to get far away from Elderton. She had enough of its tests to last three lifetimes. Deftly untying the rope from the wooden post, she hopped inside of it and grabbed the oars. Pushing away from the dock, she used all of her strength to get away from there and back to home. To her family and friends. Strangely enough, she couldn't wait to see Efrim. Glimpses of that test raised many questions she hoped to get answers for. But first...she had to get to the mainland.

Thankful for the southern breeze, she rowed in the direction of home.

CHAPTER 30

Her arms hurt even worse from all the rowing, but she made it. She approached the shores of the mainland and instantly became leary of the shadowed figure waiting at the small dock. The uneasiness that had clawed its way into her heart and mind eased away when the shadowed figure stepped into the sunlight.

"Efrim!" Liekki shouted as joy replaced the darkness that tried to seep into her. She rowed faster, wanting to be on land again. When she reached the docks, she quickly hopped out of the tiny vessel and tied the rope to the posts.

Efrim stood there with an enormous grin on his face. Their eyes met and something passed between them she couldn't place. He exhaled a heavy sigh when she reached him. He gently touched the side of her face and caressed it before dropping his hands quickly. "Kha Blaze. I knew you would survive and win! I am so proud of you."

Not wanting to think about the strange feelings she experienced whenever she was near him, she walked into his waiting arms and cried tears of joy. Liekki was extremely happy to see him as well. They stood there for a long time, enjoying the feel of each other, before pulling away. She wiped her face while taking another look at him.

"I thought I would have to walk back to Vulpo on my own. I didn't know what to expect," she admitted.

"I promised I would be right here waiting when you returned. You didn't think you were coming back then, but I knew. I had faith you would survive and win. I prayed to the spirits to watch and guide you. I've never been more happy to see they answered my whispered words."

"I'm glad someone had faith. I sure didn't." Liekki laughed, still in disbelief she survived. "Where's Brightsun? I thought she would be here, too. Being my mentor and all."

A serious look replaced the smile on Efrim's face. "She was busy. Believe me, she wanted to be here. I promised I would bring you to her."

Liekki remembered the chaos that was Vulpo when she left. She was on the run from her father and Mezal Irontail. Vulpians were being murdered. Riots took place day and night, and buildings burned. All because the spirits chose her to be their champion. How would they react now that she's back and had won? Would they treat her the same? As a pariah, or would they give her the respect and honor of doing something that even Kalama Brightsun couldn't do?

"What about the troubles that plagued our home?" Liekki finally asked. She needed to know.

"You've been gone for three and a half days. Another half day and it would have been too late for you." He handed her a leather tote. "Here. Eat something. It's a variety of cured meat and hard cheeses. It'll keep you satisfied until we make it home."

"You must have been reading my mind. I am starving," she said, and grabbed the bag. She dug into it and pulled out a piece of cured smoked meat and took a bite.

"I just knew. You're always hungry, Blaze. My duty is to watch over you and make sure you have everything, including protection. Besides, when you're hungry, it's bad for everybody."

Liekki laughed. He was right. She became a different vulpii when she was hungry. "Point made. Now tell me what you didn't want to tell me on an empty stomach."

He smiled. This time, it didn't reach his eyes. "Always a clever fox you are. The troubles are still the troubles, but not in the same way when you left."

"Oh," she said.

"Two of the sacred three are gone. Elders Nikesh and Salibas. Murdered on sacred ground. Along with all the acolytes."

Shock rippled through Liekki. To do such a thing was to go against the spirits of Vulpo and Zera, the Mother Goddess.

Efrim continued. "Elder Brightsun would have been one of them if she hadn't left to see you off. After all of Vulpo found out what happened, the chaos we knew stopped. It was all aimed toward the culprits of the unrest. Mezal Irontail and your father, Diev. Your sister, Senia, too."

Liekki's jaws dropped, and her mouth fell wide open. "But how did they know it was them?"

"Your other siblings had gone into hiding with your mother. They had proof of the dealings between your father and Mezal. How Senia wasn't as innocent as she proclaimed to be." He looked at her. "They're in custody. Collared, unable to touch or reach their magic. Your father and Mezal's personal guards were the ones who slaughtered everyone on the Sacred Island."

She knew what it meant. "That's a death sentence," she whispered.

"It is. Come on. Everyone is waiting. Kalama moved the Hasking stone to the middle of the island after everything came to light. She wanted all to see how you were doing. She put it there so all of Vulpo could track your progress. When the stone turned red, we knew you were in serious trouble. That was when Kalama kept saying she needed to reach out to you. I didn't understand, but she knew and whatever was done apparently had helped."

"I just don't get why."

"Because of what you were going through," he said. "It affected us all. The moment we realized you truly won the trials, a roar went up in all of Vulpo. Vulpiians shouted for joy and cried in the streets, Blaze. Vulpiians still remember the cursed years of leanness. We couldn't go through that again. You saved us from a hardship some wouldn't survive a second time. We gained favor with Zera because of you." Efrim stepped into her immediate space. "Now, hold on tight."

Liekki held on as tight as she could. Unprepared for the pull of his magic, she yelped when they were sucked into the swirling vortex. One of these days, she was determined to get him to tell her how he could transport himself and another. When they came through the portal he created, they landed on their feet.

Her eyes were closed as they traveled too fast. Efrim held her up as the room swirled. Liekki did her best to adjust her eyes to the light. When she opened them, she froze in her spot. Her mother and siblings were there in front of her. All of them grinning at her. Kalama stood to the side, with Icelia at her side. Everyone was there. Those who she didn't realize cared for her. The tests opened her eyes to what blinded her for so long. Efrim nodded towards them and she took a step forward. They filled in the rest and embraced in a brace of hugs and kisses and murmurs of congratulations and love.

It was overwhelming, but it was what she needed.

"Thank you, Mother Goddess. For everything," she silently prayed while amongst those who loved her.

Liekki stood in the center of the sacred island. All three clans had gathered and watched from their areas. It was an emotional time. The last time they had gathered, the outcries and jeers weren't pleasant. Her family had to run off because the other clans wanted to fight. She was amazed and still couldn't believe the outpouring now was because she won the trials.

A few days had gone by since she had returned. The opportunity to see her father had arose. He was the same. He wouldn't change, and she knew that now. Diev Nightsong was going to his death, stuck in his ways. *Good riddance, she thought.* Her mother was a different story. They reconciled their differences. Even with her siblings, they apologized and promised that they would do better about her.

She didn't even want to think about the turmoil within her clan. With her father jailed, her mother took over House Nightsong, and became the de facto leader of Clan Night. Some were mad that a vixen held the role, but she proved to them she had steel in her spine too.

Kalama came and stood beside her while she watched her mother speak to the gathered crowd. She wore an affable grin on her face, something Liekki was still getting used to seeing on Brightsun's face.

"Are you ready?" her mentor asked.

Liekki took a slow, deep breath, then exhaled. She nodded. "I am."

"You will be fine, Liekki. If you can endure the trials, you can endure these vulpii." Kalama glanced at the anxious crowd.

"This is a fresh start for us. We can't let the darkness take hold of us like it did. Not anymore. We're not completely in the clear, but the danger is not as relevant as it once was."

"I think we could all use a fresh start," Liekki admitted. "Our kind will be for the better if we can learn from this and do better as a whole."

"See, you're understanding it. This is why you are the champion," Kalama said. "Now, let all of Vulpo see who they should be grateful for."

Kalama left Liekki's side and walked to the center of the sacred island. She raised her hands to silence the clans who had gathered. She turned towards Liekki and motioned for her to come stand next to her. Efrim, ever at her side, nudged her on. He winked at Liekki when she took the first step.

"I can do this," Liekki whispered.

With her head held high and her three tails erect behind her, she strode to the spot next to Kalama. Her mentor grabbed her hand and lifted her arm up for all to see.

"My fellow Vulpii," Kalama said, her voice projected for all to hear. "We would not be here if it wasn't for Liekki Nightsong. One, even myself, scoffed and belittled. One of our own that we couldn't stand. But I've learned so much, being her mentor. Without her, we'd still be hiding in the darkness. This is a fresh start for all of us and it's because of our champion."

Kalama let go of her hand and stepped away from her. Liekki stood there and watched as all three clans stood up and faced her.

"Let us show our thanks to the one who did her best to save us when we didn't even know we needed to be saved."

Liekki watched as Kalama bowed low at her waist. It was the vulpiian way to show the utmost respect to a peer of the realm, and never in her life had she ever received a bow. Or seen anyone else receive it. Her eyes darted towards her family, Icelia, and to Efrim. They all followed Kalama's action and did the same. The sound of fabric and cloth moving in the wind reached Liekki's ears. She slowly turned and watched as each clan showed their respect and bowed low to her.

She didn't know what to do or say. Choked by the emotions running rampant within her. The things she remembered from the trials. Everything she had to endure. It was a test for her, true, but also for her kind. She wasn't much different from them. If she could change and want to be better, then she knew they could, too.

Everybody deserved a chance to want better. They still had a long way to go, but she had a feeling that things would turn out alright.

D.L. Howard is a cosmic traveler who embraces her weirdness. Never one to back down from a chance to get away, she is always traveling on a new adventure snapping pics of her escapades.

A lover of animals, she is ruled by her psychotic cat overlord Sir Crookshanks!

She finds comfort in listening to music, thunderstorms, dark and gloomy days, cold weather, curling up in a corner with a blanket and a good book.

You can find her on Facebook, Twitter, and Instagram. Don't hesitate to stop by and say hi. She loves meeting other cosmic travelers too!

Subscribe to get awesome updates on the latest news, exclusive goodies and new releases at www.dlhoward-writes.com/newsletter

The Eldritch Trials is a collection of books in the same world, but each book is written by a different talented author! If you enjoyed this story, check out the others in the collection. https://mybook.to/D8BymgW